D0052079

"Pure escapist fun."   —*Calgary Herald*

"An entertaining and vivid romp."   —*The Gazette* (Montreal)

playing with boys

"A funny, guilty pleasure of a novel."   —*Publishers Weekly*

"As Marcella, Alexis, and Olivia grapple with men and their careers, they really don't seem all that different from Bridget Jones herself."
—*The Miami Herald*

"Valdes-Rodriguez brings savvy, and sometimes savage humor, to chick lit."   —New York *Daily News*

"Entertaining."   —*Entertainment Weekly*

"Humor abounds in Valdes-Rodriguez's new novel . . . women of all eth-nicities will identify with the real-life trials of this novel's three friends."   —*Romantic Times BOOKreviews*

the dirty girls social club

"The feel of a night out with the girls . . . charming . . . undeniably fun."   —*The Miami Herald*

"A compulsive beach read . . . smart, brassy, and messy enough to make you pause mid-sunscreen slathering."   —*Entertainment Weekly*

"Delivers on the promise of its title . . . a fun, irresistible debut."
—*Publishers Weekly*

"Laugh-out-loud read . . . with no-holds-barred humor."
—*The Dallas Morning News*

"Wonderful writing, delicious humor, biting sarcasm, and impressive intelligence."   —*Detroit Free Press*

"Alisa Valdes-Rodriguez's writing style is raunchy yet refined . . . but in the end, it's the complex, finely drawn characters who make the book work."   —*Rocky Mountain News*

DIRTY
GIRLS
on
TOP

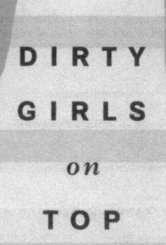

DIRTY

GIRLS

on

TOP

alisa valdes-rodriguez

ST. MARTIN'S GRIFFIN
NEW YORK

This book is dedicated to the memory of Miriam "Mia" Moreno, a Las Cruces *sucia* taken from us too soon. It is also dedicated to all women everywhere who suffer from bulimia nervosa.

www.madd.org
www.anorexiabulimiahelp.com

DIRTY GIRLS ON TOP. Copyright © 2008 by Alisa Valdes-Rodriguez. All rights reserved. Printed in the United States of America. For information, address St. Martin's Press, 175 Fifth Avenue, New York, N.Y. 10010.

www.stmartins.com

Design by Stephanie Huntwork

The Library of Congress has catalogued the hardcover edition as follows:

Valdes-Rodriguez, Alisa.
    Dirty girls on top / Alisa Valdes-Rodriguez.—1st ed.
        p. cm.
    ISBN-13: 978-0-312-34967-7
    ISBN-10: 0-312-34967-X
    1. Hispanic American women—Fiction.   2. Female friendship—Fiction.   3. Boston (Mass.)—Fiction.   4. New Mexico—Fiction.   I. Title.

PS3622.A425 D55 2008
813'.6—dc22

                                                            2008012930

ISBN-13: 978-0-312-34981-3 (pbk.)
ISBN-10: 0-312-34981-5 (pbk.)

First St. Martin's Griffin Edition: July 2009

ACKNOWLEDGMENTS

Thanks, again and always, to Patrick Jason Rodriguez, for humor and friendship; to Alexander Patrick Rodriguez, for imaginary worlds that dwarf my own; to Leslie Daniels, for forgiveness, patience, humor, strength; to Elizabeth Beier, for missing these girls enough to welcome them back; to Nely and Debra, for believing we could breathe cinematic life into these women; and to all the readers who looked at Lauren, Sara, Elizabeth, Rebecca, Amber, and Usnavys the first time and saw in them something of themselves, and wrote to tell me so—thank you for loving the *sucias* (I am quite certain they love you back).

I blame my mother for my poor sex life. All she told me was, "The man goes on top and the woman underneath." For three years my husband and I slept on bunk beds.

—JOAN RIVERS

NEW
MEXICO

usnavys

So, **YOU** *KNOW* I'm not a hoochie, okay? But an unhappy marriage can make a woman do questionable things. Things she's not proud of, things she only tells her closest friends—and even then with the understanding that, if they blab about it, they'll get their butts kicked. So it is, *m'ija*, that I am cheating on my husband at a big adobe resort outside Santa Fe, New Mexico. I have never cheated on him before, and I'm not sure I'll do it again. Alls I knew was I had to do it just this once.

My college friends, the *sucias* who've been my support network for fifteen years—since we met as freshmen at Boston University—will arrive here in a few days for our annual vacation trip, a tradition we started two years ago. Me, though? I flew here from Boston yesterday to take care of some personal *business*. A seven-year-itch kind of thing, only a little early. I am not proud of it. I decided I'd seduce the golf pro after I saw his photo in the brochure for the resort. I learned what I could about him, and I concocted my strategy. It worked.

My husband, Juan? He'd looked up at me through his smudgy Clark Kent eyeglasses over the morning paper across the breakfast table before I left yesterday, his curly black hair sticking up all greasy wherever it wasn't receding. "Why are you going early, *mi reina?*" he wanted to know. *Reina* means queen, and to him, I'm still an empress. He doesn't know about the golf pro, and I don't think you should tell him, either.

I told Juan I wanted to get to the resort early, to observe some outreach programs having to do with Latinas and AIDS in New Mexico, for my work as an executive with the United Way of Massachusetts Bay. It sounded very official when I said it, and he was duly impressed with his empress. "They've been very successful," I assured him, with a wave of my hand. "It's a model that might be emulated here in New England."

He believed me, *el pobre*. He thinks marriage *changed* me. For a while I *did* change, too, but now I know better. Listen to me. After ten years of juggling no less than two men at a time, a woman does not just up and change, even though God and the world know there's a piece of paper and shared taxes involved now. I am a "manizer" the same way my daddy was a womanizer. I was to the manor born, as the *americanos* say, and, even though I'm not proud of it, I seem to have stayed the way he met me.

Juan thinks I'm different because he chooses to see the best in people, even when it isn't there. His heart hallucinates. I know, you think that's a plus, right? Being married to a loving optimist like Juan. But *nena*, that's just *it*. Juan believes *everyone* and he does it indiscriminately. Ain't no backbone in *that*. The boy is naïve. Back when he had him a *job* (ahem), he believed all them drug addicts when they told him they were clean and sober as an Osmond now, he believed them when they said they were going to get jobs and stop doing shit like stealing cars. Then he acted all surprised when they came crawling back into rehab after getting arrested for crime and crack again. I try telling him, people don't change that much, *m'ijo*, no matter how bad you want them to. *Badly*. Yes, I know the difference between good and bad grammar; no, I don't give a rat's ass. Whatever, no?

This resort is supposed to look like a Pueblo Indian village, like in those Georgia O'Keeffe paintings, where the pastel flower petals look all coochie unfurling in their glistening glory. I think this place looks like a big bunch of caramels all stacked on top of each other, or like a dusty old stack of wedding cake. Depends on your attitude. At the moment, I've chosen candy over cake.

Chocolate, to be exact.

His name is Marcus Williams, and he's the golf pro—like an older, darker Tiger Woods in his crisp white polo shirt and khaki shorts, with that salt-and-pepper hair and that little sexy mustache. He's probably forty-five or so, but he's got him some deltoids like cantaloupes. You don't think you're going to find a fine black brother teaching golf up on an Indian reservation near Santa Fe, *nena*, but life is full of delicious surprises, *¿sí?* From what I read about him, I know that Marcus used to be a professional golfer. He retired and came to work here in New Mexico because he likes the desert but dislikes Arizona's take on black people. I've seen his car, and it's a white Cadillac, so you know he's got at least a little something-something stashed away from the days when he almost won the U.S. Open and Nike came knocking on his door. I learned all this about him on the Internet, following his comments on message boards and things like that. I plan my attacks like an army general, always have.

I should tell you, Juan don't play golf. Doesn't. He doesn't play golf. Dominos, yes; golf, no. Nintendo, yes; skiing, no. I try telling him, you will never get ahead in business inviting CEOs to play dominos, *nene*, but he's like, "I don't want to play anything with CEOs except Revolution, I want to play with my *tío* and my *sobrino* and the people I actually like." Whatever.

All my life I dreamed that I'd marry the kind of man who played him some golf, and liked to ski and went to places like Jackson Hole, okay? I imagined it, and it felt good. So, I'm not saying I'm falling in love with Marcus or any nonsense like that, I'm just saying Marcus plays golf and Juan doesn't. Marcus has a Cadillac and Juan doesn't. Marcus wears polo shirts, Juan does not. I'm just saying that sometimes you have things in your head a certain way and life spins you a different way, and you still wonder about that road not taken, only my road not taken is more like a little path for golf carts. I like Marcus, and I wonder, you know, if I'd married me someone like that, would I still be struggling to pay the Bloomingdale's charge on time. I wonder if I'd still be choosing to go to fancy dinners for work alone because I can't bear the sight of my husband in his Che Guevara T-shirt and tuxedo jacket sitting next to me. I am a woman of class and substance, and I'd like to imagine what it would be like to be married to a man of class and substance, or at least to spend some time with one. So sue me.

Oh, and the best part? Marcus likes me back. I knew he would, though, and not just because he said my Boston accent was cute. It's because I look good and I smell good and I'm full of compliments of the type and caliber that make a man feel important. That's all. Oh, and he likes some big thighs, know what I'm sayin'? You *know* how black men feel about curvy women of a generous size and proportions. Uh-*huh*. He gave me a lesson this morning, wrapping his big old arms around me to show me how to swing, holding me so close I could smell the manly spice of his deodorant and the heat of the sun on his clean cotton clothes. He eased his hand over mine and whispered in my ear, "Don't swing carelessly, Usnavys, don't lose focus on your game, girl."

I could have taken him right then, okay, *nena*? I coulda had him this morning, that's how bad he wanted me. But I had lunch to attend to in the resort café. Some things are better if you have to wait for them—including me. I sat outside, behind my big sunglasses with the golden DIOR on the sides, with a view of the kiva-shaped pool and the jagged plum-colored mountains, with my copy of *Oprah* and *Gourmet* to keep me company. I started with some baby pork ribs marinated in red chile and hoisin sauce, with a side of rainbow-striped designer coleslaw with black seeds in it. To drink, I had sparkling water with a twist of lemon, and a sweet white zinfandel. Then, because I knew I'd need some energy for the afternoon, I had the leg of lamb, marinated in garlic sage oil. There was polenta on the side, which is really grits but nobody around here is going to tell you that, baby, with tomatoes and pine nuts all sprinkled up on it. They say pine nuts are the most expensive nuts in the world to harvest, the caviar of the nut world, because it's so damn hard to get them out of the pine cones. I had a local red wine with the main meal. Even though I am not big on drinking so much in the middle of the day, I knew I might need to drift away a little bit because of what was coming. There was something else I wanted to tell you. What was it? Oh, right, *m'ija*. The rest of the meal. What was the side dish? I remember now. You would have died, girl. It was sautéed *vegetables*, which ordinarily would not sit well with me because I do not *do* vegetables, but they were tossed with a pecan demi-glace and mint. It was so good I almost decided not to go for dessert, but when I saw the light, simple strawberry cheesecake, I could not refuse.

Same goes for Marcus. Look at him. *Look* at him. You know what I'm saying. No, Marcus will not be finding out I'm married. Are you crazy, girl? He *doesn't* need to know. Four *years* married. I'm not trying to hurt Juan, the main man in my life since high school. Seriously. He's good enough at doing that all by himself, okay? He started that masochistic trend by not having him a real job, with real pay. He made it worse by deciding he wanted to quit his job as the director of a rehab center for Latino men to be a "stay-at-home *papi*." Because I, an executive with style and grace, made three times his salary. We agreed we didn't want a nanny raising our Carolina, because I can tell you from personal experience, that whole nanny thing is for people who care more about their dogs than their children. I always thought it would be me at home with the kid, not him. He's all, "Go ahead and stay home, but we'll have to downgrade a few things on my salary." I drive a BMW, *nena*, and I wasn't about to go back to a backfiring Neon with a dragging tailpipe. So here we are.

Pero, Mister Mom, how *joto*, no? I don't care how good he is with her. Watching Juan answer questions from *Dora the Explorer* with our daughter doesn't exactly make me lustful for him. Dora's all, "Do you see a monkey?" and Juan's like, "Right there, Dora!" Pointing his finger and shit. I can't stand that show. That Dora girl, and Diego too, they sound like they been drinking lead paint. I appreciate my husband. I do. Seriously. I just don't want him. He might as well dress his hairy ass up like a French maid, *m'ija*. That's how much he's turning me on lately.

I know kids need their parents to stay together and all that. I mean, I *thought* that was basically true, until I heard some guy on a progressive talk show saying how the Bible actually doesn't say squat about monogamous marriages, and how David in the Bible had him seven hundred wives and how up until three hundred years ago, polygamy was the damn norm for most of the world. I didn't believe it, and went and looked it up, and saw that it was true. All these "family values" people who thump the Bible around don't even know what they're thumping, that there was lots of humping going on in that book. That made me think. Lots of things do.

God knows I don't want to hurt our daughter (even if she does act like a filthy little tomboy), but I was raised to want a real man, a man's man, and right now I can't believe my stay-at-home *flojón* fits that description. Anyway, he's too tired to seduce me anymore, right? Girls like me? We're raised to be conquered by our men, okay? That's the verb we use for seduction, *m'ija*. It's *conquistar*. "To conquer." With his dishpan hands and aching back, Juan doesn't have the strength to *conquistarme*. It's sad.

Don't get all preachy with me about this, either. Listen. Tell me, *nena*, do real men make their grandmama's *sancocho* recipe from memory, cracking the corn cobs in half like a practiced *campesina*, with their favorite daytime talk show playing on the kitchen flat-screen? Do real men call *abuelita* in Bayamón to ask her the best way to mash the *tostones*, all the while licking yellow cupcake batter from the wooden spoon out of the pink Williams-Sonoma bowl I bought myself for Easter last year? Cupcakes he takes to

Carolina's exclusive preschool for her snack day, while I'm slaving away at the office in a *pants* suit? *Tell* me. Don't be shy now. I'd like to know. *Do* they? *Bueno.*

Mira, I know it's retro, the way I'm thinking and so on and so forth. But I, like George Washington and *esa animal con pistola* Lolita Lebrón, cannot tell a *mentirita.* Okay? It's that simple. It's like this: With the way my family goes on about it, like when my *mami* clicks her tongue like a chicken and says how disappointed she is I couldn't do better than some masculine moocher, I feel like he's taken my womanhood from me, like he done gone and cut my uterus out with pinking shears.

Marcus, when I invited him up at the end of the golf lesson, lifted his big mirrored aviator sunglasses and watched me walk all the way across the putting green to the clubhouse in the bright white sunshine, a smile of scandal and surprise in his wide-set, honey-colored eyes. I was all, swish-to-the-left, swish-to-the-right, and I wore me a pretty pink golf *skirt,* okay? Not wide-ass khaki shorts like all the other women with their flat butts. Those women look like they're about to wrestle a crocodile down or something, girl. Not me. I wore me a sexy little skirt, and he watched my *nalgas* like they was one of them golden pocket-watches German hypnotists pendulum around when they say "you're getting sleepy." My body is mad *hypnotic,* right? Five four, a size twenty curved up in all the right places, thirty-three years old, and men still be *begging* me for a piece, okay? You know I got it like that, girl. You *know* I do. I take good care of myself, that's all.

Five minutes ago, at two in the afternoon on the dot, Marcus knocked on the door to my mountain-view suite and I, wearing only my black lace body stocking, shiny black do-me pumps, a three-strand pearl choker, and the hotel-issue robe, answered. I don't wear a body stocking because I'm embarrassed of my size or anything like that. It's just nice to have something holding me all in place. After having a baby, things jiggle-wiggle a little more than a girl is used to, and this way I have the support. Anyway, it took less than twelve seconds of his nervous small talk for the thick white robe to slip off.

Whoops.

So there I was, all curves and soft brown skin. I have to tell you, I have gotten sexually bold in my thirties. If you're a modern Latina, I swear it's like you spend your whole twenties working like *loca* to get over your Catholic guilt at being sexual at *all*, just so you can be a vixen in your thirties. Marcus whispered "whoa," and stuttered after that, wanted to ask me what I did for a living, what brought me to the resort, what city I lived in, and all that kind of nonsense, but I shut him up quick. "I don't *know* you, Marcus," I said, handing him a cherry-flavored condom as I draped myself across the big bed with its earth-tone Southwestern bedspread, "and you don't know *me*. Let's keep it that way for now, *nene, ¿'ta bien?*"

When he heard the Spanish he was all, "What's a fine African-American woman doing talking Mexican?" and it was all I could do not to turn him around and drop-kick his ass back to the clubhouse, okay?

"For your information, I am Puerto *Rican*," I told him, pointing to my luscious neck with my French acrylic tips. "And the language you heard was *Spanish*. Ain't nobody in the world speak no *Mexican*, okay? Mexican? That's not a *language*, now shut your mouth before you start to look ugly to me, and let's do this thing."

I had to pull him to me after that, not because he didn't want none of mama's island papaya pie, but rather because he was all human popsicle in shock, like he couldn't move. Men dream about women doing this kind of thing to them all the time, but there aren't many *mujeres* who can pull it off, you know what I mean? So, when it happens, they get stiff as uncooked pasta. A practiced *campesina* like my girly husband has become coulda broke that boy in half with her bare hands.

Now, here we are, ten minutes into it, and Marcus has apologized for his ignorance about Spanish. "I am sorry. That was very uncouth of me. You wouldn't know I went to Yale talking like that, I suppose," he said, and I was all, "Yale?" and he said, "Yeah, I have a law degree that I don't use anymore," and that's when he told me he was a widower whose wife used to be an attorney, and that he's actually quite well-off and only does the golf pro thing because he loves golf and needs to be around people so he doesn't go crazy.

That last bit made me have to respect him, *m'ija*, and even though I don't want to, I am now seeing him as more than a piece of ass. Now he looks like a potential friend, which is no good. I mean, my husband Juan? Soon as that boy sees we've got enough money, he quits his job and stays home. But not Marcus. Marcus has enough to retire on and live comfortably, but he would rather work because he takes pride in work and likes it. Why didn't I marry me a man like this, girl? That's what I want to know. Why did I think Juan would shape up just because I bought him some nice shirts? Life doesn't work like that, and now it's too late. Or not. I don't know. You make your own life, and it ain't over until it's over.

I push the possibility of falling for Marcus out of my mind and focus on the task at hand, even though if I'm honest I'd say he looks a lot better now that I know he's a man of means and substance. He's gotten over his stage fright nicely now, too, and there's a passion to him that pleases me. I was worried he'd be wooden about this, but he isn't. He's all down on his knees at the edge of the bed, his oval face all up in my cocoa-puff, nosing around like a pig in truffles. And if you were to bottle it, I bet it'd cost like truffles, too. I'm that good.

He's making satisfied sniffles and there's the sloppy wet sound I haven't heard in a while. It has been. *Too* long. Okay? Something happens when you have a baby, *nena*, and it has nothing to do with your body. It's all flat psychological. You and your husband? You get so tired from the whole thing, all the up and down all night with the baby, all the fights over whose turn it is to change the diapers or warm up the bottle, all the arguments about the best way to do this or that, that you just lose interest in each other like that. I didn't lose interest in sex, okay? I just lost interest in sex with *my husband*. It's been three months since Juan and I knocked the booties, and I wouldn't care if we went another three *years*, I really wouldn't.

"A little more to the front," I tell Marcus. He follows instructions and, oh my goodness, girl, gets a bull's-eye. Juan, though? Please, girl. The *one time* I tried to suggest he do it differently, three months ago on a night when I worked late and got home in need of loving, he sighed and looked all beleaguered, wiped his mouth on the back of his soggy gorilla hand like I made him tired, and whined, "Do I *have* to?"

What is *that* shit, *m'ija*? "Do I *have* to?" Please, psh. How can you get busy with a man who asks you something nonsensical like that? I was all, "If there's something you'd rather be doing, then by all means, *nene*, go do it." I closed my legs to him then, and I haven't had the urge to open them to him again. It's not entirely my fault that I've wandered down the path to Marcus. It's Juan's fault, too, for not trying harder to keep me interested.

"*Así, papito,*" I call to Marcus as I run my hands over his short, kinky hair.

"I'll assume that means 'yes, Daddy,' in Puerto Rican Spanish," he mumbles. "It means 'like that, Daddy,'" I correct him. He smiles up at me as he tweaks my nipple with one hand, and I feel like I'm on fire.

I read one time that some marriages *need* affairs, because they reignite the flames that went out between husband and wife. Honestly? I love my husband because he's the only fool who completely understands where I come from. I don't have to explain anything about being a Puerto Rican New Englander to him, because he's one too. I'm hoping that's what happens here, okay? That I can take these flames that this golf pro man has fired up in me and keep them lit up like the Olympic torch until I get home.

"I want to be inside you," he mumbles, twisting out of his polo shirt, coming up toward me all sculpted muscle. He's removing the golf pro shorts, and mama is pleased to see his club's nothing less than a seven iron.

"What a boy wants, a boy gets." I arrange myself for easy access. "Gimme that putter, baby. Sink it in the hole."

"More like a driver, but who's going to quibble over semantics at a moment like this?" he asks as he slides in with a groan, and tells me how warm and soft it is. Like I didn't *know*. I'm pure melted butter, *nena*. Okay? He begins to rock me, gently, with a sweet smile on his face. I don't mean to, but I start to make some little noises. Before I know it, my eyes have rolled back in my head, and I've begun to suck my own damn finger. For Catholic girls, it's easier to be kinky with a man we don't know.

Don't think less of me, okay? I have never been a one-man woman any more than my daddy was a one-woman man. It's in my genes. I didn't sleep around, exactly. But you know how I did. I had multiple possibilities to get me through my day. My girlfriends can confirm this for you when they get here. Just ask them, any of them. All my adult life, until I got married, I juggled men, at least two at a time, as a form of insurance. If one left me, the way my daddy did, or didn't pay enough attention to me, the way my daddy did, or got his ass shot dead by hoodlums, like my brother did, there was always the other one to step in. I been like that since high school, when I first started dating Juan and realized my love for him was so big it might crush me if he ever lost interest. I kept them all at a distance after understanding that. None of them have been close to my heart except him, and now he's breaking it with his *santa madre* act. I am a sound investor—never put in more than you can afford to lose. The safest bets involve a diversified portfolio. I'm all about biology and financial planning.

The pumping gets faster. Marcus goes to work, okay? Something about athletes. They know their bodies. *Ay, m'ija.* Why does *chingando* have to feel so good? Wouldn't the world's problems be solved if sex felt more like plunging up a clogged toilet? You don't like to think God screwed up, but with the whole sex-drive thing, he just might have. Without pleasurable sex, there'd be no risk of overpopulation, no AIDS, no unwanted pregnancies, and no cheating wives.

"Harder, baby," I tell Marcus as I press my eyes closed and flex my calf muscles. I could get used to this man. Yes, I could. If I weren't married, I mean. Which I am. I am married. Have to remember. That. Oh. God. "I'm almost there."

He says nothing, and, like the husband I wish I had married instead of the one I got, does exactly what I ordered.

When we finish, he leans up on his elbow, all sweet-looking, kisses me gently on the lips, and says, with a tear in his eye, "It has been a long time since I did that, Usnavys Rivera."

"Pssh. You're lying."

"No, no, I'm not lying." He closes his eyes, flops onto his back with a satisfied, melancholy smile, mouthing numbers as he counts on his fingers. His eyes open and he regards me seriously. "Three years. It has been three years since I made love to a woman."

"What? Why? You scared of girls, Marcus?"

The tears brim a little more, and one of them traces a line down his check. He wipes it away with a strong, solid hand I'm sure doesn't do dishes all day. "No, I'm not scared of girls. Three years ago. That's when my wife died. I haven't met anyone who interested me, and, frankly, did not think I ever would. Until now."

I balk. "I'm the first? Since your wife died?"

Marcus nods, and smiles with a hint of sadness that is quickly replaced by something that looks like love. "You remind me of her. You two. You look alike. She was a firecracker, just like you."

"A firecracker," I say. I don't know what else to tell him. I remind the man of his dead wife, and he loved her, and I know he's transferring that onto me and I don't deserve it, but still. Transfers can feel real, *m'ija*. They can. You shouldn't be jealous of a dead woman, but for some reason, I am. I imagine the house they lived in, the wine they shared on the terrace, the elegance of her husband a sharp contrast to the ordinariness of mine.

"So, I hope this won't be the last time we see one another," he says. "I'd love to get a number for you in Boston. I travel out that way quite a bit. And now that I've met you, I have a reason to go more often."

I should know better, girl, I should. I realize that. This is the part where a nice person would tell the truth about her husband and child. Denial is a wonderful thing, though, when you need it. So it is that I get up and walk to the desk, and I write my cell number down on the little hotel pad of paper. I rip off the sheet, hand it to him, wondering how on earth I'm going to keep Juan from finding this shit out. I'm going to have to start policing my phone like a guard. I'm going to have to sneak and lie my ass off. What is wrong with me, *m'ija*? I shouldn't have opened this door, but what else am I supposed to do? Old habits die hard.

The man, Marcus, this beautiful man who pleased me, is crying, and he plays golf, and I remind him of a woman he loved. And you know what that all means, don't you? It *means* that even with my size and attitude and my current moral relativism, even with my head all screwed up like this and my heart flying in a thousand different directions, he just might be able to love me the way I have deserved to be loved all my life.

*l*auren

WAKE UP HAPPY, even with the little sting of heartburn. The New England summer sun beams through the custom bamboo blinds of my bedroom, leaving butterscotch stripes of light across the exposed red-brick wall behind the headboard. My calico cat Fatso dozes on the light goose down comforter between me and Amaury, my fiancé. That is correct, I said "fiancé."

My new fiancé, not my old fiancé. I am scheduled to be married for the first time, again, only this time I think it might actually happen.

Amaury's awake, his chiseled chin propped up on one of his strong hands, looking at me with his wide, brown, almond-shaped eyes with the long lashes. His gaze is soulful, intense, and filled with humor. He loves me. He is naked. Life is good. So, so good.

I reach out to touch him, my pale white finger even paler against the toasty brown of his skin, and trace the outline of the scar on his exposed shoulder; it is the size, color, and shape of a ragged penny, the entry wound from a bullet fired by a rival gang member a decade ago. I know nothing about gang life. Amaury has three of these scars on his body, and hundreds of stories. But that's all ancient history. Since he met me five years ago, his difficult life has turned around, and my okay life has gotten good. So, so good.

"Buenos días, mi amor," I say, practicing the Spanish that he has taught me. Until I met him, I was one of millions of Spanish-challenged Latinas in the United States, more aligned with my white-trash mother's Louisiana swamp people than my dad's New Jersey Cuban exile people, for the simple fact that in my formative language years, my mother raised me (albeit on Kool-Aid, Velveeta, and mayonnaise) while my father worked at the university. They later divorced, but I won't let that bother me right now. It, too, is ancient history, and she is far from this place. I will not allow the tapes of her negativity to play in my head anymore. Thanks to years with a therapist who wears fancy scarves, all those "who the hell do you think you are's" and "that Lauren, she has a mind of her own's" have been dumped in the great emotional trash can in my soul, sealed away forever.

Amaury smiles with those perfectly straight white teeth at me, and my heart flops around, squashed to smithereens once more by his unbelievable physical beauty. He grew up in a splintered blue shack in the Dominican Republic, with a dirt floor and no running water, yet his teeth are better than mine. His skin, where it is unscathed by bullet marks, is smooth and creamy, absolutely edible. That's because his mother, *que Dios la bendiga*, cared about him. I won't think about my mother right now. Why ruin a good thing?

"¿Como estás, baby?" I ask him.

He answers me, as he often does, with a scrap of memorized poem, in Spanish.

"Two happy lovers make one bread," he says in his gravelly, nearly whispered mother tongue. He takes my finger and kisses it, then scrunches bits of my long, curly red hair in his hand. "A single moon drop in the grass. Walking they cast two shadows that flow together. Waking they leave one sun empty in their bed."

"No, don't tell me!" I cry, amazed that I understood it all, blinking up at the high ceiling of my new Jamaica Plain condo. Instinctively, I run a fingertip along my lower eyelids to minimize the dark circles caused by my lazy failure to remove my eye makeup the night before. I'm working on the whole grown-up thing. I know I should remove my makeup, I just don't always do it. "I know that one. I do."

"Okay. Then I won't tell you." He leans back a little, a smile of triumph on his full, perfect lips. His sexy grin carves dimples in his cheeks. He is so adorable it's hard to imagine him as a gangster. They don't look like Amaury in movies. In a movie, Amaury might play the cute South American soccer star.

"You think I can't figure it out," I tease him.

"I didn't say that."

"You didn't have to. Your eyes said it."

"My eyes said nothing of the sort. Yours are full of mascara, which is why you can't see very well."

"Gabriela Mistral?" I ask as I rub the makeup away again, harder this time but not hard enough to stretch the skin into wrinkles. He shakes his head, and his intelligent eyes dance with my failure. A drug dealer who barely spoke English when I met him, Amaury now holds an associate's degree from Roxbury Community College in English literature, and he's working on a bachelor's degree in poetry from Emerson College. When he's not working or in class, he's reading and writing. I'm a newspaper columnist. We share a love of words. We also share a body chemistry that can only be described as animalistic and incredibly perfect.

"García Lorca?" I ask.

"*Tampoco,*" he says, shaking his head.

"André Breton?"

"*Ay, Dios mío.* Come on, *bonbón,*" he cajoles. "It's easy." Fatso the cat wakes up pissed as Amaury lifts her out of the way so that he can snuggle closer to me. She licks the spot of fur he's touched, as if his very essence offends her. *I've* forgiven him for the time he cheated on me, two years back, after one of our big fights, but my cat has not. It wasn't technically even cheating, because we were broken up for a few days. But it still hurt. For what it's worth, Amaury and I break up every six weeks or so, just because. We like to fight and argue, and we each like to be right all the time and we both like to win. This leads to problems. But not fatal problems. We always get back together within three or four days.

"Think," he says with a kiss to my forehead.

"Give me a hint," I say, through the next kiss, to my lips.

"Okay. His real name was Neftali Ricardo Reyes Basoalto."

I laugh. "No one would give their child a name like that."

"His mother did. He's from Chile."

"Alive or dead?"

"Poets never die, you know that. Your question is unanswerable."

Amaury kisses me again, longer and deeper, and I feel my body respond immediately, as it always has to him. From the first moment I saw him in a crowded nightclub, I have lusted for him, and time has not diminished his effect on me. Even his morning breath excites me. He has never smelled bad to me, which is remarkable considering how many men seem to smell bad all the time. His confident hands search my body, and he pulls me tight against him. I feel his damp, firm excitement against my thigh. I try to ignore the odd pain below my sternum. It has been bothering me for a few weeks.

"Chile?" I ask, weakly.

"*Sí,*" he says.

"But it's not Mistral?"

"More famous than Mistral."

"Neruda?" I ask, astonished that I'd spaced this famed poet out.

Amaury says nothing. Rather, he climbs on top of me with a predatory stare in his eyes, separates my legs with his own knee. He makes sure I'm ready with an exploratory dance from his fingertips. Then, without a word, he enters me.

"Oh," I gasp. My lip comes to rest between my top and bottom teeth. So, so good.

Amaury kisses and then nips at the vulnerable skin over my jugular vein, and murmurs, "Pablo Neruda. King of the love poem. You, *amor mío*, win the prize."

TWO HOURS LATER, Amaury drives me across Franklin Park in his black Lincoln Navigator with the tinted windows, toward Logan Airport, with the new Vuitton luggage he bought me in the trunk. He wears his work clothes—trendy dark jeans from Express Men's, and a FUBU shirt with several large gold chains and colorful Santeria beads around his neck. As the new East Coast regional director of street teams and MySpace publicity campaigns for Wagner Records' Latin division, he might not be a gangster anymore. But his posture and style are still street enough to make my heart race with his bad-boy vibe. He drives a little too fast, steers with one hand as the other rests on his crotch or holds his Apple iPhone to his ear. He speaks Spanish, lightning quick, and I can't tell what he says, exactly, something about shipments and numbers. Work talk.

We stop at a Dunkin' Donuts in Roxbury, and he tells me to wait in the car. I obey, even though I hate how he sometimes feels entitled to tell me what to do. Maybe it's my outfit that is making me cranky. My size eight dark jeans are too tight; the green lacy thong flossing my ass cheeks doesn't help. Note to self: Never wear a lacy thong when you're about to sit on a plane for five hours. It's masochistic. The soft black scoop-necked black DKNY T-shirt is too low-cut, too, and I keep having to adjust myself so my purple bra isn't showing and the sparkly silver DKNY letters stay on my boobs instead of on my belly. Because my size is up and down by twenty pounds and three dress sizes all the time, it's hard to remember what fits and what doesn't. I try to stretch the waistband on my jeans a little at the waist with my thumbs. I pull the thong out of my ass, and stuff my boobs back into the shirt. All better.

Sort of.

Amaury returns moments later, still talking on the phone, with a breakfast bagel, egg, bacon, and cheese, and a large iced hazelnut coffee, heavy on the cream with a packet of artificial sweetener dumped in. For me. These are my favorites, and he knows it. As I take them, I admire the twinkle of my large diamond engagement ring, a ring far superior to the one my last fiancé, Ed the Bigheaded Texican, gave me. I take the pink straw into my mouth, and sip. The sun, the coffee, the ring, Amaury's soothing rumble of voice, the reggaeton pumping softly from the speakers. It's all a dream come true for me. I am in love with this man, and my life is excellent.

He finally ends his call when we near the airport. Instantly, the phone vibrates to let him know he's got a text message. He checks it, holding the screen away from me, bites his lip, and puts it away quickly, his face betraying no hint of what it might have been about. Amaury is a good poker player. I've watched him do it. You never know what he's thinking. My blood speeds up with the memory of the cheating incident, which I found out about from calling every number stored in the memory of his old Razr phone. I realized then that my lack of trust was part of what drove him away. I'm trying to be more trusting. You can't have a good relationship without trust. Not trusting a man can be a self-fulfilling prophecy of infidelity.

"You ready for your vacation with your *amigas*?" he asks me as he slides the SUV up in front of the crowded American Airlines drop-off area, and slides his free hand up my thigh. We're double-parked, but so is everyone else.

"Very," I say, as his hand makes its way to the apex of my legs. "Don't start," I say, wriggling a bit. "You trying to torture me?"

"I just wanted to give you something to remember me by," he says, in Spanish.

"That'll do it," I say.

He leans over to kiss me. "Have a good vacation. You deserve a break." He knows work has not been going well for me. I keep hoping my column will get moved from the Lifestyles section of the *Boston Gazette* to the news section, where I'd have a wider variety of topics to write about, namely politics and immigration, but the powers that be don't seem to think I'm needed there. My editor and others seem just fine with the news columnists at the *Gazette* being all male, and all white, and mostly conservative. Why muddy those pristine waters of opinion with a progressive Latina voice? That would be crazy.

"You deserve a break, *cariño*," he says, vibrating his hand against my crotch for one titillating moment before snatching it away. "It's going to be great." He cuts the engine, jumps out, and opens the back to get my bags, leaves me there all hot and bothered. For a second, I wonder if it would be acceptable to relieve my sexual tension by myself in a public bathroom stall. I've never done that before, but it might be sort of interesting to try. Then again, I might end up like Larry Craig. I hear the text chime go off again. His phone is in the cup holder between the seats. I glance back. Amaury is hauling my bags to the crowded curb, stuck behind six talkative old women in saris. I grab the phone and sneak a look at the message.

WHEN U CMNG? T Q-RO. BESOS. MC

My moment of sultry excitement disappears. I don't want to feel panic. Maybe it's nothing. Maybe it's for work. Lots of people in the Latin world sign off with *"besos"* and it doesn't mean it's sexual in nature. It's a much more affectionate culture, his. I need to remember that. I take a deep breath, and silently recite the mission statement my therapist gave me. *I am confident and trusting. I know good things will come to me. I am surrounded by white light and kindness and compassion.*

I lower myself to the street, weave through the East Indian contingent, and join Amaury on the sidewalk. We embrace, and kiss.

"Hey, yous twos, keep it movin'," bellows a uniformed police officer. Amaury tenses, and I feel him wanting a fight.

"Don't," I say. "It's not you. It's since 9/11, everything's different here. Remember?"

"I know," he says, adding in Spanish, "but these fuckers always want to keep my kind down."

"Olvídalo," I say in Spanish. Forget it.

"Fóquin cops," he grumbles.

"I'll see you in a few days," I say.

"Don't drink too much," he says. "And don't cheat on me."

I stare at him, trying to see if he's kidding. I can't tell. "You're joking, right?" I ask.

Amaury shrugs. "Sometimes you drink too much."

"No, I know that. I meant about the cheating thing. Why would you say that to me?"

"Just don't cheat on me, that's all." Is my fiancé projecting?

The policeman asks him to get moving again, this time in a sterner voice.

"I'd never cheat on you," I tell him. "I love you."

"I love you too," he says, eyeing the cop. "I have to go now." He moves away after brushing my breast hard enough with his hand to indicate intention and pride of ownership, but without a last good-bye kiss.

I watch him walk back toward the SUV. He turns to smile and blow me a kiss before walking around to the driver's side and getting in. I watch as he instantly picks up his phone and checks the texts. He seems to have forgotten I'm here. I walk through the crowd until I can look back at him and see his face. I squint to see his mouth as he talks into the phone. I can tell exactly what he says.

"Hola, mi amor."

Hello, my love.

Maybe it's nothing. He greets lots of people that way. Maybe it's for work. Or maybe it's his mom in Baní. That's got to be it. His mom, *que Dios la bendiga.* He's been with me so much lately, we practically live together. It's probably nothing. So why does the air feel thicker, like someone stole all the oxygen?

"You all right, lady?" the cop asks me. "We gotta keep this area clear."

I shake myself out of the panic state, reassure myself that Amaury is nothing like my last fiancé, whom I caught cheating on me with a sleazy teenager. I was hiding in Ed's closet, and saw the whole thing. It's hard, once you've been through something like that, to ever trust a man completely again. Any man.

"I'm fine, thanks," I tell the policeman.

But as my heart races and adrenaline floods my body, as Boston spins around me, I'm not so sure it's true.

rebecca

ANDRE AND I sit on leather pueblo-style patio chairs on the sprawling back porch of our cozy new 1,800-square-foot adobe weekend house in the artist colony of Tesuque, New Mexico, in a lush green mountain valley just outside of Santa Fe. The house sits at the top of a peach-colored mesa—a flat-topped hill—and over the top of the tumbling tangle of vegetable and flower gardens we can see the entire verdant valley stretching out below us, and the purple mountains that rise beyond. The cloudless sky is a brilliant blue, cobalt really. The air still carries last night's chill, and a fire burns in the freestanding pottery chiminea nearby. The morning brings a bracing chill of fresh mountain air. Miles from any freeways or main roads, it is absolutely quiet here. Just the crackle of the flames, the soft, round sounds of mourning doves in the sagebrush and poplar trees, and the quiet patter of the stream running along the north side of the house.

"Gorgeous," Andre says, as he sips local piñon coffee from his thick brown pottery mug. A silver carafe of the coffee steams on the leather-topped table before us, next to a platter of sliced mango and watermelon and a basket of warm blueberry muffins baked for us by our very nice neighbors, retired diplomats with young children, down the road this morning. I never tire of my husband's British accent, or his deep voice. He is very tall, London-born with Nigerian parents, and this morning he wears chino pants with a light lime-green sweater that sets off his beautiful, nearly ebony skin.

"It *is* beautiful here, isn't it?" I reply, taking a deep breath of clean air and gazing down upon the land where my family has lived since the sixteenth century. I am so pleased to finally have a home of my own here. Our main residence will of course continue to be our four-story brownstone in Boston's South End neighborhood, but I will make every effort to visit our northern New Mexico hideaway often.

Andre looks at me and smiles. The goatee and mustache suit him, now that his facial hair is salted with white. He looks quite distinguished and fatherly. "That's not what I meant."

I look at him and wait for him to explain. He has that flirty look in his dark, nearly liquid eyes. "You," he says simply. "You are the gorgeous thing I meant."

I went for a run early this morning, and now, freshly showered, wear a long white linen skirt with a matching sleeveless button-down blouse with a pink denim jacket. I feel pretty, natural, and healthy. The breeze ruffles my dark hair, which I wear in a longer than usual style, a layered bob slightly lower than my chin. We are on vacation. We came to New Mexico from Boston two weeks ago to shop for furniture and art for the new house, in anticipation of my reunion with my college friends at a resort not too far from here.

"Thank you," I tell him. No matter how long you've been married, you should never lose your manners with your partner. If more people remembered to treat their spouses with the respect and dignity they reserve for strangers, fewer marriages would end in disaster. "You are pretty easy on the eyes yourself."

Andre rises from his seat, smiling, and comes to stand behind me. He wraps me in his arms and kisses the top of my head. "But I am not the one carrying our child," he says.

I tilt my head up to him, and we kiss.

"It's really going to happen this time," I say as I place my hands protectively over my still-flat belly. I am only two months along, but it is further than I've made it with the last two pregnancies, both of which ended in miscarriage.

Inside the house, the phone rings. Andre goes to answer it, leaving me alone with my beloved high desert. I want to move back here to raise our child when the time comes, which is part of the reason I've been considering selling my magazine, *Ella*, to a multinational conglomerate. I cannot imagine raising a child, particularly a partially Spanish child, anywhere but here. Andre could relocate his software company anywhere, even Santa Fe, and with the recent round of layoffs at Intel and other local high-tech companies, there'd be no shortage of qualified employees.

"Rebecca!" calls Andre from the open French doors leading into the great room and kitchen. "For you, darling."

"I'll take it inside." I go to him, and take the silver cordless from his hand.

"It's your mother," he whispers with a cringe, one hand guarding her from hearing him. "I'll just tend to the garden a bit."

"Hello, Mother," I say, as warmly as possible. "How are you?"

"Your father doesn't know I'm calling," she hisses.

"Is he there?"

"No."

"Then why are you whispering?"

"You know how he feels about this," she says, referring to the fact that my father, a short, swarthy man the white population of this country would regard as a minority but who does not see himself that way, has publicly disowned me for marrying a black man.

"I know, and I see it only as more proof that you were always the smarter one," I say. *Though not smart enough to leave him*, I add silently. *Though not smart enough to treat me and my husband with the dignity and respect we deserve.*

"I just wanted to call to tell you I'm sorry I won't be able to come up and see your new house," she says.

"I didn't expect you would."

"But thank you for inviting me."

"You're welcome."

"Next time, don't send a card. He might see it."

"Fine."

My mother sighs, and she sounds old. I love her, and hate her at the same time. I pray to God that when I have children of my own, they never feel this way about me.

"Have you been taking your insulin?" I ask her.

"Well, that's just it," she says. "I'm tired of it, *m'ija*. I don't want to do that anymore."

"Mother. You have to take your medication. You know that."

"Sometimes I don't want to."

"Please don't talk like that."

"I told *el patrón* the other day he should start adding those organic tortillas to his line, you know? I told him that's what everyone else is doing. The organic, and the wraps, you know, with the sun-dried tomatoes and the basil."

"That's good, Mother," I tell her, cringing at her use of the Spanish phrase for "the boss" to describe my father. "You're right. I hope he listens to you."

"He always listens to me."

He just doesn't publicly acknowledge that most of his ideas are yours, I think. "That's good, Mother," I say.

She sighs again, and I fear for her. Lately, she has sounded so depressed. "Mother, would you do me a favor?"

"What is it, *mi hijita*?"

"Go see Doctor Candelaria and ask him about putting you on Paxil or Xanax."

"What's Paxil annex?"

"Never mind, Mom. Just ask him."

"I don't want to go to the doctor anymore," she says, weary. She needs some good news in her life. She has never completely forgiven me for breaking my vows and divorcing Brad, my first husband, and I don't think she'll ever come to accept Andre as her son-in-law. But I do think she would love a grandchild. I should wait until I've passed the three-month mark, but she seems so down.

"I have some good news," I tell her, before I've had time to stop my mouth.

"What is it?"

"I'm pregnant."

Silence. I can hear her inhale, long and slow, and blow the air out again. She only does this when she is trying to keep herself from getting angry. My shoulders tense instantly.

"Did you hear me?" I ask.

"Yes. Of course I heard you."

"You're going to be a grandmother."

"No, I'm not," she states flatly.

"*Excuse* me?" I say.

Her voice quivering, she tells me, "You sinned against God when you divorced Brad. He was a good man, Rebecca. And you sinned against your family when you married that *mayate*."

"Don't call him that."

"The Lord does not look kindly upon those who sin and do not repent," she continues softly, in a tremulous voice.

"What are you trying to say?"

"I am saying that with any luck, you'll lose this one just like all the others," she says in a low voice.

I gasp, and pull the phone away from my ear as if it has burned me. I press the End button, and sit there, stunned. I look around, at the thick adobe walls painted lovingly by Andre and me in muted tones of the desert. At the hammered tin frames around the large mirrors on the walls. At the local paintings, colorful and joyful, of northern New Mexico scenery. At the pottery, and the Navajo rugs. We painstakingly created this oasis in my home state as a testament to the love I feel for this place, for its people and, yes, for my family and ancestors. I feel the tears sting the inside of my nose, and behind my eyes.

Andre comes back in, and finds me like this. "Oh no," he cries. "What is it? What did that monstrous harpy say this time?"

I tell him. Andre sits down next to me on the leather sofa and holds me in his arms.

"Darling. Listen to me. You mustn't pay her any mind," he says. "She's an idiot. You have to accept that, Rebecca."

The phone rings again. My mother's number appears on the screen. She hates to be hung up on.

"Don't answer it," I tell him.

"I think I must," he says.

Andre takes the phone from me, and presses it on. "Mrs. Baca," he says. "I am only going to say this once. Do not call here again." He pauses, listening, and then replies. "What am I going to do if you do? Here's what I'm going to do. I'm going to call Snoop Dogg, Wayne Brady, Clarence Thomas, and all of my fellow Negro gang members, and we are going to come to your house in our—

"I don't know, darling," he says to me. "What is it Negro gangsters drive, anyway?"

My jaw drops. I am astonished that he's speaking to my mother this way. But she deserves it. "Hummers," I say. "Lowrider Hummers."

"Smashing. We'll come to your terrifying barrio in our lowrider Hummers and we'll shoot the place up with our . . ." He pauses and looks at me again for help.

"Gats?" I suggest.

"Right. We'll drive by and shoot up the terrifying barrio with our Scary Black Man Gats and gangster ways. Cheers."

I laugh, in spite of myself, as he listens to her again. He nods sarcastically—furious, really—as he listens, as if she makes some kind of sense. He is the single most educated, elegant, and refined human being I have ever known. A brilliant man who heads a company estimated to be worth more than $70 million. My parents, meanwhile, own a tortilla company that gives them enough to feel rich in New Mexico, but which wouldn't buy them half a townhouse on my block in Boston.

He says into the phone, "What's that? You don't live in the terrifying barrio, Mrs. Baca? You live in Tanoan? A Tanoan? What is that? Some kind of tequila-drunk Mexican ghetto, certainly."

I can't control the laughter now. Tanoan is a lily-white, gated country-club area in the northeast heights of Albuquerque. In addition, my mother finds nothing more offensive than being assumed to be Mexican. She believes, as I once did, that we are purely Spanish. As in white Europeans, purely. Our family tree, researched in part by my friend Cuicatl, indicates otherwise, however; almost all of our female ancestors were Native Americans from the region.

Andre stares at the phone now, in mock confusion. "Fancy that," he says. "The line has gone dead."

I lean against his strong shoulder. "It's probably for the best," I say.

"Absolutely." He looks around, at the spacious gourmet kitchen and the gorgeous Edward Gonzales portraits of women on hillsides, and the Jacqueline A. Fleming landscape paintings. He smiles at me as if nothing were wrong at all, and says, "Now, my darling girl, let's get you packed up and over to the resort, to go see your enchanting girlfriends—the people who actually care about you. Shall we?"

sara

ONE OF THE TWO incredibly skinny makeup artists dispassionately powders my nose as if I were a sculpture, while the electrical grip softens the lighting in the studio to make me appear less tired. The stylist fluffs my blond, shoulder-length hair and sprays the bangs and layers into place— again. When he's done with that, he adjusts my light blue button-down shirt, which matches my eyes, and then he fixes the chunky silver and turquoise necklace.

I didn't realize I looked tired, *chica*. But that's what Elizabeth, my best friend and the producer of my weekly home-decorating and cooking show,

Casas Americanas, just told everyone into their little black headsets. "Sara's looking tired. Cut!"

Now? *Oyeme, now* everyone is running around like *pollitos* with their heads cut off, trying to make me look fresh and young again. Five years ago, this kind of thing would have bruised my ego, but not anymore. What ego? I have no ego anymore. Are you kidding? When you work in TV, you learn to take yourself with a grain of kosher salt.

My assistant, Lourdes, trots out from the shadows with a phone in her hand. "Sara! Call for you. It's someone named José?"

Everyone in the studio makes a teasing "ooooh" sound, like they're in the fourth grade. For the past two days, I've been getting calls from "José" here at work, and everyone is dying to know who the new guy is. Little do they know he's not a new guy at all. Nor is his name José. I calm my heart, which races at the mention of the call. He shouldn't be calling me here. It is gutsy and reckless that he would. But he has always toyed with me like this, kept me on the edge of bliss and self-destruction. He turns my adrenaline on like a faucet.

I pretend not to care.

"Please tell him I'll call him back *en un ratito,*" I tell her. "I'm working here."

"She'll call you back, José," Lourdes says into the phone. She says his name like a schoolgirl teasing a boy on the playground. You think the people who work for you might be a little more mature, ¿*verdad?* Not so here. She presses the phone off, and raises a suggestive brow in my general direction. "Sara and José, sitting in a tree . . ."

"What are you, six?" I ask her. "Let's get to work here."

"Seriously, Sara," cries Lourdes. "You have to tell us who it is."

"No, I don't. Let's get this thing in the can already." Assistants make adjustments to the stage and equipment, and fit me once more with the earpiece.

"Am I beautiful again?" I ask, my voice traveling from the enormous boom mike hanging over the kitchen-set island into the ears of my minions. I pose sarcastically and bat my false eyelashes. You have to wear grotesquely thick makeup you'd never wear in public when you're under studio lights, *chica,* but it looks *completamente normal* when the show runs.

"You look perfect," says Elizabeth. I hear her in the tiny, flesh-colored speaker in my ear.

On cue, everyone scurries from the set. It's a kitchen, *sabes*, done in bright colors with a mix of Mexican rustic elements and 1950s deco pre-Castro Cuban elements gleaned from photos of my parents' house in Miramar that I used to pore over as a child. The counters are done in hand-painted Mexican ceramic tiles, blue and white and yellow. The Sub-Zero custom refrigerators are made to look like the old capsule-shaped Frigidaires from the 1950s. My pots are hammered copper, and the mixing bowls I use are made of terra cotta and black clay. The cabinets are carved wood, stained in primary colors, the tops of them decorated with clay vessels and figurines and assorted colorful folk art from the heart of Mexico. Mexican iron and tinwork decorates the walls. Through the fake windows on the studio wall over the counter behind me sway artificial palm trees that look real on the small screen. It is all very festive without being gaudy, and, judging from our growing viewership nationwide, resonates with many different kinds of people.

"Ready, Sarita?" asks Elizabeth.

"As I'll ever be," I call out. *Don't think about him, Sara. Just do your job. Don't think about how people will react. Don't think about how you're going to explain this one.*

Prep cooks swoop in and replace the minced onion from the last cut with a fresh one, the soiled bowls with clean ones. They wipe the counters, adjust everything just so, and Elizabeth begins to count down. "We're rolling in five, four, three, two, one." In her jeans and flannel shirt, the outfit I teased her for borrowing from that communist propagandist Michael Moore, she points at me from across the black floor of the studio beyond the camera. The camera is manned by Valentín Garza, our newest hire, a strapping, dark-eyed twenty-one-year-old college graduate and soccer player from San Antonio who is so hot he makes me wish I were younger. The lights shine down upon me, and I'm on.

"Hi there! Welcome back to *Casas Americanas*. I'm your host, Sara Behar-Asis, and in today's cooking segment, in honor of the Fourth of July and the all-American cookout, we'll be exploring one of my favorite Cuban recipes, the Cuban hamburger. No, I'm not kidding, *chicos*! We eat hamburgers in

Cuba, just like here in the States, but we do it with a lot more flavor and a lot more pep. That's no surprise, right? We do everything with more *sazón*, ¿sí? Right.

"So, the first thing you'll need is this, about a half a cup of quality bread crumbs. You can use any kind of bread you want, but I prefer crumbs from a loaf of crusty Cuban bread. My grandmother used to make these for us in Miami, and you could smell them cooking all the way in the backyard, where I'd be swimming in the pool, and I'd come running for them. *Verdad que sí, chica*, running. Okay. So you take your Cuban bread crumbs like this, all finely crushed. If you don't have any of that, you can use French or Italian bread. *Lo que sea.* So you take the bread crumbs like this, and you soak them in about a quarter cup of milk. I use whole, organic milk, because that's me, but you'd be fine using lowfat or nonfat if that's your thing. I prefer flavor, and I make up for it on the treadmill in the morning. Okay, *bueno*. Next thing we do is take a big bowl like this and just mix everything together. Here's the everything, okay? You ready? You writing this down? If not, no worries, just check my Web site at www.sarascasasamericanas.com."

I try not to look at Valentín as he eases closer and moves the camera expertly around me and what I'm doing. He's so fine, *chica*, with those luscious Tejano lips that remind me of the actor Jay Hernandez. He's so fine that sometimes I like to imagine what that kind of attentiveness would be like in bed, ¿sabes? But I don't look directly at him, because there's nothing worse than when the host of the show looks away from the camera, unless she's got a studio audience, which is where we're headed next year. *Qué chévere, ¿no?* So far, we've been able to shoot the show in Boston, where we live, but I'm thinking about moving the show to California. I've always wanted to live there, in the land of palm trees and mountains.

"*Bueno.* Okay. Here's the ingredients. A pound of ground beef. I use kosher because that's how we are in my family, we're Jubans as you know, but you use whatever floats your little boat, *chica*. Next you add one egg, half a teaspoon of paprika or chile powder, a teaspoon of Thousand Island dressing, another teaspoon of ketchup, a quarter teaspoon of fresh ground black pepper, two teaspoons of salt, a teaspoon of ground onion, more if you like onion, ¿no? I like to add a clove of crushed garlic, too. Put the bread crumbs in there *así*, and then you just take your hands—don't be shy now, roll up those sleeves, *mamita*—and you just smoosh it all together *así*, like that, until it's all good and mixed together. If you have kids, let them help you with this part. My boys love to get their hands into the mix. Just make sure everyone washes up before *and* after, with soap and hot water. But you knew that already, *¿no?* I thought so.

"Okay, now. After that, you cover the bowl with plastic wrap, and you put it in the fridge for at least two hours. *¿Está bien?*" I put the new bowl into the yellow fridge, and take another one out of the pink fridge, my routine.

"Now, through the magic of television, we've got some of this delicious mixture that's been chilling for *dos horas ya*, and I'll show you what we do next. You take a round cookie cutter, a big one, five or six inches across, like this one here. You mash the meat mixture down on a board or a plate, just like this, and then you cut perfect little circles. You heat up a grill in the backyard, or, like I'm doing here, a skillet inside, and you lightly grease it with *manteca*, which is lard, if you have it and like it, or butter, or even olive oil. I like extra-virgin olive oil myself. And then, presto, *así*, just like that, you add your meat to the pan, and you fry it up like a regular hamburger, to whatever you like, rare, medium, well, whatever, and then you take it out and serve it on whatever kind of hamburger bun you like. You top it with chopped raw onions, and you serve it with French fries, but not the ones we're used to here. They're skinny fries, okay? And not because they make you skinny. They don't. Because *they* are skinny, like *frites* in France. I'll show you how to prepare those when we come back." I try to look relaxed, and smile directly at the camera.

"Cut!" calls out Elizabeth. "That worked. That was good."

The crew descends upon me again, and, like picnic ants, clean up to prepare for the next segment.

"Anybody got Tylenol?" complains Elizabeth.

"*Oye, pero ¿qué te pasa?*" I ask her.

"I've got a headache. Stress. We're hardly sleeping with the baby waking up all night." Elizabeth and her wife, Selwyn, recently adopted a baby boy from Africa.

"I know it doesn't seem like it will ever end," I tell her. "But trust me, they sleep through the night eventually."

"Promise?"

"Claro."

"Selwyn will be happy to hear that. She's like a different person lately."

"Mira," I tell her. "After work, we're on vacation, *chica.* A weekend in New Mexico with our *sucias."* I am so glad Rebecca chose New Mexico for the retreat, because I can check it out as the possible future home of the show. I am also considering Los Angeles and Scottsdale, Arizona.

"Thank God for vacations," says Elizabeth. "I need it."

"When are you guys leaving?" asks Valentín. I love his youthful male voice almost as much as his face, okay, but you can't tell someone that when they're twelve years younger than you and you are their boss.

"Tonight, after this," I say.

Valentín looks right at me. "I'll miss you," he says. "Maybe when you get back we can have lunch. Without José."

Ay, Dios mío, chica. I don't know if he meant it like it sounded, but if he did, this boy's got balls to match his face. Strong, and confident. He has been flirting with me nonstop since the job interview, and everyone notices it.

"Speaking of José," I say. "We're taking five, right?"

"We're taking as long as it takes for the Tylenol to kick in," says Elizabeth.

"Bueno. I'm gonna go make a call, be right back."

I sneak off to my car, which is parked in back of the sound stage near a Dumpster. I dial his number. He picks up after half a ring.

"So you finally found time for me?" he says by way of greeting.

"I'm sorry," I tell him. "It's been crazy, trying to get everything tied up before we leave for New Mexico."

"You should stay home," he tells me.

"I'd be lonely without the girls," I say.

"I'll come keep you company."

"You know we can't do that," I tell him.

"No one would have to know."

"The boys," I say, referring to our twin sons. "They'd talk about how Daddy was home. They'd tell everyone."

Roberto is silent on the other end of the line, for a long moment, and then he asks, "You swear it's girlfriends you're going to see? And not some *comemierda?"*

"No *comemierda,"* I assure him.

"You better be telling the truth."

"Roberto, don't start."

"I know. I'm sorry."

You see? He's working on the whole temper thing. The old Roberto wouldn't have apologized, *chica*. Not if his life depended on it.

I tell him I haven't been with anyone since he fled the country five years ago, after accidentally killing our beloved housekeeper during an ugly fight with me. We used to have ugly fights. But they were just as much my fault as his. The justice system in this country is stacked against the men. No, seriously.

"I'll come to New Mexico," he says. "I'll sneak into your room like when we were in high school."

I smile at the thought, the memories. "*Ay, mi amor.* I'd love that. But I don't think it's a good idea."

"Why not?"

"Well, what if one of the *sucias* saw you?"

"So what? Let her see me. They'll know the truth eventually."

"And what is the truth, exactly, Roberto?"

He blows air out of his mouth and I can visualize his face—rugged, handsome, tired, loving. "The truth is that I love you, you're my wife, I'm your husband, we're a family, and to hell with everyone else."

I think about how my girlfriends would react to knowing that I was talking to Roberto again. Not well, I can tell you that much. My friends and family think he nearly beat me to death, and I admit he roughed me up a little, but I'm not so sure anymore it was as bad as everyone acts like it was. I slipped down icy stairs. *That* did the damage. That's what caused the miscarriage. But you know how these super-feminist women get, *¿verdad que sí?* They put everything on the man. I bought into it for a while, too. I didn't want to admit it, but I missed Roberto after he disappeared. We were close, *¿sabes?* He was the love of my life. It has been hard raising the boys alone. When he called me, and I have to be totally honest here, I was thrilled, not scared. I still love him, and I always will.

I see Elizabeth come out the back door of the sound stage, looking for me. Our eyes connect and she motions for me to come back inside. I try to look normal.

"Baby," I tell Roberto. "I gotta go."

"You always have to go."

"No, I know, I'm sorry, *mi amor*, but I'm at work and we're wrapping up a segment. I'm almost done. I'll call you later. I promise."

"At work," he says, doubtfully.

"Yes! I'm at work. Where do you think I'd be?"

He says nothing.

"Be careful," I tell him. "You're going down that path again."

"What path?"

"The jealous rage bullshit path."

Again the blowing out of the air, and a sigh, and a deep inhale. "You're right. I am. You're right. I won't do it again."

"I love you," I tell him as Elizabeth starts to walk toward my car. "I have to go."

"I love you, too. When can I see you?"

Elizabeth is at the door of the car now, motioning for me to roll down the window. I smile and whisper to him, "Baby, I don't know. Soon. Okay? Soon. I promise. But I really have to go now."

"I miss you," he tells me.

"Me, too," I say. "Good-bye, baby. Call you later."

" 'Bye."

I end the call and stash the phone in my purse, nervous as a teenager caught in her room with a cigarette. I open the car door and ask Elizabeth, in a voice that sounds too cheerful and forced, if her headache is better now.

"Who were you talking to?" she wants to know. She studies my face, and I smile in hopes that she can't read Roberto there.

"Huh?" I pretend I haven't heard her in order to buy myself more time to think of an answer.

"Who was that on the phone?"

"The phone? Oh." I wave my hand dismissively. "Just a friend."

She smiles slyly now. "José?"

"Maybe." My shoulders tense with the lie, but I toss my head back a little and try to seem relaxed. I wish more people understood the struggle of real love. In this country, everyone wants you to give up on people too easily. People divorce for the smallest things. I'm not saying what happened between me and Roberto was small. That's not what I'm saying. But I do think people change, and I think these past few years have been good for Roberto. He's a different man now, but I know Elizabeth and my other friends well enough to know that they will never believe it possible.

We start to walk back toward the door of the studio. "So," she says. "Who is this guy, Sara? Usually you tell me everything, but you've been so secretive about this one. It's making me very curious."

"Don't be. It's nothing. Trust me."

"Nothing? You come hide in your car for a phone call and this is nothing?"

"I wasn't hiding."

She just looks at me. I look away, and say, "He's just a friend. Okay? Let's leave it at that."

"You have that twinkle in your eye," she says. *Pero Dios mío*, I feel like such a schmuck lying to my best friend. I don't know how much longer I can do it. I shouldn't be talking to Roberto. I probably shouldn't. I don't know. I'm confused. Confusion is familiar territory for me these days.

"No twinkle," I insist.

"Twinkle," she insists back, opening the door for me and holding it.

We go back to the set. Elizabeth takes her place with the crew, and the assistants come to arrange me for display once more. Powder, brush, hairspray, adjustments to my clothes.

"Okay, guys. Do I look beautiful again?" I joke into the microphone. Valentín, who is circling nearby checking the lights, leans close enough for me to smell him. He smells like trendy cologne, like the Banana Republic.

"Absolutely," he says. "So, what about that lunch?"

I shake my head. "I don't think so."

He lowers his head, and his voice, and nearly whispers in my ear, "I'm going to keep asking you to go out with me until you say yes. Just be aware of that."

"*Oye, mi amor,*" I tell him, longing for him though I know I shouldn't, hating myself for lying to Elizabeth, in sick, crazy love with my husband, but looking very together and camera-ready beneath the studio lights. "You have no idea what you're up against."

cuicatl

ÓRALE, **BRO. WITH MY MANAGER** and homeboy Frank on his
Yamaha behind me, and me in my Levi's 501s, combat boots, and my black
leather biker jacket, I roar my Harley off Interstate 25 toward Albuquerque,
with a hunger growling in my belly. I'm gonna drop Frank at the Hyatt
downtown, the hotel where I always stay when I come to play this city with
my band, and then I'll mosey on to the resort to meet my *sucias*. I don't know
if I'd even think of those women as close friends anymore, our lives are so
different than they were in college, or even five years ago. It sucks that life
does that to people, but that's the way it is, man. Those chicks are all coupled
up, with kids, and jobs with suits. It's cool. They're cool. But the life I lead?
It's way different, *pues*. After this retreat with them, they'll all go back to
their jobs and families or whatever. But me? I'll head to Phoenix with Frank,
to meet up with the guys in the band, to kick off my twenty-two-city North
American tour at U.S. Airways Center. I'm going to be promoting my new
album *Americanita Me*, my third and most wacked, esoteric, experimental album to date. As much as I'd like my old friends to share the high of standing
on stage before a sold-out crowd of screaming *chingón* lunatics, there's no
way they'll ever really understand.

As I ride against the hot summer wind, secure in the sense of Frank on
the road behind me, watching my back, I get a snippet of a melody in my
head, right across my brain like a scorching pink tattoo. "Picture yourself on
a boat on a river, with tangerine rivers and marmalade skies . . ."

I rasp the words past my lips, where they rise as a steam inside my motor-
cycle helmet. I can't remember the rest right now. *Chíngame*. How does that
shit go again? . . . *with tangerine rivers and marmalade skies*. And then what?
No sé. Ni modo. Two lines are enough. Enough to get me steamy under my
helmet. A Lennon and McCartney steam, all past my head and into my hair.
My itchy, long, black and green hair. I imagine the Beatles young and tiny,

in miniature black trench coats, scrambling across my scalp like lice. Scratching my itch. To have had your itch scratched by John Lennon, man. Yoko had it made.

Órale, pues.

I pull into the drop-off valet area of the Hyatt, and Frank roars his metal beast up next to mine. He pushes the black helmet from his head and shakes out his shoulder-length, mostly gray hair. You'd never know this *loco*-looking, fifty-year-old Aztec warrior had a law degree from Yale to look at him right now. You'd never know he has ten Armani suits in his closet. Right now, he's way grizzly, all hippie-looking and wild-eyed, with grit in his teeth from riding eight hours across the desert Southwest and a laugh in his light brown eyes. We been on the road two days, from Los Angeles, where we both live. He takes his leather jacket off and shows off those nice arms in a sleeveless T-shirt. He looks good for his age, man, with those Mexica tattoos. He's got nice, brilliant eyes, which is why I've trusted him this long to represent me. By brilliant I mean this dude's mad smart. But not smart like most lawyers in the entertainment industry, where they're vampire smart and want to suck the blood out of everything in sight; he's smart and wise. Gentle and tough. He's not the kind to go into a meeting all macho or full of attitude like most of the lawyers I've met since signing my first record contract five years ago. He's calm, and he thinks about the shit he's going to say before he says it. Sometimes you can see people start to squirm, just waiting for him to say something. He doesn't get angry like I do, or if he does, he handles it elegantly and controls it. If you're like me, you need someone like Frank to keep you in line, to make sure you don't fuck everything up by saying some shit you'll regret later. If it had been up to me, I'd have done this whole pop star thing all fucking wrong. Frank made sure that didn't happen, just like he made sure I didn't run off the highway from Los Angeles to here. He's like my guardian angel, or like my big brother, my best friend, my lawyer. That's hilarious, by the way. I never thought I'd think something like "my best friend, my lawyer." But, *órale*. Life isn't always what you think. He's made me a millionaire, and I'll never forget it.

"Damn, girl!" he says, rubbing his hip with a hand. "I don't know how you do it."

"You did it too, homes," I tell him.

"Yeah, but my old ass *hurts.*" He grins at me, and no, it's not a perfect smile. It's a little lopsided, and after all the fake white teeth of the music industry, his real teeth seem a shade too gray. But it doesn't matter, man. A guy like Frank? He's regular-looking, but you can come to think of him as handsome if you know him well enough. I know him real well, you know? I feel that something I've been feeling for him lately. A little tingle of something. He's seventeen years older than me, though. I don't think he's ever seen me in that romantic way. We started our relationship in the same Aztec dance group back in L.A., him as the elder man. It's always kind of been that way, him seeing me as a kid and taking care of me. I don't want to say he's like my dad, because my dad, *pues.* First of all, my dad doesn't understand me or what I do. He thinks the Mexica movement is ridiculous and all he wants is to have people think of him as American. I haven't had a real conversation with either of my parents since I was a little girl. They never went to college. You don't think that by getting your education you're building a wall between you and your mom and dad, you know? Everyone, all your counselors in elementary school on up, all your teachers, they're always on you to go to college to get a better shot in life and all that shit. But then when you come from a family that never went to college, it's hard. The counselors never tell you that. They don't prepare you for the inevitable loss of self you, as a kid of unread parents, get when you read too many books and start to think differently about everything. Mom and Dad? They try to understand me. They love me. But mostly they love going to the casino.

"*Órale,* then go on in there and get your old ass a massage," I suggest. He smiles at me gently and puts a hand on my shoulder.

"You better get going, Cuicatl, before it gets any darker." He worries about me.

"*N'homb'e.* I can handle the dark," I say.

He eyes me uncertainly. "I just want to make sure you get there in one piece. I can't let my superstar be out there on her own. You sure you don't want me to go with you?"

"I thought your old ass hurt."

He laughs. "Yeah. Touché. I'm still happy to ride out there with you."

"What about your ass?"

"It's so damn numb at this point, it wouldn't matter," he says. I have a brief image in my head of me, holding on to his ass. I shouldn't think of Frank like that, should I? I didn't used to. But lately, the more we hang out and talk about books and music, the more I want him.

I shake my head and try to seem like I don't want him. "Thanks, Frank, man. But no. No way. I have to do this on my own. This is women-bonding time, dude."

There's a long pause as he considers what to say next. It's not that he doesn't have anything to say. You can tell looking at those eyes that there's a lot going on in there. It's that he wants to make sure he says it right.

"I know your women friends mean the world to you. I respect the hell out of it, you know that. I think it's good that you have this group of strong women you stay connected with. I wouldn't want to get in the way of that, and if I rode out with you, it would only be to the door of the resort and then I'd disappear."

"I'm fine. Don't worry."

His eyes worry for a moment. "You're strong. You're capable. You know I'm not some *machista* prick trying to tell you that you can't do things on your own, because you're the most capable person I've ever known."

"*Pues*, stop worrying, then."

He sighs and fidgets for a moment. "It's not you I worry about. It's other people. You need to remember that you're *famous*, Cuicatl. You have to be careful. There are freaks out there. I don't think it's sunk in yet that you shouldn't go places alone."

"Nah, dude. I'm fine. Thanks, though."

"Okay," he says, holding his hands up in surrender. "No problem. I don't want to get in your space."

Really, though? He could have come with me. But I don't want him to know I have plans to hook up with a guy I have sex with when I come to New Mexico. He's sort of a groupie. I got a few boy-toys in cities around the world. I try to keep that side of me from Frank, because even though he's my friend, and my manager, there's a part of me that feels like he's real dignified and ethical. I mean, shit, he rode all the way out here with me just to make sure nothing bad happened. I'm not sure I'm that good a person, you know?

"*Bueno*," he says with a pat on my back. "*Cuídate*. Call me when you get there."

"Don't wait up, bro."

"You know I worry."

"You should stop. You worry too much. *Bueno*, Frank, I'm going," I tell him. "I already kept these chicks waiting too long as it is. It's been fun riding with you."

He steps off his bike and comes to give me a hug. It lasts a little longer than usual, and I take my time, enjoying the herbal scent of his sweat. It's been a while since anyone held me who knew me before *la fama*, you know? Before I got famous. That pre-fame friend kind of hug is different. When people know *about* you before they *know* you, like they've heard your music or read articles on you, it's different. They *project, ¿sabes?* What they wish they were, or what they hate, whatever it is they have an issue with, that's how they interpret you. You can never be a real person to someone who knows you *after* you've become famous. That's why I doubt I'll ever get married now. Too many people act like they like me because they want something from me, know what I mean? I'm a hen in a world of foxes. Can't trust any of them.

He says, "Call me when you're ready to ride to Phoenix. I'll just be here by the pool, reading books that scare the *gabachos*."

"Like what?"

He gets a mischievous look in his eyes and digs through a pack on the side of the bike's saddle. He holds up a book with a blue-green cover. I read the title: *No Longer a Minority: Latinos and Social Policy in California.*

"That's some heavy shit, *chato*," I say with fake disappointment, imitating my parents, the way they respond when they see me with books like this. Frank laughs, because he's like me. He is the first in his family to go to college, too. He knows how it is.

"Heavy lifting is good for the soul," he says.

"Just lift with your legs, not your old ass, okay? I don't need a manager in traction."

"Cuicatl," he says, the way you'd say a kid's name after they've done something cute and irritating, half adoring, half annoyed. "You're the craziest girl I know."

"That's what everyone says."

"Have a good time out there." He puts the book away and turns to face me. There's more he wants to say, but he's not going to let himself. I know him well enough to recognize the way his neck tightens up when he's with-holding.

"*No te preocupes*," I tell him. He looks at my face, at my eyes and my lips, and, after seeming like he wants to step toward me, he backs away instead.

"Tea with honey," he calls out as he disconnects his knapsack from the back of the bike. "Take good care of those vocal cords. There's a lot riding on the shows next week."

I act like I'm not nervous about the tour, and shrug it off. I rev my bike's engine, warming her up to hit the road again, and yell out to him. "What-ever, man. Hey! Don't get crazy with the local girls, *hombre*."

He laughs as if I've told him not to have too much fun with a colonoscopy. "Don't worry. There's only one woman for me."

"Who's that?" I ask.

He shrugs and locks up the bike, turns to walk toward the entrance of the hotel. "None of your business, kiddo. Just a girl from back in the day," he says, dreamy. He's so *pinche* secretive sometimes. I wouldn't be surprised if he had a whole family he kept secret from me. I wonder who she is. There were lots of women in the movement back before Frank ended up managing me and spending most of his time with me, and they all dug him.

Once I've watched Frank enter the hotel, I head back onto the freeway. The engine is bass-heavy, with a dissonance that moves my soul. On the headphones I blast Béla Bartók, the dead Hungarian composer who drew upon Eastern European folk and Middle Eastern sounds in his music. I have just jumped from the Beatles to Bartók and back again, see? After this, I'm cranking that jam "Lean Like a *Cholo*." I love that fucking song. *That's* the part of it these people don't understand, that music is not mine, it is not yours. Genre means shit, man. It is ours, it is out there, floating forever on the wind, and people like me, we're just the conduits. Music is universal, and I don't care who the fuck wrote it, as long as it makes me feel good. No, wait. As long as it makes me feel *something*. As long as it makes me *feel*.

My legs are wrapped around the body of the Harley, and the vibrations work their way through the black leather seat, through my jeans, and on-ward, through my slash of womanhood and into my soul. I am nothing but vibrations. Everything is. We are all vibrating, all the time, in harmony and dissonance with the sounds of the stars, these stars right here, the ones that peek out through the purple velvet of the darkening New Mexico sky. In the sky, with diamonds.

My hands grip the machine through my gloves, and I fly. Frank and I toked a little in the rest stop bathroom back in Gallup, some good Jamaican shit, and I'm still feeling the buzz, still flying like an eagle. I giggle because I realize this might be making my thoughts a little more intense and hard to chase for you. I giggle because I imagine you trying to follow me, like a child after a dragonfly. Dragonflies can fly up to forty miles per hour. I learned that watching TV in a hotel. I'm always watching TV late at night in some hotel somewhere, insomniac on the road before a show, nervous. I watched something about animals that fly, and there was the dragonfly, booking like a motherfucker down the air over a river. I'm like that, my wings buzzing, the road beneath me like slow black water. I am free. You can't catch me. Ha!

I look down at myself from outside my body. I can see and feel everything, everywhere. The desert, my body. We are one and the same. Dust to dust. I speed ahead, feeling the g-forces. The faster the better. They like to say you can't ride high, but that's bullshit. I ride better high, man. I do *everything* better high. All the greats were like that. Mozart, Charlie Parker, José Alfredo Jimenez. It was drink, or drugs, man. That was the creative fuel. That's why the shit I do is outlawed in this uptight nation. They don't want original thinkers, creativity, because my kind are impossible to control, and lately in the United States that's what the shit boils down to, man. Control. Mind fuck. Mind control. Nothing new, though. Just new weapons to do it more efficiently, *y nada*. I can't think about it too much anymore.

I come to a stoplight in a place called Bernalillo, balance the big, heavy bike between my legs, weight on my left foot. I wear shiny black thigh-high boots, with spiked heels. I rev the motor. It sounds like a thousand jaguars growling. Pure power. I can't tell where the bike ends and I begin, and this is a form of magic, too.

A purple lowrider pulls up next to me, the paint sparkly with gold flecks, the seats filled with men, five of them, all of them Mexica, beautiful with their brown skin, bare heads, and dark eyes, their tattoos and their anger. I love them instantly. My people. With the red helmet over my face, there is little chance of them recognizing me. So what if they did? I'd be keeping my name "out there," as Frank says, wherever the fuck out there is.

That's what it's about anymore, right? Being seen, being famous for being famous.

The men look my bike up and down. They look me up and down. I rev for them and smile. They smile back. One licks his lips at me. Yeah, yeah. Indian magic. Aztec prince. But young. They can't be more than twenty-one, *ésos*. I'm twelve years older than that now. Hard to believe, man, how fast time passes and then there you are, up the hill heading toward the crest that takes you to fuckin' forty.

"You dudes look *bién firme*," I call out. They look surprised. I'm a crazy brave girl, right? Frank would hate that I'm talking to these *vatos*. But fame or no fame, I won't be trapped by fear. Nothing scares me anymore. Or as my mom might say, "Doesn't nothing scare you no more, *m'ija*. And that scares me." I have been to the mountaintop. I have lived the dream I had. I could die and I'd be happy because I did what I set out to do. How many people can say that? And how many are living the lives of quiet desperation Thoreau wrote about?

"*¡Qué viva Mexico!*" I cry. The driver gives me a thumbs-up.

We are ancient, powerful, strong people who own this land, this America that the intruders tried to tell us is theirs by birthright, this land that the newspapers and cable news channels try to say is being taken over by Mexicans. Fuck that. We Mexicans are Native Americans, we were the first people to come to this place, and we are not taking it *over*.

We are taking it *back*.

The light turns green, and I peel out.

I round the corner and take the twisty narrow road down the valley toward the resort. The wind feels good on my neck.

I stash my bike in the parking lot, take my army-store duffle bag from the back, lock the helmet onto the Harley, and walk toward the front entrance. I take the place in with my eyes. Upscale, glamorous, dark brown, a spa resort in the center of the desert, just exactly the kind of place conservative, sophisticated Rebecca would pick. I get to stay at so many places like this now, as part of my job, that I prefer roughing it in nature when I have free time, for a little variety, you know? Or just plain being home, eating homemade yogurt and my own brown rice cooked with vegetable broth. But I understand that my friends don't have the life I have. It wouldn't be fair to ask them to go camping. They might break a nail.

Órale.

A timid, apologetic young man with a resort name tag opens the door for me. I thank him, and he asks me if I am me, his eyes all surprised. I say yes. He asks me where my entourage is. I laugh and say, "You lookin' at it, bro!" He asks for an autograph. I use the valet desk's battered ballpoint pen to sign a bank receipt he has crumpled in his pocket. His balance was twenty-six dollars, which pisses me off because they don't pay average workers a living wage in this fucking country. You go to a place like Canada, or Switzerland, or Norway—and I've been to them all—and the average worker there has a nice house, and his kids go to a good school, and he has free health care. Dude thanks me. I shake his hand and make a point to look at him in a way that imparts respect and dignity.

I check in under my fake name, another precaution of fame and its many crazy-ass stalkery types. I hit my room. Take a long piss, freshen up my makeup, ditch the leather jacket, and head downstairs in my jeans, boots, and a white tank top without a bra.

I had my boobs done three years ago, on a whim. I've always been pretty slender, and had the flat chest that goes along with a naturally skinny body. I always wondered what it would be like to have real *chichis* all out to here, you know? So I fucking bought them and got them slipped in through holes they cut in my armpits. Sounds gross, but you know how it is. I'm all healed up now, but I'll admit the shit hurt for a few months like nothing I ever felt before. They look pretty good on me, too. I didn't go overly huge or anything, just a regular C-cup. I don't need a bra. Because they are new, and made of something artificial, and stuffed underneath my muscles, they stay put and stay up on their own pretty well.

The new tattoos, a dragon on the small of my back and a flowered choker on my neck, are nearly healed. I find my black book, and my phone, and I call Joaquin's cell. He's got the outgoing ring programmed with one of my songs. Gotta love your fuckin' groupies. He picks up on the third ring. I tell him I'm in town and ask if he's free. *"A toda madre,"* he says, which is basically a way of saying of course he is. He's a college student, some kind of perpetual grad student involved with politics and I forget what else, a real angry kind of guy involved with clandestine movements and underground newspapers that never materialize. I tell him to meet me as soon as possible at the resort. He says he'll leave in a couple hours. After I hang up, I feel guilty, like I'm cheating on someone. It's got to be the dope. I need to stop smoking, man. I need to stop getting all fuckin' *prendida*, lit. It makes me mad paranoid.

I find the door, and me and my boobs head downstairs, humming Bartók with a *chuko*-dancing backbeat, to find my five estranged friends from college who don't know what the fuck it's like to be me.

rebecca

I USE MY WHITE, square paper cocktail napkin to sweep the offending dust and soot from the woven seat of a chair near the fireplace on the patio outside. I don't sit on dirt, as a rule. I realize that, in my red linen matching shorts set from Talbots, a size two and accessorized with a brown leather belt, matching brown Rockport sandals, plain gold studs, and a simple gold neck chain, a white sweater tied around my shoulders, I am dressed much more sensibly than my friends, who still seem to think they're in their early twenties.

"Ooh, that looks good, *m'ija*," says Usnavys, eyeing my virgin margarita. "I gots to get me one of them when I'm done with this." She holds up her half-empty mojito, with the mangled stalk of mint crushed at the bottom. They've all got them, mojitos. It's been our little group's favorite drink for the past few years.

I should tell you, Usnavys wears a black tube dress, tight as a sock. She looks like a bloated blood sausage, and her feet soufflé over the tops of her tight pumps. Everyone told her she looked great, including me, because that's what girlfriends do. I told all my friends they looked wonderful, and they told me the same. Elizabeth, a beautiful black Colombian woman who inexplicably and unnaturally prefers women to men, is in her one-piece

Speedo swimming suit and a sarong, wholly inappropriate for cocktail hour. Sara, the Cuban blonde, is wearing something kaleidoscopic and loud, in hot pinks and purples. Lauren's cleavage keeps falling out of her DKNY shirt, which is too big for her. Her jeans, meanwhile, are too small. Cuicatl, who just got here, wears greasy jeans and a white tank top thin as gossamer, without a bra. Her tattoos are everywhere, even up her neck.

"Some of those new?" I ask Cuicatl, pointing to her body art without revealing how repulsed I am by it.

"Yeah. This one, too." She stands and lifts her shirt to show us the sunflower around the navel in her flat belly.

"It's beautifully done," I say. It's not exactly a lie. It was well done, for a tattoo. I don't think it looks good on her, but I do think the artist knew what he or she was doing. I feel my face flush, which it does not ordinarily do. Must be the pregnancy hormones.

"You look boiling hot, Rebecca," says Usnavys, reaching out to unbutton the top button of my blouse.

"What are you doing?" I ask, leaning away from her.

"Usnavys! She's married," quips Lauren with a cynical grin.

"Oh, please," says Usnavys to Lauren. "Don't flatter her." Then, to me, she says, "You look like you're burning up, girl. We gotta get some of those buttons down. You're all buttoned up like Mary Poppins."

"I'm fine, thank you."

"Leave her alone," says Cuicatl. "She's fine."

"God, the air smells good here," says Elizabeth, with a deep inhale. Lesbian or not, Elizabeth is the best diplomat in the group, after me. She has deftly changed the subject here, and united us in the common pursuit of breathing.

"Isn't it great?" I ask. They all murmur approval.

"You done good, *m'ija*," Usnavys tells me. "This is my kinda place."

It is summer, June, early evening, and the sun has begun to set. As is always the case in the New Mexico desert, the air temperature is dropping quickly as darkness moves in from behind the mountains to the east. There can be as much as a thirty-degree difference between day and night here.

The mix of hot and cool air kicks up a bit of wind, fragrant with alfalfa and the sedimentary scent of Rio Grande river water, and with it, more dust.

I suffer from a bit of hay fever, and feel an urge to sneeze. I stifle it through will and concentration; I don't appreciate public sneezing, and it is out of consideration for others that I refrain from it as often as possible. The breeze rustles the thick green leaves on the gnarled, twisted old cottonwood trees along the river, about a quarter mile to the east of where we sit. Their limbs sway like the arms of giant conductors working through a slow bit of Beethoven. Exquisitely beautiful. On the smooth dirt path below, men drive in from the golf course in their little white carts. One of them, a stunning black man I recognize from somewhere, smiles and waves in our direction. I see Usnavys lift her hand and wave back. He looks like he's in lust.

"What's that about?" I ask.

Usnavys shrugs. "I took me some golf lessons."

"How was it?" asks Lauren. Then, without giving Usnavys time to answer, she says, "I hate golf."

"It was fun," she says. "Why you hate golf?"

Lauren shrugs. "I just don't like it. It's like billiards, only you can't see the holes."

"I like your hair, Rebecca," Sara tells me. "You're definitely a longer-hair girl."

"Thank you," I say. "I like it short, too, but this is nice."

Sara reaches out and touches my bangs. "But don't you want to cover those?" She stares at the inch-wide streak of silver hair in my bangs.

"I like them," I say, fingering the hair.

"You don't think they make you look old?" asks Sara.

"No," I say slowly, willing myself not to say something I will regret. I remind myself that Sara is blunt by culture and upbringing. She probably has no idea she has offended me. My Caribbean Latina friends are always touching me and making personal comments. It's just the way they are.

"I think they make her look distinguished," says Lauren.

"Ain't a woman in the world wants to look *distinguished*," says Usnavys.

"Except Madeleine Albright," adds Sara.

"Ain't a woman in the world wants to look like Madeleine Albright," says Usnavys. Then, to me, she says, "Why don't you cover that up, *m'ija*? Take ten years off, like that." She snaps her fingers.

"I like the way it looks."

"It looks good," says Lauren, with a hand pressed to her chest like she's got food stuck in her throat. "Leave her alone. Jesus."

In truth, I stopped dyeing my hair because the chemicals might harm the baby. But they don't need to know this. They don't know I'm pregnant.

"I think it's very attractive," says Elizabeth. I'm not sure this is what I want to hear from our group's lone lesbian, but I thank her nonetheless.

"*Órale*, you could go green," jokes Cuicatl, who has green streaks in her jet-black mess of hair. She changes hair color more than anyone I know.

"I'll pass on the green, thank you," I say. "Though it looks fabulous on you."

"You do look amazing," Sara tells Cuicatl.

"Your boobs rock," says Lauren. "What'd they cost?"

"Twenty grand," Cuicatl tells Lauren. "But you could do it for half that."

"You think I need it?" asks Lauren.

"No!" Cuicatl cries, wanting to make sure Lauren knows that's not what she meant. "I'm just saying, since you asked. You look great. I mean, do it if you want to do it. But you don't need to."

"Me? I am coloring this hair until I die," says Usnavys. "I don't want to look like my mother, okay? I don't. And when the carpet starts to match the drapes, you can bet I'm coloring that shit, too."

The cocktail waitress comes to take orders for the second round of drinks. Everyone's chatting with everyone else, and we've got almost too many little conversations going on now for me to keep track. It gives me a headache trying.

"Oh!" cries Sara, looking directly at me. "How's your house in Santa Fe? You guys closed on it?"

I nod. "I love it," I tell them. "It's just right. You can stay there anytime, you guys. Think of it as yours."

"You are so lucky," whines Usnavys into her glass as she downs the last of the mojito. "How many houses you got now?"

I freeze because I don't want to answer this. Usnavys acts like it's all luck that gave me what I have. It's not. It was hard work that got me here.

"Let's see." Sara starts to count on her fingers. "Her cape on the Vineyard."

"Her condo in Whistler," adds Usnavys.

"The London apartment," says Elizabeth.

"If it's in London, it's a flat, darling," says Sara, with a miserable fake British accent. Why do Americans do that?

"Come on, you guys," I say, uncomfortable as I always am when they start to talk about my lifestyle. It is likely that I have the most money of all of us, but that comes with hard work. They should know that. It did not come easy.

"And your Boston brownstone," concludes Usnavys. "Did we miss any?"

"No," I say.

Usnavys counts on her fingers now. "What the hell you need five houses for, girl?" asks Usnavys.

"Lay off her already," says Cuicatl, who, to my knowledge, has a pretty nice house of her own, in Santa Monica.

"You married you a good man," Usnavys says, as if it were only Andre's money buying us these things, and not mine. As if I married him for his money, which I didn't.

"So did you," I counter. "Juan's a good man." The others agree with me.

"You *had* to bring him up, didn't you?" Usnavys accuses me in a joking manner that doesn't feel all that jokey to me. "We got all talking about your house here and your house there, and you go right into how's my unemployed husband in the apron doing. Thank you, Rebecca. Thank you very much."

"He's a stay-at-home father," says Sara. "As a former stay-at-home *mamita*, I can tell you. *That's* a job. That's the hardest job in the world."

"I read that a stay-at-home parent's worth is valued at more than seven hundred thousand dollars per year," says Elizabeth.

"Then I should quit my job, too," gripes Usnavys. "With both of us valued at seven hundred grand, we'll be millionaires, like you."

"Money isn't everything," says Cuicatl.

"Easy for you to say, Miss Pop Superstar," pouts Usnavys. Her eyes follow the golf cart with the cute man, and he turns to look at her once more, blowing a kiss.

"That must have been some golf lesson," I say.

"You know how it be, men see this, they want this," says Usnavys, running her hands along the lumpy sides of her sock-dress. Everyone laughs, except me. I feel sorry for her. Everyone thinks Usnavys is really confident, but

I think it's all a front of some kind. I think underneath all that she must know how unhealthy she is, and she must be uncomfortable in her own skin.

A group of successful-looking businessmen in their thirties and forties sits nearby, business casual, and several of them look over at us frequently. Of course they do. My friends—and I say this with pride and amazement—are moderately attractive. All of them. Even Usnavys, who is heavier now than she has ever been. She has a pretty face, and a perfect nose. She could be stunning if she lost the weight. Which is unlikely.

Usnavys digs into a large cheesy plate of nachos and looks closely at me. "You want some?" She gestures to the nachos.

"No, thank you." I have raw almonds in my purse. I shall eat seven of them between now and bedtime, no more, no less. I am on a sensible diet aimed at optimal nutrition and minimal weight gain.

I make a mental check of my body language, and realize I've covered my belly—a dead giveaway. I cannot tell even the *sucias* of the pregnancy yet. I consciously relax my pose and rest my hands on the armrests. Your posture and gestures say as much about you as your words, sometimes more. It has always amazed me that people don't take stock of their nonverbal communication skills better than they do.

"So," says Usnavys. "I have to tell you all about my new project."

Everyone waits for the rest. Usnavys sits up and leans toward us.

"I've got me a blog."

"A blog?" Cuicatl asks, with a curious, interested face.

"A blog," she confirms, digging a small, lightweight laptop out of her large handbag.

"They got wi-fi here," she says. "I'm gonna show you guys what I been up to."

"I've seen it," I tell her. "The girls at work read it religiously."

"Really?" Usnavys looks thrilled and surprised for a moment, before returning to her tapping on the small computer. "What do they say?"

"They enjoy it," I say. "They think you should give workshops."

"Tell them thank-you for me." She concentrates. "Okay, it's www .usnavysrivera.blogspot.com. Here it is!"

The others gather around to read it. I resist, but they force me over. I read along.

How to Slice a Mango

I don't know what it is about all y'all gringos and oral sex, okay? But the verdict is in and the verdict says y'all done got a whole big lot to learn from your Latin brothers, and especially from the *dominicanos,* okay?

I am not a racist, and I am not being mean. I'm not trying to offend, just trying to inform, *m'ijo.* The Latin man, when he sees a woman spread open in all her labial glory on the silk sheets of his lair, looks her over hungrily, like he didn't get no food for the past two weeks and you and your glistening, hairy pussy are the ripest, juiciest mango that boy ever saw.

What's that, gringo boy? Did I say hairy? Yes, *m'ijo,* I did. And I don't appreciate how you get all shocked George Clooney bland-faced bullshit on me when I say it, either. Get over it, okay baby? Because that's tip number one I want all gringo boys reading this to take away from here today: If you want to eat the mango like a real Latin lover, get your JFK Junior cheeseburger ass used to some real mango hair, know what I'm saying?

Latin men don't want their women all bald up in there like children, *nene.* Uh-uh. It's just all you damn borderline pedophile *americanos* who dig that waxy baby look. Latin men like us beautiful women the way God made us, and that means hairy and coiffed and clean and sweet like candy, and our men are not afraid to get a little extra floss on them back teeth—know what I'm saying, Mister Donny freakin' Osmond?

Now get flossin', *nene.* Damn.

Sara and Elizabeth howl in approving laughter when we're done.

"Oh, my God," says Lauren.

I smile, but cannot bring myself to laugh. I find the piece offensive and horrifying.

"What on earth inspired you to do such a blog?" asks Elizabeth.

"*M'ija.*" Usnavys finishes off her drink and motions with a pointer finger extended toward the ceiling for the cocktail waitress to bring her another. She preens.

"I love being married. Y'all know that, right? I got me a man at home who loves me, and a daughter I would die for. I have everything I ever wanted. Technically. But . . ."

I feel my shoulders tense at this final word. I am absolutely, positively sure I do not want to hear what's coming. I wait for what comes next.

"But?" asks Sara, with a frantic twirl of her hands, the "get on with it" signal, as if she were pantomiming starting the engine that is Usnavys's mouth.

"*But,*" continues Usnavys, a nod here, a look there, preen, preen, preen, "you guys know how I spent the years before my marriage."

Usnavys dabs the corner of her mouth suggestively with a fingertip, and holds up three ghetto-manicured fingers, wiggles them like grubs. "I had me no less than three—*uno, do', y tre'*, okay?—men at a time. It kept me busy getting *busy*. It also kept me from ever getting bored with any one of 'em. If there was the one who liked to go down and the other who didn't, but who liked it through the back door—" She pauses, shivers with the memory. "If I felt like doing role-play, there was the one who liked that shit. If I wanted a full-body massage, there was the one I called for that."

"You slut," jokes Lauren.

"More power to you, girl," says Cuicatl. "That's how it should be."

"Watch your mouth, Cuba-gringa," Usnavys snaps back at Lauren.

"You had a male harem," says Elizabeth to Usnavys.

"I prefer to say cabal," Usnavys answers quickly. "That way I can think of them as my *cabalers.*"

My friends laugh at this, and I can tell by the slightly unfocused look of their eyes that the alcohol has begun to kick in. It's so obvious to the person who is not drinking that others are getting tipsy, even though they sometimes deny it or can't tell. I smile to be polite, appreciating the wordplay but not the intent behind it. Usnavys has the most remarkable intellect. You'd never know it to listen to the casual street-slang she uses most of the time, but behind that barrio-girl façade is a brilliant woman with a formidable vocabulary.

Says Usnavys, "I think I might have me a case of the sexual ADD, girls. That's what I'm sayin'. I miss Back Door Ben. I do. Juan don't play like that, you know what I'm sayin'?"

I cringe. Back door? Does she mean *anal sex?* Good Lord.

"Sexual ADD?" repeats Sara. Delighted. They are all delighted by this woman's depravities. How can they not see that she is crying out for help in several ways?

"I always had variety," says Usnavys. "No time to get bored. But marriage? Bores a girl to death, okay? That's the damn *truth*."

I feel like I have listened to enough of this. It's time to break my silence. "I disagree," I say with a cough to follow up. "Marriage can be very positive for one's sex life."

"*Pero*, of course you'd say that, *m'ija*," says Usnavys. "You have the perfect marriage and the perfect rich stud for a husband."

"That's right," says Cuicatl. "And he knew you *before* you got successful. I can't meet men anymore. You'd think I could, going all over the world, but I can't. I mean, I meet them, but the vibe is all fucked up."

Silently, I argue with them. It would be tacky to engage in such a thing as conflict at a retreat intended to solidify our bond as friends. I rephrase my thought: "What I mean is that I think marriage can remain a haven for a healthy sex life, if the partners are open-minded and well matched. Communication is essential. Good communication, in other words."

They all stare at me as if dumbfounded.

"What?" I ask.

"You are the only person in the world who can make good sex sound so damn *boring*," says Usnavys.

Sara laughs first. Then Usnavys and Lauren. Cuicatl lets loose, too. Elizabeth mercifully does not laugh at all, but rather turns her attention back to Usnavys and asks, "Why did you decide to aim this blog of yours specifically at Anglos? That seems a little unfair."

"Anglo is not a race," I remind them. "It refers to England. Andre, technically, is Anglo."

"Understood," says Elizabeth. Then, back to Usnavys, "Why aim it at . . ." She looks at me. "What should we call them, then?"

"Non-Hispanic whites, the way the census does," I say.

"Non-Hispanic whites," repeats Elizabeth. "Why aim such a blog at a race of people? It seems unfair."

"Maybe because after the Puritans and the Mormons and shit, they need it," suggests Usnavys.

I am not going to try to set them straight anymore. I don't know why I even bother to finesse labels in a country that so consistently gets it all wrong.

"Sexual ADD, girl." Usnavys grins and clinks her glass against an invisible one in an imaginary toast before guzzling. "I'm not saying I'm some kind of a 'ho, okay? I'm just saying I have been there and done that, and that, and that, and a woman draws her some fine conclusions based upon empirical evidence."

"Oh, my God," I say. My head has begun to pound.

Usnavys continues her racist diatribe, unaffected by my pained facial expression, or the manner in which I rub my temples with the tips of my index fingers. "I have so much time to sit around thinking about the old days, you know?" She looks up at the sky, lost in reverie. "The old dating days with all my various men, and so on and so forth, and I started to write it all down so that I'd have a good record of it in my old age. So I'd have something to remember when my memory was gone and I had my hands down my pants at the nursing home. And I realized that the ones who were the worst in bed were them white boys."

"That's ridiculous," I tell her. I feel my composure slipping. I smile to indicate that I am not trying to be antagonistic, but rather an active participant in the conversation.

"Okay, Miss Rebecca. Answer me this," says Usnavys to me. She pigeons her neck like a ghetto girl. When she angers, or when her adrenaline kicks up, Usnavys reverts to the barrio girl she was before college (supposedly) smoothed out her rough edges. "Who was better? Brad, the white husband, or Andre, the black husband?" She makes an arrogant face that tells me she thinks she already knows the answer.

Brad is a non-Hispanic white man from Michigan. He was fairly bad in bed, with a penis that might have filled in for a tampon in a feature film, but I am not going to discuss that here. I don't think it would be appropriate. I also do not believe his sexual inadequacy had anything to do with his *race*.

"Andre is a superior man in every way," I conclude, diplomatically.

Usnavys laughs at me as if she has read my mind. "I knew it! The black man *wins*."

"*Pues, claro que* Andre is better in bed, obviously," says Sara with a know-it-all shrug.

"How is that obvious?" I ask. "Don't be ridiculous."

"He's black," says Usnavys, as if I have asked a stupid question. For what it's worth, Usnavys's own father was also black, from the Dominican Republic.

"That's moronic," says Cuicatl. She and I have had our differences over the years, but lately we have been more alike than not on most issues.

"Whatever, *m'ija*," says Usnavys to Cuicatl. "In America, black is black. Maybe not in Nigeria or England or what-have-you, but here, you know how it is. Trust a *mulata* on this, okay?" She seems to float away for a moment in her thoughts, comes back with her eyes ablaze, and adds, "The thing with black men is that they don't go down on you the way Latin men do. A lot of them won't do it at all, especially the Jamaicans. How 'bout Nigerians, Rebecca? Do they bite the beaver?"

I balk. Andre is exquisitely skilled at oral lovemaking. But they don't need to know this. Cuicatl looks pissed. "Don't answer her," she tells me.

Usnavys continues, "Never mind. I don't want to make you have a heart attack right here." She laughs kindly at me, and continues, "Please, girl. I don't know what they teach them down in Jamaica, but don't go looking for a man there unless you want to spend your life without ever engaging in cunnilingus."

"Is that an airline?" jokes Lauren. "Could I work there? I hate my job."

Sara shakes her head in disagreement with Usnavys. "Not all Latin men eat you, Usnavys," she says.

"Trust me," she says with a world-weary sigh. "I am *aware*."

"Mexican men hardly do it at all," says Cuicatl. "The ones from deep Mexico? Hardly. Too *machista*."

Usnavys shrugs. "Whatever."

"No!" shouts Sara. "*Te lo juro, chica.* Cuicatl's right. There are studies about this. I've seen them."

"People *study* this?" I say, disgusted.

"And you *read* it?" Cuicatl asks Sara.

Sara nods. "*Fíjate.* It breaks down like this. Of all Latinos, men from Mexico are the least likely to perform oral sex on women. It is a documented *fact*."

"Really?" asks Cuicatl. "That sucks. My people need enlightenment."

"Shh," I say, hoping she'll stop scandalizing the men at the next fireplace. They keep looking over at us with increasing interest. And mockery. Of course they do. They probably think we are for hire.

"What? If it's true, it's true," says Lauren.

"You don't have to broadcast it to the world," I say in a low whisper I am certain my friends will interpret as frigid.

Usnavys rolls her eyes at me. "Loosen up, Mary Poppins," she says. "Let your freak out, *mujer*."

"Here?" I hiss. "Have you lost your *mind*?"

The others act as though I have not spoken at all. Usnavys addresses Sara now: "You might be right. My experience with Latinos is pretty much with Puerto Ricans and *dominicanos*." She bites her lip as she remembers something, and her eyes roll back in her head in ecstasy. "*Ay, m'ija*, and Cubans. Oh, my God, *m'ija*. *Los cubanos son buenísimos*. They are the best in the world. Oh, and there was one Panamanian guy who rocked my world, you remember him?"

"Mr. G-spot?" asks Elizabeth. She wiggles two fingers as if she were searching for something deep inside of someone. Someone female. I feel sick. I have nearly reached my saturation point with this conversation. I've been moody and a little tired lately, for obvious reasons, and I don't have the energy at the moment to tolerate this nonsense.

"Yep." Usnavys beams.

"I've heard the Cubans lick it more than almost everyone," says Lauren.

"Not all of them," adds Sara.

The women laugh uncomfortably, because none of us want to ask her if she's referring to the murderous Roberto. We act like he doesn't exist, even though he does, somewhere out there, hiding under his rock.

"This entire conversation is ridiculous," I say softly. "I can't believe a group of accomplished women can't find something more interesting to discuss." Then again, they're drunk as skunks.

"My vote would be for Dominicans," says Lauren. "Amaury does it like no one I've ever known. Oh, my God. Yes. That's my vote. Dominicans."

There is a strange silence, and then Elizabeth leans in toward Lauren, and says in Spanish, and in a low voice that I can hear even if no one else can, "That's only because you haven't tried *colombianas*."

Lauren takes a long, hard drink and pretends Elizabeth hasn't spoken. She addresses the group again. "He's amazing at it, but you know what's really fucked up?"

We all wait for her to continue, me with great dread.

"What's fucked up is I think Amaury is cheating on me again," says Lauren. Okay, that's it. That's the final straw for me. Every year, it's the same sob story from this woman. I have little patience for people who can't get their lives in order, especially at our age. I do not believe in perpetual victimhood. I don't care what happened to you in the past, it is your job to live in the present as the person you wish to be.

"I'm sorry," I tell my friends. I touch my temples for emphasis and believability. "I'm getting a bit of a headache. Must be the altitude. I think I'll go to my room for a bit to lie down."

They wish me well, and, relieved, I separate from the group at last.

cuicatl

IT IS SATURDAY, and I've been at this resort for almost twenty-four hours.

Joaquin stands there with his arms hanging down, like he doesn't know what to do with me. He's waiting for me to make the first move. That's how it is when you're famous. The men are scared of you. You are the alpha dog, even in the bedroom. I sit on the edge of the bed in my hotel room, and wait for *him* to make a move. I'm confident as hell on the stage, but here? It's different here. Here, I want to be seduced, devoured. I want the man hungry for me, and unafraid. It's been a long time since a man did that, just came at me all *pinche* hungry and shit. Not since Gato, and even he couldn't do that once I got the record deal and he didn't.

"How you been, *chata*?" Joaquin asks.

"*Órale, pues.* Good, it's all good, man." We stare at each other, uncomfortable. Five years ago, this kind of thing, the whole groupie *vato* thing, was interesting, maybe even enjoyable. But I'm getting too old for it now. It's not interesting anymore, the starstruck man in my room. I want it to grab me, you know, but it doesn't. I have nothing to say to this dude, man. I just want to get me some sleep. I just want someone to lean against while the TV plays a movie in the dark, someone to talk about politics with. I want a companion who doesn't think of me as famous Cuicatl. Someone who thinks of me the way I think of myself, as the goofy girl from Oceanside who got a lucky break and doesn't know how the hell she got here.

"Can I give you a massage or something?" he asks, all wimpy and eager to please me. Suddenly, I regret inviting him here. I don't know what's changed, exactly. Maybe I'm getting too old for this. Maybe the ganja's wearing off. That's probably it. I got the mad munchies, man. I want me a bean burrito with brown rice.

"Sure." I roll over onto my belly and wait for him to come next to me. It takes a few seconds, but then his hands are on me, tentative, inexpert, and freezing cold. It's like being touched with uncooked tofu from the refrigerator. On the bedside table, my BlackBerry alerts me to a new e-mail, and the phone chime rings. I reach for it and check to see who's calling. Frank. I put it on speakerphone and leave the device next to my head on the bed, with a look to Joaquin to silence him.

"*Oye*, Frank, wassup, man?"

"Hey girl. Just wanted to make sure you made it out there okay."

As I listen to his voice, I wish he were here. With me. We wouldn't have to touch. Just watch a movie and eat room service. I'd like that. He knows me. He knew me before all this. I try to sound the way I always sound with him, even as my feelings for him shift beneath me like a chord modulation. "*Pues*, dude, what do you think I'm gonna do? Roll off the road? It's only twenty miles away, c'mon."

"I know. I just wanted to make sure you knew there was someone looking out for you."

"*Órale*. Thanks. I appreciate that."

"*Bueno*, Cuicatl, you take care and have a good night. Call me if you need anything."

"Yeah, sure."

"I mean it. Anything at all, *estoy a su orden*, you know that."

"Thanks, man."

We hang up, and Joaquin says nothing. He just keeps rubbing my neck like he doesn't mean it, then my shoulders. I pull my shirt over my head without sitting up, and he continues on my back. When I've had enough of this heartless groping, I roll over. He runs his eyes over my new, gravity-defying breasts and grins.

"They're bigger since I saw you last time," he says.

"Yeah, a little."

"They don't even flop to the sides like normal tits," he says. "They stay put."

"Yeah. That's the idea. I wanted porn tits."

"I'm surprised you'd do that, actually," he says, with a look I've seen before. People are always surprised by whatever I do. I think it's because they see me as an extension of themselves, like they don't really know me. They think they do, but they don't. I've heard it when I released pop songs, from the *roqueros* who thought I was selling out. People want celebrities to be just like them, and when we're not, they hate us for it.

"Why don't you think I'd get a boob job? I did it, didn't I?"

"Cosmetic surgery and all, you know, the *hermanitas* in the women's studies department are always talking about how it's misogynist to mutilate yourselves for patriarchy." Even as he says it, he's drooling over my boobs. He's a *pinche* hypocrite, like everyone else I know in the movement. Did you see how he called them *"hermanitas"* instead of *"hermanas"*? That's diminutive. He's a hypocrite, like almost every Mexican man I know with a college degree.

"They're full of shit," I tell him. "Empowerment comes from being true to thine own self." I take a deep breath and close my eyes for a moment, not in the mood to have this discussion. I'm so over it.

"You *do* look hot," he tells me with half a grin. I want this to be over with. I want him gone.

I sit up and kiss him, mostly so he'll stop talking about the bitter feminist control freaks at the university. It's an okay kiss. There's nothing spectacular about it. That's been the rule with sex since I dumped Gato, *¿sabes?* I have sex the way I run on the treadmill when I'm on the road and don't know the city well enough to go for a real run. I approximate running, right? Just like I approximate intimacy. When I'm back in Los Angeles, I run on the beach, or in the hills. But I'm hardly ever home anymore. I don't make love anymore, either. It's different now. You think you're going to connect with more people when you get famous, right? But for me the opposite has been true. I connect with fewer and fewer people, behind my wall more and more. Not better or worse, just different.

We go on messing around like this for a while, and then he squeezes my *chichis* a little and before I know it, he's taking his clothes off and I'm taking my jeans down even though I don't think I'm wet enough to do anything yet. I should really try to go down on him or something, but I don't feel like it. I'm still a tiny bit high, and a little drunk, and seriously, homes, mostly I'm fucking *tired*. This is going to sound stupid, but all I want to do right now is fucking cuddle with somebody who likes me for me.

He goes down on me, and does a half-assed job that I don't feel like correcting. He's got his tongue up under the clitoral hood and the shit hurts. He might as well be chewing me up like a piece of sushi.

"*Ya, ya*, that's good," I say. "Let's do it."

He puts the condom on, and in it goes. It feels all right. Not great, you know? Just okay. He's okay. He gets that glassy look to his eyes, staring at the different pieces of me like I'm meat in a grocery bin. Boobs, pussy. His eyes go back and forth, his mouth a little half-cocked like he can't believe he's doing this, like he's watching himself from a great distance. He's with me, but he might as well be masturbating. There is no connection here. He can't bring himself to look me in the eye, like the underdog he thinks he is. He goes at it for less than a minute, no longer than that, and then he's done. Just like that. A damn Minuteman.

"Shit," he says, with a slap to his forehead, still not exactly looking at me. "I'm sorry. I didn't mean to do that."

"Better luck next time," I say. I just lie there staring at the ceiling, feeling very alone. More alone than I've felt in my entire life. This can't be all there is, surely. I chased this dream, this crazy dream of fame, and here it is, and I'm lonelier than ever. That wasn't in the script.

"Can I do anything for you?" he asks, all *pinche* embarrassed and ready to beat himself up. "You want me to use my mouth again?"

"No, please don't." I roll over and close my eyes against the sight of him. I wish he'd never come. I can't keep doing this anymore. This is the last time. I'm better off with a vibrator and memories.

"What?" he asks. I can hear him putting his clothes on. "Was I that bad?"

"Pretty much sucked, yeah," I tell him. "But don't worry, I won't tell anyone."

Next thing I hear is the door slamming shut. Whatever, man. I know he's pissed, but I'm too bored to care. I walk to the bathroom and take a long, hot shower. I dry off, crank the air conditioner, and crawl into the bed naked. I like it cold when I sleep, with the covers pulled way up over my ears.

As I start to doze, my body gets on my case for not relieving myself of the sexual tension I feel. So I let my hands go to work on me. I do the usual routine, and let my mind wander free. Then, as I'm about to come, my brain plays a weird-ass trick on me, right? It conjures up the image of Frank. I think of his sinewy shoulders, his soft, long hair that smells of patchouli oil. I think of his beautiful brown skin and the way it crinkles in rays from his eyes. I think mostly of his eyes, so deep and intelligent, so peaceful and accepting of me, so caring, the way they laugh when they connect with mine, and I imagine them staring into my soul as he and I share our bodies. There would be no servant in the equation. We are equals. It's his soul I want, that thing behind his eyes. I want to see him seeing me, really seeing me, for who I am, naked and completely vulnerable. I want Frank to be inside of me. I shudder and shudder for the longest time, convulsing in the fantasy of making love to my manager and homeboy. "I love you," I tell the fantasy Frank. In my mind, he kisses me gently as he moves inside of me. I tell him again: "I love you, I love you, I love you."

A man almost twenty years older than me, and in love with a mystery woman. A man who will always think of me as a kid, even when I'm fifty. What gives, man? What is *that* about? *Chinga.*

elizabeth

SATURDAY NIGHT, LATE. I am present on the patio in the voluptuous enveloping darkness and cricket song of the desert, to watch Lauren. All of our other friends have long since gone to their rooms to sleep. The flames from the fireplace cast a flattering orange light upon Lauren's face. It ripples across the strong cheekbones, the full lips, the dark brown eyes. The flowing red curls of her hair. The pale skin with the constellation of freckles across the nose. The sparkly white T-shirt with the crowns and rhinestones all over it, the trendy jeans. She is like Guinevere from an Arthurian legend, wild, so far away even though she is right here next to me.

She is so very beautiful, a mythical princess in her tower. I want to use my finger to trace the outline of her mouth, to connect the dots of her freckles. As I watch her, my khaki hiking shorts and dark gray tank top feel too tight. I also ate a buffalo burger with green chile and sharp cheddar cheese on it earlier, with curly fries, and it all seems to be taking its time digesting. I will eat lighter tomorrow.

I pull the light brown shawl closer around my shoulders, and sigh again. I try to do it quietly, but the need to hold her is too large to contain. I have loved her for fifteen years, selflessly, silently, sadly. Love like the lonely, blind walk of a desert caterpillar in search of a blade of grass upon which to become a butterfly.

She catches me watching her and blinks at me for a long moment, longer than normal. I have never had the courage to tell her in direct words. The mystery remains this: Could she love a woman? I have never asked her. I have assumed not, for the simple fact that she has always chosen men, with their scratching beards, horrid breath, and rotting goblin feet. But this look, this wavering, this hesitation in her wounded, intelligent eyes, this small, slow opening of her ripe mouth before it curls into a smile? Perhaps. And this is the word held in the back of my throat now: Perhaps. Perhaps she could love me after all.

I watch her shape-shift in the half-light like some sort of mythical creature. Soft Lauren, hard Lauren, each side of her flashing for such a small moment across her open, unguarded face. She shows it all. Every feeling swims fast behind her eyes and then is gone, like minnows flashing in the sun on the surface of a pond. She hides nothing. I do not think she realizes this. It is the part of her that attracts the victimizers. They see what she feels, what she thinks. The men she chooses more often than not use her transparency and vulnerabilities as a road map leading them toward the construction of her destruction. I want, have wanted, to turn her away from the cliffs they lure her toward, back into the sun and the valley.

With her insightful cutting remarks and comments, Lauren comes across to many as tough, even cruel. But I see what she really is. Just like the victimizers, except that I would not use it against her. Innocent, a child in so many ways. Hopeful, wounded, walking her life on the tips of sharp nails, leaving a footprinted trail of her own blood in her wake, weakening on the path she has chosen, and never knowing that it doesn't have to hurt. That love, life, all of it can fortify. Appease. Adore. Cherish. Make stronger.

I love her.

I have wanted to rescue her from that pain for more than ten years. Never more than now. Now that I am married, to a strong-legged poet from Oregon named Selwyn, for five years married now, with a son of our own. A child Selwyn seems not to want, now that he has come to us from Sierra Leone. When I first saw the baby, I fell in love with him. Desperate love of a magnitude and shape I have never known nor had ever imagined might exist, so massive were its proportions against the sky. I would take bullets, knives, anything for this boy of mine. I would happily slice myself to death if it meant ensuring his tiny, defenseless soul would survive in the cruel, unfeeling world. Not so with Selwyn's feelings for the child. Selwyn does not like little boys—or any children, as it turns out—any more than she likes men. I wish she had realized this before we brought one into our lives.

I love Lauren with a different intensity than I love my child. Different sorts of love, but with the unconditional, potential selfless hurtingness of it. A gargantuan love smeared across the stars. Love her. A love impossible.

Now it seems Selwyn finds any and every excuse to stay late at work and leave me alone with our boy. She is a poet and a professor, and her work is not as demanding as she makes it out to be now. In the beginning, it was any excuse not to change his diapers. Not to run bottles of formula beneath the warm water from the kitchen faucet. Now that we seem to be going through our days like robots, a good morning here, an obligatory kiss there, and then the separation, she seeks opportunities not to have to hold him, or feed him, or read to him. She seems to have no feelings for him at all, which has made me despise her. I regard her as a predator in our home now, and sometimes wish I had fangs to bare at her.

I have never felt more alone than I do now, when I should feel filled with family, now, married with a child, and I hear nothing but the sound of the wind blowing through the emptiness of my soul. I stumble through it and wonder: Why did I do this? How do I extricate myself?

"What are you thinking about?" Lauren asks me, munching on a basket of red and blue corn chips with chipotle dipping sauce. "You look so melancholy." For the past few hours, she's been eating like mad, then excusing herself to the bathroom, returning with the strong scent of toothpaste on her breath. I know what it means. She needs help. I want to rescue her from this, too.

"It's a long story," I tell her.

She nods and does not push me to tell her more. She accepts what I've said. And that's part of why I love her. Lauren Fernandez. Many see her as prickly, horribly difficult, and self-loathing, even crazy. I see another side to her. A great humor, and a forgiving nature. That is what it is that gets her into so much trouble, the fact that she can accept nearly anyone, in any condition, without giving up on them. She continues to sip her beer, and I sip my martini. We don't speak, and it is comfortable, just this warmth from the fire as the air cools around us, just the crack and pop of the embers as they spit and glow.

I sense it all the time, but now that she is next to me, close enough for me to smell the flowers and soap of her perfume, the mint of her toothpaste, the musk of her neck, now I know this love will never disappear. I thought I could forget her, move on, find another way to love myself out of being in love with her. There is nothing as painful as being in love with your straight friend. It is worse than Romeo and Juliet. Worse a million times over, because it is a one-sided love. I thought Selwyn, with her swagger and her cold, hard, predictable love, could fix the way I thought of Lauren constantly, cure me of aching for decades for a straight woman who is one of my best friends. It has not worked. Lauren's heat continues to curl through me, leaving goose bumps in its wake. Her humor slices me into a million pieces of beautiful, draping lace.

I feel my cell phone vibrating in my pocket, but I don't want to look at it. It will probably be Selwyn, with a question about how to make the baby stop crying. She hates the sound of his pain and tears. I don't think I should have to guide her motherhood nonstop like this. She has called three times today already, accusations in her tone, frustrated that I left her with Gordon, our baby. Upset that she will eventually have to teach him to pee standing up, a bridge to a world of masculinity she never wanted contact with. Resentful. I think she should have to figure some of these things out for herself. I will ignore the phone. I will watch Lauren. And imagine. And hope.

And hurt squirmingly, like a squirrel beneath the tires of a truck, unable to breathe, or move, or live. Nothing hurts like love unrequited. A love impossible. Completely impossible. You wish you could cut your heart out with a machete when the pain gets this huge. Now, when it is the least possible, a love doomed to die as surely as an air bubble at the bottom of the sea.

Lauren looks at me. There is a question in her eyes. There always has been. After several long seconds, I look away, focus inward, look at the trees in the distance to avoid the heat of her eyes. I can't believe she held my gaze that long. She looked strong. It unnerved me. I have never seen her look so strong. A strong Lauren would be unstoppable.

"Liz." Her voice is steady. There is no question in it, just a statement of fact.

I look back at her, and she has leaned closer. Toward me. Her arms uncrossed from her chest, hands on her knees. Open. I take a deep breath. This is the night. I am going to tell her, and just see what she says. There are possibilities. I have long thought it was impossible, but half of reality is our perception of it. If you tell yourself something is possible there's a good chance it will become so. I think of how to say it, and then, to my surprise, she says it for me.

"I know how you feel about me," she says. I feel the slow rush of my pulse turn inside out in rainbow colors.

"You do?"

"Sara told me, ages ago." She looks directly at me over the top of her beer, as she drinks the last of it. She smiles, the soft light of the fire flickering at the front of her eyes, the minnows at the back telling a new story. They look like mermaids now. What kind of smile is this on her pretty lips? Is it pity? Mockery? Lust? All three? I can't tell. She is devious.

"And how *do* I feel about you?" I ask her, rhetorically. I try to sound calm, cool, and I fail. Delirious failure. Delicious failure. Why is my pulse racing so? I am at the precipice of such a steep drop. I can't do this. I should not talk about this. I am married. But in my heart? In my heart? In my heart I've always belonged to Lauren.

Lauren laughs at me.

"What?"

"You're nervous," she says. Toys with me. Her eyes, her body language. She is flirting. I am not imagining it now.

"Yes," I tell her. "I am."

Lauren sets the bottle down on the table, and continues to smile at me. "You want me," she announces. Flat, simple language, spoken in the lubricated tones of a drunk. A gross approximation of what this beastly, beautiful thing is that I actually feel for her. She reminds me of a college girl, and not just because I've known her since then. She is like a girl at a frat party, taking a dare.

"It's more than that," I tell her. "You wouldn't understand. Let's not discuss this."

Lauren shrugs. "What could be more than wanting? Wanting is everything. Wanting is . . . overwhelming." She spreads her arms for emphasis. "Huge. Wanting is drastic. Massive. It has driven people to their deaths."

She is drunk. This is not the right time. Her perception is a funhouse mirror, all off. I know better than to share secrets with drunk women. Drunk *straight* women. It is never the same the next day as it is in the inebriated night before.

Lauren stares into the night. "Fucking Amaury," she gripes. "I keep calling and texting. I know he's cheating on me again. He never answers, you know? He's ignoring me." She has tears in her eyes.

"I should get to bed," I say.

"No, don't go." Lauren reaches out and puts her hand on mine. She looks at me, hard. "Liz. Listen to me." Not drunk enough to slur her words yet. Maybe she is not as far gone as I thought. "I want you to know, I think you're beautiful."

The breath stops in my mouth. I swallow it, will it into my lungs, force myself to breathe. "You do?"

She nods. One time. Slowly. With a Cheshire grin.

"Let's walk," she says as she bucks her head in the direction of the trees and the river. "I want to talk."

Against my instincts, I stand up, and follow her unsteady form down the stone steps, toward the dirt walking path that leads into the darkness. On the path that leads to the trees, we walk, side by side, for a full minute or more, without speaking. The darkness gets thicker the closer we get to the growth of trees alongside the river. There are so many stars it makes me gasp. I've never seen such intense, red-black star-smear. I look around. Nothing. No one. I am pleased with this. Content that we are alone. I stop walking and turn to her. She grabs my hands in hers.

"Why are you doing this?" I ask. "Is it because you're hurt that Amaury might be unfaithful?"

"Doing what?" she says, sly, flirty, moving in closer. "I'm not doing anything bad. Am I?" I want to step back, away from danger, from possibilities of pain. But I don't. I let her come close. Close enough to smell the beer on the mint.

"You're self-destructive, Lauren. If that's what you're doing, don't get me involved. Seriously, Lauren. Is that what you're doing? Trying to hurt him back? Even the score?"

"No." She says the word with an upward twist at the end of it. Cute, childish. Flirting the way straight women flirt, in that they try to lose their power for the benefit of a man. "I'm trying to save myself," she says enigmatically.

I take another deep breath, and speak it. As I have practiced it many times. "Since the first time I met you," I tell her, "I've wanted to save you, too."

"How cliché."

I laugh. She's right. "You know me and English," I say.

"Oh, please. That excuse won't work with me, girl." She tries to kiss me, lurches toward me, and I duck away.

"Lauren, what are you doing? You're straight."

My eyes are adjusting to the darkness, and I can see her own eyes shining at me. Narrowing in thought. "Yes, I am. I'm straight."

I drop her hands, and she wraps them through mine again.

"But," she says. "I fucking *hate* men."

"How cliché," I say. This time, she laughs. It hurts to think that this is her motivation. A negative motivation rather than a positive one. Nothing good begins this way.

"I just wonder what it would be like," she says. She moves closer. In my pocket, the phone vibrates again. I ignore it. I shouldn't. I let Lauren place her head on my shoulder. I feel the soft curves of her face along my neck, and then the lips puckering, a gentle kiss to my neck. "You smell really good," she says.

I look at the sky. There is a crescent moon. A few puffs of clouds. Stars like I have not seen since I was back in Colombia, thousands, maybe millions of them. I forget my doubts, my fears, and realize with a shock of happiness that Lauren is kissing my neck. I turn my face toward her, and kiss the top of her head.

"I love you," I tell her. "I have loved you for so many years. Do you understand?"

"Mmm-hmm." She stands up straight again, and faces me, close. Closer. And then it happens, this thing I have imagined for so long.

Lauren kisses me.

Funny, I had always thought I would be the one to kiss her.

It lasts, a movie kiss, only better. The best kiss of my life. I feel the center of me melt, burn, melt and burn, and I ache to touch her along each curve of her body.

We stop, and she laughs.

Laughs.

My heart would stop if I could make it stop. It would.

"What is funny?" I ask her.

"Nothing," she says, backing away. "It's just, your lips. They're so soft. I've never kissed a woman before. You don't realize how used to facial hair you get until you don't have any there."

In my pocket, the phone vibrates. I grab for it, and try not to cry. A woman. She said she has never kissed "a woman." I should have known better. That is all I am for her. A female mouth to kiss just to see how it compares to the hairy mouths of her real life. She found it amusing. Looked at it like a scientist, compare and contrast. I have made this mistake before, seducing straight women, and I know how it ends. It never ends well. It always ends badly.

I pull the phone up to where I can see it, and look at the caller ID. Selwyn. It's two in the morning in Boston, I realize with a jolt. This might be an emergency. To distract myself from the heartbreak Lauren is offering me on a silver pillow, I answer it.

"He won't stop crying," she yells into the phone. "This fucking *baby*, Liz. I can't take it with him anymore. I need some fucking sleep!" She sounds crazed, and frantic. You'd think she was on the top floor of a building on fire.

"Where is he?"

"In his fucking bed, that's where. Why haven't you answered the fucking phone?"

"Please don't speak to me like that," I say, listening to my son howling for me in the background. "Calm down. Don't curse."

"Don't you lecture me, Miss I'm-going-on-vacation-while-you-suffer-with-the-demon-from-hell."

"Have you taken him into the bed with you?"

"No, I haven't."

"Try that."

"Ferber says not to, you know that. We can't do that."

"Ferber was a counterintuitive sadist," I say. "Just comfort him, Selwyn."

"I don't want to comfort him," she says, plainly stating the fact of what I have suspected about her for months. Now she is whining. "I want my own fucking sleep, in my own fucking bed."

"He's lonely," I say. "He's so tiny, Selwyn, just a little tiny person."

"A little tiny man, who wants to be the center of the world the way all of them do."

I feel the tears come, for the son I am neglecting to be here with these friends from college, to be here trying to make a straight woman, a drunk straight woman, fall in love with me. Selwyn is as hateful toward men as the people who despise homosexuals are toward us. I can't believe I never saw it before. I am the worst mother in the world.

"I'll be home as soon as I can," I tell my wife. "I can't get a flight out tonight, but first thing tomorrow, I'll come."

There is silence. "You don't have to fucking *do* that."

"Can he hear you? The words you're using?"

"I don't know. I don't care."

"Yes, I am aware. I know you don't care. Just try to do the best you can for him, fake it if you have to, hold him, rock him, let him feel your human warmth, that's what he needs more than anything else. Please, Selwyn, do it for me."

"Yeah, like you do so much for me, right?"

"What is that supposed to mean?"

"It means that ever since Gordon came into our lives it's all about *him*. He's all you seem to care about."

"You're tired. I'm going to assume you don't mean what you're saying about your own son."

"*Your* son. I never *wanted* a son."

"He's your son, too."

"Not legally, he isn't. Yours is the name on the papers."

"Just hold him, Selwyn. He's a baby. He needs love. Even if he is a boy."

"Fine," she says, angry.

"If you don't, he might cry all night," I say, hoping to play on her own narcissism now. "You need your sleep. Just do what it takes to get him back to sleep so you can have some peace, Selwyn, you deserve that for watching him all on your own."

I hate myself as I say these words that I don't believe. Hate myself for allowing this cold woman to care for a child who needs love, a child whose parents both died of AIDS, a boy who miraculously escaped the disease himself, but who was doomed to poverty and neglect in an orphanage not fit for stray animals. He deserves better than this woman, this pampered woman from her middle-class family in America. What does she know of poverty? Of suffering? Of racism?

"Fine," she repeats. "I'll do it."

"I'll be home tomorrow."

She returns to fury, yelling madly, "No, don't *do* that. Don't *give* me that guilt trip, Liz. I'm not buying it. Don't try to make me feel like an inferior parent, okay? I'm not buying it. I'm not."

"I'm just trying to help."

"Just do your little retreat with your little straight friends, and I'll deal with it. But you owe me, big time, when you get back."

"Selwyn?"

"What."

"Promise me you won't hit him."

Silence again.

"Did you?" I ask her.

"A little swat on the behind now and then won't kill him."

I feel sick. "You *didn't*."

"I did."

"Selwyn! How could you?"

"He's fine. Look, stop it. Just stop it. You do it your way, I do it my way."

"Well, if that's the case, why do you keep calling me for help?" I am so angry my hands shake.

Another silence, and then she says, "You're right. I won't do it again."

And with that, Selwyn hangs up on me. I turn toward the resort, and I begin to run. I just want to be in my room, to pack my things and call the airline to see if I can get a flight out tomorrow instead of on Monday.

Lauren follows, asking me what's wrong. I don't answer, or even look at her. I can't bear it. I resent her now. For experimenting with me. For preventing me from answering the phone before it was too late to save my child from Selwyn's hand. For being the lure that got me to this resort in the first place. I should have been home with Gordon.

I should have been there for him.

usnavys

I **CAN'T SLEEP.** Yes, I feel *guilty*, okay? I just talked to Juan on the phone to ask him how his Saturday went, and he was so nice and loving, asking about this and that and whatnot and reminding me of my mother's birthday, and I was all in my head, like, "What the fuck is wrong with me?" I shouldn't have done it. But now that I've done it, I can't stop thinking about Marcus and what he might mean to me. He's called me three times already, and he's sent me flowers to my room. And not just any flowers, okay, *m'ija*? A big bouquet of expensive flowers with a box of Godiva chocolates and a card with a poem in it. Some romantic nonsense, right? Now what am I supposed to do with that, I ask you? I wasn't supposed to fall in love with the golf pro, *nena*. I wasn't even supposed to let that man in, here, into my heart. But he pushed his way in there, and now I've discovered that just because one man goes in your heart it doesn't necessarily mean that the other one is going to get his ass up and leave. So I'm thinking about two men, one of them my damn husband, and I feel like I went and killed somebody, that's how guilty I am.

He wants to spend all day with me tomorrow, before I go back home on Monday. He wants to take me up some tramway on the mountain and whatnot, like all romantic and so on. I don't know if I should do it. I don't know. I already told him I was single, so that was my first mistake. Now he's courting me, and he wants to take me on a date. I can't remember the last time Juan took me on a date. I don't think we go on dates anymore, unless you count taking the whole family to the Stop and Shop and bickering over the frozen foods. Whether we *need* four Sara Lee pound cakes, can you believe it? I should tell you, I agreed to go with Marcus. I don't know how I'm going to swing it, because it's the same time I'm supposed to be horseback riding with my girls. I tried horseback riding in Connecticut a few years back, but the trainer told me I was too heavy for the tired old horse, and that was that. Maybe that's it. I'll tell them girls I'm too voluptuous to go riding with them, and I'll retire to "my room" and sneak out the front door with Marcus. Or maybe not. Maybe I'll nip this thing in the damn bud and go back to being somebody's wife like I'm supposed to and we'll pretend it never happened. Choices, choices, girl. I don't know.

So to keep my mind off what a crazy bitch I've become on this trip, I'm sitting at the desk in my hotel room, writing me a blog to post and enjoying the room service fruit and artisan cheese plate, with nutty peasant bread. I have to remember to be better about blogging on time. It's been a few days since I put something up there, and I know my loyal readers will be getting restless for more. You don't think I'm gonna have me all these readers for something as specialized as a sex blog for gringos by a plus-sized Latina, but you'd be surprised. I think the only reason most people be logging their sorry asses onto the Internet is sex, *m'ija*. I really do.

Here's what I done got so far, okay?

Now, for everybody's favorite topic: Toys! When I was a little girl growing up in a Puerto Rican family in the projects of New England, I was only allowed to play with girls' toys—dolls, kitchen sets, toy food. I was not even allowed to ride a bike, people. And I'm not like some really old bitch, either, okay? I'm only thirty-three. But my moms, she didn't want me on a bike because she thought it might ruin my virginity. *Lo puedas imaginar.* There are still Latina mothers who think like that. She didn't want me to wear sneakers, either. Nope. I got me some shiny-ass patent leather shoes, and dolls. Not that I minded. I think it went a long way toward making me the sexy, feminine woman I am now.

But today I am writing about the concept of hypocrisy in the way Latina mothers forget to tell their daughters about another sort of toy altogether once they get to be adults. And not just mothers, but sisters and friends. I am talking about sex toys, *m'ija*. That's right. Vibrators, dildos, what-have-you. I never heard of them until I got to college, and even then there was a sense of shame about it. But here's the truth: Girls need toys. Toys for girls. As women, we should reclaim our right to toys, to playing alone, to having fun with our womanhood. There are studies that show that the more a woman pleasures herself, the more fun she has once she hooks up with a man. In other *palabras,* women who learn to fly *sola* can get higher faster when they're with a man. Everybody still be talking about the Jackrabbit, but I'm here to tell you that's old news, girlfriend. The one you have to get? The Stormy Wicked Lover. That's right. Get yourself on that Internet and order you up one of them things, okay? You won't be disappointed. The Lusty Larger Latina would not steer you wrong, *m'ija*. Go play, and do it without shame. Let me make it simple: It's the women who never masturbate who don't have orgasms with men, okay? That's what I'm talking about. I don't have studies to prove that last point, but I have a feeling about it, okay? Women need us some toys. There is no shame in it. And men? You should never, ever be jealous of a toy. Healthy people have private sex lives that involve only themselves. It's like when we're kids. Sometimes it's fun to play with others. And sometimes it's fun to play alone.

My fingers are getting tired from all that tappity tapping on the laptop keyboard and so on, so, grabbing the large green bottle of Pellegrino from the room service tray on the bed, I take a stretching break and open the door to the little balcony in my room. It's late at night, and there ain't nothing making noise out here but the bugs. I like the fresh air. Swigging straight from the bottle, I feel like an old-time cowgirl. I'd rock me some pigtails, okay? And a little checkered shirt all tied up in the front like Daisy Duke? You know it. I'd look good. I could see me living somewhere quiet like this someday. I grew up real urban, you know? Like all you heard at night was sirens and people yelling at each other or fighting or what-have-you, and now I still live in the city. I could live anywhere I wanted to on my salary, but I choose to stay in Mission Hill because I like it there. I like the city vibe and I like being around my people. But this whole clean-air, peace-and-quiet vibe is growing on me. I look up at all the stars, and they look like good-quality salt sprinkled across the heavens.

Then, just like that, the silence is broken by the sounds of something rustling around in the weeds under my balcony. At first, I half expect to see Marcus down in the bushes with a ukulele or some shit, to serenade me. But then I hear a woman's voice mutter something, and then what sounds like footsteps in the grass. I lean over my balcony and squint my eyes. I can't believe what I see, *nena*. It's Sara, all dressed up in a red conservative dress and medium heels, trying to walk but getting her heels stuck in the moist ground with every step, like she's in quicksand. I'm about to call out to her when I notice that she is looking over her shoulder all guilty-like, like she doesn't want anybody to see her. I know that look, okay? Please, girl. I spent this whole trip with that look wanting to sprout off my face. Who am I to ruin a girl's secret? I'm not going to ruin that for her. I do wonder who the hell she's going to screw, though. It's gotta be one of the men who works here, and I hope it ain't the golf pro. Huh-uh, no *way*. Marcus best not be cheating on me, or he'll get a taste of woman's fury, Puerto Rican style.

I hurry back into my room, and close the door to the patio, feeling like a whodunit sleuth, all adrenaline. I close the curtains, and look at the laptop. Not. Important. Okay? Listen to me. There will be time to finish the blog tomorrow. Or maybe it's fine the way it is. Why am I so nervous? I got me a theory. You start lying and cheating in your own life, and pretty soon everybody around you starts to look suspicious, too.

I peel the nightie off, throw on my cocoa brown velvet jogging suit, the one I think looks like something a movie star might wear in one of them photos in *People* magazine where they got their hair back in a messy ponytail and they're coming out of a Starbucks and whatnot and so forth, with a cup of something that will probably be all they'll put in their puny stomachs all day. Hey, if you can't dress like a star on the red carpet, then you dress like a star in their off-hours. Right?

I get my fancy designer Ecco sneakers on, the only kind I think a woman can and should wear with any self-respect, really, and a white scarf on my head and dark glasses with matching white frames, even though it's nighttime, and then I call down to valet for my car and I tell them to rush it if they want to get them a good tip.

I get to the valet stand and find my rental Jaguar idling, waiting for me. I ask the parking boy if a woman fitting Sara's description left recently and he said he just saw her drive away not a minute ago. I ask him what she was driving and he tells me it was a green Ford Taurus. I know that car's a rental, honey. Nobody drives them a Taurus otherwise. I stuff a twenty-dollar bill into the valet boy's hand, and off I go in my Jaguar, chasing the taillights of the Taurus down the winding, narrow road out of the resort, in the direction of the city.

lauren

OKAY, SO, LIKE, I don't know exactly how pathetic a loser you have to be to piss off a lesbian who has been in love with you for fifteen long and devoted years. A woman who is one of your closest friends and has sworn her undying love for you. I figured if there was anyone in the world who wouldn't reject the ever rejectable me it would be Elizabeth.

But as it happens, she is, at this moment, running away from me as if I were dipped in anthrax rather than hotel-issue sage-scented body lotion. Like, a *Run, Lola, Run* type of running. A loping, Mel Gibson *Apocolypto*, bloody, oozy, crappy kind of run. Okay, it's not exactly running. It's more of a graceful trot at high speed, because she moves like a gazelle.

In spite of having made myself vomit three times since I got here last night, and five times today, I'm drunk enough to feel the world tilting, to realize that it feels like a horror movie in here. You know the drill. There's the dark and creepy hallway that seems to get longer the more I walk, with Elizabeth like the little wild-eyed dwarf that keeps trying to lure you to your doom.

"Liz!" I call after her.

My voice sounds distant to me as it bounces off the muted neutral walls of the hotel. Liz ignores me and puts her phone to her ear again. I can't hear what she's saying, but from her tense body language I would guess it's not good. That wife of hers, from what little I understood of the conversation they just had, is a total and complete bitch. Who the hell has to be reminded to hold a crying baby? I swear to God, there are people in the world I'd like to just kick the shit out of sometimes. Selwyn is one of them.

"Wait for me, Liz!"

She turns to look at me with a tortured expression. I stumble after her, but she won't stop. I race ahead, my head unusually large and wobbly, and I intercept her at the emergency stairwell. She hurries away, and nearly sprints to a second set of elevators. This is so dramatic. I'm a drama queen, too. Yay, goody. She presses her phone off, puts it back in her fanny pack, and looks at me like a lover scorned. I'm not sure I could be gay, but I sure as hell want to find out. It was awesome to kiss her. I mean, it was soft and smooth and her lips tasted like vanilla ice cream. It was so different from the harsh biting stubble of Amaury. I could get used to it, couldn't I?

I want to find out.

Elizabeth presses the elevator button over and over, hoping she might escape me this way. I force my way in between her and the wall. She won't look at me.

"What?" I ask. "What did I *do*?"

She doesn't answer.

"Come here," I say. I grab Elizabeth's face with both of my hands, and I kiss her, hard. Too hard, and our teeth crunch together through our lips. Oops.

"Ow!" Her hand comes up to her mouth. There is a tiny drop of blood on her lip, and for some reason—some sick reason—it excites me. The elevator comes, and the doors slide open. No one inside. She steps in.

"Sorry," I mutter, and follow her.

When the doors slide closed again, I keep kissing her. I push her up against the wall of the elevator and shove one knee up between her legs in their khakhi shorts. She relents, opens them. I get a flutter rush in my belly.

"No," she protests, softly.

"Yes," I insist. She has tears in her eyes. I feel cruel, and for the first time in my life of romance, I feel like am the one utterly and completely in charge. I force myself on her.

I don't know exactly why I'm doing this, except that I am drunk enough to think it's sensible, and ambiguous enough in my own sexuality at the moment to find it thrilling to act like a man. I hate Amaury. And Ed. All of them. Men. Fucking *men* have all the fucking *power*, and I want that fucking power, okay? If it means making myself over as a man, then shit, maybe that's what I have to do. I could solve all my problems at once if I went lesbo.

She pushes me off of her. "Don't, Lauren." Her tears spill over to her cheeks. The elevator door slides open, and she hurries out. I follow after her. "Go back to your room," she says. "Go back to Amaury."

"Fuck Amaury, that stupid motherfucker," I slur. I tag along, a smile on my face. I feel high and obnoxious and crazy. I like challenges. I like being in situations where I have to prove to people that I am worth their time and energy. I like it when people reject me. It gets my adrenaline going. It makes me feel alive. It is also familiar.

Liz stops at the door to her room and sticks the key card into the door. She doesn't look at me as she slips through a crack she hopes to keep narrow enough to keep me out. I push my way in, past her.

"Don't," she says, weakly.

"No," I correct her, vaguely aware that my speech is slightly sloshy. "*You* don't. *You* don't."

I enter the room and we both stand in the small vestibule, looking at each other. She is absolutely beautiful. I don't think I have ever known a more beautiful woman in person. She is pretty in the way movie stars and pop stars are pretty, that whole other level of unattainable prettiness and symmetry. People who don't know her are always shocked to find out that she is gay, because of the stereotype of lesbians as butch or ugly, and all that. Liz is the furthest thing from that. She used to be a model, and she is something of a local celebrity in Boston. Even five years after quitting her job as an on-air news reporter, and after moving to Colombia for a year to try to be a poet, she is still recognized everywhere she goes.

"What?" she says, fingering her tank top along the neckline. "Why are you looking at me like that?"

"You are so pretty," I say with an envious pout. "It's unfair."

Liz rolls her eyes and walks away, toward the main room. "Oh, please, Lauren. It figures you'd say something like that."

"Like what? What did I do? I thought I just complimented you!" As I raise my voice, the chest pain returns. What is it? I ignore it.

Liz sits on the side of the bed and looks at me with laughter in her eyes. "Oh, my God, Lauren. Can't you hear what you're saying?"

I stare at her, dumbfounded. What is her problem?

"When you say it's not *fair* that I'm pretty, that's like screaming 'I'm straight' at the top of your lungs."

"How so?"

Her hands fly up. "Because! Only a straight woman could view another woman's beauty as *unfair*, because only a straight woman would view herself as being in competition for a man."

I think about this. "Not necessarily," I tell her.

Elizabeth leans forward and puts her head in her hands. Like someone who is about to cry. Like someone with a headache. Like someone who would rather be anywhere but here. She looks destroyed. She looks like my dad used to look when he got tired of me. This thrills me somehow, and only strengthens my resolve to make her like me again.

"No," I insist. "I mean, couldn't it also mean that I saw you as competition for other chicks?"

"*Chicks*, Lauren?"

"Yeah. Chicks. You know. Bitches. 'Hos and tricks."

Elizabeth stops rubbing her temples and freezes. Then she looks up with a very different look on her face. A smile. She laughs. "That's funny."

"Anyone seems funny when you're married to Selwyn, I bet."

Liz smiles sadly and lifts one brow. "I have to go back tomorrow."

"No you don't," I say.

"I do. She can't do it alone."

"She's not alone, she has Gordon."

Liz laughs again. "God, you're funny."

Her compliment makes me feel cocky. Speaking of cocky? I am *wishing* I had a cock right now, because it occurs to me that sex with another woman might be ultimately unsatisfying to me because neither of us would get a good hammering. There is nothing better in the world than a good hammering.

Dammit. I can't do this now.

How do women do it with other women? With fingers and tongues and so on? I know those things can be very effective, but, and I have to admit this, there is that animal part of me that just really, really needs that final act with the male part entering and exiting. I can't imagine it going any other way. I can't imagine that Liz is going to be content to go through her entire life without ever wanting or engaging in the in and out with a man. The thought that I might live like that depresses the hell out of me, so I shuffle it quickly and efficiently out of my mind.

Uh-oh. Even as I think this, this thought that is probably best categorized under the "reasons why I'm actually straight" tab, Liz is looking at me differently now, as if she thinks we have a chance after all. The pain in her eyes is draining away. It is being replaced by a peaceful kind of joy because I made her laugh. And it seems really fucked to hell that she is changing over to wanting me at almost exactly the moment I am starting to have second thoughts, and second thoughts about my second thoughts, which, and I'm not sure about this, could qualify as fourth thoughts or third thoughts depending on which mathematical paradigm you chose to use.

"She really *doesn't* have a sense of humor, you know?"

"Who?"

"Selwyn."

I make a face that reminds me of Rachael Ray making a mistake. "Oh, please. That's old news. I could tell that dyke had no funny bone the minute you brought her to meet us."

"Really?"

"Uh, yeah. Hello? Lesbian mullet?" I start to cough, and not because I think I'm funny. Rather, my chest and throat feel heavy and weird again. I feel like there's a barbed lump of something stuck under my sternum.

"You okay?" she asks me.

"Fine. It's the thought of the mullet," I say.

Liz smiles with guilty pleasure. "Her hair is pretty bad."

"All business in the front, all party in the back. Jesus, Liz. No one has hair like that except guys in Calgary, and maybe Saugus."

Liz laughs again, but cries at the end of it. "She's not a completely bad person, you know."

"You deserve better," I tell her. I say this to all my girlfriends. But from the way she's looking at me now, I realize that she has misinterpreted it to mean that I think she deserves me. That I think I am better than Selwyn—which I am, but not because I think I should marry Liz. I should marry Ward Cleaver. Except that he's dead, or gay, or already taken, or something like that.

"What are you thinking about?" she asks me, her eyes all soft poetry.

"You," I say. It isn't exactly a lie. Not exactly.

She looks at me with pure longing now. I have not seen her look at me like this, not this directly. I have known she might, but it has never happened. "You mean it?" she asks.

"Mean what?" I am such an ass.

She points to herself; specifically, she points to the space where her heart would be. Grins. God, she's gorgeous. God, I'm straight. "This," she says, indicating herself. She is so hopeful. And I am so drunk. So, so drunk. Almost puking drunk, actually. I think it will be okay. I'll just try it. I'll just pretend I'm a man. Maybe I'll be pleasantly surprised and end up realizing it's exactly what I need and have been looking for.

"Yes," I tell her. I know it isn't true as I say it, and yet I can't help it. She is one of my closest friends. I cannot bear the thought of hurting her, and as screwy as it seems right now, I think that rejecting her would hurt her.

She stands, and comes to me now. I close my eyes and imagine that I am okay with this. It doesn't frighten me. And then, as if planted in my mind from somewhere else, a thought comes to me. *If you can masturbate, you can be with a person of the same sex.* Right? It really isn't all that different. Is it?

Liz stands close to me, facing me, and her eyes stare into mine without blinking. Naked eyes. There is so much there it actually seems to suck the air out of me for a moment. So much. All of our history as friends, and all of the feelings she has kept hidden from me for so long, all of it is there, and I feel it stab me.

"Lauren," she whispers. It isn't just my name. It is a sigh. A mantra for her. "I love you."

"I love you, too, sweetie," I tell her.

But even as I say it, again, I know it is not true in the way she *thinks* it's true. I love her as a friend. Thus, the "sweetie." If I felt romantic love for her, I wouldn't have said that. I said it the way you'd talk to your friend who's about to get married to a man, to help calm her nerves about the dress being a little too tight, like you'd finish it up with "you look amazing, he'll think you're *so* totally hot." I feel excitement because I am about to try something I have never tried, for the sake of maybe seeing if I can change teams for the sake of my stability and sanity.

But I do not feel the excitement, that animal lust and thrill that I get when I am in this position with a man. Position? When I'm about to get it *on* with a guy. Then, in those times, I feel an ancient kind of excitement, a natural pull back toward my evolutionary roots, and strong drive to procreate. That, for obvious reasons, is lacking here.

She kisses me. It is pleasant, and I kiss her back. It escalates, to a passionate kind of kiss, and she is tender at first. I can almost believe she is a man, if I close my eyes. I feel her shiver and she pulls me closer, kisses me harder. The feel of her breasts against mine makes it nearly impossible now to imagine she is a man. There is also something decidedly estrogenic about her breath. There is no mistaking it for man-breath. Unless she were a man with breasts, which would be . . . disgusting.

I open my eyes and look at her. Her brown skin and beautiful eyes. I wish my waist were as small as hers. I wish my breasts were as large. I wish my shoulders had the soft shine to them that hers do, I wish I had legs that went on forever like hers. I close my eyes again, hoping I'll be able to go through with this. I don't want to let her down, as crazy as that sounds. I imagine we're in a movie, one of *those* kinds of movies, and that the guy will be here any minute to relieve the tension. I tell myself this is just a game. I let her kiss me, and I enjoy it as much as I can, even though I can't stop thinking about the way her collarbone is so much prettier than mine beneath her skin. Mine, you can hardly see at all.

Her hands begin to wander up and down my back, and around, to my breasts, which, I must say, are about two cups smaller than hers. I push my insecurity away, and try to imagine she is a man. I go with it. She is so good, so freakin' expert, at touching them I almost cry out. Of course she is. She has the equipment herself. I mean, men have nipples, too, of course, but they don't often seem to know what to do with *ours*. They do this obligatory squeezing thing, like the way they'd palm a basketball, and then move south to the parts they view as the goods. But Liz? Damn. Liz *knows* what girls want. She finds the nips on the outside of the shirt, and teases, pinches, touches, all the while kissing my lips, my neck, and then she is down in front of me, lifting my shirt, kissing her way up my belly to the chest.

And I feel, groove along on feeling and being present in my own skin. Soon, through the feeling, the space between my legs has grown oozy. Beyond wet. Throbbing, sopping. She is so good. I have heard that you can have an orgasm from nothing more than nipple stimulation and I have never believed it. Until now. I get close, more quickly than I thought possible, and Liz seems to have a sixth sense about what I am feeling, because she pulls away just at the moment where it would have been too late to cross that line.

She stands up straight again, and kisses my lips.

"I have thought about this so much," she tells me, her deep, sexy voice tinged with just a hint of her Colombian accent, a lovely voice, but not a male voice. I don't know what I'm doing here. But I'm starting to like it. This scares me. A lot.

I open my eyes and look at her. Being as hot as I am right now, and seeing her beauty, I am overcome with the urge to please her back. But I am. Not. Gay. Okay? Let's just get that part out in the open. I am straight as the side of a refrigerator. I *know* that. But I could be, for this moment in time. I don't think it's something I could stick with for very long. Like the time I joined the Japanese club in college and pretended I was interested enough to actually do the work to learn the language. But I knew, even from that first meeting, that I wasn't going to stick it out.

We move from the vestibule to the bed, and continue. Off with the tank top and boy shorts. Off with the plain white underwear and bra. Then, bam. What a freakin' body this woman has. I'd kill to have a body like this. I can't believe she could find me attractive, seeing as she is perfect *Playboy* material. I pretend as I am touching her that I am simply touching myself, or that I am a man touching me. I know, that sounds weird. But it works for me. She smells good. Even "down there" she smells good. And the thing that surprises me the most is that she smells a lot like a man. I mean, I think that men and women don't smell all that different in their nether regions. The whole thing about women smelling bad is a myth, I decide, unless they don't clean themselves, but that is also the case for men. And dogs. And camels. Pretty much any living thing, unwashed, reeks.

She removes my Bebe sparkly T-shirt and my jeans. Then my ridiculously fancy lace thong and the matching bra, both light brown. I try to cover myself up.

"Why are you doing that?" she asks, with a truly confused look on her face.

"I feel fat," I tell her.

"Lauren, please. Not here, not with me. You don't have to do that." She pulls my hands away from where I try to use them to shield my private parts, and I let her. It is strangely freeing, the way she doesn't seem to care if I've got a few extra pounds on me.

We spend what feels like an hour simply exploring each other. And then, there comes the moment where I place my fingers into her body. She is warm, and wet, and she groans and begins to speak softly in Spanish as I do it. I am surprised by this, because of all the *sucias*, she is the one who never seems to use Spanish at all, even though she was the one raised with it. I've reached a part of her none of us have seen, and I don't mean physically.

She stops me, and flips me over, aggressive now. She goes to work on me, now. All I can say is this: It is true that women are better at oral sex on a woman than a man could ever be. She knows what to do, and she does it well. Before I know what's happening, I've climaxed. She knows exactly when I finish, and she stops without being asked. She holds me for a moment, until I pull away from her, feeling guilty and confused. All I want to do now is leave. But I have to please her back, right? That's the right thing to do.

So I keep doing it, doing to her what she's done to me, and she lies back and lets me. It feels like my fingers are in the middle of a big, warm sponge. It's not a thing I like to actually do to myself, because of the fact that there are so many more nerve endings in my fingertips than inside. I end up focused on the wrong sensation, and a little grossed out by the inequity of sensations. I usually use something else inside myself. But now, inside her, it's totally different and not at all disgusting. Well, maybe a little disgusting if I think about it too hard. But not all that disgusting. Not as disgusting as I thought it would be, is what I'm trying to say, and yet even as I say it I feel weird. What is happening to me? Why am I doing this? It's crazy!

I look at her, the way she arches her back, the way she props herself up on her elbows for a moment to look down at me, the way she rolls her eyes back in her head, bites her lip and falls back to the mattress in surrender. She looks like a porn star. I look at the graceful movements of her hips as she rocks herself toward climax around my fingers and across my mouth.

And now I get it.

I *get* what it is that men find so infinitely fascinating about us. With men, it is simple. In out, up down, and do it enough times and they get to where they need to go, pop off. They leave their seed and they move on in their emotionally clueless way. But with women? The dance of it is so beautiful. The tensing and release, the circular motions, the eternal connection to the creative forces of the universe. I guess you could say that the older I get the more I agree with the religious humanist vision of the world, the one that says God is nothing more than the creative forces of the universe that science has begun to quantify. Which makes no sense right now, I know. But it actually does. See, here and now, generously moving my dear friend Elizabeth toward fireworks, I understand something about her, and about me as a result, that I have never allowed myself to believe until now. Women are intrinsically holy. We are sacred. We are holier, and more sacred, than men. The universe made us like that, and men know it. That's why they work so hard to contain our infinite power.

Shit!

It is an epiphany that holds the promise for real change in my life. If I can only come to feel awe for myself in my everyday life as I feel awe for Elizabeth and her power right now, I might have the strength to find a good man.

Or to be happy alone.

Elizabeth shudders through her starburst, and when she stops moaning and flinching and twitching, I crawl up to put my head on the pillow next to hers. I kiss her tenderly on the lips. I tell her what I was just thinking, probably because I am drunk.

I tell her about her universal, creation-drenched beauty. About how I have spent so much of my life feeling inferior to men and feeling like I needed one in my life to make me complete. I tell her it has caused me to accept bad men. She listens, and I feel her gaze growing terrified. I thought she'd be happy for me. I thought we would bond in this realization of mine, but I realize too late that it is hurtful to her. I realize too late that I am talking to her as I have always talked to her—as a friend, and not as a lover.

She begins to cry quietly, just a tear rolling down the side of her face onto the pillow.

"I'm sorry," I say. "I am such an ass."

"You're not an ass. You're *straight*," she says. "Even after this, even after what felt like love to me."

"It *was* love," I say, trying to think as clearly as a drunk, miserable woman like me, a bulimic love addict and self-hating human being who has just used one of her best friends as an experiment, can think.

Her face twists with agony. "Then why are you still talking about men? Why are you still talking about the men you might pick? Or being *alone*? My God, Lauren. You were just with *me*. It's all I've ever wanted, to be with you."

She is really crying now, and she has pulled the sheet up over her and wrapped herself apart from me. She stares at me with bloodshot eyes.

"My God, Lauren. Don't you see how much you mean to me? That I would do anything for you? I would die for you. I would. I would do anything. Anything. I have never loved a woman as much as I love you. Never. And it has never gone away. As much as I've tried to take it out of me, it's still there. What more do you want? I could give you everything you want and deserve. But you just lie here telling me how excited you are that you finally realized you could be happy alone."

I think about her question as I reach for my jeans and T-shirt on the floor. Realize that I am going to leave, and that I'm probably going to find junk food and eat buckets of it before sticking the backside of my toothbrush down my throat to retrieve it. I also realize that leaving makes me more like a man than I thought. I now understand what it is they find to be so scary about us, too. A man would never break down weeping like this, talking about being together as a couple after what essentially amounted to a one-night stand. A man would not do that. A man would want to run away, just like I do right now. Women talk a lot. I realize that this must be draining, too. The way we talk too much and demand so much commitment and emotional investment, when maybe all the guy wants is to have sex. It's too much for me right now. Way too fucking much.

I start to pull my pants on.

"I love you," she says again, in a pathetic way that only angers me.

"I appreciate that," I say. There is nothing more to say. I sound so much like the many asshole men in my life I surprise and amuse and disgust myself.

I understand why they do it, though. I totally do. Who wants to be lectured and bitched at by a woman who feels more than he does? I don't. I don't need it. And there's another thing that becomes clear to me right now. I understand why men freeze up and don't talk about their feelings in these situations. They're flat terrified, that's why. I mean, who can counter this kind of emotion and intensity with anything halfway soothing to the crazy woman talking at us? She's not interested in hearing my side. She's totally wrapped up in her side, and in her imagined version of how this was supposed to be. We are so judgmental and controlling, women, aren't we? That's the exhausting part of us, and at this moment I totally understand the complicated dance of men and women better than I ever have before. They are fascinated, and terrified, by our power. They want to feel it and be close to it, but they don't want to be destroyed by it. They want to sample, but not be owned. Jesus, that's the part women never realize. They think men are just selfish. But I'm not being selfish right now. I'm being the person I was earlier. Nothing in me has changed. The only thing that changed is Elizabeth's perception of how I should behave and feel. She can't control me, so she's crying, as if that will help change my feelings. I feel angry about being manipulated. A man would never do this. This whole crying, manipulating bit—that's my job. Not my partner's.

I don't tell her what I'm really thinking, and that is this: She might love me and she might be able to give me a lot of what I want, but she will never, ever be able to give me the one thing I really and truly do want: a good man to love me without hurting me in the process, because he finds me holy.

sara

I'M DRIVING A rented Ford Taurus through the New Mexico night, on my way to meet my husband at a hotel in a part of town known as Old Town. I've just begun to sing along to the Celia Cruz CD I brought from home, filling the car with the scent of my sugar-free watermelon chewing gum, when

Roberto calls me on my cell phone. I welcome the call, turning down the volume on the car stereo; it's scary out here, very desolate and dark, with only one or two other cars on the freeway with me.

"Hey, baby," he purrs. *Óyeme, pero* I love this man's deep voice. It soothes me and excites me at the same time.

"How are you, *amorcito?*" I ask him.

"You know, instead of coming up to my room, sneaking around like we're some kind of forbidden lovers instead of a proper husband and wife, meet me in the bar downstairs."

I look at the green digital display on the dashboard clock. It is nearly two in the morning. "Is it still open?" I ask.

"Did you not just hear what I said?" he snaps back.

"I heard you," I say, slowly, measuring my words not to offend him. "I was just saying, it's late, and you never know with these small cities. That's all. I didn't mean anything. I'm sorry."

He answers angrily. "Do you think I'm so stupid that I wouldn't check first to see if the bar is open before asking you to meet me there?"

I feel the old familiar pattern of tension building up. I am aware of it, much more so now than I used to be, but instead of finding it repulsive, as I should, I find it attractive. A moth to the flame. I know I should turn the car around, hang up, refuse to engage in this kind of situation, but the temptation to fix us at last, for the sake of my children, our children, is too strong.

"You didn't *ask* me to meet you anywhere," I shoot back, my voice trembling a bit with the excitement and danger of standing up to him. "You *told* me. But that's what you always do, anyway." I mutter this last part, hoping he doesn't hear it.

"Oh, yeah, right," he fires back, sarcastic. "That's right. That's what I *always* do. Boss you around, huh? Like it was me who told you to sell the house in Chestnut Hill, right? I'm the one who made you do that. Our *house*, Sara. What did that say to the world, eh? That you didn't think I'd ever come back. That you didn't want me to. That you believed I was guilty. That you were single and on your own, eh? That's what you wanted everyone to know, especially all the men."

"Don't be ridiculous. That house was too big for just me and the boys."

"Oh, you and the boys? That's how it is, huh? Like I'm not even their father anymore, right? You and the boys. The single mother act, eh? And I made you buy that little town house in Brookline, right by the hospital, so you could meet a doctor and seduce him? Eh? I'm always the one pushing you around, eh? Is that what your little friends told you to say about me, Sara?"

"What the hell are you talking about? A doctor? I never met any doctor."

"I'm the one who made you start working so many hours with that show, it was all me that made you think you should ignore your kids and work like a man. Is that it?"

"Don't be ridiculous," I tell him. "I know this is all very stressful, but Roberto, this is no way for us to begin again. I know you're upset. I understand. I don't want to fight with you. I thought we were beyond this."

There is a silence. And then he sighs. "Look. I didn't fly all the way here from South America to fight with you, either, Sara."

"I know." I feel my pulse slowing down a little.

"Please understand that I've been traveling for almost twenty-four hours." Now he sounds calm, and flexible. Normal. It is amazing how quickly his moods can shift. I'd forgotten. It was like living in a monsoon one moment, a dust storm the next, always thrilling and a challenge, like a puzzle. "I'd just appreciate it if you'd have a little more respect for my intelligence."

I consider arguing, because his accusation feels so unfair to me. I did not disrespect him. I had a legitimate concern, and if he were a normal man he would have answered with a simple explanation that he'd called and the bar was open. But I realize he has given *some* ground here, at least in his own mind, and so I decide to give some ground right back. That's the key to a healthy relationship, no? Giving in now and then.

"I know," I say. "And I'm sorry." It's a lie. I'm not sorry because I don't have anything to be sorry *for.* Except maybe for agreeing to see him again. This is starting to feel like a very bad decision. Like the queen mother of all bad decisions. So, why does it excite me?

"Okay, then," he says. Then he asks me where I am. I tell him I've entered the city now, and have reached the interstate interchange. "Good. You're about five minutes away. I'll go down now. The guy at the desk told me they have great mojitos at this bar, but I don't believe it."

"Well, it isn't Miami," I say, referring to our shared hometown. He laughs with me, and says he wants us "all" to move back there someday. *Dios mío,* but

I love this man's laughter. It makes me feel more than joy, it makes me feel successful when he laughs. He isn't the type to laugh just to be polite. If you can make Roberto laugh, you've really done something special.

"You know," he says, his voice smooth and steady, "if we ever went back there, no one would bother us, Sarita. I know some people in the local police department, exiles, people who help our kind when we need it."

"What are you trying to say? You know corrupt cops?"

"No, I know honest cops who'd understand I didn't do anything wrong."

"Oh." I shudder. He did, after all, kill Vilma. Even if it was an accident. That was wrong. He surely knows that, doesn't he?

"I am telling you, Sara, we'd have no trouble there. I thought you were going to move back there to do your little show."

"I missed my friends. I felt like I needed them. It didn't feel like home anymore. I came back."

"You don't need them anymore. You have me again."

"Yeah," I say. My voice is weak. I don't know if I want him. That's the thing. I just don't know. And why is it always a choice—my friends or Roberto?

"Hang up and drive, baby," he says, lovingly, gently. "Concentrate on the road. I don't want you getting hurt."

As I PULL the car into the hotel parking lot, I look at myself in the dim light in the rearview mirror and smile. *"Felicidades, chica,"* I tell my reflection. "We're both finally growing up."

I lock the car and, as I walk toward the fashionable boutique hotel in my now muddy red pumps, congratulate myself on finally healing my relationship with Roberto. There is hope, *sabes*. No, it's not perfect. But it's better, so much better now. For a long time, all these counselors and my friends tried to pump my mind full of these ideas about how abusers can never change. This one counselor even tried to tell me that Roberto was some kind of a psychopath, can you believe that? Only they don't use that word anymore. These days, they say a man has "antisocial personality disorder." It didn't sound like the Roberto I knew, and I resented them stuffing their psychobabble down my throat.

But what do any of those people know about real love, anyway? They know nothing, that's what. They're too American about love. Most of them are lonely or have their own problems. Sometimes, you have to actually believe the vows you took, for better and for worse, and sometimes you just have to stick with a man until he changes. I swear to you, most of the people who go into social work or become therapists do it because they're the ones who are screwed up, not their patients.

I smile as I open the door to the bar, and enter the dim, modern space with the dark wooden floors and the red velvet sofas and chairs. A hearth fire roars in one corner, and jazz tinkles over the sound system.

There are a few people scattered around the room, speaking in hushed tones, and I spot Roberto right away, sitting in a secluded booth that has long, thick drapes hanging from the ceiling and knotted at the sides. Excitement bubbles through my belly, and my pulse accelerates. Love. It's the feeling of being swept off your feet in love with someone. I am still in love with my husband, even after all we've been through. How many women can say that? Eh? How many? Not many.

He sees me, and smiles at me in that roguish way of his. He is all man. He is the same Roberto that turns heads everywhere he goes, with curly brown hair and dark green eyes, the man with a jaw so square you could make drafting blueprints with it. The only change in him these past five years has been for the better. He was always fit, but all these years working as a waiter in Argentina have made him even buffer than he was before. He looks tanned, too, and healthy, with just a sprinkle of white at the temples. I wave. He waves back, and for some reason his smile feels a little insincere. Probably my own paranoia. I have to learn to let go of it completely. He's right about that. He's also right when he tells me I have to forget all the nonsense the counselors and my friends have told me about him, if I want to heal and move on.

I get to him, and we have no use for words. We simply embrace. And hold each other. For a long time. Then, he kisses me one time, softly, on the lips, and looks me up and down.

"You look healthy," he says, with a bit of a sneer. He pats my hip. "A little rounder, but that's what happens to women anyway, no?"

Suddenly, I worry that I'm fat. "You look the same," I tell him as I suck in my gut, the gut I'm sure is pouring over the top of my panties in lumping rolls now.

He surveys my breasts now. "Gravity does what it does," he says somberly. Then, as quickly as the somber mood had hit, he's cheerful again, and pulling me in for another kiss. "No matter what time does to you, you're still the most beautiful woman in the world," he tells me.

"Thank you." Why don't I feel happy about this? It was a compliment, wasn't it? This man just told me I was the most beautiful woman in the world, so why do I feel like pouting?

"Sit, Sara. Have a drink."

I do as he says, and look around at the trendy bar, at the roaring fire and the faux-sixties decor. It suits him. "Well, this was a lovely idea," I say, gesturing to the curtains as I slide into the booth seat next to him. "You can close them up if things get steamy, for privacy." I bat my eyelashes at him and kiss him. He backs off me.

"If things get steamy, it won't be here," he says, a look of disapproval on his face. "We do that upstairs, in the room, like respectable people."

"Sorry," I say, with only a trace of sarcasm. Roberto is big on being respectable.

"Did you bring the money?" he asks in a low tone.

"Of course," I tell him. In an earlier phone conversation, he'd told me he was running low on cash in Argentina, and asked me to get him some from what used to be our funds. I've got ten thousand in cash for him in my purse. He stares at me. "What?" I ask in Spanish, our language of privacy. "You want me to hand it to you here? Like *that* won't arouse suspicions."

"Watch your voice," he says. He smiles falsely and shoots me a threat with his eyes. Oh, no. I didn't think I'd ever see that face again. Maybe my friends are right about him, I think as I get a rock in my gut. He leans close, and commands me to "keep it light."

"Look who's talking. I'm not about to count it out for you here on the table. Unless that's what you want." I try to look strong to let him know I'm not the same Sara I was five years ago, that I'm not going to just sit here and take abuse from him anymore.

"Cut the shit, Sara."

The cocktail waiter comes now, with two highball glasses filled with something that looks a little pink and fizzy. Roberto's ordered for me, as he always does. I used to like it, how I didn't have to make decisions. But now I'm getting used to making my own choices. I won't risk bringing that up now, however.

"That looks good," I say. "What is it?"

The waiter answers. "Oscar's Big Night."

"Oscar's Big Night," repeats Roberto, as if the name were idiotic. "They told me this was the house specialty here."

"What's in it?" I ask the waiter, trying to seem like a normal woman, and not one who has just been cursed at by the man everyone else in the world thinks tried to kill her once, a man who is living in Argentina under a fake name, using papers he got from some of his father's associates in the Cuban exile underworld in Miami.

"Well, it's strawberries, fresh strawberries, with grenadine, cream, ground ginger, and ginger ale."

"Sounds yummy," I say.

"Thank you," Roberto says dismissively to the cheerful waiter, letting him know he's worn out his welcome.

He eyes the front door for a moment, and then warms to me at last. "Come here," he says, pulling me in for a real kiss. Like his laugh earlier, his warmth makes me feel triumphant. I close my eyes and breathe him in, feeling the comfort of home on his lips. As I open my eyes I catch a smear of brown velour as a pudgy woman in a headscarf hurries across the main room toward what appears to be a smaller room in the back.

"I guess we're not the only losers hitting the bar at this hour," I say.

"Hurry up and finish your drink," he orders me.

"I just got here," I protest.

He eyes the room where the white-scarf woman disappeared, worry on his face, but looks perfectly peaceful when he turns back to me. "I know, baby," he says, all charm and admiration now. "But the thing is, you look so amazing, so sexy, I don't think I can wait."

"Wait? For what?"

He pulls me in and kisses me again, and nuzzles my neck playfully before biting it a bit too hard. "I need you. Now."

I wish to God these words did not thrill me. But they do. What can I tell you, *chica*? True love is complicated.

usnavys

OH, NO, SHE *DIDN'T*. She *didn't*. I'm sitting in the small, dark back room of the bar at this hotel that thinks it's better than it is, in a dusty-ass town that *Forbes* magazine keeps saying is the new Austin, and I can't believe my own eyes, *m'ija*. Sara just got her ass out of a booth she was sharing with Roberto, the man who nearly killed her and *did* kill their maid, and she's looking all lovestruck and they're holding hands like they're some kind of normal couple. I could slap her, but my guess is she'd like that shit too much, right? She'd probably want to marry me if I hit her. Crazy woman. I mean, how else do you explain her being with him? What is she *thinking*? She's not. That's what. She's *not* thinking.

Now, you *know* me, right? You *know* I grew up in the projects, that I had my own brother die in my arms when he got shot for being a good kid when only the bad kids ruled the barrio, and I am telling you right now that I have seen a lot of bad shit in my time. I know bad shit when it shows up, because I have the powerful radar like that. I would not be where I am if I had not developed that sixth sense, as I told you, but nothing the orishas could have done prepared me for this.

I think I'm going to faint, right here at the bar next to this stank-ass, toothless biker dude who keeps looking at me like I'm a juicy steak.

"Don't even think about it," I tell him as I whip my cell phone out of my handbag. He keeps leering. "Seriously, I know karate," I tell him. "And I ain't afraid to use it."

He looks away now. *Thank* you.

I speed-dial Lauren on her cell. No answer. Then Elizabeth on her cell. She picks up, all depressed and groggy sounding. I ask her if I woke her up and she says no, that she is so heartbroken she doesn't think she'll ever sleep again.

"I'll hear all about it later," I tell her. "Right now, spare me the melodrama, because ain't nothing in your pampered lesbian life worse than what I am about to lay on you, girl."

And then I tell her about Sara and Roberto, including the fact that I am in another hotel, in the city, watching Sara love on him.

"That's impossible," she says, all alert now, okay? She's awake and done feeling sorry for herself, *now*. "I work with her every day. Maybe it's someone who looks like Roberto. She has her type, you know? There's this guy José she's been talking to."

"Okay, listen to me. Listen to me good." I get up, slap a twenty on the bar, and follow in the direction Sara and Roberto went. I spy them in the lobby area, and so I duck behind a large potted tree. "You want an indication?" I hiss into the phone as I peer at them through the fronds. "How about the fact that she and Roberto are waiting for the elevator right now, and she's making out with his ass like she's some hoochie on *Blind Date*."

"Are you sure?"

"Yes, I'm sure! Do not doubt me right now, Liz. I'm not in the mood. This is serious."

"But it doesn't make any sense. Why would she be seeing him again? She's not stupid."

"They're getting in the elevator. Oh, my God. He's gonna kill her ass." I feel a wave of panic flood my body. "We have to do something."

"Hold on. Calm down. It makes no sense, what you're saying."

"Shut up about making sense, *m'ija*! Our friend is in the elevator with a killer. A stone-cold killer, girl!"

"Well, get in there with them. Save her."

"Are you *crazy*? That man's a murderer! You think he's gonna want to spare *me*? Pssh. Please. He doesn't even *like* me. If he kills people he loves, what's he do to people he hates? He probably gets all Jeff Dahmer on them, that's what. He'll eat my eyeballs with barbecue sauce."

My cell phone chimes in my ear to let me know I just got a text message. Like I got time to sit here reading text messages, okay? I don't *think* so.

"So you're just going to let him kidnap her?" asks Elizabeth. "You can't do that."

"Listen, *m'ija*. It looks like she went voluntarily, okay? She's all licking on him and shit, and she's all smiling and touching his butt with her hands. Ugh. God, I think I'm going to be sick."

Another chime in my ear, another text message.

"Okay. Okay. Listen, Usnavys. Usnavys?"

"Oh, my God, the door is closing and she's in there with him. Shit, shit, shit! What am I going to do?"

"Tell security."

"Okay." I come out from behind the tree and start to look around for a security guard, or a police officer, something.

"No, wait!" cries Elizabeth.

"What?"

"If she's with him, and they arrest him now, they might take her, too. Enabling the perpetrator, or whatever they call it. I can't think right now."

"Girl, the way I feel right now, I am so pissed off at her that they can keep her, okay?" I say. By now the two uninteresting women working behind the front desk of the hotel have begun to stare at me, looking at each other like I'm dangerous. I remove the sunglasses and the scarf so I don't look as weird.

"No, no, we can't do it like that. There has to be an explanation."

I watch the numbers over the elevator door light up. One, two, three. Up they go. My friend and a killer. This is so terrible, girl, you have no idea. They stop on the eleventh floor.

"They're on the eleventh floor," I say. "I'm going up there."

"No, don't."

"I'll give them two minutes to get to their room, and then I'm going up."

"Be careful. Why don't you let me come help you?"

"It's too far."

"Just wait until she comes back down."

"In a stretcher? Oh, hell no. That girl has a problem. She's one of them battered wives, *that's* what it is. The kind that keep going back because she thinks he'll change."

"Be smart, Usnavys. For all we know this could be something the detectives set up to try to catch him."

I say, "Like a sting or something?"

"Exactly. You ever think about that?"

"Only one way to find out. I'm going up there."

"It's not smart."

"Please. They try anything, they're gonna get a big helping of *boricua* justice, okay?"

"Usnavys, be reasonable."

"*M'ija,* you got no idea what I've been through in this life." I rub the place on my lower back where it has begun to ache.

"Yes, I do know what you've been through in this life. You tell us all the time."

"I'll call you later. Call the others and tell them."

"I don't know. I think we should talk to Sara first."

"Whatever, girl." I get ready to hang up on Elizabeth. "I got me an elevator to catch."

As I wait for the elevator, I check the text menu. Two messages, both from Marcus. I delete them without reading them. If I get out of this thing alive, I'll call him later. But right now? My own problems don't bother me right now, okay? I don't have *time* for my own depraved bullshit right now. I just *don't.*

roberto

MY **SARITA. SHE DOESN'T** look as good as she used to. She's getting a little thick in the legs, and even though all those magazines talk about how she has the same classic good looks as Martha Stewart, it should be noted that Martha Stewart is a Holstein cow. She is a size fourteen, and at the rate she's going, Sara is going to follow. The women in Argentina are fit, all of them. It is a great country. Here, in America? Women let their age show.

"You shouldn't eat so much," I tell her as I watch her in my hotel room. "You're looking thick. And old."

She stops removing her clothes and stares at me. I can tell she wants to say something, but she's not going to. The smile she had on her made-up face has gone. Good. That's what I was hoping for. She's learned from living with me the importance of obedience in a wife. It is always so much easier when only one half of the marriage is in charge. The male half. Any other way, and you invariably run into problems. I ask her what she's waiting for, and tell her to continue stripping. She peers up at me like a sad dog.

"Don't look at me like that," I tell her. "You're still pretty, understand? I just think you might put a little more effort into how you look, because you could be beautiful again if you wanted to."

She makes that face like she's going to start a fight with me. I thought she said she was learning to be better about conflict.

"I would like to talk about what you just said, because it did not make me feel good," she says. "I don't say this to upset you. I just think it's important to talk about our feelings as they come up, in a calm way."

"I didn't come all the way to New Mexico to talk," I remind her. She asks me if I came all the way to New Mexico just to tell her she was fat. I remind her that I did not call her fat. "I came to New Mexico to make love with you again," I say simply.

"Couldn't find anyone to have sex with in Argentina?" she asks. She is playful again, in her eyes at least, but still does not remove her clothes.

"Don't speak to me that way. *Por favor.* I mean it."

"Sorry. I am sure you'd never find anyone to keep you company in a country like Argentina."

"You are sorely mistaken," I tell her, as I look at her breasts and her hips, and begin to rub myself a bit through the gray slacks.

"So you've been with someone else?" she asks. She still has not resumed removing her clothes, so I go to her, to pull them off. She smiles. She always liked it a little rough.

"I plead the Fifth," I tell her. She pouts a little. "Hey," I say, lifting her chin with my fingers. I stick my finger in and out of her mouth and she sucks it like a good girl. I poke her chest with my now-wet pointer. "*You* are the one who made this happen. *You* are the one who decided I was some cold-blooded murderer."

"I can't believe you've been with other women. It hurts to hear that."

"Please," I say, easing the red dress up over her head, and the panties down. She lifts her feet one at a time, like a child being undressed. She starts to remove her high heels, but I stop her. "Keep them on."

She nods, sheepishly, and looks a little scared and excited. When she does things like that, so sweet and gentle and obedient, it just makes my heart melt. Women need to understand that a man needs to feel necessary for their survival. I feel like protecting her from everything in the world. That's the Sara I fell in love with. The one she should always be, if she knows what is good for her. I think back on all the dark-eyed Argentine beauties I've had in the past five years. Too many to count. And the thin, horny teenager who comes every Tuesday and Thursday morning now, to do my laundry and whatever else I want her to do. Sara doesn't know how good the sex has been for me in Argentina, but that doesn't matter. I am not really here for the sex. I am here because I love Sara, because she belongs to me, and because I am not about to lose my sons, my heirs, to the lies and propaganda of the foolish women in Sara's life. I tell her, "It doesn't matter. I don't love anyone but you."

She stands before me now, in her bra, and I can see that what looked like chub is actually muscle. She has lines in her arms and legs that she never had before. Sara used to be soft. Now, she seems hard. I am surprised by this.

"What?" she asks. "You want to criticize me again?"

"No, no. You look strong. You been working out?" She never used to enjoy exercise at all. She tells me she has been taking karate with Usnavys, and Pilates and yoga. I can't help laughing. Her fat friend is taking self-defense classes?

"What's so funny?" she asks me.

"That fat bitch thinks someone might actually want to rape her?"

"Rape isn't about sex, Roberto. It's about power. Rapists attack elderly women."

I put my finger over her lips now. I am not in the mood for one of her lectures. Seeing her naked has put me in the mood for other things. I sit on the edge of the bed, unzip my slacks, and tell her to get on her knees and suck me. She does, like a good girl.

"Look at me while you do it," I tell her. She rolls her eyes up at me. She looks so helpless. She looks like my slave. God, I love when she looks like that. Here she is, Sara, the woman who thinks she's such a big shot out in the world with her own TV show and her crazy friends, the same woman who used to think she would put me in jail for doing nothing but helping put her in her place, and look at her now, eh? She's just a woman, just a woman like every other woman.

I grab her hair and pull her face down hard. She takes me in all the way, all of me, and gags. I can feel her pulling to get away, but I keep her there. She likes it, too, I can tell, because she starts to use her free hand to touch herself on her damn clitoris, the part she's always trying to get me to pay attention to, the part all her crazy feminist friends are always talking about like it was some kind of magic button. I am starting to understand why so many of the Africans and Muslims cut it off. It's nothing but trouble. She looks up at me with the crazy rage she gets when we fuck.

"You like that?" I ask her. I can tell she does. Her breasts hang lower than they used to. They are still lovely, though. I yank her up off the floor, and bend her over the bed, spread her wide, enter her hard and fast before she's ready. She gasps and looks back at me, surprised and hurt, and then she just kind of bites her lower lip and goes limp on the bed, a rag doll in my control.

When she puts her hand down to touch herself again, I bat it away. I will not be insulted like that. I should be enough for her, more than enough. I steady her in front of me, and continue until I am about to come. I pull out and shoot it all over her.

"Get dressed," I tell her. I don't want to look at her, naked and shameless in front of me like that.

"But I didn't get a turn," she says sweetly, a smile that I'm sure she thinks is cute playing across her face. She thinks I'm going to help get her off. I will not. A woman has to *earn* that. After all the misery she has caused me, she doesn't deserve it.

"That's what you get for disrespecting me," I say.

"How did I disrespect you?" She doesn't make any move to get dressed. I think she believes I'm joking. I am not. She just lies there, naked, looking at me with defiance all over her face. I am sick of it. Women in Argentina? The younger ones from the poor neighborhoods? They know how to behave. Not this one. This one will never learn.

I pull up my pants, stride over to her, and hold her by the shoulders. Her eyes widen with surprise and then, once she realizes I am serious, fear. "One? You assumed I was an idiot who couldn't call the hotel bar. Two? You made fun of me when I asked you if you brought the money. *My* money."

The rage building inside of me is too much as I remember how she humiliated me. I am sick that she would laugh in my face about the money. After all, it is entirely her fault that I am broke now.

"You think it's easy for me? Living on the run, like some kind of fugitive, struggling to pay rent on my shitty apartment in Buenos Aires while you're over here living like a queen off the money I worked hard to earn?"

"It was our money. You left the country. For all we knew, you were dead."

"No, it was mine. You were my wife, but you didn't earn the money, Sara."

"I do now," she tells me. "I make as much now as you used to. Probably more."

This comment and the defiant look on her face infuriate me. She took everything from me, and now she brags about all her money?

She still hasn't put her clothes on, and the shameless way she's running her hands over her own body makes me sick. She's trying to kiss me, and pull me in to her, telling me she doesn't want to fight, she wants to "make love." I want her off of me. *Off.*

I slap her. She seems surprised, and frozen. It feels so good, I do it again, and grab her hard around the neck. She doesn't hit me back, the way she used to, which is good. I let her worry I'm going to strangle her. Finally, she may have learned something.

"Don't you *ever* think you're better than me, *¿oíste?* Don't *ever* say that again."

She glares up at me with tears in her eyes, but doesn't fight back. She's learning. "I understand," she says. Now, like a good girl, she gets dressed. She doesn't look up at me again, even though I keep talking to her and her tears flow quietly down her cheeks. She looks so small, so helpless, so injured. The spot on her face where I hit her is glowing red. She sniffles again and again. I feel terrible now.

Terrible.

I shouldn't have done it.

"Sara," I say. I come to her, now that she has her clothes on, and I try to comfort her. "I am so sorry. I don't know what is wrong with me. All the flying. I'm a little jet-lagged. It won't happen again."

She looks at me. "You're right," she says. "It won't happen again. I promise you that. I won't *let* it."

By that, I am sure she means she knows she has a long way to go before she is the perfect obedient wife I need.

"That's my girl," I tell her. "That's why I love you."

elizabeth

FOR THE FAREWELL DINNER Sunday night at the resort, a dinner I dread because I will have to face Lauren and pretend all is well, Usnavys and I have coincidentally dressed alike, in nearly identical sleeveless linen resort dresses from Liz Claiborne, mine white, hers black. If you socialize with the same people long enough, I suppose you start to shop in the same places. We walk toward the restaurant, tense with anticipation, knowing that we have agreed to confront Sara in front of everyone as a form of intervention. I try to focus on this task. I try not to feel sick over Lauren, how I still love her, but now hate her, too.

"Be strong," I tell Usnavys. "And whatever you do, remember that harsh words will not help. We must strive to be loving and understanding."

Usnavys turns her head to look at me. "You are the only person I know who uses 'must' and 'strive' in everyday speech."

"It's my English."

"No, *m'ija*. Your English is better than half the native-born idiots' in America. You should be proud of that." She pauses. "You okay, girl?"

"I'm fine," I tell her. I've spotted Lauren. I hate the way she avoids looking at me.

"You look sad."

"I'm not," I lie.

The others are all at the table when we arrive. Lauren, in a simple beige skirt and matching T-shirt, ignores me, like everything is fine. Rebecca, in black linen pants with a light gold sweater, studies her menu. Sara sits next to Cuicatl, looking at a *New York Times* article about her upcoming tour the way an adolescent might look at a school yearbook. Cuicatl wears another tank top with jeans. Sara, wearing a light cotton blazer in a shade of yellow that matches the lightest strands of her hair, is trying to conceal the marks on her neck with a patterned silk scarf.

Everyone looks up as we take our seats, and various greetings are thrown around. We each had this afternoon to ourselves, so we take a moment to catch up on everyone's spa treatments or, in the case of Lauren and Rebecca, a shopping spree to Santa Fe. Usnavys said she had another lesson with Marcus, the golf teacher she can't seem to stop talking about, but I did not see them when I went for a walk earlier, along the hilly perimeter of the resort's golf course. Maybe there's another part of the course somewhere else.

"You would not believe the crazy money this woman spends," Lauren tells us, her mouth hanging open, still in shock, as the rest of us peruse the menus. How can she act like all is normal? How? I look away from her, to my menu. This restaurant has some truly interesting offerings, like blue corn tempura vegetables. Too bad I'm not hungry.

"Oh, no," says Usnavys. "I'd believe it."

"Lauren, please," says Rebecca, with her customary dislike of the spotlight. I understand how she feels, and sometimes I wish Lauren would just keep her huge mouth shut. Right now, I don't want to hate her, but I do. I hate Lauren. Passionately.

"No, seriously." Lauren leans forward, excited. She includes me in the friendly confidence of her conversation as if nothing has passed between us, as if we did not make love to one another. She speaks excitedly, in a fast tone. "We went to a bunch of galleries? And she's looking to get some art for her new house out here. So, I'm thinking she's gonna drop, what, like a couple thousand on some paintings or something—which would totally destroy my bank account if I did it, you know?"

"Lauren, please." Rebecca is giving her the "shut up now" look. She really doesn't like to brag. If you didn't know Rebecca was wealthy, there would be very little to give any indication of it. She is polite to a fault.

Lauren continues, her vulgar disdain for the feelings of others quite obvious to me now. "But no-oo. She didn't spend a couple of thousand on some paintings. She spent, like, what was it, Rebecca?" I'm quite sure this time, when she made eye contact with me, she flinched a little. But just a little. She won't let this bother her. Funny how something that feels like it could ruin my life has scarcely left a dent upon hers. I focus on not crying.

"That's *enough*." Rebecca blushes, angrily. In my mind, I flee this place. I would like to be in my room, alone with the hotel television and room service, able to cry into my pillow. But I'm not one to feel sorry for myself for too long, and this incident with Sara has at least temporarily pushed my own crisis out of the way. I had planned to go home to Gordon today, but Sara's crisis made me change my mind. This morning Selwyn seemed better with him.

Lauren grins at Rebecca, in a way that to me seems oddly flirtatious. It angers me. She says, "That's what I said when they rang you up at that one place, where you got the yard sculpture of the bronze horse, and then at that other place where you got three doors imported from India."

"They were antiques."

"Okay, whatever. But the total bill for one day's shopping for her new house—which isn't even her primary residence, as they say in real estate—was sixty thousand dollars! That's nearly my yearly salary."

Usnavys shrugs and pretends this sounds like chump change to her, because she likes to present herself as much wealthier than she is. If you were going to guess that anyone in our group was an actual rich woman, you would probably guess Usnavys.

"Marcus spent nearly that much on his car, in cash," she says.

"Who is Marcus?" asks Cuicatl, who has, until now, been conspicuously quiet and meditative, almost as if she doesn't feel like she belongs here.

"The golf teacher she keeps talking about," I say.

"If I didn't know better, I'd think you had a crush on him," Lauren tells Usnavys.

"Yeah? Well you do know better. Let's get back to talking about Rebecca's antiques."

"*Chinga, mujer,*" says Cuicatl to Sara. "Sixty thousand? That's mad cash for one day's shopping."

"Oh, please," Sara tells Cuicatl. "You've spent more than that in one day, surely."

"I know, but it was on music equipment," says Cuicatl defensively. "Or charity. Not on antique doors."

"To each her own," says Rebecca.

"Got that right," snaps Usnavys.

I think about it. "You know," I say to Lauren, trying to engage her as if we were merely friends. I do this mostly for the benefit of the others, because I don't think I could bear for them to know what happened between me and Lauren. They would lose all respect for me. Maybe at some other point in time I'll be up to sharing it with them, but not now. Now, I have to pretend everything is exactly as it was when we all sat over our drinks, that first night here. I force a smile at Lauren. "You and I are the only ones here who would be surprised by that kind of spending."

She eyes me nervously, almost guiltily, as if she expects me to confess. "You mean we're the only ones who aren't loaded?"

I look at Usnavys and shrug as if my heart were not still broken. I've never done such a good acting job. "Well, I mean you and Usnavys and I are the ones who live on regular salaries."

"Excuse me?" Usnavys sits up like a princess who has lost her tiara. "I do quite well, but seeing as I'm supporting a family all by myself, I do not have as much disposable income as I was formerly accustomed to."

I suppress a smile. Whenever she feels threatened, Usnavys speaks this way, in very proper English. It took me a while to be fluent enough in English to pick up on it.

The waitress approaches and asks if we "ladies" are ready to order.

"Dinner's on the house," she tells us.

"What?" asks Sara.

"Not the house, exactly," says the waitress. She lowers her voice to a whisper and comes in close. "It's on Marcus, the golf pro." She looks at Usnavys. "He said you were a special friend of his."

Usnavys gasps, and we all look at her. It is obvious that she is interested in this man. I have seen that glow in her eyes too many times before not to recognize it now. This is familiar territory with Usnavys, and we know it.

"Special friend, huh?" asks Lauren.

"I have no idea why he would arrange to pay our bill," says Princess Tiara.

"I just had to say something," says the waitress. "He's such a doll, and we're all, I mean, all the girls who work here, we're always trying to get his attention, you know? I mean, here's a millionaire who decides to work at the resort because he loves golf and the desert, and that's about it. He's a catch." She puts a hand on Usnavys's back. "You're very lucky."

We all look at Usnavys. She ignores us and sips her drink.

"Yeah, congratulations," says Cuicatl to Usnavys.

"For what?" Usnavys shrugs. She stares the waitress down. "He is *not* my man, okay? Now, when you finish gossiping about your coworkers, I'd appreciate it if you'd do your job and take our food orders."

"Sorry," says the waitress. "I just thought—"

"Well, stop thinking," says Usnavys.

"Ready to order?" the waitress finally asks.

We all agree that we are. Rebecca starts, after no one else seems to want to be the first, ordering the Southwestern Caesar salad and water to drink. Usnavys chimes in next, requesting the grilled elk brochette, the crayfish bisque, and the veal and blue corn lobster tempura. To this she adds a Diet Coke, and more bread with butter.

"She's eating Noah's ark," Cuicatl whispers to me. I do not react because I think it is cruel to attack someone based upon what they eat. Cuicatl has long been a vegetarian, unafraid to let us know how she feels about our carnivorous habits. I'd be more inclined to attack Usnavys based upon the fact that Marcus seems to think, at the very least, that she is available.

I speak up next. "Yes, I'd like to start with the seared scallops, and I'll also take the margarita shrimp."

"Good choice," the waitress says. I wonder if they ever tell a diner they have made a bad choice. "Anything to drink?"

"Just water."

The waitress moves her eyes to Cuicatl.

"Does the Thai summer roll have any animal products in it?" she asks the server.

"No."

"I'll have that, and the barley-stuffed green chile. And another Tecate. Thanks."

Lauren orders next, and I can't bear to listen to her voice. I am crushed by her very presence at the table, by the very act of her ordering food and me imagining it going between her beautiful lips. She gets the pesto green chile shrimp wonton, the corn and coconut soup, and the margarita shrimp, the same thing I ordered. I hope she didn't do it on purpose. And, being Lauren, she also orders a gin and tonic. If I could, I'd toss it far from her.

Sara orders last, getting the green salad and the rotisserie that includes chorizo sausage, chile chicken, beef rib eye, and lavender salted shrimp. "Do you have a drink called Oscar's Big Night?" she asks.

"Of course," says the server.

"I'd like one of those, please."

The waitress leaves, and Usnavys reminds us that we were talking about how much money Rebecca spent. "I love living vicariously through you, girl," she says. "I hate being poor."

"No one here is poor," says Cuicatl, with a distant, thoughtful look in her eyes. "You want poor? Visit Haiti or Brazil. All of *us*? We're lucky."

"It's not luck. It's hard work," says Rebecca.

"And luck," says Cuicatl. "The 'hard work' thing is an American myth."

"Hogwash." Rebecca frowns, and Lauren laughs at her.

"You did not just actually say 'hogwash,' did you?"

"So what if I did?"

"Her inner hick is coming out," says Sara.

"We all have secret people that ought to come out," says Usnavys to Sara. Again, the two share a look.

"You have something you want to tell us about the golf pro?" I ask her, thinking it is unfair for her to be so condemning of Sara when she herself appears to have a crush on a man who is not her husband.

"Me?" She looks stunned. "You kidding? I'm not talking about *me*." Usnavys focuses her eyes on Sara with laser-beam intensity.

I gulp down a bit of my drink, and summon the courage to confront Sara, to get it over with. Clearly Usnavys doesn't want to talk about her admirer. Might as well dive right in to the topic none of us thought we'd ever talk to Sara about again: Roberto.

"So, Sara, have you heard from Roberto lately?" I ask her. I try to sound natural. I know her well enough by now to know that when she smiles this strenuously and begins to turn pink in the cheeks, she is lying. We all have that one thing that gives us away. She starts to twirl a piece of her hair with her fingers. Now I know we're in trouble.

"No, why would you ask?"

Usnavys folds her arms across her chest and harrumphs.

"I wouldn't like it if you lied to me," I say. "Just like I know you wouldn't like it if I lied to you. Especially not about something this serious."

"And dangerous," adds Usnavys.

Suddenly, the other women in our group seem to stop and pay attention, as if they were wondering what might come next.

"Because we love you," I say. I don't want to scare Sara into silence here. I want to help her.

"What exactly are you talking about?" Cuicatl asks me and Usnavys. "Danger and love? Roberto?" She looks scared.

"Shh," Usnavys tells her. "Let the woman talk."

Sara looks like she wants to run. I put my hand on hers, and try to get her to look me in the eye. "I'm just asking, because . . ." I can't think of anything to say.

"Because a little bird told us you've been seeing him again," Usnavys finishes for me. She looks furious. "Okay, *nena*? There. I said it."

"What?" cries Lauren.

"I have no idea what you're talking about." Sara looks very uncomfortable now.

"Oh, I think you do," says Usnavys. And then, before I can stop her, Usnavys has opened up her mouth and told Sara everything, that she followed her to the hotel, that she saw him, that she almost "died" when she saw Sara get in the elevator with the man who killed her maid. "My God, Sara," cries Usnavys, her voice rising with anger and worry. "When that man tried to kill you, we were there for you, we nursed you back to health, we were the ones by your side, and now I have to see that you're seeing him again? You might as well just slap me across the face, okay? You might as well just beat me down."

"What?" asks Rebecca. She looks rapidly around the table, at each of us, stunned. "Sara's seeing Roberto again?"

"No," says Sara.

"Yes, you are. Why are you lying?" asks Usnavys.

Sara looks terrified now, caught and scared. She coughs into her hand one time, a sure sign of a lie in her. The other women in our longtime group of friends watch in disbelief.

"Why would you do that?" asks Lauren. "Sara, you didn't. Did you?"

Sara says nothing. Her dropped head and slumped shoulders say it all.

"Where has he been?" asks Cuicatl.

"Argentina," says Sara in a soft voice. I take this to be her confession.

"Argentina?" I say at the same time as Lauren. She locks eyes with me and smiles, as though in victory. I wish she would disappear.

"What the hell is he doing in Argentina?" cries Lauren. "And why the hell didn't he just stay there?"

Sara's voice is faint, almost girlish, and this frightens me. "He's been working as a waiter. He's been trying to change."

"Oh, my God," says Cuicatl. "So you did. You saw him."

"I saw her see him," says Usnavys. "Why don't you crazy bitches believe a sister sometimes?"

"Where?" asks Cuicatl.

"Here. In Albuquerque. Last night."

"You followed me?" Sara asks Usnavys, hurt and incredulous. "You shouldn't have done that."

"I'll file that under pot and kettle," snaps Usnavys.

"He's *here*?" cries Rebecca. "Roberto is *here*? You brought him *here*?"

"He's not *here*. Not at the resort. He's gone back to Argentina now."

"This is crazy," says Lauren. She makes brief eye contact with me, but hurries to look away. I want to cover her with kisses again. "I can't believe I'm hearing this. We saw what he did to you."

At this moment, the conversation is interrupted when Marcus appears across the dining room with a bouquet of flowers and walks over to us. Or, specifically, he walks over to Usnavys, and gives them to her. He's flanked by a couple of other men, both of whom seem as well-to-do and gentlemanly as he does. There is something very gentle and almost feminine about Marcus that instantly draws me to him. He is a good man. I can tell from his posture and from the light in his brown eyes.

"I hope I'm not interrupting anything," he says. "But I wanted to give these to you myself. For playing such a wonderful game this afternoon."

Usnavys almost blushes. She shoots a look of panic around the group of friends, but it is replaced so quickly by a false bravado that you would miss it if you weren't focused on her face the way I am. "Girls, this is Marcus, the golf teacher."

I see Usnavys fiddle with her wedding ring as Marcus shakes our hands and introduces his two friends. I see her palm the ring just long enough to take the flowers and set them in the middle of our table. When he hugs her, it lasts a little too long, and he gives her a kiss on the cheek that is more than friendly.

"Ladies, enjoy the rest of your evening. We're off to Santa Fe to the opera." He looks at Usnavys now. "I'll call you when I get back."

I watch the emotions tug across her face. She likes this man, and this makes me feel an actual pain for Juan, who is one of the nicest people you could ever meet. "Have a good time. Thanks for these."

Marcus leaves, with one last longing glance at Usnavys, and she slips her finger back into the ring. I think I am the only one who notices she took it off. My God, I think. We all have secrets here at this table. You think you know your friends, but in the end, I suppose, many of us are harboring secrets.

"What was *that*?" Lauren asks Usnavys, pointing a finger casually in the direction of Marcus's exit.

"What was what?" shoots back Usnavys.

"You *know* what," says Lauren.

"He's cute," says Rebecca. "I wonder what Juan would think of him."

"You seeing him?" I ask Usnavys.

"What?" she asks, offended. "Are you crazy? Of course not. I'm a married woman."

"Doesn't stop lots of people," says Lauren, with a hard look at me. But that was different, I want to cry out.

"Yeah, well it stops *me*, okay?" says Usnavys. She is not convincing enough to make me believe her, however.

"He likes you a lot," says Rebecca to Usnavys. "It's obvious."

"*¿Y qué?* Everyone likes me a lot, *ya tú sabes*."

"It looked like more than that," I say.

Usnavys rolls her eyes dismissively. "Whatever, okay? It was nothing. It was a man who teaches golf and he probably fell in love with me, and you can't blame him. That's what happens when I take this body out into the world, okay? It's nothing new. They be lining up for a sniff, okay? Not my fault."

"How's Juan, anyway?" asks Sara. We all look at her in surprise, as if she doesn't have a right to participate in the turn the conversation has taken.

"Juan is fine," says Usnavys to Sara. "Better than you. And much better than Roberto." Detour over. Back to business.

"We'll talk about Marcus later," Lauren tells Usnavys. "But now, we need to resolve this Roberto thing. I can't let you do this, Sara. I can't."

"Maybe we will, maybe we won't," snaps Usnavys at Lauren. "Now, where were we? Oh, that's right." She stares at Sara. "We were talking about how we all saw what Roberto did to you for years and we're not about to sit back for a repeat performance."

"You saw what you wanted to see," says Sara. "You didn't know the whole story."

"You don't mean that," whispers Rebecca. She places her hands over her belly, as if she were sick, or afraid of being punched herself. All of us have these shocked looks, like someone just came over and smacked us, one by one, across the face.

We all watch as the expressions wash over Sara's face, one after another. First anger, then fear, then humiliation. "I don't know what to say."

Lauren scowls at her. "This is insane, Sara," she says. "You know that?"

Sara takes a deep breath that seems angry, and begins to speak. "I know. I realized that last night. It was a moment of weakness. It was stupid. I've been lonely. It's hard to explain. You get in the habit of loving someone, you know? And then you have children." She looks at Usnavys. "You know what I'm talking about, right? When you have a child with someone, you are bound to that person forever."

"That's not necessarily true," I say, wondering why no one in this group ever really seems to think of me as a mother. Is it this way because Gordon is adopted or because I'm gay? Or both?

"How could you, Sara? After everything he's done to you?" Lauren is furious now. "He killed Vilma. He broke your bones!"

"Sometimes, we love people even when they hurt us," I say to Lauren. She knows I mean her and me, and backs off, probably in fear that I'll reveal to the group what happened between us Friday night, which I never would.

Sara begins to dab the tears from the corners of her eyes with her white cloth napkin, leaving black spots of mascara there, and tells us a sad story of confusion, her own confusion. She masks the weeping in her voice very well, a woman practiced in the art of making everything seem fine. She tries to make it sensible, this sick, undying love she has for a murderous madman. It will not make sense to me, not now, not ever. I try to understand her, because I care for her and consider her to be my best friend. But Roberto is severely homophobic, and violent, and there is nothing Sara can say that will make me believe he has changed.

"As your friend, as someone who actually cares about you," I tell her, "I am saying you have to get help. Not tomorrow. Not next week. I know you think he can change, and I know you love him. I understand that. But I covered enough of these stories back when I was in news to know that these men never change. You can't go back to this man. He'll kill you, or the boys. You're better than this, Sara. Think of your children."

She looks me right in the eye now. "I will never see him again. I promise. I swear."

"How can we believe you now?" asks Usnavys. I hold my hand up to silence her, but she pushes on. "I saw you with him last night. I know you looked like a woman in love. You can't just change your mind like that."

"He was cruel to me last night."

We sit, in stunned silence now. I don't know what to say. Sara pulls back the scarf and shows the marks on her neck.

"He did that to you?" asks Lauren. Sara nods.

"You can't see him again," warns Rebecca. "You absolutely can't."

Cuicatl gets up, throws her napkin on the chair. "I'm sorry," she says. "But I just lost my appetite." She starts to walk away, shaking her head.

"Don't go, Amber," I call out to her. I realize too late that I've used the wrong name on her again. I will never get used to the new name she has given herself. She stops and turns to look at us. I think she's crying. In all the years I have known her, I have never seen Cuicatl cry. If I were asked to give a list of the toughest women I know, she would be somewhere very near the top.

"I can't think straight right now," she tells us. "I just can't." Cuicatl gives Sara one last sorrowful look before leaving and says, "I love you, ¿sabes? But I can't watch anyone kill themselves. It's not ethical. You're a grown woman, and you will do whatever you want. But I can't be party to it."

"You can't just give up on her!" I call out. Everyone in the restaurant is staring at us now. I try to keep my voice down.

"*Mira*, okay? I'm stupid," says Sara. "And there's a big part of me that knows I probably seem stupid to people who don't know what real love feels like, which is why I never told any of you. I knew you'd react like this. I knew I couldn't count on you to understand."

"Don't know what real *love* feels like?" Lauren asks, insulted.

"Real love hurts sometimes," I say to Lauren.

"Couldn't *count* on us?" asks Rebecca, power and intelligence radiating from her face and posture. "Sara, with all due respect, we are the *only* people you have been able to count on in all of this. We were the ones who helped you get your show off the ground. We're the ones who committed to standing by your side, no matter what. We're the ones who babysit for you, who talk to your parents when you don't feel like it. We're your real family here. Not that, that . . . monster."

This time, it is Sara who gets up. "I don't expect you to understand," she says. "I just want you to believe it's finally over." Tears pour from her bloodshot eyes. "Until you've been in love like I've been in love, it's impossible for you to get it."

None of us make a sound as she turns and walks away. By the time the server brings the six courtesy-of-Marcus entrées five minutes later, there are only four women at the table—but almost none of us are hungry.

"I can't believe this is happening," says Rebecca in a forlorn tone. "I don't even know what to say."

"We have to do something," says Usnavys, reaching for the butter. "Before it's too late."

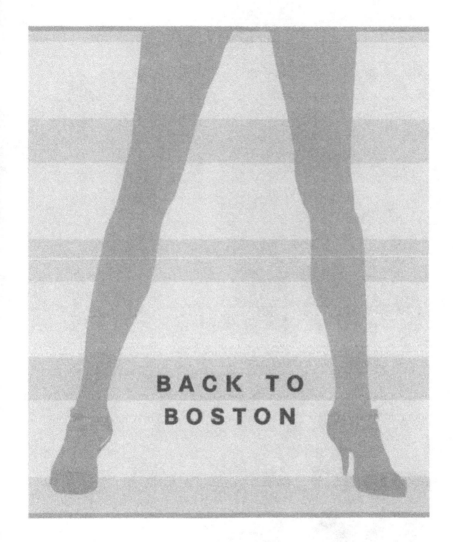

BACK TO
BOSTON

rebecca

IT IS A SUNNY, expansive late Monday morning when the shiny clean black Lincoln Town Car limo takes me from the resort in the desert to the Albuquerque airport. Andre is on business in Chicago, and he'll be back in Boston tomorrow.

The car's interior smells like new leather, one of my favorite scents. It makes me feel sophisticated and elegant. I've worn a new black ensemble— pants, shirt, and jacket—I bought at the J. Jill store, part of their wonderful "travel" line of clothes that pack well and do not wrinkle, yet manage to make you look great anyway. I have slip-on sandals on now, for ease of removal at the security checkpoint, and a pair of warm, fuzzy sleep socks tucked into my neutral Hartmann carry-on bag. The Elias Rivera painting of Guatemalan women I purchased for the Boston brownstone has been shipped home, and everything is as it should be. In *my* life, anyway. I don't know about my college friends.

Honestly. Sara's poor decision-making, Lauren's gluttony, Usnavys's depravity, Cuicatl's politics and breast implants, Elizabeth's pouty flirting with Lauren. It's all too much to consider at the moment. I cannot find room for it, not yet. On the whole, this weekend was supposed to be restful and bonding for us. I am not sure we accomplished anything. Only Cuicatl seemed genuinely happy. I longed so much to tell them of my joyful news, but my resolve to remain taciturn about it was strengthened by the suffering of my friends. Misery loves company, not the good news of others who are more fortunate and have been able, through sense and hard work, to craft a functional life plan for themselves.

As I watch the wide, arid land slide past the window of the car, I feel a twinge of melancholy at leaving my home state, and yet at the same time I can't wait to leave. It is the curse of those of us who are from here yet harbor ambitions greater than might be fulfilled here. It is nearly impossible to be ambitious in New Mexico, at least on a grand scale. I had considered relocating the magazine here, but I worried that it might be nearly impossible to stay up-to-date on trends and fashion in New Mexico, which is part of the charm of this timeless, self-identified place. New Mexico moves to its own slow, unique rhythm.

Nonetheless, it is very much time to get back to work. I retrieve the BlackBerry from my briefcase and dial my assistant.

"Get me on the phone with Muehler," I tell her, referring to the man at the head of the magazine division of the multinational media consortium hounding me to sell *Ella* for the past six months. He has called me several times over the weekend, which I find both admirable (he is a workaholic like myself) and offensive (he should have phoned once and waited for a return call rather than calling repeatedly).

I wait on hold while Marianne places the call for me. She is my third assistant this year. I have a hard time retaining people, not because I am a difficult boss, but rather because so many of these shiny, overeager girls lie in their interviews about their career ambitions. The first assistant of the year left for an internship at *Redbook,* and the second took a job as the personal assistant of a very famous male movie star after arranging for an interview with him in our pages.

Soon, Bob Muehler is on the line, barking his name with self-importance. He is abrupt, yet friendly as is required in these matters. If I'm not mistaken, he sounds like he's chewing food. How rude. I tell him I would like to discuss my thoughts and plans regarding the future of my magazine, but in person.

"Great. Come down to New York, we'll put you up, I'll take you to lunch."

"No," I say. "I was thinking it would be much more convenient if you'd come to Boston. I have been traveling a lot lately." You have to make them work for what they want, and the truth is, I am not sure I want to sell. I have many questions for Muehler before I'd do so. If he is serious, he will come to me.

"You bet," he tells me. "You back in town?"

"I will be, as of tomorrow."

"I'll make it in the next week or two. I'll have my girl call your girl, and we'll make it happen."

"Good," I say. "Girl?"

"Beantown. That'll be fine, just fine. You a Red Sox girl?"

I pause, already hating the way this man has pulled our business conversation into the male domain of sports. Are they even aware of doing this? "Not really," I say. *And I am not a girl, I'm a woman.* "I run a fashion magazine, not a sports outfit."

"Alrighty," he says, with a tone that communicates to me that he thinks I am uptight. I hear him suck his teeth. He wouldn't be the first to think I was harsh or uptight. I am not uptight. I am forthright, and direct, and honest—a businesswoman. I see no need to act like a man or pretend to be interested in male pastimes all in the name of business. If anyone should be out to prove that he can straddle the gender divide in this negotiation for a women's magazine, it should be Bob Muehler.

"We'll see each other soon," I say. "Good-bye, Bob."

I try, whenever possible, to be the first person to hang up in these conversations. It is always the person with more power who makes the first move to end the conversation. Nothing irks me more than wishy-washy people who don't know when to end a conversation, or those needy types who keep you on the phone even after you've clearly hinted or even stated that it is time to hang up. I sigh, and close my eyes, meditate on my spinal alignment, center myself once more.

Speeding along Interstate 25, I make a couple more phone calls, including one to Andre at the Drake Hotel in Chicago, to ask his opinion on the sale of the magazine. I am not one of those women, like my mother, who look to their husbands to approve of their every decision; rather, I am fortunate to be married to the smartest person I know, businesswise. He is of the opinion that it would be fine to sell and move on to new ventures. "You've done what you could do there, and you have so many good ideas. You shouldn't be afraid to try something new."

He could be right. He's probably right. It's not that I'm bored, exactly, with *Ella*, but it does feel less exciting now than it used to. I've moved on.

I make a couple more calls, and try to convince myself that the slight ache in my lower back is nothing. I check the office voice mail, then my e-mail. It is afternoon in Boston, and already my in-box is stuffed with messages. The only bad thing about a vacation like this is that when you return from it you have enormous amounts of work to catch up on. As I read one particularly distressing note from one of my copy editors—about a factual error in a reported piece on the author Sandra Cisneros—I feel a sharp electric spasm of shooting pain in my back.

"Oh, my God," I whisper to myself. I place my hand on the painful spot and try to massage the knot out, telling myself this pain, so familiar, so miserably familiar, is nothing. Nothing to worry about. It's nothing more than fatigue from walking so much, and from golfing nearly all afternoon yesterday. I've read that as your uterus grows with a baby in it, you get these kinds of pains as your bones spread to clear space for the baby. It is totally normal, I assure myself. I focus on my e-mail messages; to my relief, the pain abates.

Half an hour later, I stand in the first-class passenger line at the American Airlines ticket counter in the Albuquerque airport, waiting to check my two larger bags. The ache has returned, stronger now, and with each breath I feel a tugging in my lower belly, beneath my hip bones, radiating to the small of my back. I tell myself it's just residual soreness from horseback riding. Right now, I would tell myself any manner of half-truth if it meant staying on task.

The woman takes my luggage and gives me a boarding pass, and I feel dizzy, and grasp the counter to steady myself.

"Ma'am? Are you all right?" she asks me.

"I'm fine." I feel beads of sweat forming on my upper lip and forehead, and I am overcome with the urge to sit down. It's nothing, I remind myself. Only stress. That's what it is—it must be.

"Okay." She sounds doubtful. I stumble away and up the escalator to the security checkpoint, which is mercifully airy and uncrowded. This is one of the many things I love about New Mexico; you have everything you could possibly want here—with the exception of an ocean, of course—and you never have to toil in lines or traffic jams in a state with barely more than one million inhabitants. I will seriously consider moving back for good, especially now that *Forbes* magazine named Albuquerque the number one city in which to do business in the nation, thanks to affordable real estate and good tax incentives. It would reduce my stress to live here. I must de-stress. I mean, look at me, dizzy and ridiculous with worry.

The ache has spread from my back to my lower abdomen by the time they call the first-class passengers to board. Is it nothing? Is it? I bite my lower lip and say a prayer silently. *Please, God, don't let it happen again.* I follow this with a Hail Mary and an Our Father, and I do not worry or care if I look crazy muttering prayers in an airport. Surely I'm not the first.

I board the plane, take my aisle seat, and try to relax the ache out of me. But the pain doesn't go away. It gets worse. It feels just like intense menstrual cramps, now coupled with a sudden wave of nausea. I look around for a bathroom, momentarily so spacey I forget where they are. The aisle is filled with bodies as people board the plane. I'd have to swim upstream against them to get to the lavatory. Another pain, this time a shock of it, as though I'd been zapped in the gut with a cattle prod.

I shouldn't have ridden the horse. This is the horse's fault. Of course it is. That must be what this is all about. I should have pretended to be afraid of it. But the girls were so insistent, and I didn't think a horse ride could ruin a pregnancy. So, is it their fault, too? Why can't I breathe right? I'm a healthy woman. After all, I have continued to work out as always. It must be the horse, then. Not me. Not my fault. I believe healthy women were meant to exercise throughout their pregnancies. But there was a lot of jolting on that horse. Not my fault, not mine that I am having a . . . no. I am not. I am not. I will *not*.

I stop myself mid-thought, and remind myself that I don't know if this cramping is something to worry about. It might be just a normal part of a normal pregnancy. No sooner have I thought this than I feel a warm gush of liquid come from between my legs. That is not normal. This much I know. This familiar flow, this draining of my dreams. Dear God. Oh, dear *God.*

I bolt up from my seat and push past the people coming in.

"Excuse me, please," I say, the tears forming in my eyes as I curse the girls, the horse, this wet misery that has come to visit me once more. I try to caution myself to take it easy, to wait for some evidence that this might be a miscarriage before I convince myself that it is. I will not—cannot. It is not my fault.

"Watch where you're going," a large woman says as I shove my way past her. She elbows me.

"I'm sorry," I say, and my voice sounds too high, too weak—not mine, someone else's, somewhere else, so far away. "It's just that I think I'm going to be ill."

A balding man with sympathetic blue eyes speaks out now. "Sick woman coming through," he announces. He holds people back out of my way with large red hands. I charge ahead, slide into the narrow bathroom, and close the accordion door behind me, locking it. I pull down the black travel pants, and my underwear. At the sight of blood, so much blood, too much, my legs grow weak. I collapse onto the toilet seat, and just sit, staring at the bright red gelatinous stain on the panties. I take a wad of toilet paper and wipe between my legs. I look at it, saturated with thick, dark blood. Lifeblood.

"No," I whimper. I feel my legs and hands begin to tremble as I feel the flow dripping, steadily. "Dear God, why?"

My mother's words come back to me. *You will lose this one, too.* She can't be right! I can't let her be right about me and this child.

"Dear God, please don't let this happen to me again," I whisper. I hold the paper to my leak, and try to keep the baby inside, my muscles straining in vain. The baby is no bigger than a grain of rice, so I wouldn't even be able to see it, but I look anyway. Is it there? My poor, poor child? It just looks like period blood, only heavier and thicker. There are clots that look like chunks of dark red gelatin. Is that my child? What monster am I?

The cramping has grown worse. I don't know what to do, so I just sit and cry, and bleed into the latrine. Outside the bathroom, I hear the front door of the plane being closed and locked. It is too late to leave the plane now. I am trapped in this hell.

I am having a miscarriage in the airplane bathroom.

I search the small bathroom for something to stanch the flow, and find a stash of large feminine napkins, bulky ones, that seem old-fashioned and ridiculous. I stick one on the stain of my underwear, and check the outside of my pants. The blood has only barely penetrated the dark fabric. No one can see it from the outside. I pull the pants up and look at myself in the bathroom mirror. Pale, clammy, horrified. This can't be happening, and yet it is. Again. Why? Why *me*?

The flight to Houston will last about three hours. I don't think I need to exit the plane, cause a scene. I should be able to handle it. I have done this all before. At this early stage in the pregnancy, it really just ends up feeling like a very heavy period, a pain I deserve for riding that horse. I can get off in Houston and seek medical attention. I can catch another flight home tomorrow, or later this evening, after making sure I'm okay. I will suffer now, for whatever it is I've done wrong. I want to die with my baby.

"I am so sorry," I say to the spirit of my unborn child.

I return to my seat just as the flight attendants finish demonstrating the proper use of a seat belt. I take my seat, buckle the belt loosely around my defective hips and lower belly. I will not cry. I will not allow myself to cry here and now. It would not be appropriate.

And yet the questions persist. Why? Why does God want this to happen to me? I don't want anything but to have a child. I consider calling Andre to tell him what's happening, but the flight attendant has been clear—no phones now. It is better this way, anyhow. I don't want to burden the passengers around me with my loss.

I take the dark glasses out of my purse and put them on. This will help to mask the tears, should they decide to come against all my coaching to the contrary. Silently, I recite the alphabet backwards, to distract my mind from thoughts of failure, misery.

And then, as the plane shudders out of the gate to prepare for takeoff, I use all the strength I have to keep from having a breakdown. I tell myself I can do this. I have to. I have to be strong. I've come too far and worked too hard to be a failure at anything more. I will suffer now with stoic grace, because there is nothing else to do.

elizabeth

IT'S GOOD TO be back in Boston. As I hurry from the darkening Beacon Hill street where I rent my parking space, where I've stashed my Toyota Tacoma truck, to my home—where Gordon, the most wonderful baby in all the world, waits for me!—I marvel at my peaceful, picturesque old neighborhood. The narrow, twisting roads of brick pavers, the arboreal canopies. I try to find comfort in the white window boxes planted with colorful flowers. I am all cried out, as they say in this country of sensible and sometimes twisted clichés, my soul soft and used as a twisted dishrag. I can't wait to see my son, the only bit of constancy and unconditional love in my life. I can't wait to forget Lauren among his chubby folds and silly babbling.

I wear comfortable gray hiking cargo pants, Ahnu multisport sandals, and a soft blue J.Crew T-shirt—I cannot remember whether it belongs to me or Selwyn. By the time I drag myself up the stone steps of my town house, across the tiny porch, and to the red wooden door of the three-bedroom home I share with my wife and our ten-month-old son, I am tired and wired at the same time, the kind of energetic exhaustion I get on trips, where I need sleep but don't get much. I'm ready for it to be over, ready to grip my life again.

I take a deep breath and focus on seeming normal when I go through this door. I look around for a moment, to remember who I was before I left here and had an affair with a dear friend who is eternally straight and might never be a friend again. I am not the same. I will never be the same.

The air of Beacon Hill is refreshingly moist and thick after the thin, dry air of Rebecca's desert. I stand at the threshold, enjoying the humidity for a moment longer. My skin drinks the water in, and for a moment I am more insect than woman. I have an urge to scurry up the nearest tree, to hide in foliage. To avoid my life, all that I sense is coming. But in I must go. Into my truth, to face myself, my wife, to see if she can taste the salt of another woman upon my tongue. If she can, and if she asks me, I will not be able to lie. Even if she doesn't ask, I might not be able to hold this thing inside.

It is nearly seven in the evening, and Selwyn is home with Gordon. My beloved boy. I see the lights on inside. To another person, one who did not know us, the cool white glow of lights might symbolize stability and peace, a refreshing home. In a healthy marriage, I imagine the person in my position, the person who has been away for a number of days, would be excited to return home. In a healthy marriage, I might even take this chance to sprint up the steps and through the door.

I stick my key in the door, and turn it slowly, a knife in the back of my union. I have betrayed her. I drop my keys on the antique wooden entry table, and survey the living room. Unfolded laundry scattered on the sofas, toys across the wooden floor like colorful shrapnel. A weekend away, and they've been able to commit this much damage? Why is laundry impossible for Selwyn to dry or put away properly? Why does she prefer to live amidst towering stacks of half-damp clothing? It makes me tired. And angry. She does not respect this house, or me. Or Gordon. She expects to be waited on, because she grew up spoiled. I never realized, until I left on trips and returned to the messes, how much more I do around here than she does.

I find them in the kitchen. It looks like she has not washed dishes since I left; they, like the clothes, sag in towers. There is a smell of old milk, and jarred pasta sauce. Rotten broccoli. I was hungry a moment ago, hoping to make myself a turkey sandwich and eat it with Sun Chips and a Sprite, but my appetite is gone now. Now? I feel sick.

Selwyn is wearing jean shorts and a ribbed gray tank top with a navy-blue button-down open over it. I am not surprised we've dressed somewhat alike; we often do, after so many years together, sharing clothes. She is a runner; her arms are beautifully toned, and tan, and she has let her hair grow out a bit since moving here. She still looks a lot like a young boy, yet her skin glows with health. Gordon sits in his blue-and-white high chair, and Selwyn feeds him something slippery from a spoon. She looks up at me standing in the doorway. I smile at them the best I can. She sort of smiles back. But not really. It is more of a sneer. I know—and hate—that look. She is looking at me with mistrust.

"Welcome home," she says with a flat tone, an aggressive tone, accusing me of something. Of what? It doesn't matter. This is how it always is. My spine tingles in preparation for a fight or a hard, fast sprint away from this place. She is not happy to see me, and she has something she wants to argue about, I can tell by the tight look of her thin lips, by the heaviness and curl of her brow over her eyes. This is her way. She baits me with these expressions on her face. It is our little game.

If I were to fulfill my duty on this dysfunctional merry-go-round of ours, if I'd follow our well-worn script, I would take her expression as a signal to ask her what is wrong. Then she might say "nothing," but continue to fester. I would push for an answer, and then out it would tumble, words like flopping, dying fish on the sand, an ocean of woes, all the problems she has with me, offense stacked upon offense, a tower of offenses brought upon her by me in a home of untidy towers. It will all be my fault, of course. It always is.

I am not going to follow that script with her right now. The baby has changed me this way. I respect the rights of Gordon not to bear witness to adult arguments, and for that reason I have never openly argued in front of him. Selwyn does not share my opinion on this, and is content to fight anytime, anywhere, with anyone listening. She even went so far as to tell me once that she thought it would be good for Gordon to hear us argue, because "it would prepare him for real life." I, conversely, hope for more from life for Gordon than this, what we have.

And therein you shall find our greatest ideological divide, as far as I can tell. I do not want Gordon to grow up thinking that ugly conflicts are inevitable. I want my son to grow in light and love, with confidence and security, for I believe that the healthier my relationships are in his presence, the healthier his relationships will be when he is old enough to have them himself.

I walk across the shiny white tile floor of the kitchen, going through the motions, and hug my wife. She smells of unwashed skin, a greasy smell. I try to kiss her on the lips, but Selwyn turns her head at the last moment, giving me her cool cheek instead. I wonder for a moment if she knows about Lauren, but there is no way she could. Rather, this is her general displeasure with me. Nothing more.

Gordon's eyes sparkle as he sees me, and my soul melts like warm butter. He dribbles a bit of mushy brown rice down the front of his navy blue T-shirt and begins to bounce in his seat, happy.

"Mami!" he cries. He holds his arms out for me to pick him up. He is speaking pretty well now, a handful of small words, and calls me Mami. Selwyn is Mama. I scoop Gordon out of the high chair, and hold him close to me. I kiss his cheeks and the tight black curls across the top of his head. He smells of Aveeno baby wash, clean and warm.

"Someone had a *bath*!" I say, amazed that Selwyn found the energy for it.

"He got filthy at the park," spits Selwyn, by way of explanation and accusation. A loving parent might say something like this with a grin. But not Selwyn. She says it with a scowl. She still doesn't seem to understand that getting dirty is part of being a child. She wants Gordon to remain clean, to do things the way an adult would. It has been this way from the beginning with Selwyn, who found Gordon's parasites and skin disorders, from having lived all of his early life in unsanitary third-world conditions, disgusting. I had to be the one to pick out the lice and nits, to administer the medicine, to sit up with the baby while he cried in abdominal misery. More than once, saying she was unable to tolerate the sound of the baby's cries, Selwyn left to get a hotel room for the night. I should have moved on from her then, but I wanted to see if it was a phase, whether or not we could ultimately come to live and love together as a family. It has not improved.

As Selwyn criticizes him, Gordon seems to pick up on it. His face looks sad, confused, and I have the urge to grab him and take him away from this woman.

I consider saying something like "that's what kids do," but I have said this sort of thing so many times now, I have come to believe she either doesn't hear it or doesn't want to believe it. No use in conversing with a wall.

Selwyn has never been flexible. It was one of the qualities I loved most about her in the beginning, her strength and assertiveness, her ability to speak her mind in the face of any sort of opposition. Selwyn struck me then as fearless. Powerful. I felt so safe with her for it. The flip side of this personality, however, has been her seeming inability to ever admit she has made a mistake, an unwillingness to apologize. Even to a child. Even to a spouse.

I think better about what I might say now, realizing I am tiptoeing across a minefield. I ask which park they went to, and she tells me. We only talk about Gordon, how he was when I was away ("a demon"), how challenging it has been for Selwyn ("I'm so tired"), what the baby ate or did not eat.

"It sounds like you two had a good time bonding," I say, even though it is not true. I am hoping that by suggesting such a thing it might actually become true. I am a TV producer with the heart of a poet. An unhealthy optimist.

I have a possibly fatal ability to make semi-good situations seem perfect to myself. I am also able, on occasion, to perform the opposite task, making a questionable situation appear large and dangerously bad. Sometimes, with me, it is hard to tell what is real and what is story. A poet above all else.

That is how I ended up in Lauren's arms, I think. Because even though I knew the truth of who and what she was, there was a part of me, the poet in me, that rewrote reality as it unfolded. I believe I developed this gift as a result of watching my father beat my mother when I was very young. I imagined him better than he was. And when we moved away from Colombia to get away from him, I imagined that my new nation, a place of confusing sounds and attitudes where my mother struggled in ways I'd never known her to, was better to me, an Afro-Colombian girl poet, than it was.

I found faith in the way I imagined things could be, often to the detriment of truth. This is why I was able to stay in the closet for so long on the job in Boston, where I was a TV reporter. I simply imagined that I was not me, every time I went to work. I imagined I was a more acceptable version of me, one that wasn't strange and scary to most of the rest of the world. So it is that now, as I stand here in my kitchen, looking at my family, I don't know anymore, just don't know anymore, whether what I feel for Selwyn, the derision and disapproval of her tepid mothering skills, is real or imagined. Am I being too hard on her? Is she crying out for help? Am I deaf to her needs?

"I don't know how much we bonded," says Selwyn. "But we sure spent a lot of time together."

As my wife rolls her eyes and sighs in exasperation at the memory and thought of dealing with a baby, I feel an intense, chilling dislike for her permeate my soul. How can anyone complain about raising a beautiful child like this? A complete innocent, a helpless human being entrusted to our care? A child who, if not for us, might still be languishing in a putrid orphanage in Sierra Leone, or worse? It confuses me intensely. For my part, I wake up every day thankful for the fact of Gordon in my life, grateful that he was gifted to me, awed by the responsibility of it, and humbled by his sweetness and trust.

"You seem tired," I say to Selwyn. "I appreciate you taking care of Gordon while I was away."

She says nothing, just seethes in my general direction. Pops her back, rolls her head, stretches with all the empathy of a cat.

"I got it from here," I continue. "I'll put Gordon to bed. You deserve a break and I deserve some time with this yummy little boy."

Selwyn nods, and gets up, tossing the napkin to the tabletop in surrender. "I'm going for a run," she announces.

"That sounds nice."

"Love you," she says absently.

I cannot bring myself to answer with the same.

I am relieved she is leaving. I can see relief on her face, too, at the thought of leaving. As I cart Gordon from the kitchen to the nursery for a fresh diaper, I wonder how much longer Selwyn and I will be able to avoid the obvious—that to be happy, we must eventually live apart. That to be good mommies, we cannot stay together.

lauren

I SIT IN the blue backseat of the smelly white cab, all the way from Logan Airport to my fiancé Amaury's sister's house in Jamaica Plain, picking at the slash in the vinyl seat the whole time, ripping it bigger, fingering the threads of its fibers like hair. I take a break from vandalizing the cab now and then to scarf down the breakfast bagel and glazed bear claw I got at the Dunkin' Donuts in the airport, washing them down with another iced hazelnut coffee. At least I am consistent in my poor eating habits. And at least I look good. Even if I'm a panicky mess.

I'm wearing one of my "weekend casual" outfits from Ann Taylor in Copley Place, to give off the illusion that I am a professional woman who holds it all together, like the skinny models on the company's Web site. Charcoal gray capri pants, with a short-sleeved wraparound top that knots at the waist on one side, sassy little slingbacks. I have my hair down and wild, and my makeup is fine. I *look* normal. That counts for something. Right?

I should go home first, I know, and take care of *me*. I have suitcases in the trunk, and a fat cat in my condo who probably needs feeding, now that his big bowl of dry food might have run out. I left a big bowl of water, too, and a toilet open, just in case. (I know, not ideal, but who can afford a kennel?) Actually, I *should* go to Sara's house and try to talk some sense into that pathetic woman before she ends up in jail, or dead, or worse. How could she go back to that guy? *How?* And then, after that, I should go to Usnavys's house and try to talk some sense into her, too, before she ruins a perfectly good marriage by falling in love with some black Republican chucklehead golf pro thousands of miles away. What is *wrong* with people? Are we all dashing into early midlife crises? Jesus.

Please. Like I'm one to talk, right? I am starting to feel insane. Freakin' insane, understand me? Crazy as shit. Not that shit is crazy, but you know what I mean. I have been calling Amaury the whole weekend, without a single call back. He hasn't picked up. He hasn't replied to my text messages. I've e-mailed him from my laptop—nothing. It's like he's forgotten me completely since leaving me at the airport. I feel invisible. I *hate* that feeling more than anything in the world. I'd rather get slimed and mauled by the monsters in that old Michael Jackson "Thriller" video. I'd rather break a finger by sticking it into David Blaine's mouth for six weeks, on a pogo stick. Anything. Something. Something that I know will heal. Invisibility, though? That is a form of death.

The tunnel lights zip past, because underneath the water of Boston is this amazing leaky anthill of freeways in tunnels, and then, once we're out, the nighttime urban Boston landscape of brick buildings, parks, subway stations, and pizzerias. Whose city is this? Not mine. Why don't I feel like I belong anywhere when I'm alone like this? I know. You don't have to tell me about how bad it is for a grown woman to derive most of her sense of self and existence from another human being. If he loved me, I'd belong here. As it is, he's made it his city, and me a ghost inside of it.

I dial Usnavys on my cell phone, to see if she's heard from Sara. My cell battery is nearly dead. Of course. I forgot to charge it. I don't remember normal things like that. I might bring up Marcus, but I don't know how, or if I have enough battery power. I hear Usnavys's daughter, Carolina, whining in the background, and the TV sounds like it's on. When and if I have kids? I am not going to let them watch TV. Ever. And they're not going to whine like that. Ever. No, really.

"No, *m'ija*, I haven't heard from her. I call and call but she never answers the damn phone. I'm gonna go over there pretty soon if she don't pick up. Doesn't. I can't be worrying myself to death about that woman." See? Everyone is a better friend than I am.

"How's things?"

"Around here? I don't know. We need to talk." She sounds depressed.

"About Marcus?"

"Sort of."

"I knew it."

"You didn't *know* it."

"I did."

"Whatever, okay?"

"You love him?"

"I can't talk right now."

"Sounds top secret," I try to joke. She doesn't laugh.

"It is," she whispers. "He sent me tickets to Montreal."

"Montreal, Canada?"

"No, Montreal, India. Of course Montreal, Canada, *nena*."

"Why?"

"Please. Why? Think about it, girl."

"Usnavys! *No*. You can't." I'm stunned to be the sensible friend, for once.

"I think I might go."

"No! Poor Juan."

She sighs. "Please. Poor *me*, okay? Poor *me*. You have no idea."

"I don't understand. I thought things were good."

"We need to talk, like I said, girl."

"Wow. Okay. When?" Sadly, I find it comforting to think that my friend's marriage isn't perfect. It makes me seem more, I don't know, normal somehow.

"How about now?" She sounds so sad. If I were a better friend I'd do it, I'd go help her. But right now? Right now I have to be selfish.

"I just got off the plane," I tell her. Then I lie. "I'm exhausted, and I planned to go home and take a nice relaxing bath and maybe catch a Lifetime movie."

Usnavys gets snippy now. "Well, you let me know when you have an opening in your schedule, okay, *m'ija?*"

Great. Now I feel guilty. Not even my lie was noble enough for her. She really needs me. A good friend would go to her right now and help. That's what she'd do for me. Anytime any of us are in trouble, Usnavys is the first one to jump in her rented BMW and rush to our sides with boxes of baked goods.

"Tomorrow. Okay?" I say.

"Fine," she says. She sounds awful. "Whatever."

"You gonna be okay?" I ask, amazed that I have been this thoughtful. Amazed that *she* needs *me*. It is always the other way around.

"I'm always okay. You know that. Go take your bath, *apestosa*. You stink."

We say our good-byes, and I end the call. God, I'm an asshole. I just *am*.

I totally am. I know the way I *should* be, and it looks nothing like this pitiful person I actually *am*. I almost wish I didn't know how fucked up I was, because then I could just go around feeling okay and still being fucked up. As it is, however, I know I'm fucked up and can't seem to do anything about it. How fucked up.

We pull up in front of the sagging old triple-decker with the trash-strewn yard and the mangy stray cat under the porch. Amaury's flashy black Lincoln Navigator is in the driveway. Have I mentioned how much I *hate* that car? It's got hubcaps that keep moving when the car is standing still, like that's gonna fool somebody. He thinks it's classy. *This* is what I'm talking about. But I thought I'd remodel this man, make him what I wanted and needed. He will never coach T-ball in the suburbs. He will never drive a sedate Volvo. He will always be a baggy-assed crotch-grabber—his own crotch, and other people's crotches. So why the fuck do I still love him? Don't answer that. I don't want to hear it. I love him because he's *there*, and if he weren't, I'd be alone, and alone is too scary to contemplate.

"Wait here," I tell the driver. "Keep the meter running. I'll be right back."

"Whatever, lady," says the driver. I have no idea what he looks like. That's how self-absorbed I've been on this ride. He has a thick New England accent, like a cabbie in a Ben and Casey Affleck movie. What's *that* about? I didn't even know cabbies talked like the actors who play them in movies, but this one does. Go figure. Maybe he's an actor. He blows air out like I make him impatient and tired. Why must everyone do that around me? Even the cabdriver realizes what a total loser I am? I guess it's obvious.

I take the rickety steps to the apartment two at a time, anger flooding my system. I am about to explode with invisibility. I seek resolution. This is so wrong, him ignoring me for days on end. I deserve to exist.

I knock on the door. Hard. Three, four, five hard bangs, until the knuckles of my hand sting. Time passes slowly. No answer. I knock again, and hear some giggling and rustling sounds behind the door. I bang again.

The door opens, slowly and with a creak of swollen wood. Must have been raining while I was away.

Amaury's sister stands there, all Caribbean curves with her huge ass and tiny waist, in her tight red jeans, flip-flop sandals, and her Adidas T-shirt, her long dark hair pulled back in a high, tight ponytail like the most beleaguered genie in all the world. She holds the door open just enough for me to see her, but not so much that I can see what lies beyond.

"Hi," I say.

"*Hola,*" she answers in a tone that oozes judgment. She has one brow cocked, as if she is amused, surprised, and uncomfortable, all at once. Those women, mothers and sisters from traditional Latino families? They are a woman's worst enemy, ready and willing to protect men from justice.

"Is Amaury in there?" I ask her in Spanish.

She narrows her eyes at me. Takes a deep breath, sighs it out again. "Yes," she says. She leans forward toward me, her posture nearly combative. "But he's busy."

"He's busy?" I ask, incredulously. "He's never busy. Don't lie to me."

"You should go home," she tells me. There's something in her eyes, a Latina-from-Latin-America sort of code of some kind. She looks tired. She has looked tired since I met her.

"What's going on?"

"Nothing. He's just busy. Go home, Lauren. It's late." She begins to shut the door on me.

The adrenaline intensifies in my veins. I push her out of the way. She tries to stop me but, failing, settles for cursing in Spanish. I am stronger than she is. Physically, at least. Emotionally is a whole other story. Emotionally, she's a rock. I don't understand how she does it, with three kids who are all fucking up in their own unique ways and a husband who works so much he's never home. She works as a nurse's aide now, after putting herself through night school to learn first English and then how to draw blood. She is solid as marble, that woman, and apparently made from a completely different strain of human being than was the lovesick American weakling that is me.

Inside the apartment, it smells of onions and peppers sautéed in olive oil, maybe beef, too. Amaury's sister is a wonderful cook, and manages to have a homemade dinner of *comida criolla* on the table for her family—and Amaury— every night, which might explain why her adolescent sons are both starting to resemble giant basketballs with legs. Her skinny teen daughter, meanwhile, appears to have assimilated to the degree that she has ceased eating altogether.

"Amaury?" I call out as I walk down the narrow hall toward the living room. "Where the fuck are you?"

I hear him say, "Oh, shit!" in English. I hear a girl giggle. I feel ice in my veins now, ice and venom. A girl. A girl who is not me. A visible girl.

I barrel into the living room and find him sprawled, shirtless and in baggy jeans, on the sofa with a remote control in his hand. His feet are bare and his toenails look like they belong on a dog, all yellowed and too damn long. Why do I love him? Why? He's watching some cheesy Spanish-language show on Univision. *Because he's there.*

Sitting in the room with him is one of the basketball nephews, who is about fifteen, and a narrow, busty girl who looks to be the same age. She is very pretty, a blond mulatta type with green eyes, and for a moment I am jealous of the way her tight, cheap Rave-type polyester blouse strains over her perky young boobs. She wears low-rise jeans, and even when she's sitting there is zero belly protruding over the top. She's lovely. Then I realize she's the nephew's friend and I'm crazy. I mean, I realized I was crazy before, but I guess this jealous reaction just sort of underlines it for me. He'd never get with a girl that young. I must be going crazy.

"Hey, baby," says Amaury as he sees me. He stands up and smiles broadly, dances over to me in that way he has that melts me in a million places. His Saint Benedict and Saint Thomas Aquinas medals, worn on chains around his bare neck, tinkle against each other. He holds his arms open and pulls me in for a big hug. "I missed you! *¡Mi amorcito!*"

The girl adjusts her hair and clothes and gives me the surly sort of look teenagers always give grown-ups. She must be Amaury's nephew's girlfriend. Seems like just yesterday that kid was a little boy, now here he is, shaving, with a girl. I mean, shaving. With a girl. Not shaving with a girl. Though maybe he is. I have no idea what the crazy kids are doing these days.

"Who's MC?" I ask.

"What?" He looks confused, but like he's faking it, too.

"MC. The woman who keeps texting you."

Amaury looks from me to the young girl on the sofa. He smiles at me, but his eyes show that he is thinking up a lie. I know that look. "MC, baby?

That's just a woman I work with. She does street team work up in Vermont, at the colleges. We had a meeting on Friday."

"I don't believe you."

"Have you been drinking?" he asks me. He puts an arm on my shoulder, all concerned-looking.

"How come you've been ignoring me?" I ask Amaury. I realize with a jolt of patheticness that I have my hands stuck to my hips—my fists, actually—just like that bossy Lucy chick from the Peanuts cartoons.

"What?" he tries to look like he doesn't know what I'm talking about. "No one's been ignoring you, Lauren. Let me smell your breath."

I start to cry. "Don't play stupid with me. You know I've been calling you and calling you. What's going on?"

Amaury kisses my cheeks and my lips, and I am so happy to be visible again I almost forget to be mad. He dances with me, pokes me in the ribs to try to get me to laugh. Charms me, as he so often does, trying to get me to leave the bad mood behind. Maybe he's right. Maybe I'm overreacting. I've been known to do that. In fact, it is all I'm known for, really.

"I've been busy, *mi amor*," he says. His face is twisted up in forced sincerity. "You know how it is. Cuicatl's new record hasn't been hittin' the way they want, and they been on my ass to do better, to get the word out quicker. They got the tour starting soon, you know? I've got all the new rock in Spanish artists, too. It's been crazy. I got Maria Cristina to help me out. My sister wanted some help this weekend with the boys, and so I delegated. That's all. You're always telling me to delegate. Remember?"

I stare at him, searching for any inconsistency, any contradiction that might betray the harm he has done me when I wasn't looking. What he says makes sense.

"Are you sure?"

"Yes!" He sounds exasperated. "Seriously, Lauren. Get ahold of yourself."

"I'm sorry," I say. I expect pain from love, from life in general, and when it doesn't come I usually find a way to manufacture it. I've been to enough therapy with non-Latina white ladies to recognize my ways, but not enough, apparently, to know how to change them. I wonder if I am manufacturing this crisis now. Probably. I have heard that healthy people in relationships give each other space and time to be themselves, by themselves. I was only gone for a weekend. And weekends are Amaury's busiest times, when he's out at the clubs, and at the radio stations, promoting Cuicatl. Could be I'm overreacting. It's what I do best. I'm so foolish.

"You could have taken a couple of seconds to call back," I say. I feel my shoulders sag, and I recognize that the face I give him now would be more appropriate on a whipped dog.

"I know, *mi amor*," he says, mirroring my pout the way a mother might do with her sad child. "I know, *ya, ya*." He takes my head onto his chest and strokes my hair, like a parent. Which only makes me feel worse, because it highlights just exactly how I've been acting like a child.

"I missed you," I tell him.

"Did you have a good time, baby?" he asks, still stroking my hair. "A good time *allá* with *las sucias* in *Nuevo Mexico*?"

"I guess."

"I didn't call you too because I thought you'd be busy partying, girl. You said it was a weekend for the girls, no?"

He kisses me and tells me that he was just helping his nephew and the girl with their math homework, that they both are facing repeating the same grade next year if they don't get their scores up. I ask him why they are all watching television, then. He says they were taking a little break. "That's all, baby." He says that's why he had told his sister to tell whoever it was to go away if it was for him. In the interest of the kids' education.

"I'm sorry if she didn't let you in, *mi amor*," he tells me. "I didn't think you'd be back so soon. I thought it'd be Fantasma, or Miguelito."

"But I told you I was getting back tonight. I left you a million voice mails about it!" Why does this all feel so creepy? What is wrong with me?

"I forgot." He does a silly dance to cheer me up. "You know me. I forget things. I thought it was Sunday for half the day today. Then they got back from school and only then I remembered it was Monday." This man has a photographic memory, practically. He forgets *nothing*. My unease returns. I feel crazy.

I fidget some more, because it gets me attention. He hugs me and tickles me. I look at the kids. The boy looks guilty and scared; he can't hold eye contact with me. But the girl? She just looks damn mean. Her arms are crossed over her large chest, and she is staring at me with pure hatred in her eyes. She is one of the traditional chicks who will aid her brothers in breaking hearts.

I have no idea why. I guess people just hate me. I don't blame them, really.

"Let me take you home," says Amaury.

I allow him to rush me from the room, past his sweeping sister, down the stairs to his Navigator. He pays the bored cabbie to leave. I allow him to drive me to my condo, and, once we're there, I allow him to follow me into the bedroom.

"*Ya, ya*," he says, still trying to comfort me. Only now his hands are on me. He's removing my clothes. I allow him to. He takes a pair of very high heels from my closet and tells me to put them on. I do.

"*Ven,*" he says, instructing me to walk with him over to my dresser. He turns my face away from him, and we both stand facing the mirror on the wall. "*Así,*" he says, bending me at the waist. I brace myself against the dresser with my hands. I watch in the mirror as he unzips his pants, and lowers them just enough to expose his pelvis. He licks his fingers and rubs them over me, his lower lip held in his teeth. He tells me my rump is delicious, and I begin to rock against his hand. He slips a finger, then two, then a whole bunch of them into me, and the pain is good, in a sick kind of way.

"Ow," I cry. Then, "Don't stop." Yup. That pretty much sums it up, doesn't it? I could be off saving my best friend's marriage, or helping save my other friend's life, but instead I've chosen this cheap, fake-porn sex with a domineering, brilliant man I know is lying to me. Some friend I am. Some woman.

He pounds his fist against me, over and over, and I look at myself in the mirror. It looks like I'm being punished. It turns me on. How sad. Some part of me, the brain, recognizes that this is not love. I watch as he removes his fingers, puts them in his mouth. He tells me I taste good, and I beg him to take me. He tells me he loves me, and I—for the moment anyway—make the idiotic choice to believe him.

cuicatl

I WAIT ON the sofa in the living room part of the Presidential Villa at the Royal Palms Resort and Spa in Phoenix, watching Lou Dobbs make an ass of himself on CNN. *Pinche* dumbass motherfucker can't stop talking about the dangers of Mexicans, like we're a disease instead of human beings. Keeps talking about how terrorists are coming over the border from Mexico, when not a single one has ever done anything like that. He thinks we're the same people because, to him, we're all brown. Idiot. Isn't it amazing, homes, that this kind of racist bullshit still plays on American television? *Pues*, you'd think we were past it. He has no idea that all over this country, people like me are staying in places like this, with careers like mine. He has no idea I just cleaned up in an indoor-outdoor shower. He has no idea the luxury of the life I lead, thanks to *mexicanos*, man. Without *mexicanos*, this country would drop dead, and this *idiota* is talking about us like we're mangy pit bulls. I raise my middle finger to the television, and decide to say something unkind about this man from the stage tonight, even if it pisses off my record company.

A soft knock comes at the front door of the two-thousand-square-foot house that will be my home until tomorrow, when I fly to El Paso to do it again, and then to Las Vegas, and Los Angeles, and San Diego, and on and on. I jump up to open the door, and find Frank, freshly showered and in his manager-wear—a beige linen suit with a white shirt. Dude cleans up nice, man. No tie tonight, which is smart, given the way the air feels like a blowtorch coming through the door. It's fucking *hot* in Phoenix in the summer, man. I don't know how people like it here. Or do they?

"You ready, princess?" he asks me. "The car's waiting."

"Give me one second," I say. As usual before a show, I'm in basic Levi's and a T-shirt. The costumes will all be at the arena, in my dressing room. I shuffle to where my plastic slip-on sandals are, and put them on.

"Can you believe this *cabrón*?" Franks asks, jutting his chin toward El Idiot

Dobbs. "His wife's a Mexican, too." He picks at the grapes in the massive fruit bowl the hotel sent me a few minutes ago.

"No way!" I'm stunned.

"Serious. She is."

"Uh-uh!"

Frank nods. "He never talks about it."

"Dude's a total and complete prick," I say. "That he's got a Mexica wife only scares me more."

"Have mercy on him. Writing's on the wall, Mexica are taking our land back, and the old guard white men are scared to death," he says. He relaxes his face and shoulders as he speaks, and I can see that he really isn't bothered by the cable news diatribes against our people the way I am. He's confident we're winning. "They know what they did to us in the past, and they're afraid we'll do it back. It's like when you hit somebody and then you flinch and wait to get hit back, man."

"But we won't hit back."

"*Órale*, no, of course not. *Pero* these savages on CNN, they don't know that. So they gotta broadcast fear. How else they gonna control all the poor people?"

"Trying to get everyone on the scare bandwagon with them." I point the remote at the television like a gun and shoot Dobbs off the air. It feels good. I grab an apple out of the bowl, rub it clean on my jeans leg. "*Vámonos*," I tell Frank as I grab my bag. It's another freebie from a fancy designer. I don't even know or care what brand it is. It's all the same crap, really, all made in sweatshops, by children. "Let's go."

"They need to do to him what they did to Imus," says Frank, continuing to talk as we cross the lush grounds toward the front of the resort. "But that's the problem with our people, no? African-Americans have their Sharptons and the other leaders who make noise when someone wrongs them. Imus says something, boom, man. They're all out in the streets with TV cameras on them. Mexica and Latino people, though? We got nobody doing that."

"Good point, *vato*," I tell him. He's right. Frank is often right, and he makes me think about things I never thought about before. "We gotta work on that, no? We gotta get a spokesperson network going."

"Just make sure they *look* right," he says. "The people they call to represent us now for the news shows? No, no, no. Have you seen them?" A maid and a gardener look up as we pass, and they recognize me and start whispering. They won't come right up and ask for an autograph. That's the thing with the permanent slave class we're bringing in from Mexico to do work for less than minimum wage. They're so scared they don't even talk in public, man. Shit. Some days you don't want to be recognized, ¿sabes? I smile back at them so they don't think I'm rude. If I were feeling more generous, I might have stopped to talk to them. But right now, I'm angry about Dobbs, and I need to conserve energy for the concert tonight. Some days you just want to be regular for a while. Some days you wish the whole system weren't so fucked up. Some days, you think life would be a whole lot easier if you were happily ignorant like my parents.

"I usually try to avoid TV, Frank." I dig the apple-free hand through the bag and find my enormous sunglasses and position them on my face. I find a baseball cap and slap it over my head, too.

"Smart woman. They usually get these crazy-looking women with colorful hats to talk for us on CNN. Or they get some woman who looks like she hasn't had a bath in a week, with dirty eyeglasses. That doesn't help."

"What's wrong with hats?" I ask, motioning to my hat.

Frank laughs. "Nothing, if you're on *Sábado Gigante*. But on CNN you ought to look like someone on CNN, ¿que no?"

"What does someone on CNN look like?" I ask, playing devil's advocate for him.

"In a suit and tie."

"A woman in a tie? Like Paula Poundstone? That's not going to help, either, man."

He laughs. "Okay. You know what I mean. A suit and pearls. They need to have that inside-the-beltway look to them."

I agree with him, and look at him in a way that lets him know I admire the hell out of his brain. I also like the way this man looks in the late afternoon sunlight, all grace as he walks, with his long hair down and those experience lines radiating from his eyes as he smiles at me. He is beautiful, and he's smart, and he thinks like I do.

"You nervous?" he asks me, squinting at me in the sun. "First tour in two years."

"Eh," I say, like I'm cool with it. I can't find the words to say back, but not because I'm nervous. *Bueno*, of course I'm nervous, but not for the reasons he thinks. It's not the show that scrambles me up right now; it's Frank.

He seems to notice I've been looking at him. He says nothing about it, but looks away with a secret sort of smile on his face that makes me wonder, you know, if he knows what I've been thinking about him. How I've been feeling about him. He must. I'm obvious about the things I'm feeling, and he's as good a judge of my moods as anyone who has ever known me.

The white limo waits for us in the shaded area in front of the resort. Frank opens my door, and in I go. He comes after. Usually, he sits across from me on these rides—at least that's how it was two years ago, when I was dating my former drummer.

This evening, though? Dude. This evening Frank sits next to me, so close our knees touch.

A**T THE SIGHT** of the shiny new arena, with the concave glass front, my heart beats faster. I almost forget about the way Frank's leg touches mine. There's already a line of kids snaking around the front of the arena. Mostly, they're brown like me. I've got some other kinds of fans, but the bread and butter of my business, man? My own people. Damn, man. I love my fans, the way the girls try to dress like me and the guys try to look so strong and cool. Some of them have pillows, like they've been camped out. I still can't believe anybody would do that just because of me and my music.

I look at Frank with a giddy smile, the kind a silly girl would have. He beams back at me and touches my hand. Squeezes it, actually. "You'll be great," he says. "Don't worry."

"Thanks, man," I tell him. This is the point when you let go of the person's hand, right? But we don't. Neither one of us. We keep holding on to each other like that. It's not sappy or super-romantic, and we don't even look at each other. We just look out the window as the limo slides around to the entrance at the back, and then down the ramp with all the security guards, to the door where performers go in. The tour bus for my band is already here.

Frank releases my hand when the driver opens my door. We don't say anything about it. He follows me up the steps, down the hall to the door with my name on it. Inside the dressing room there is another fruit basket, tofu, bottled water, more food than I could ever eat. *Órale*. Why do they do this? There's also a couple of bouquets of flowers from the record company, and balloons. Oh, and my wardrobe, all clean and hanging on a rack.

"*Bueno*," says Frank. "I'll be back in a bit. There's some people from Wagner here, Joel Benitez and some others. I'm going to go make sure they're happy."

"Thanks, man," I tell him. I wonder for a tiny second if he's going to kiss me, but he's gone before I have time to finish the thought. I head off with some of the band members to do a sound check on the stage in the empty arena. It all comes back to me now, the thrill of the stage, the rush of having fans sing along with you, thousands upon thousands of them. The sound system is good, and we're going to be fine.

I head back to my dressing room to get transformed into a pop star.

By the time Frank gets back to my room, nearly an hour later, I'm dressed, and the makeup artist and hair stylist work their magic on me as I sit in a chair at the well-lighted mirror. In the mirror, I see Frank check me out. He definitely does. Maybe it's just the costume, which is sort of like a sexier take on the typical Aztec dancer outfit for women. I have a long, shiny turquoise skirt, slit down the sides all the way to the waist, decorated in intricate black and gold patterns all across the front and back panels. I've got the shell bracelets on my ankles, only instead of the usual flat moccasins I wear short boots with super-high heels, very sexy. On top, I've got pretty much a bikini top, but a *muy* fancy one, black with blue and gold designs. It is tiny, and insubstantial compared to the massive necklace, all beaded and hanging. I designed the costumes for the show myself, with the help of real designers, of course. There is something very powerful and Cleopatra about it. I feel like a queen.

"You look great," Frank tells me, as they paint my eyes dark. He seems like he doesn't want to come across as leering in any way, like he's very guarded about anything sexual he might feel for me. Like he's worried he'll offend me.

I want to tell him he looks great, too, but at that moment, Joel Benitez, the man who gave me my first record deal, comes into the room, looking fatter and older than the last time I saw him. We all shoot the shit for a while, and then, before I realize what's happening, the stylist fits the massive feathered headpiece onto my skull, then the cordless mike is attached to me, adjusted just so, and the stage manager and all my entourage lead me down the hall, toward the stage.

I see the guys from the band, shake everyone's hand. We go over the set list, then they take their places. They begin to play the droning intro to my Bartók-inspired piece first, without me. I hear a low roar from the crowd as the music starts. A minute later, I tumble onto the stage, all raw energy and fury. My ten backup dancers follow, and begin the chant and blessing dance.

"What's up, Phoenix!" I shout into the microphone. Again, a dull roar. I think I've caught them off guard, so I ask again. Again, the same low cheer. "Come on, *chingazos*! You can do better than that!" I yell. But they don't do better than that. I squint through the bright lights, into the auditorium, and see empty seats. Many empty seats. My heart feels like it falls through my belly to my bowels. I am used to sold-out shows. That's how it was for album one, and album two. This place, dude? It's maybe half full. *Maybe*.

I try to focus on the people who *are* here, rather than all the thousands who haven't bothered to come to see me again, and give the best damn show of my life.

LATER, WHEN IT'S all over and no one has had the *cojones* to tell me the bad news I already know, Frank sits with me at a small, dark restaurant called Fate, in downtown Phoenix, sharing some fried tofu at two in the morning. I'm drained. The crowd was not only smaller than usual, but not as receptive as I'm accustomed to. The rejection of my public was more painful than any romantic breakup I've ever been through. I feel like dying.

"It wasn't what we expected," he tells me, stating the *pinche* obvious.

"No shit," I say. "Who dropped the ball here? Where was the promotion, man? I swear, Wagner fucked up this time."

He studies my face and takes a deep breath. "Cuicatl, listen to me. They put more into promoting this than the others. We had the MTV special, the radio blitz, we had T-Mobile with the whole cell phone promotion, everything. But . . ." He pauses and looks like he doesn't want to finish his sentence.

"But *what*?"

He looks down a moment, and tells me in a soft voice, "But control groups are coming back saying the new material is too inaccessible."

"What the fuck does that mean?" I rage. " 'Too inaccessible'? Speak clearly, Frank. What are you saying?"

He places a hand over my own and squints for a moment, as if the panic and pain I feel right now were his own. The echo of my own words rings in my ears, and I realize how bratty I've sounded. I'm taking it out on him, and it isn't fair.

He takes a deep breath, and says, "It means that even though you and I know you drew on Bartók and Ravel, even though I love the whole tone-poem take you did with the new record, and the fact that you used seven languages in your lead single, it's too much for the public to understand. It's the best music you've ever written, and that's the problem. It reminds me of Amel Larrieux. She is almost too good now. Her pop start is what the company wants, but she's moved on. It's like that."

I stare at the tabletop and swallow my food. "Are you telling me I got too good to be popular?" I ask him.

"No. I'm not saying that. You sold almost ten thousand tickets tonight. You're still popular. You're just maybe not as popular as you were before. Because people in this culture like brand names to be reliable."

"Ten thousand? That's nothing," I whine. I glare at him. "Brand names? Is that what I am now?"

"In a way, yes. People go to McDonald's, they know what they're going to get. They go to Crate and fucking Barrel, they know what they'll get. They buy a book by Dean Koontz, they know what they'll get. It's like that with music, too."

"That's fucked."

He shrugs and nods at the same time. "That may be, but it's capitalism. That's how it works, I'm afraid."

"So I'm just supposed to make the same record over and over?"

"Not necessarily. Look, try not to get upset."

"Yeah, okay, my career is over, but I can't get upset."

"It's not over."

"Fuck!" I feel like a failure. I am humiliated by my own expectations, by the way I feel disappointed. I have never wanted to become attached to success, in the event it went away. I always told myself I didn't need it, but I know right now, as the dread sets in, that I do. "I should have known this. I should have done better than that."

"It'll be okay. I just wanted you to know that Wagner's not thrilled with advance sales so far."

"Wagner doesn't have feelings," I say. "Corporations aren't people."

"I realize that. I should have said the executives at Wagner."

I stare at the top of the table and try not to cry. "It's the same everywhere?" I ask.

"It's the same. The tour, the album, even radio play is petering out. The new single isn't even in the Hot One Hundred. I'm sorry."

"Fuck. What the fuck?"

He looks at me with compassion. "People just don't like the new stuff as much as they liked the old," he says. "Sometimes that happens when you take a big chance and do something new. Sometimes you stumble. But I know you, Cuicatl. You won't fall. You never do."

I am not convinced he's right.

usnavys

Mama Got Herself a Present, *M'ija*

This is *not* me in the picture, okay? I look better than that girl right there, even though we're about the same size. I think she forgot how to smile, *nena,* but whatever. Anyway, that's not the point.

The point of today's post is to let all my *comadres* of a certain girth and whatnot and whathaveyou know about a site that sells mad-fresh lingerie for us *mujerones.* I'm married now, as you know, and I got me a little baby girl, and after a lifetime of having more than one iron in the fire—if you know what I mean—I'm finding it a little hard to settle down. So I bring in props and we act things out—or I do, anyway. Juan's a little shy, but what the heck do you expect?

It's called Big Gals Lingerie, and even though I hate that word, "gals," because it makes me think of Elly May Clampett and that stupid-ass show with the Jethro guy who's all stupid as a lamppost, it's a good place to go if you're looking to spice things up.

I been spending up a storm over there. Juan's not complaining, though, and you know the boy's a cheapskate.

In the first chapter of *Dirty Girls on Top,* I'm wearing a full body stocking, black, all up and down my many wonderful curves, and there's a certain man who can't keep his paws off me.

Just remember: Big women are sexier than small women. Latinos know that. Now it's time for everyone else to figure that shit out.

Catch you later.

M'ija, I don't know what is wrong with these suburban homebody women, okay? They stare at me whenever I show up at the front door of the preschool class, to pick up my daughter, Carolina, from her French-language immersion day school, all amazed and shit, like they've never been witness to a plus-sized woman of grace and style. I don't have time for their Pilates-gossip nonsense and whatnot today, because after I get Carolina home to her dad, I'm going over to Sara's to check if that crazy woman is alive. Then I'm meeting Lauren to tell her all about how I cheated on my man, because even though you know how I am, all independent and tired of Juan's mess, I feel like I should have told somebody so I don't choke on the secret like a cat on a chicken bone. Why pick Lauren, you ask? Because she's the least normal and together of my friends, and so I think she has the least room to judge me. She's also my best friend. And I'm also going to tell her I've already packed my bags for that trip to Montreal with Marcus. I am going to ask her to be my alibi to Juan. I already told him she wants me to go up to Canada with her on some assignment because she doesn't feel safe in Montreal on her own, and, thanks to my Haitian neighbors growing up, I've got a little bit of French skills to lay down. Juan's all, "She's scared of Montreal? That's stupid," and I was, like, "That's Lauren for you."

I lean into my hip in the bright white hallway of the school, and try to appreciate all the crayon drawings and yarny art things taped to the walls. It smells like some low-rent Pine-Sol or something. You know what I'm talking about. That cleaner you get in the ghetto market, with a teddy bear on the label, that's 80 percent water and the rest is purple formaldehyde from China or some shit. Me? I like the crisp cleaners from Williams-Sonoma that smell like grapefruits.

We're waiting five minutes until the children are released to us, and every mom here is all busy sizing up every other mom here. You think we outgrow this in high school, girlfriend? *Hell* no. Women are evil to one another for our entire life spans. I bet we get to the retirement home, shuffling around with walkers, and we're still checking out each other's asses to see how we measure up. That's some stupid nonsense. You just stare at those other women and wonder if they have sex with their husbands anymore, or if they got mad stretch marks under their yoga pants. You wonder, it's human nature. But this Chinese formaldehyde smell ain't natural, I am telling you that right now. You think they'd use them some nicer kind of cleaner in a place like this, right, *m'ija*? But no. Cheap-ass Pine-Sol, straight up and undiluted. I mean, I like my home to smell clean, and I don't believe in those organic cleaners that don't leave a fresh scent, okay? But this is too much. My kid's school smells like a damn dog pound.

Speaking of dogs. I *worked* like a dog all morning, catching up on things for my job as the director of public relations for the United Way of Massachusetts Bay, dragging my ass to hell and back in that corner office and loving every minute of it. It's two in the afternoon, the hour when the carriage becomes a pumpkin again. For the rest of the day, I will be a mom to a tomboy, with all the stress that represents. I work extra-long hours on Fridays and "telecommute" (read: pretend to work from home) so I can have Wednesday off to pretend to be a real woman. I always come prepared with a white paper sack from our favorite *panadería*, full of sweet empanadas filled with apricot jam and smothered with powdered sugar. It's our Wednesday ritual, me and Carolina, to eat these on the way home. I want her to have positive associations with school.

Juan uses this time to do the grocery shopping, which just makes a pain in my ass, okay? I want to do the shopping, and it isn't just because I hate the way he conveniently forgets my Pepperidge Farm Mint Milano cookies every week. It's because I have the uterus.

I use my slick new phone to send Lauren a text message asking her to come by the house tonight for dinner. I don't have the patience to have a whole phone conversation with her crazy ass right now. She is a woman who takes a lot of energy, and I'm preserving myself for *la loca de* Sara. *Dios mío,* but what is happening to us?

I look up just in time to see the Hot Dad coming toward us in his baby blue doctor's scrubs, Top-Siders, and his trendy glasses and goatee, his slick hair back in a ponytail. Normally I don't like me some men with long hair, okay? But this one? He's got it goin' *on.* I noticed him right away the first time I saw him. I think he's from India. Maybe Pakistan. One of them countries where people are dark with fine features and that straight, shiny black hair that smells like curry sauce in the sun. He's got an angular face like a handsome shoebox, with these big, dark eyes that look like he wears mascara, only he doesn't look *joto* or nothing like that, is what I'm saying. Anything. He's all man.

I stand up straighter and flip my straightened hair back, taking time to twirl one long strand of it around my pointer finger. Don't ask me why, but men go crazy for that shit. Hair twirling. Please, *m'ija.* Whatever, you know? They think it means you're into them. They think this because all the men's magazines tell them that's what women do when they like someone. Maybe other women, but not me, *m'ija.* If I like me a man, I go for it. I get his number, I track his ass down, and I make him mine. That's all. But I know enough about the rules of the game to know how to play it in the way they expect me to. So I twirl and try to remember his damn name. He's a doctor, but I can't remember his last name right now. He looks at me and I smile and bat my lashes all Bambi at him.

"Hello, doctor," I purr. "You look very substantial today."

He looks at me curiously. "Usnavys. Good to see you."

I take some business cards for my blog out and hand them around to the other moms. I hand one to the doctor, too. He looks at it and seems to blush. His skin is nearly black, like licorice, so it's hard to tell.

"I didn't know you were a writer," he says.

"I dabble," I say.

"Dabble?"

"You know, dibble here, dabble there. I don't write so much as I educate, *m'ijo*. Okay?"

"Ah." He eyes the card with an amused smile that has nothing condescending about it. "An educator."

I turn away from him now, disinterested and haughty. It's best to cut them off when they least expect it, and to leave a little mystery for them to unravel in their big old man-hands. Men like to fix things, right? *Listen* to me. They like your shit to be *difficult, m'ija*. A man tells you he likes things easy, he's lying, *¿oíste?* Difficult. *That's* what they like. Especially these educated, smart ones. If you make it too easy for them, they lose interest and go off in search of another challenge. Here's the secret: Keep them wanting, *m'ija*. Keep them wanting and keep them on their toes, bobbing and weaving, dodging like that fine-ass boy Oscar De La Hoya. *That's* the key.

Mira, you ever see that *Dog Whisperer* show? Well, yeah. I watch it, but not for dog tips, okay? I watch that little bowlegged Cesar Millan whisper to dogs and whatnot because the same tricks you use to fool dogs into doing what you want them to do can translate over into men. Make them beg, *m'ija*. Make them want to *please* you. You stay one step ahead, in charge and in control, and just watch them fall in line. I'm telling you. The shit works, okay? It works. A man don't want nothing more than to be made calm-submissive in your presence, his nervous eyes focused on your every move, taking his cues from your lack of excitement about him, and your lack of eye contact.

I look around this school and sigh. It gives me the creeps, *chica*. So, you might ask, why did Juan and I pick a day school for Carolina that was so chock-full of white folks? That's easy. I did my research and found out that children who went to this particular school tended to be the same children who got accepted to the top private elementary schools in the area. And children who attend the top elementary schools in the area tend to go on to the top prep schools, like Milton Academy or Andover. And, as we know, kids who go to the top prep schools tend to be the ones who get into Ivy League universities. And those are the damn people who go on to rule the world, *m'ija*. I intend for Carolina to rule the world. That's what I'm saying. This crazy preschool is step one.

The door to the room opens, and we all go inside. The children are still playing around the room, with paints and blocks and that kind of thing, and some of them are on the little playground accessible through a back door in the classroom. I look around the room. Carolina isn't here. Of course not. Given the choice of playing dolls or drawing pictures like a little lady, or going outside and peeling the bark off a tree with her teeth, my daughter will invariably choose the latter. It's disgusting.

"Hello, Miss Clara," I say to the assistant teacher.

"Bonjour," she answers with her voice all high and stupid like Miss Julia Child's or something. *"Comment allez-vous?"* She sounds like a cartoon character trying to speak French. I almost say something about how pretentious it is for her to continue with the French on the parents. I almost remind her that ain't nobody in the world give a shit about no French anymore, but whatever. I'm not in a mood. No, wait. I'm in a mood, but it's a mood to retrieve my child and get my ass home.

I go out the back door of the classroom onto the playground and look around. I don't spot her right away. This scares me. I have this constant fear when she's out of sight that something terrible will happen to my child and no one will notice. You hear horror stories. Once, when I came to pick her up here, they couldn't find her. She was hiding in the wall. That's right. In the damn wall. She had figured out a way to remove the vent cover and crawl into the duct. No one had noticed. I don't know if I've mentioned this, but in addition to climbing trees and beating up boys, Carolina has a Neanderthal's gift for making tools out of whatever is around. Tools she uses to dismantle the world. There's something in her that craves destruction.

I hear a commotion in a corner of the playground, and spot Carolina's nappy head bobbing up and down. Her hair springs out all over her head. What happened to the pigtails I made her this morning? She destroyed them. That's what she does. She is jumping wildly, with a look of pure joy on her face, while a little blond girl next to her cries and yells at her to "stop killing Muffy."

I stride over to where the children are and investigate. Carolina appears to be stomping a light purple stuffed bear to death. She looks demonic. The bear wears a pink dress and bows on her ears, which I can only guess is the main reason my daughter hates it.

"Carolina!" I shout. "What you think you're doing, *m'ija?*"

My daughter stops jumping and looks at me, little mouth wide open, guilt all over her face. She looks like one of them kids in a movie, where they act surprised but know they're cute at the same time. Like one of them—those, sorry—kids who grows up to be anorexic and on drugs with Danny Bonaduce. She knows she got it going on, even without the girly clothes. My daughter is beautiful. And naughty. Look at her. She might not know exactly what she has done that was wrong, but my tone of voice lets her know she's in trouble. Another mother, one of the ones from the huddle, runs over to the crying child.

"Wakefield!" the woman says to the girl. "What's wrong, honey?" What the fuck kind of a name is Wakefield for a girl? A first name, *nena*. The mother is all whiny, too. How a woman can sound so weak is beyond me, *m'ija*. I can tell you this, though. Ain't no way her kid's gonna feel safe in the presence of that kind of whining. This is one of those families where the kid is in charge. Not good, okay? The child should never be in charge. You ruin children that way. Those are the kids who end up running away and living in the park with purple hair, okay? The ones who thought they were in charge and then, around the time they turned twelve or something, realized they actually weren't and decided their parents had been lazy and lying to them all these years. Those are the ones who grow up to kill squirrels and cats and open them up with pins in their fur like taxidermists. Those are the children I won't let Carolina associate with.

The woman spots her child's toy mushed up under my daughter's feet. Her lower lip trembles and she looks like she's going to cry. These people are too soft, *m'ija*. They don't know what struggle is. They don't *know*.

"Oh, my God!" whines the mother. "Muffy!"

"Get off that damn bear," I say. Carolina makes a face to let me know that even though she is going to do what I asked her to do, she doesn't like it and doesn't care.

The mother looks at me in shock and horror. Puts her hand over her chest all dramatic. "We don't *curse* in front of *children!*"

"Why the hell not?" I answer as I grab Carolina's hand to keep her from harming the bear further. "They gonna hear the words, *nena*. You think they'll never hear these words? Please. Better they learn them from us than from some street urchin. We tell Carolina that sometimes people use angry words because they're pissed off."

"Damn right," says my child.

"Oh, my God," says the weakling as she stoops to pick up Muffy. "Unbelievable."

"Your God whatever," says me. I break into a string of Spanish curse words now. "There's your language immersion, okay?" I tell her. "Give that child some words she can use in the real world, okay? Now if you'll excuse me."

The doctor walks past with his incredibly skinny little boy in the high-water brown jeans and gray top, and smiles at me. Approvingly. He approves. I like him. I ain't never been with a man from India, *m'ija*. It might be interesting.

"E-mail is on the blog," I remind him.

He holds the card up. "Yeah," he says. "Right. The educational blog."

"What's a blog, Daddy?" asks his skinny little boy. That boy walks all on his toes like some kind of geek. You kind of hope he beefs up eventually, because it would be sad to go through adult life that narrow and mismatched, on your tiptoes.

The Muffy Bear Mom squints her eyes at me as if I were the most disgusting human being on the planet. *Y qué me importa.* Please. Like I care. She turns to her child, her voice as shaky as her lower lip, all ready to cry and shit. Puh-lease. "Come on, Wakefield. Let's get out of here."

She marches off, all offended. I don't care. Sometimes I think I should just take Carolina out of this school and put her in public school where the immigrant children are polite and well-dressed and ready to learn because their parents understand what it is to struggle and they teach their kids what it means to work hard and succeed in spite of the trials and tribulations. But I won't put her in public school if I can help it. We need to stick it out until we take over all the shiny institutions, *m'ija*. That's my motto. Get yourself greased up, insinuate yourself into their world until they get so uncomfortable they either move on or start to play by your rules.

"Come on," I tell Carolina in Spanish. *Loud* Spanish, too, okay? "Let's go home. This place is making me *tired*."

I turn and take a delicate, powerful step in my heels. I like the solid sound of my feet on the ground. Carolina steps along after me.

Step one, m'ija.

You just watch, okay? In thirty years, we'll be *running* this school. And when we do? Mmm-hmm. You can bet it ain't gonna be in no *French*. It's gonna be in *Spanish*. A language people actually *use*.

WE GET HOME and Carolina immediately runs to the kitchen in search of her father. She finds him there, wearing his Levi's and that Chairman Mao commie star T-shirt he thinks is funny, unloading groceries from the stinky food co-op. His glasses are dirty, as usual, and his hair's a mess like he's been out in the wind. But his smile is new. He looks real happy, girl. I mean *bién pero bién feliz*, okay?

"Hey, kiddo," he says, and he lifts our daughter up and twirls her around until she laughs. "How was your day, Caro?"

"Good, Daddy! I killed Wakefield's stupid ballerina teddy bear."

"Good for you," he says, then gives me a look that I take to mean "What the hell is this kid talking about?"

"I'll explain later," I tell him.

He dances over, humming. "Hey, *mamita*," he says, coming in like a predator to give me a kiss. I give him my cheek. He comes around to my lips and forces a kiss on them anyway. "Can't get away from me," he says, joking. "No, no you can't. I'm your biggest fan, girl."

"You never know," I tell him. "I might get away yet. Did you remember the cookies?"

He digs through one of the wholesome brown paper bags and hands me a damn banana. "I have some good news for you," he tells me.

I stare at the banana like it's my worst enemy. "You *better* have good news after that trick you just pulled with this *plátano*, okay?" I tell him. "I want me some *cookies*." I start looking in the cabinets for something better to snack on.

"I got a call from Paul."

"Paul, as in your old boss Paul?"

"Yeah," he says with a big old smile. He sets Carolina down at the kitchen table and tells her he's going to make her a peanut butter and apple snack.

"So, what did Paul want?" I ask Juan.

As he multitasks making a snack and putting food away, my husband tells me that his former boss is opening a new rehab center for Latino men out in Lawrence and he needs a director to oversee both it and the Boston facility.

"He wants *you*?" I ask.

"Don't act so surprised." Juan looks really proud of himself. "He wants to pay me almost double what he used to pay."

That still doesn't come close to what I make, *m'ija*, but it's something.

"So," he says. "What do you think?"

"I think you should do it if you want to," I say. I don't want him to think he's gotta work for my sake, right? I want it to be genuine, coming from him.

"But what about Carolina?" he asks.

"What *about* me?" whines our daughter.

"*M'ija*," I tell her, "why don't you go play Barbies for a little while?"

"Because I hate Barbies."

"Dollies then," I suggest.

"She hates those, too," her father reminds me. He jovially pantomimes someone ripping the head off a doll, as our charming girl has done so frequently.

"I am *aware*," I tell him. "But it doesn't hurt to keep trying to make her normal."

"Don't say that," he says. "Really. Don't."

"Why does Mommy say I'm not normal?" asks Carolina with a frown.

"She didn't mean it," Juan tells her. "Now, why don't you go to your room and play trucks for a while?"

"Yay!" she says.

"Go play trucks, then," I say. "Daddy and I have to talk." Carolina gamely gets up and goes to her room. When she's gone, I add, under my breath, "But don't blame me when you end up *mariquiqui*." I find some chocolate Goya biscuits in the pantry.

"I think I'd like to work outside the home again," says Juan. "And I hear you loud and clear about you staying home."

"I'll go down to part time," I tell Juan as I stuff a biscuit in my mouth. "I could do that."

"Is that what you want?" he asks. He comes over to me and takes my hands, biscuits and all.

"You know it is." *M'ija*, he is looking really good to me right now. Really good. Like he just sprouted him some new balls. I reach around and hold onto his *nalgas* with my hands. Maybe I won't go to Montreal after all. Maybe it's all good here at home.

"Wow," he says. "It's been a while since you did that."

"It's been a while since you wanted to work," I say.

"I work around here."

"Whatever."

He kisses me, and it's just like old times, girl. It's a real kiss, with the open mouth and the whole thing. "You think she'd notice if we went in our room for a little while?" he asks.

"Yes," I say. "Later, *m'ijo*."

"Okay."

We kiss again. I am so turned on by Juan possibly being a director of something again that I almost can't control myself.

"There's something else," he says.

"What is it, *papi*?"

"I think we should do a list, for weekends, if I'm going to be working again."

"What kind of list? Sexual positions?" I ask, sliding my hand around to the front of him.

"No," he says with a little laugh and then, as I touch him there, a little groan. "A list for chores."

I stop, cold, girl. "Chores?"

"You know, laundry and cleaning and all that."

"That's what housekeepers are for."

"I think we should save more money, Usnavys. We're not putting nearly enough away in Caro's 529."

It's like I done run up against a damn wall, girl. All that love and whatnot and what-have-you that I felt for the boy not ten seconds ago? Gone. Okay? *Gone.* I start daydreaming about walking around Montreal.

"What are you trying to say? That I won't keep house good enough? Well enough. I won't need your help."

"It's a lot of work," he tells me, like I'm not a woman. "Hard as physical stuff is getting for you lately, you'll need some help. I figure, I'm working, you're working, we split it fifty-fifty."

Oh, no, he *didn't*. I give him one of my cold stares, girl, and I tell him I am too busy to discuss this nonsense with him right now and whatnot. And then I leave the kitchen and go to my bathroom off the master bedroom so I can break something in peace. I didn't think he'd ruin it, girl. I didn't. But that's just it, right? He doesn't think I'm woman enough to take care of my own shit. He thinks I'm too fat to mop the floor. That's what it is. Damn. Girl, I'm glad I had sex with Marcus, okay? I'm *glad*. I'm glad I'm going to see him again this weekend.

I look at myself in the mirror. It's a shame that boy doesn't appreciate my great beauty. I'll have to think about this later. Right now? I have to go visit an old friend in the police department, and then I got me a delusional Cuban Jew to go rescue.

sara

AY, *DIOS MÍO*. Roberto just called to make sure I wasn't sleeping with anyone. Now that he's landed in Buenos Aires again, he wants to make sure I'm being faithful in Boston. He acts like I didn't blow him off, *chica*. I told him it would never happen again, that *we* would never happen again. I should have been clearer with him about what I meant. I meant I never wanted to see him again. Ever. He misunderstood, somehow.

You look at me now, in my office at the studio in Waltham, in my gray Boston University sweats, with the beautiful pink St. John's suit hanging on the hook on the bathroom door, brought to me by wardrobe for today's shoot, you'd think I was mature and unafraid of the world. I look like a professional, successful woman, getting ready to do her show, no? But I'm scared to death, *chica*. I am. What Pandora's box have I opened by reestablishing communication with Roberto after all this time? He wants to talk to the boys, and I won't let him. All I can say is that stress and loneliness make for big mistakes. I need to change our phone numbers, but I'm afraid that if I do, he'll hunt me down and hurt me. Love, *Dios mío*, is crazy.

I'm sitting cross-legged on the red canvas Crate and Barrel sofa in my office, flipping absently through some glossy upscale home and gardening magazines that have piled up on the rustic wooden coffee table, looking for ideas for storage in small apartments. I wonder how Elizabeth will act when she gets to work today, knowing what she does about me and Roberto. No sooner have I thought this than Usnavys barges into my office like a plus-sized tornado in a shiny shirt. I was not expecting her. I smile, in shock.

"Aha, found you," she declares. She marches over to me in a clackety-clack of heels and yanks the magazine out of my hands before hugging me. It looks like there is powdered sugar on the front of her shirt. She feels my forehead, as if checking for a fever.

"What are you doing here?" I ask. "I mean, it's nice to see you, but it's a little surprising."

"I'm making sure you're alive. I know you're crazy, but I didn't know if you were dead crazy or alive crazy."

"That's very clever," I tell her, as I remind myself to be patient with someone who thinks, however misguidedly, that she is helping me. "But I don't need you checking up on me. I'm fine, and I will remain fine."

"So you broke up with him? You sure now?" She helps herself to the loveseat.

I stare at her with more hostility than I imagined I could feel. "Yes. As a matter of fact. But I never really got back together with him, so I don't know if I even had to."

"Here's what you have to do, okay? You have to call the police and get him in jail, where his ass belongs."

"I don't know. I'm not sure it happened like that." But the truth is, I *am* sure. I just can't justify the truth with me falling into the trap of being with him again.

She sits on the sofa next to me and takes my hands in hers, searches my eyes. "Fine. Okay. Whatever, okay? Here. Look at this. I brought you something. To jog your memory."

She plops her shiny leather briefcase on the coffee table, opens it, and extracts a manila envelope. She pulls large photos out of it. At first, I think they are black-and-white autopsy photos. Then she tells me they are pictures of me, taken by the police, when I was found unconscious at my home the day

Roberto killed Vilma. Oh, and by the way, *chica*? It was no accident. I know that now. I *knew* it before, but I guess I didn't want to *believe* it.

"How did you get those?" I ask, angry and embarrassed. In the photos, I look like a corpse, all covered with blood and bruises. It's like something you'd see on a TV show late at night, an unsolved mystery.

"I have friends in the police," she says, in a way that implies these are friends she might have slept with at one point in time. "Some boys here and there."

"Well, why are you bringing those to me?"

"To remind you."

"Of what?"

"Of the fact that this"—she points to the photo—"is not love."

"I understand. I know. But I wouldn't even know how to get out of it now if I wanted to," I tell her. "He's going to find me. You know that. No matter what I do. I've cut him off, but he knows where I am. He's so possessive. He'll get me." I begin to cry.

"Not if he's more scared of you than you are of him, girl."

At that moment, we hear a knock on the door and look up to see Valentín standing in the doorway, gorgeous as ever. Usnavys gives me one of her "aha" looks as she quickly collects the photos and stashes them once more in the envelope. I dry my eyes and compose myself.

"I think the answer just walked in," she whispers with a wink.

"What are you talking about?" I whisper back.

"Am I interrupting something?" asks Valentín.

"You know what they say in Spanish, *m'ija*," she tells me. "*Un clavo saca otro clavo.*" It means "one nail replaces the other," and refers to the way carpenters get rid of troublesome rusty nails whose heads have broken off—by hammering another nail into the space on top of it. "You're not interrupting, honey," she tells Valentín. "You're just in time."

"I don't know," I mutter, wishing she hadn't called him "honey."

"Sometimes, you need a new nail to build you the house you need," she says. "Trust me on this one."

"I can come back another time," he says.

"I was just leaving," Usnavys announces to Valentín as she gets up with much flourish. "Oh, lookie at the time, I'm late. I'll leave you two alone to discuss work. And whatever else comes up."

She walks past him and eyeballs him up and down.

"Very nice," she says to me, about him, as she leaves.

"What was that?" Valentín asks me once she's gone, with a laugh in his eyes. *Ay, Dios mío*, he melts me with that look.

"That was my friend Usnavys. She means well."

"I wish *you'd* check me out like that," he says, flirting openly with me as he usually does. "How come you never do?"

I check him out, casually, jokingly. "How's that?" I ask, trying to be playful, trying not to show the horror that rose in me at the sight of the photos.

He wears nice, dark jeans, an expensive brand, black leather loafers, and some kind of striped, trendy button-down shirt that looks like the sort of thing you'd find at Urban Outfitters. He's got a diamond stud in one earlobe, and a nice, pretty face that is almost always neat and clean. Oh, did I mention he's smiling at me with the most beautiful full mouth I have ever laid eyes on? Twenty-one, *chica*. He's only *twenty-one*. I must never forget this.

"So, can I help you with something?" I try to sound all business, no play, not to reveal the unclean thoughts washing over my brain.

"Just wanted to make sure you got here okay this morning, that's all," he tells me. "You seemed a little off yesterday, a little preoccupied. So. You know."

I pick up my little white coffee cup and take a sip of the black brew. Finally, some good, strong Cuban coffee, *chica*. *Así*. That watery stuff they served out in New Mexico at the resort, all flavored with pine nuts, just didn't cut it for me, I'm afraid. I need my jolt to the central nervous system. My battery acid. My *café cubano*.

My hand trembles a little, and I hope he can't see it. This happens now, the shaking, the nerves, and it's not the caffeine. I don't know what's wrong with me, *chica*. I hate it. I try to control it but it just happens anyway. Maybe I'm getting Parkinson's. My *abuelita* always used to talk about having *un ataque de nervios*, and now I know what that is. Roberto, that's what.

"No," I say.

He takes a seat on the red loveseat opposite mine, left vacant by Usnavys, spreads his feet out wide, places his big hands on his knees. God, his skin looks young. The skin of his face has no wrinkles. It looks plump, fuzzy, and edible, like an apricot. He's got a shadow of stubble on his chin that I think makes him look very sexy.

"I found a great new Italian place, real cute and small, hardly anybody knows about it, out in Hyde Park. It's in a mini-mall, but once you're inside, it's got mad character."

"We've been through this already." Mad character? *Coño, pero* he even *talks* young.

"I know." He grins. "It's fun. I feel like going through it again."

"Valentín. Please."

He affects my accent and timbre now. "You're too young, Valentín, just a baby, blah blah blah." He's laughing at me.

"Well, you *are*."

"Age is just a number, *chula*."

Ay, Dios mío. I love the way this man calls me *"chula,"* so very Texan, so very sweet. He has a Texan accent that makes me crazy. It's not fair. I don't need or want to feel this way about a *niño*. Like I haven't had enough drama in my life? *Por favor.* I say nothing and try my hardest to seem strong.

He speaks up. "Okay. So, if you won't have lunch with me, you wanna get dinner later?"

I shake my head adamantly. "I don't think we should get dinner, either."

"You don't *think* we should. Hmm. Not *thinking* is not the same as not *doing*. You can *do* without *thinking*. You can *think* without *doing*. So. So, that's *not* a no. Awesome!" He looks happy as a school kid on the first day of summer break. "So if it's not a no, that's a yes. *Too* cool."

Slowly, hoping I won't doubt it later, I say, *"Well.* It depends on where you want to go. If you want to go to Arby's I'd have to say it's a no."

"Arby's?" He wrinkles his nose in disgust.

"Or McDonald's."

"That how it is, girl?" he asks. "You think so little of me." His cocky grin tells me he doesn't really believe I think very little of him. It tells me he knows I think the world of him. He knows. *Ay, Dios mío*, what am I going to do with this? Not good. Not good. What if Roberto finds out?

I try to seem annoyed, *oíste*. I think I fail. *"Pero,* you know. Young men don't always have the best taste in restaurants."

He doesn't answer, just looks at me as if he's getting just a wee bit tired of the whole thing with me. He gets a semi-serious look on his face that takes my breath away. There is a man in there, inside of him. And that man is deadly beautiful. *Chica*, there's something magical about men at the age of twenty-one, something of the boy, something of the man. It's the perfect age for them, physically. They are primed and ready to reproduce. *Look* at those eyes.

He says, "Anywhere you want. You pick. I pay."

"I don't know about that."

"Good. Not knowing is better than no. Right? Totally. That's still not a no. Let's say we go straight from here, after shooting."

"No. Not tonight. I have plans." It's true. I have to take the boys to a baseball game, Little League.

"Then tomorrow. Wednesday. Middle of the week, safest day of the week. You like blues?"

"Blues?" Being a mom, my first thought is *Blue's Clues*. Then I remember the other kind.

"There's a great band playing at Tobacco Road tomorrow. They got the best burgers in town, Sara. Now come on, girl. I know you like *burgers*. You're never too old for a good burger."

Live blues, a burger, and Valentín. Sounds perfect. So why do I shrug and make a face like I don't think it sounds fun at all? Because I don't deserve it, because my life is too complicated for this poor boy.

Valentín gets up and hurries to the door. "I'm leaving before you have a chance to say no." He puts his fingers in his ears as if he doesn't want to hear anything I might have to say. "La la la la la. I can't hear you. We'll take my car. 'Bye."

"No!" I shout. He stops and looks back at me.

"I'm going to pretend I didn't hear that."

"Weekdays are bad for me. I'm a single mom, remember?"

"Oh, right. But don't you have a live-in nanny?"

"I make a point of being home for my boys on weeknights to help with homework and that kind of stuff."

"So Saturday, then. It's a plan."

"I didn't say that."

"I *did*. And you haven't disagreed yet. So I am going to run away now, before you have time to shoot me down again. Saturday, at this amazing tapas place in Cambridge. I'll pick you up at your place."

Smiling to myself, I look up to see Elizabeth staggering into my office in her jeans and button-down yellow shirt, looking haggard. She should have reported to work an hour ago. She is crying. I grab a box of tissues and rush to her side.

"Liz? *Pero ¿qué te pasa?* Are you okay?" She shakes her head. I invite her into the office, which is proving so popular today. "What's going on?"

And she tells me why she's late and what is going on. "I know you've got your own stuff to deal with, Sara, but Selwyn's leaving me. She left a note this morning. I'm getting divorced. I should have called, but it's been a crazy morning, completely crazy."

The bubble of flirty Valentín warmth I was floating in pops now, and I come crashing back to my real life with a painful thump. *Ay, Dios mío, chica.* I don't know what it is about human beings that we can't just stay in one place. That we are always moving on in search of something else, something new, something better, something.

Not knowing what else to say, I get up and hug her.

Sometimes, that's the best thing. Not speaking.

"There's something else, too," she tells me, all choked up. I lead her to the sofa and we sit side by side. I hear her draw a deep breath, blow it out. She says, "I slept with Lauren. In New Mexico. While you were seeing Roberto."

Ay, Dios mío, chica. I gasp.

"Okay, *mi amor,*" I tell her as I try to think of something else to say. "Nice to know it's not just me who does stupid things."

It's the best I can come up with.

rebecca

ANDRE, CLEAN AND HANDSOME in his tailored gray suit and crisp white shirt, drives in silence, away from the women's hospital. I sit in the passenger seat of our new shiny white Range Rover, the car we bought together because it had room for children. The thought of children brings tears to my eyes. I look out at Huntington Avenue, at the people waiting for the bus, how they smile and chat as if the world were not crashing down around us. There is something horrible about the cheerful green grass and ebullient trees of the edge of a park, and I try to control the crying. How the world can go on celebrating when I am mourning is impossible to understand.

I was strong all day, as we sat in Dr. Jacobs's office going over the blood tests, talking about the miscarriage and looking over the forms from the emergency room in Houston. I dressed festively, in a yellow Talbots blouse and black slacks (best to cover any possibly leaking blood) because I did not want to have any more reason to mourn. I did not want to show weakness. I did not cry when the fertility specialist told me that there was nothing wrong with Andre. I did not so much as sniffle when he looked right at me through his bifocals, over the top of his shiny wooden desk, and told me that the deficiency lay with me.

"You have an incompetent cervix," the doctor told me. "Ordinarily, this can be treated with a procedure called a cerclage, where a small stitch is made to hold the cervix together."

"So there's hope?" I asked.

"Ordinarily. But yours is not the ordinary case. Generally, with an incompetent cervix, we see the miscarriage in the second or third trimester. With you they've happened quite early on. Tests show that this is likely because you also have a malformed uterus."

"What does that mean?" I asked.

"It means that it is quite likely that any pregnancy you have will conform to those you've already suffered. I would advise you under these circumstances to use some form of birth control to prevent future pregnancies and miscarriages."

Incompetent. Malformed. Suffered.

"I can't, I don't know," I stammered, unable to understand completely why such misfortune was mine.

I stare now at the streetlights as they flicker on, and realize evening is upon us. A light drizzle has begun to fall. The good news, the doctor told me, was that I was in perfect health otherwise, and that I should recover just fine from the miscarriage—physically anyway. He suggested I see a psychologist to cope with the mental and emotional anguish he sensed I was feeling.

"Count yourself lucky, considering that this miscarriage took place largely on a cross-country flight, that you didn't get an infection or some other complication. You are a lucky woman, Rebecca."

Lucky? I did not feel in the slightest bit lucky. Incompetent? There are many words people who know me would use to describe me, and nowhere on anyone's list would you be at risk of locating the word "incompetent." I have spent my entire life focused on becoming the single most competent person I know. I am efficient, reliable, punctual, honest, direct, diplomatic, and measured. I am not *incompetent*.

At last, as my dear, sweet, patient, and loving husband eases this enormous beast of a car to a stop at a red light, the emotional dam breaks inside of me, and the tears flow. I hear my own voice, high and small, come out in a sort of depleted whimper. I am crying. I feel my lower lip slide between my top and bottom teeth, and my knees come up to my chest. I am curled like the fetus I and my incompetent uterus could never sustain. I hear a long howl, and realize it comes from my own chest. It is the ugly, horrible sound of my heart breaking.

"I am a failure," I cry. "I can't stand it, Andre! I can't fail. I *can't*."

"Rebecca, it's all right." I feel his hand on my shoulder, and I look at him. His eyes are shiny with tears of his own, and wide with an unspoken fear. He has never seen me break, because I never have. Not to this degree. With the divorce from my first husband, Brad, there were moments of doubt and fear, but nothing that compared to now. I don't think he ever thought, until this moment, that I could fail at anything. It overwhelms me.

"It's *not* all right," I snap. "I'm incompetent, Andre! *Incompetent*. You heard the man. That's what he said."

"That is the scientific term for what's going on," he tells me. "It wasn't meant as a personal assessment of your character, Rebecca."

The light turns green, and behind us the impatient denizens of Boston begin to lay on their horns. Andre turns his attention back to the road, but leaves his warm hand on my shoulder. I want to bite it. I don't want it there. I am tired of being touched by this man, of the failures of our coupling. Sex, making love, the thing that started with such intensity and tenderness at first, has become a chore for us, and painful, every thrust a reminder that I am not really a woman after all. I am an *incompetent* woman. I am not, for all my trying and striving, for all my accomplishments and accolades, good enough for the duty God gave all women.

"I'm not good enough," I wail. "I'm a failure."

Andre's face turns quickly toward me again, concern wrinkling his brow. "Nonsense, darling," he says. "You are certainly good enough. You are not a failure. This happens to lots of people, Rebecca. There are solutions. It's not the end of the world."

"Yes, it is." I begin to rock in sobs. I want to turn away from these windows, from the way everyone can see me. I feel exposed and incompetent. "Why me? Why?"

"It will be all right, Rebecca. I promise you. Just try to get hold of yourself."

"How? How is it all right? It's easy for you to say that, there's nothing wrong with *you*. You're not *incompetent*, are you? You're not *deformed*."

"I thought we were in this together."

"But why? Why me, Andre? Why me?"

He says nothing for a moment, steering us toward our brownstone home in the South End. I hear him draw deep breath after deep breath, his way of centering himself before speaking. It is usually one of the things I love most about this man, his impeccable nature and tremendous self-control. But right now I wish he would just let go and express his anguish like a flawed human being—like me. I don't enjoy grieving alone.

"I don't know why it happened to us," he says, ignoring the fact—the scientific fact—that it is me, not us, with the problem. I am the incompetent one, not us.

"Andre, just stop it!" I shout.

He says nothing.

"Stop acting like it's okay!" I shriek at him. "Stop acting like this is a minor problem that we can solve. We can't solve the fact that I wasn't built right. We can't solve the fact that my body won't hold a baby. Oh, my God! I'm like a ship that won't float."

He remains silent as I cry. The wetness comes from my nose, disgusting. I find the tissue packet in the glove box and blow my nose. I am shaking with rage, and sadness. I look at him, the way he stares straight ahead with his jaw set. How can he be so calm in the face of this tragedy? I reach out and punch him in the arm. I do it before I realize what I've done. I have never hit anyone in my life.

"What are you doing? Rebecca, get control of yourself! Don't be ridiculous."

"I hate you!" I scream. "I hate that you don't understand how terrible this is for me."

"Of course I understand how terrible it is for you," he says. "It's terrible for both of us, Rebecca. I understand that. But there's more to life than reproducing. Look at all you've done. You're amazing."

I sock him again, my fist landing with a solid whump against the meat of his arm. He recoils from me this time, a shocked look on his face. In the five years since I've been with Andre, I have never seen him look at me like this, accusatory, shocked, disappointed, and afraid. I suddenly fear my marriage is going to fall apart because of my incompetent cervix and malformed uterus.

His voice remains calm, betrays none of the fear in his eyes. "Rebecca! Stop it. I'm trying to drive here, and you're not helping matters by slugging me."

I hit the window instead, fully intending to break it. But it does not break; rather, it stays solidly in place and instead it is my hand that feels broken. I stare at my neatly manicured nails, and notice the red polish has begun to chip on two of the fingers. Of course it has. I have become incompetent in all regards now, is that it? I am no longer in control of my own life. I begin to cry harder. I try to get a handle on myself. I try to breathe deeply and count to twenty, all of my old tricks, but the counting feels oppressive, as does the interior of this car. I want to fling the door open and run into traffic. This terrifies me. I have never felt this way in my life, and I know—I absolutely know—I must wrestle control back from this incompetent version of me who has usurped my life for the moment. Why is this happening to me? I place my forehead against the cool solidity of the glass and press, press, willing the bone of my skull to burst through my skin, horrified that I would want such a thing to happen. I will myself to stop blaming and hitting Andre because even though it feels good for the time being, I know it isn't right. It isn't his fault we can never have a child the way normal married couples have children. I know this. It isn't his fault. It's mine.

"I'm sorry," I cry in a voice so high and nasal I scarcely recognize it. "I don't know what's happening to me. I just, I just feel like I'm just falling apart."

Andre remains calm and very British. "Understandable, darling. Totally understandable. Just try to hold on to it until we get home, right? Once we're there, I promise you, you can pound on me all you wish and I'll just stand there like a scarecrow. Maybe with a pillow in front of me, if you don't mind, to protect the soft bits."

I smile in spite of the horror of the situation. "A pillow? You're so English and proper."

He smiles at me and rubs his bicep where I hit him. "Good *God*, Rebecca. It bloody *smarts*. You throw a good punch, you know that?"

"Sorry."

"No need to apologize." He hesitates, thinking about what he is about to say. This is another one of the traits I most love about him, this English ability of his to think a thing through before speaking. I hear the air get sucked in through his nostrils, and he holds it a moment before releasing it in a sigh that is the prelude to what he is about to say.

"Okay. I said earlier I know how you must be feeling, but the truth is there is no way I could know that. I don't know. I can understand and empathize with you, but the pain you feel is probably something I will never know, and I'm sorry to have presumed to know. I have always hated it when people told me they knew how I felt when the fact of the matter was they did not, and never would. So I will give you that, Rebecca. I am here, and I am hurting, too, but I do not know what it is to be you right now. I am here for you, and I love you, and I acknowledge your pain. But I can't do more than that."

I don't speak again until Andre deftly parallel parks the large car into the meager space at the end of the block, between a Mercedes and a BMW, without so much as a bump to either. *He* is competent. Perfectly fit and fertile, able to parallel park without hesitation or error. I would never have gotten the car into this space without some fight between the steering wheel and my brain. I see now that my incompetence has been there all along, permeating every facet of my behavior. It was I who refused to see it, until now.

I continue to cry pitiably, lost in my own tortured agony, weak and slouch-shouldered—as opposed to the crisp upright posture that is usually my calling card on the streets of Boston—as we walk to our house. The street is patently beautiful, with the grass and flowers and fountain on the median, and the neat flower boxes in the windows.

The street is so pretty, but none of that registers as delightful now as it once might have; now, it registers as an affront, a reminder of the thin, gaping donut of flesh I have in the place of the thick, nurturing cervix of normal women. I plod forward, this foot then the next, wondering when I will go numb and retreat from this pain into a world of efficiency and businesslike energy to move forward. I need that.

Andre cups my elbow in his large hand, steadies me on the sea of my own melancholy, leads me up the steps and through the front door to the tune of the competent tinkling of his platinum keyring.

"Here now, we're home, let it all out, darling." He leads me with a hand on the small of my back to the red velvet antique settee in the front sitting room. "Just sit here and ponder my criminality a moment," he says. "I'll be right back and ready to be your punching bag."

He leaves me there, feeling guilty and horrendous for having hit him at all. I look around the room, at the fine antiques, oil paintings, and thick Persian carpet in jewel tones. How many times I've imagined our baby crawling from Daddy to Mommy across the plush swirls and whirls of this carpet! Now it will never happen. How many times I've imagined this house filled with the sounds of a baby, and then a toddler, and then a preschooler, and a young child with an overstuffed backpack and mittens clipped to a warm winter coat. My God, why have you done this to me? Is there a God at all? It is a horrible thought, and I erase it quickly from my mind. I have been a devout Catholic all my life, and even though He is testing me now, I must not turn away from Him.

Soon, Andre returns, out of his business suit and comfortably padding in sports socks, dressed in a dark blue sweatshirt and matching pants. He carries a king-sized pillow from the bed, one with a golden and navy blue sham on it. We bought the bedding together, specially designed for us by a boutique shop on Newbury Street.

"Okay, love." He holds the pillow in front of him like an iron shield. "Let's have at it, then."

I stare at him and shake my head. My hands tremble as if they were dried leaves skittering along a gutter in a wind. Nothing I do stops the tremors, and soon they spread from my hands along my arms and into my torso, down to my thighs. I am shaking all over.

"Andre," I say. "I'm sorry I hit you."

He stands for a moment, unsure. "Does that mean you haven't immediate plans to do it again?" How I love the way he raises his eyebrows, the humor dancing in his eyes. For a nanosecond I remember the attraction I felt for him years ago, the simple, incomparable attraction I swam in, free and uninhibited, enjoying his eyes, his face, his body, his soul, for no other reason than the fact that I loved him. Since then, since trying to have a baby with aggressive determination, I had stopped seeing Andre as a man, a flirt, and I had come to see him as an extension of me, as the provider of the sperm. It got so technical and cold, so matter-of-fact, so sterile.

"Of course I won't do it again."

He lowers the pillow, and a wry grin plays across the left half of his mouth. "You're sure, are you?"

"Yes, I'm sure."

He asks if he can make me some tea, but I don't want anything. He cautiously takes a seat at my side, on the sofa, and clears his throat, his hands folded on his lap. We don't speak, and the silence is so complete that when he swallows I hear it, and cringe. I do not like to hear the goings-on inside people's throats or mouths.

After a couple of minutes he raises a hand, then his whole arm, turns toward me, reaches out and holds me, just holds me. I let him, leaning my trembling body stiffly against his at first but then, once it becomes clear that there is no pity in his gesture, relaxing into his embrace with a tenderness I thought I'd forgotten.

"You won't leave me, will you?" My voice is soft, but steady, and I can hear his sharp intake of breath at my words.

"Never. Never, Rebecca. Don't be silly." He continues to hold me, unwavering.

"But I can't give you a baby."

"I would rather have a life with just you than all the babies in the world." He pauses, and I feel his torso vibrate with a silent chuckle. "Of course, no one in his right mind would want all the babies in the world, would he? So many soiled nappies. That's not a life, now is it?"

"I know you've always wanted children. A family. And your parents! They're dying to be grandparents."

"Shh," he says. "I have all the family I've ever wanted, right here, right now. Enough of this, now. I love you. I will always love you. Like it or not, Rebecca, you are quite stuck with me, regardless of the state of your cervix."

The silence returns. We stay like that, rocking gently, for five, maybe ten minutes. Then he releases me, pulls back just a few inches from me, searches my eyes with his own, as if looking for a clue, and speaks.

"Now, I don't want you to misconstrue what I'm about to tell you, Rebecca." He pauses. "But we *could* use a surrogate."

The word echoes in my ears. Surrogate. We have never spoken it. We have not really even let the doctors discuss it in any detail with us, because of my religious beliefs, and I've always had the impression that Andre, a recent Catholic convert himself, was as spooked by the thought of it as I was. I hate the word as he says it, and yet as it echoes back to me from the empty corners of our home, I soften toward it. A surrogate would carry the baby to term, but the baby would be ours, mine and Andre's, biologically mine. It isn't my eggs that are incompetent, after all, only my cervix. Technically, I could procreate with the help of another woman's womb, but I am not sure I'd want to face God in the afterlife having done so. It's bad enough that I defied the Church by divorcing Brad to marry Andre. Jesus is forgiving, this I know, but might there only be a limited amount of forgiveness to go around? My mother certainly thinks so.

"You know I can't do that," I tell him. I resist the compulsion to make the sign of the cross for even having thought it. Andre sighs and raises his eyes toward the ceiling, blinking back his impatience with me. "It isn't allowed."

"The Church again, is it?" He sighs, frustrated.

"You know the Catholic Church opposes surrogacy."

He draws a breath, opens his mouth, and stops for a long moment before blowing the air out again. He is stopping himself from saying something. I have seen him do this many times. His calm and diplomacy are two of the most admirable things about him, yet at this moment they irritate me.

"What?" I ask. "Spit it out."

"Nothing."

"No, it's something. Tell me."

"I am thinking that as much and as deeply as I respect your beliefs and your faith, and even though I've gone through all the religious education classes and the arduous ceremonies to become a Catholic so that I could share that with you, I must be honest and let you know that I continue to think . . ."

He doesn't finish. Rather, he drops his hands into his lap, laces the fingers together, and stares at them.

"You continue to think *what*?" I demand.

He takes a deep breath through his nose, as if drawing the strength to continue. "I continue to think that the Catholic Church, while beautiful in ritual and long in history, with so very many things to love about it, does not always have the best track record when it comes to issues of fairness and justice, Rebecca. There is God, and truth, and the eternal essence of faith, and then, in my opinion, there are men, who can, at times and if not guarded, corrupt these things toward their own ends, ends that are usually political in nature as far as I can tell."

I feel my body tense away from him. "What do you mean?"

"Well, the Crusades, for one. The Inquisition, for another. Surely there were good Catholics during that time who said, 'You know what? I don't think this is what God wants us to do,' and history proved them right, Rebecca. That's all I mean. I mean that maybe the Church is not at the furthest point along in its evolution. Perhaps there is still some room for growth."

"I don't know."

"Please, Rebecca, just hear me out. The whole thing of not allowing women to be priests. Then the whole thing about the males not being able to use their bodies to their full potential, sexually, which, if you ask me, is unnatural, and so you end up with all of these sex scandals with children."

"I can't believe you're saying this to me. What does any of that have to do with our situation now?"

"Everything, Rebecca. Listen to me. The Catholic Church, if it had its way, would not have allowed us to be married. You do understand that, surely? You'd still be married to Brad if you were inflexible in your interpretation of the teachings of the Church."

"So? That's different."

"Is it?"

"Brad and I got an annulment. The Church does not acknowledge the marriage anymore, even if my mother does."

"But look at what you're saying! The shame you've endured. Needless shame."

"How can you say that?" I ask him.

"Listen to me, please. Please hear me. We broke with the Church every time we used birth control before we started trying to have a child. I don't see any reason why you shouldn't do it again, for something this important to you."

"But this enters a different realm, Andre. Science and procreation."

"Birth control is within that realm."

"But there you aren't necessarily thwarting God's will."

"That's not what the Vatican thinks."

My face reddens in humiliation. "I understand. You're right. I am a hypocrite. I should never have taken the pill."

"No! That's not what I'm saying at all! I'm saying that the Church has a misogynist streak. You know that."

"It's a matter of opinion, but yes, I can see why you might think so."

"Me and lots of other people."

"I understand. You're right."

"I'm not insisting here that we do it, all right? I am doing nothing more than presenting the case for surrogacy. I happen to believe that two or three hundred years from now, much of the thinking in the Church surrounding these issues will have changed. It will have to. They had to admit, however grudgingly, that the Earth was round. Right?"

"You might be right." I feel queasy, and exhausted. I don't know what to think anymore. My values and beliefs were one area I could count on to see myself as upstanding, but these past six years have challenged me in my relationship to my faith. I am sickened that the Church I love so much cannot be more forgiving toward women like me, and yet I know I can never leave it.

"You're okay with someone else having our baby?" I ask him, in a tone that comes across more judgmental and incriminating than I intended.

"It would be *our* child, Rebecca. How our child gets here is not the important part. It's the eighteen years that follow, as far as I can tell, that really matter."

I hear the words. They sicken me. But I know that what he says is true. I also know that parenting doesn't end after eighteen years, but now hardly seems the time to quarrel.

"But a stranger, Andre? Surely you can understand why the Church opposes it. You have your baby in the womb of a stranger. It's completely unnatural. It's not God's will."

"If it weren't God's will, would people have been able to think it up, Rebecca?"

"I don't know. The same could be said for the atomic bomb."

"That's just it. Maybe God wanted the atomic bomb, to keep us from destroying each other. God wouldn't have even allowed surrogacy to develop, would he, if he was going to oppose it? Maybe it isn't God who opposes having a child the only way one can, in our situation, maybe it's a bunch of old Italian men . . ."

"Andre!"

"I'm sorry, but that's the truth, isn't it? It's nothing but a bunch of supposedly celibate old men running about in dresses and funny hats, writing this proclamation and that, telling the women of the world what they can and cannot do, but not allowing them to have any power to have any say of their own."

I gasp. "It's sacrilege, what you're saying."

"It's common sense and you know it."

"I don't know, Andre." I am so weary.

"Who says it has to be a stranger? Surely we know someone who might be willing to help."

"That might be worse, don't you think?" I ask. "What if she didn't want to give the baby up after all? What if she felt like the mother? Or what if the baby thought of her as the mother? Or a disease! What if it turned out she had a disease, like AIDS?"

Andre rubs his temples as if to ward off a headache he seems to think I intend to give him. "I don't know. I've only just now begun to think of it. I suppose the only requirement would be that she be healthy and mentally sound. Surely there are tests for all of that."

"My God."

"I know, darling. Don't worry about it now. I should not have brought it up now."

"No, no, that's okay. It's okay. I might do it, if it's the only way," I tell him. My voice is small, weak, nearly as incompetent as my cervix.

"It appears to be."

"Then we might have to use a surrogate," I say, hardly able to believe my own voice has formed this sentence.

"We don't have to, Rebecca. I respect your faith. Our faith. I will let you make this call."

Andre smiles at me, with a glistening residue of sadness around the eyes, and takes my chilly, trembling, nearly brittle hands in his warm, soft ones. He holds them, as if wrapping them in prayer, allowing the warmth and calm from his own body to radiate over into mine. His warmth is divine, and even though sex is the last thing on my wounded and healing body's mind, I want to dissolve into him, to be at one with his strength and peace.

He looks into my eyes, and I feel the old Andre returning to me. It has been so long since he looked at me like this, completely open. He holds my hands for maybe five full minutes, just looking at me, holds me until I am warm, rubs my hands until they stop shaking.

Then, one at a time, like a gentleman, he kisses them and sets them back in my lap, never taking his eyes off mine.

"I would never presume to tell a woman what to do in your situation, Rebecca. Least of all you. What I *would* presume to tell you is that no matter what you decide, I love you madly, and will for the rest of my life."

Tired of fighting my own frailty, my own imperfection, I fall at last into his arms, and we remain that way for the rest of the evening, without talking, just him holding me, stroking my hair, keeping me safe and warm, until, without realizing it, we have both fallen asleep on the sofa, exhausted by the tragedy. Not the tragedy of being unable to sustain a pregnancy; rather, the tragedy that we appear to have failed, for the past two years, to understand that two married people, completely in love with one another, are a whole family, whether they have children or not.

cuicatl

I **SHOULD KNOW** better than to read the colorful non-news of *USA Today*, but it's what has been delivered to my doorstep at the hotel, and I take it. There, on the front of the Lifestyle section, is a piece about my miserable concert ticket sales and declining album sales. The article says, as if it were fact, that my waning popularity "is possibly evidence of a shift in mainstream sensibilities, away from the exotic and Hispanic, and back toward the tried and true American."

"Fuck you!" I shout at the paper. "Could it be that my new music is just too fucking weird for the public? Could that be it? Could you treat me like any other person with a pulse? Why do you have to make me your fucking spokesperson for the entire Latino world? *¡Chinga tu madre, cobarde!*"

Across the room, Frank watches me. He slept in my room last night, on the sofa, to keep me company. He thought I might have a breakdown of some kind, and so he made popcorn and we watched a Ben Stiller comedy that I liked until they had Mayan stereotypes in it. He held me a little during the movie, just a friendly kind of fatherly hug. I wanted more. But I held back. It didn't seem like the time to bring it up. I have to deal with my own shit before I can pull him into it with me. It's only fair.

Frank doesn't say a word now, as the tears flow from my eyes. He walks over to me in his jeans and T-shirt, rumpled and sleepy, and takes the paper from my shaking hands. He throws it in the trash after looking at it.

"They are wrong," he says. "You have to know that."

At that moment, his cell phone chimes with a Los Lobos song. He answers it, gives me a concerned look, and takes the call outside. I use the chance to change from my shorts and tank top into jeans and a T-shirt, too. We're flying to Las Vegas today, for my show tonight.

Frank returns with a grim look on his face. He asks me if I'm packed. I am. "Then let's go," he says. "The car's waiting to take us to the airport."

When we get to the airport, Frank directs the driver to the international terminal. "Homes," I say, "last I checked, Vegas was in the United States." *USA Today* might not agree, given that the city has a Spanish name.

"We're not going to Las Vegas," he says as he opens the door to get out. I follow him into the sun.

"What do you mean we're not going to Las Vegas? I have a show there tonight."

Frank hoists my bag over his shoulder and gives me a sad look. "No, Cuicatl. You don't. They called this morning to say it was canceled."

"What? Why?" I feel like I'm going to fall over. This is too much. Too much for one day. This can't be happening.

"They didn't sell enough tickets, and now, thanks to all the bullshit from people like Dobbs about immigration, you've got the Minutemen and all those stupid motherfuckers up there picketing and making a scene, saying you should go back to Mexico."

"Fuck them!" I cry. "I'm from San Diego!" What is *wrong* with this fucking country?

He comes to hold me, and kisses me on the cheek. "*Cálmate, chica,*" he says. "Listen. I thought about it, about what they're saying. Maybe they're right."

"What?"

"Maybe those confused, ignorant, hateful sons of bitches are right."

"I don't understand."

"We're going to Mexico," he tells me. "Right now."

"Right now?"

He looks at his watch. "In an hour, actually."

"Why?"

"Because," he says sagely. "Before there was Mexico City, there was Tenochtitlan. And before there was Cuicatl the superstar, there was Cuicatl the woman."

"I don't understand."

"You can't let them take your history," he says, holding up one finger. "And you can't let them take your soul." He holds up another. "That's what I mean. I don't care how comfortable the American bigots are getting. We're going to Mexico so we can both remember what's truly important in life."

EARLY IN THE AFTERNOON, we land in the dense pink smog of Mexico City, a city that seems to stretch on forever out the window—the second-biggest city in the world. The airport is a crazy mess of people, and I try to duck their attention beneath my sunglasses and scarf. Frank stands between them and me, and pulls me through without incident. He rents a Japanese hybrid car from a vendor near the airport and drives us expertly through the crowded, polluted, almost unfathomably huge city, stopping at important ancient sites along the way, describing them to me from memory. I feel completely safe and completely taken care of with him. He has studied the history of our people, and he's been here many times. He knows exactly where to go, and what to say. He tells me about the Mixtecs, the Nahuats, the Mayans, and the Toltecs. And I stare out the window at a gigantic, swarming world of nineteen million people, a world that knows and cares little about my life as a pop star. It is very comforting, actually.

Frank finds a public parking lot and hands the attendant a wad of cash. He tells me we're going to walk across the plaza to the Zócalo.

"What if people recognize me?" I ask.

"So what if they do? No different here than in L.A."

We get out, and I follow Frank through the crowded streets, two blocks to the edge of the gigantic Plaza de la Constitución. It is a dreary-looking place of gray cement, and reminds me of all those scenes of protests in East Germany before the wall fell, except that here the gray is broken up with the bright colors of the vendors selling their food and drink and trinkets.

"Where we walk, this was Aztec ground," Frank tells me. High above my head, a massive Mexican flag waves in the breeze. The air is filthy, like Los Angeles but a million times worse. He stops beneath the flag, and we look around. "This," he tells me, "is the third-largest public square in the world."

"Wow," I say. It's a stupid thing to say, I know that. But there is nothing else to say. I want to drop to my knees in honor of my ancestors. I want to cry.

"Tenochtitlan was huge," he tells me, as we continue walking toward the enormous cathedral. "This is where it used to be, right here. When the Europeans got here, before they built any of this, there were two hundred thousand people living here already. There weren't many cities that size anywhere in the world yet."

I look out at the undulating crowds of people, and I get chills. Mexico. Here they are, millions upon millions of human beings, almost all of them living with much less than I have, and we are all united. My history lies here, maybe also my future.

We return to the car without speaking, just experiencing the majesty and importance of this place. Back in the car at last, Frank drives through the city, slowly, telling me more. "It was multiethnic, and multicultural, even before the Spaniards got here. There were many different kinds of people living here. They had fresh water. They were meticulous, too, bathing twice a day. There were four zones in the city, and every zone had about twenty districts. They called these districts *calpulli*. They had huge streets, and each district specialized in some kind of craftmaking or arts. The Spaniards were shocked to see all of this. They'd never seen anything this sophisticated or gigantic. They didn't know what to make of it, Cuicatl. Just like they don't know what to make of you now. We scared them then, we scare them now. And through it all, we endure. We *endure*."

I stare out and feel my breath slowing down. I feel my hands relax as I make contact on the spiritual plain with my ancestors. Frank's face is set in a powerful repose. I am floored, man. Chilled.

He goes on. "There was trading that went on here every day, tens of thousands of people. The Spanish who came here could only compare it to Sevilla, and they said it was twice as big. We Mexicans had had indoor toilets and garbage collectors long before Europe. We had a sewage system where we sold human waste for fertilizer: the first recycling program. This was long before Wagner Records or rock and roll. Before your hits and misses. Before almost everything."

Frank continues to drive, and eventually, we end up parked twenty-five miles away from Mexico City, in the humidity of Teotihuacan, at the site of one of the world's most impressive pyramids and ancient cities. We walk to the base of a giant pyramid. The noise of the city is gone. Everything seems to be covered in a growing moss. I can hear the colorful tropical birds in the trees.

There are a few people here, but not many. Frank begins to climb the largest pyramid with me, and, after stopping to tell me it is called the Pyramid of the Sun, he climbs silently. He doesn't need to say a word. With every step on the ancient gray stones, I feel myself transcending my own selfishness and shallowness. I connect with each step to a world much larger than before. There is so much more to the world than me. There is so much more than CNN and Lou Dobbs, so much history that is not American. There are so many tens of thousands of years that my people lived and prospered without the biases and prejudices of my current nation. There is music, and music is eternal, whether people buy it or not. I have earned enough in the past few years to live off of for the next thirty. I do not have the worries of most of the people in Mexico, in the postcolonial world that has tried, and failed, to rob us of our past. How can you rob us of the proof of the pyramids? How can you rob us of the brown of our skin?

We get to the top, sweaty and tired. Frank sits on a step, and I sit next to him. Quietly, we link hands and gaze out over this place.

"Tell me about it," I say.

He points to what looks like the main road through the pyramids and ruins. "That was called Avenue of the Dead. It used to go all the way to those mountains back there. All the pyramids you see here were designed with astronomy in mind. They were aligned just so, with the planets and the stars."

He goes on, telling me of the Olmecs who likely built the city, of the different names the Mayans had for the place, of the confusion among scholars about the Toltec impact on the city because the word "Toltec" to the Aztecs meant "great craftsmen," and didn't necessarily mean the people of the same name.

"But what about the human sacrifice?" I ask him.

"Ah," he says. "Did you know that every civilization, in its early stages, has practiced human sacrifice?"

I did not know. Frank tells me, "In Genesis 22, God asks Abraham to sacrifice his son Isaac on Mount Moriah. The Japanese did it, the Chinese. Everywhere in the world, at some point in history, people did barbaric things to one another."

"*Chinga,*" I say. There is so much to learn. I sit, listening to Frank talk about the different cultures of the world, and the various ways they invented to kill people in order to appease God.

"The ancient Phoenicians sacrificed babies," he tells me. "The Druids in what is now Ireland did it like crazy. The Vikings, even the Hindi." He talks of the Hebrew Bible mentioning the same sort of thing, with babies cooked on hot stones to appease the gods.

"That's fucked up," I say.

"It's the eternal risk of magical thinking," he tells me. "One of many risks of magical thinking, actually. Anyway, what's worse? Ritual sacrifice of a few people to the gods, or Bush's 'collateral damage' of nearly a million murdered Iraqi civilians in the name of oil?"

He grins at me, those lines radiating from his eyes like rays of the now-setting sun. "Think about what it means, Cuicatl. It means that by and large, most people around the world have been stupid and gullible. Most people are followers." He looks at me as if this concludes something about me.

"What do you mean?"

"You can't take anything the public does all that seriously. You can't let the tastes and behaviors of a time influence how you see yourself, or how you create art, or what you do."

I think about this. He puts an arm around me, and pulls me closer. I bury my head in his chest for a moment, and then I grab him and kiss him lightly on the lips. He seems too surprised to kiss me back. It is our first kiss.

"I love you," I tell him.

"I love you, too," he says, uncertainly.

"No, I mean I love you. Like I *want* you, Frank. The way a woman wants a man. I have these feelings for you. I've been wanting to tell you, I just didn't know how."

He looks at me a good, long moment, and then his face erupts in a huge smile. "Really?"

"Yes, really! Please, I'm not going to make something like that up."

"*You* want *me*?" He seems like he can't believe it.

"Yes. I do."

"Thank God," he says, suddenly relaxing. He adds, with a grin, "Any god."

"What do you mean?"

He kisses me this time, softly at first, and then with a little more passion. When he stops, he laughs to himself and shakes his head. "Do you know how long I've wanted you, Cuicatl? Jesus H. Christ. You are the most compelling, sexy woman in the world."

I pretend to slug him. "You never said anything."

"We work together."

"So?"

"It wouldn't be right."

"Frank! You never, I mean, I would never have guessed. You could have made this a little easier, you know. It was hard to tell you!"

"It didn't feel like the right thing for me to bring up. I thought it would be better to wait and see if you felt it. It didn't seem, I don't know . . . Professional, I guess. I'm such an old man, you know? I didn't think, you know . . . You have all these young studs after you."

"But they don't know me," I say. "Not like you do."

He says nothing, just looks into my eyes with that relieved smile that threatens to turn into an all-out laugh again.

"Come here," I say. I pull him close again, and it feels so right. We continue to make out, like teenagers, on top of the Pyramid of the Sun, as the sun goes down. The air is chilly and dark when we stop, and he whispers.

"In the United States, they practice ritualistic sacrifice, too. They do it with celebrity. The American media likes nothing better than to build someone up to godlike status, only to kill them for the collective catharsis of the self-loathing masses. Britney Spears, her heart upon the platter, her life taken from her for our salacious needs."

I stare at him, in shock. He's fucking right.

He's always fucking right.

"This is why I love you," I tell him. "You make me think in ways I never thought before."

He kisses me lightly, and says, "The danger comes when a celebrity allows himself or herself to believe the good things the press says about them before they are led to slaughter. If you don't believe your own hype, if you never allow yourself to look at your own life through their barbaric eyes, then you can never be destroyed."

He kisses me again, gently. I am overwhelmed with love, and happiness, and peace. We are the last ones here. And as a nearly complete darkness falls over us, we remove our clothes, and just like our ancestors before us, we make love at the top of the world.

lauren

I **SIT AT** the granite breakfast bar in Usnavys's cozy upstairs kitchen, in her Victorian house in Mission Hill, listening to the new ice maker in her stainless steel refrigerator plop through its duties. I try to wrap my brain around the fact that my friend wants me to *lie* to her sweet husband for her so she can have an affair with an idiot. Juan is having a late dinner with a potential boss, and Carolina has been bathed and put to bed in a set of blue Batman footie pajamas that made Usnavys cry. And now, after what seemed like an hour where the little girl kept finding any excuse to get up and join us here, the child seems to be snoozing for good.

"Could she just once wear the pink nightgowns I bought her?" my friend asks me, dabbing her eyes with a paper napkin. She's wearing her own pink nightgown, with a matching chenille robe and slippers. She looks like a round cupcake with a Dominican salon blowout. I feel overdressed in my work clothes, a navy skirt from Barami that I've had for years and which was the only clean thing I could find, and a rumpled beige blouse that has sweat stains in the pits and smells like a dead dog. Why I can't look and smell like a normal working woman, I have no idea. I try, but the clothes don't try *back.*

On the counter by the refrigerator, the stainless steel Cuisinart coffeemaker issues a soothing burble to let us know the Bustelo is finished percolating. Usnavys waddles over to prepare two large white mugs of it. I ask for mine with nonfat milk, but she doesn't have such a thing in her home and, in fact, seems offended at the *thought.*

"I have cream or half-and-half," she says, as if these were fighting words.

I take my coffee black, and watch her dump what seems like half the carton of the cream into her own before stirring in four spoonfuls of sugar.

"I think Carolina looked cute in the Batman," I say. This does not please Usnavys. She gives me the death glare.

"Cute? She looks like a *marica* in training, that's what she looks like. Those pajamas have a weenie hole in the front. A weenie hole, Lauren."

"Cut the kid some slack. *Damn*," I say. "They're just pajamas."

"First it's the pajamas, then she's dating Angelina Jolie."

"That wouldn't be the worst thing in the world," I offer with a shrug. "Lots of grandchildren."

Usnavys resumes her seat. A large box from the corner Dunkin' Donuts sits open on the table. I had two and feel torn. Part of me wants to barf already, but part of me wants to eat a few more first. Usnavys grabs her fourth.

"I had no idea it was so much work getting a kid to go to sleep," I tell her. I don't really want to talk about Carolina, but it beats having to tell Usnavys I don't want to be her fall guy.

"Me neither. Usually, Juan does it."

"Must be nice, having a hubby who takes on so much." I cringe at how clumsy I've been in defense of Juan.

"No," she says. "That's just *it*. That's why I'm going to Canada, Lauren. That's just what I wanted to talk to you about. It's *not* nice that he does everything around here. It makes me feel like less of a woman."

"Well, that's just silly," I tell her. "You're all woman, and everyone knows it."

She shakes her head. "Listen to me. You know how they have that word for when you make a man all faggy? Emasculate? Well, why don't they have a word like that for when the man wears your damn ovaries around his neck like dog tags?"

I cringe at her use of the word "faggy," but, like so many things about the woman who I consider to be my best friend, I let it go. "How about defeminize?"

"How about he did it to me, and now it looks like he's doing it to Carolina, too?"

"That's not fair," I say. "Caro's fine."

"Please," she complains through a mouthful of powdered sugar and cake. Crumbs fall onto the front of her robe, but she doesn't notice. "My girl-child makes them idiots that wrestle crocodiles look pussy."

"Maybe you should talk to him about how you feel, before you go to Montreal."

Now she tells me that whenever she tries to talk, all they do is fight. "He's bitchy, *m'ija*." She takes a chocolate glazed from the box next, and turns it around and around in her hands as if looking for the best place to sink her teeth in for the first bite. "Plus, Montreal is all about the nookie, too, okay?"

"Marcus was good, eh?" I ask. I feel terrible asking, because I think of Juan as a friend. But Usnavys comes first and, let's face it—good nookie is always worth discussing.

"*So* good."

"Details," I demand, and she gives them.

Mostly, it comes across that he does what she tells him to do, which, I think, is counter to her whole wanting-to-be-a-wifey-at-home thing, but I don't want to argue with her. There is no one in the world you are more likely to lose an argument with than Usnavys Rivera, because she will never concede to your point, even when she knows you're right.

"I'm glad you like him. I am. But do you have to use me as your alibi?" I ask, wincing as I grab another cruller. "I don't really want to, I mean, I'm no good at lying. I'm really not."

Again with the death glare.

"But I will," I continue, afraid of her now. "If you really want me to."

"I'd do it for you," she says. "God knows I've done a lot for you."

I sip my coffee, and wonder if now would be a good time to tell her about sleeping with Elizabeth. I need to tell *someone*. It's bothering me how I don't think we can be friends anymore, and how I never imagined I'd actually have an orgasm with a woman, and how I don't know if this means I'm gay now. I feel disgusted by it all, but mostly with myself.

Usnavys changes the subject for me, frowning. "I miss me some men, Lauren. I do. I just don't think I was cut out for this whole monogamy thing, not like this. Not the way it's turned out. I didn't think marriage would be like this."

"What did you think it'd be like?" I try not to obsess about the purging, but I feel so fat now. I need the relief of the vomit.

"I don't know. I thought I'd stop wanting other men. I thought I'd be happy all the time. I thought he'd get a better job and I could be a housewife."

"I don't know what to tell you, having never been married myself, and with Amaury likely to back out before we ever formalize it." What I want to tell her is to stop complaining and appreciate what she has. But you can't say that to a friend. Your job, as the friend, is to listen. That, and eat the donuts.

She points the last bite of the chocolate glazed at me. "You keep talking negative like that, it'll come true."

"But," I continue, ignoring her jab, "if I were to advise you, I'd say it's probably best that you talk it out and make a decision one way or the other. You're married, or you're not. I don't think it's all that honorable to cheat on your spouse, I don't care if you're a man or a woman, it's just wrong. And you have a child. It hurts her, too."

"Yeah," she says. She sips her coffeed cream and looks a little lost. "Thanks for listening. I had to get it off my chest."

"I'm sorry I couldn't be more help."

"No, you were good. It was good. I feel good now."

"You do?"

"Pretty good." She digs through the box for the jelly donut next. "Which leads me to ask you if you're feeling good after sleeping with Liz and getting all *lesbiana* on me."

I gasp as I sip, and end up spitting coffee into my hand. I stare at her over the top of my mug as I wipe the coffee on my leg. "How did you know about that?"

"Please, girl. We're *sucias*. We figure these things out. I saw you looking at her like a hunter, and I know that she's had the hots for you for a long time. I know you do some stupid shit sometimes, like falling in love with Amaury."

"What's wrong with Amaury?"

"Two words. Low. Life."

"He's not as bad as you think."

"Please, girl. I got me a sixth sense about things. He's *worse* than I think, okay? That's the truth. He's bad news and I don't want to be on your doorstep when the headline comes. You're better off with Elizabeth."

"I thought you hated lesbians."

"What? No. Why would you say that?"

"You're so worried Carolina's going to end up one."

"That's because she's my daughter."

"Oh," I say, sarcastically now. "So you only hate lesbians if they're your own children."

"Something like that."

"Very enlightened," I say.

"Just wait till you have kids."

I give up trying to get her to see her own hypocrisy. "Did Elizabeth tell you?"

"*Hell* no, she didn't tell me. It doesn't take a rocket scientist, *m'ija*." For the record, I have always hated that saying. I tend to find people who use it unimaginative and boring.

"So you're just pretending to be a rocket scientist?"

"What? No. But you asked me how did I know, and I'm saying. I figured it out. You did Elizabeth. How was it? Fishy?"

"God, 'Navy," I say. "Could you be more obnoxious?" I know I'm being defensive.

"No," she says.

We look at each other, the taboo topic hanging heavy in the air between us.

"So?" she asks. "Was it any good?"

"I don't know. It was okay, I guess. But I'm not gay and I don't want to do it again."

"So why did you do it in the first place, *¿'tas loca?*" she asks me, again.

"What?" I pretend not to have understood her, just to stall and buy a little time to think of an answer that isn't too lame.

"I said why did you have sex with Elizabeth when you knew you weren't gay and you knew she was in love with you? That's crazy, *chica. Eres completamente loca.*" She points the finger to the temple and turns it.

I glance around us, worried that Carolina might walk in and overhear the conversation.

"She sleeps like a log," says Usnavys, reading my mind.

"I don't know. Just do me a favor and don't go blabbing about it to everyone, okay? I don't want it out there that I'm some kind of lesbian lothario."

Usnavys cackles. "Lesbian lothario!" she shouts. "That's good. I like that."

"Shut up!"

"What?" She shrugs with her chin tucked up into her neck.

"What?" I echo in disbelief. "Like you don't know? This is embarrassing, okay? I feel like an asshole."

"Okay, and like telling you I cheated on my husband isn't embarrassing?"

"Not for you. I don't think it is."

"It is. I know you don't think I have a conscience, but I do."

"You just said you didn't regret it."

"Regret is a wasted emotion, *m'ija*. But I can feel guilty without regret, and embarrassed without regret."

"So we're both lotharios then."

"But not *lesbian* lotharios. That's *your* specialty."

"I don't want to talk about it. I really don't. Let's talk about you cheating on Juan again. I liked that better."

Having exhausted the donut supply, Usnavys gets up and roots around in the cabinets until she finds a box of Goya coconut cookies. She comes back to the table eating one. "I'll drop it, but first you have to tell me why you did poor little Elizabeth."

"I don't know, okay? I don't know." Truth be told, I *do* know. But I don't feel like sharing the fact that I was wasted and lonely and nearly suicidal and hoped that I'd develop a taste for girls so that I wouldn't end up miserable with men for the rest of my life.

Usnavys guzzles her coffee, and goes to refill it again. "Have you talked to her since?"

"Like, one on one?"

"Yes. Like one on one."

"No. She hasn't called me."

"What do you expect? You break her heart and she's the one gonna call you? I saw how devastated she was at our last dinner."

"I don't know. I'd just say, given the fact that I was the last one to talk to her, that the ball's in her court now."

"Or lack of balls."

"Yeah, okay, whatever. She *could* call."

"Have you called *her*? You should call *her*."

I shake my head no. "The whole thing is so freakin' awkward," I tell her. "I wouldn't know what to say. 'Hey, Liz, sorry I had sex with you and realized it was a huge mistake. Wanna go play racquetball?' Or maybe she'd like to go underwear shopping. That's a fun activity for two women who don't know exactly what to say or feel for each other anymore."

"You two need to fix this. I can't have *all* my *sucias* falling apart. So, you are now under orders. Fix it, *m'ija*. Or I'll fix it for you."

This, and everything else. I got some things that need fixing, for sure. I don't even pay my bills on time, even though I have the money. I seem to operate on this anticipation of everything running out. Deficit psychology or some shit. I just let the bills pile up, or worse, I hide them in drawers and forget about them until something happens like I'll come home and the electricity will be off, or the phone, or the cable, and I have to call and they're like, "You haven't paid your bill in three months," and I'm dumbfounded because I had kept telling myself there was time to get around to it, after, you know, after I sent Amaury some desperate, depressed text message, or ignored my friends.

Have I mentioned even I am getting sick of myself like this? I think it's about time I grew up. It would suck, flat suck, to get to forty and still be operating like an irresponsible yet delusionally ambitious college kid. So I sigh, rub my forehead, and tell Usnavys, in the hopes of starting a new era as Responsible Lauren: "I was drunk. Okay? *That's* why. It's a terrible excuse, but it's true. That, and I think you might be right about Amaury."

Usnavys makes a dismissive face. Like she doesn't believe my excuse *para nada*. "What else is new, *nena*? You're *always* drunk. I've resigned myself to your alcoholism. But I'm glad you're seeing the light about Amaury."

I pretend to be offended and surprised, but the truth is, she's right. There is entirely too much alcohol back in my life. I got over it for a while, then I got suspicious of Amaury and beer looked great again. Beer looked like Gael Garcia Bernal in a pair of boxers, on his back, on my bed. That's how good beer looked, girl.

"You need to lay off that shit, Lauren."

I know Usnavys means well, but I want to smack her smug face. I hate when people lecture me about what I need to do or not do. I am not an idiot. I'm well aware of what I need to do. I just don't do it. Can't they see that? I tell her, "Let me make sure I have the list of things I need to do right. I need to call Elizabeth, fix things with her, and stop drinking. Anything else?"

"Dump that lowlife before he kills you."

"Okay. Is that all?" I give her a defiant, annoyed look.

"It'd be a good start."

We hear the latch on the front door downstairs coming undone, and the door chime signaling Juan's return home. Usnavys instinctively brushes the food crumbs from her shirt front and sits up straighter.

"Guess that's it for talking about you for the night," I tell her.

"We can still talk about the lesbian lothario."

"No, thanks. Oh, unless you want to congratulate me on the good deed I did today."

"What good deed?"

"I agreed to mentor a Latino student group at one of the gifted magnet high schools." Usnavys is always getting on our cases to mentor Latino youth. "I am practically the last speaker of the school year. I am supposed to go in tomorrow to inspire them. They're supposed to be amazing, real studious and ambitious, but some of them are from troubled homes."

"Congratulations," she says, still looking nervous about Juan's arrival "Seriously. That's good. I'm glad."

Juan calls out a hello in a soft voice as he rounds the top of the stairs to the living room. "Anybody home?" He comes to her and plants a kiss on top of her head. I see him survey the donut box and the cookie container, but he says nothing. How many of us can say we have a man like that? She's stone *crazy* to let him go.

"Hey, Lauren!" he says, coming to hug me.

"Hi," I say, guilty.

"How's the coffee klatch?"

"Hi, baby," says Usnavys, on autopilot of the wifely sort. I smile like a jerk, like nothing's wrong, and feel dirty for knowing more than he does about the true state of his marriage. Usnavys asks him how it went, and he smiles, triumphant, and gives an enthusiastic thumbs-up. He is very cute, by the way. A cute, fit man who is madly in love with Usnavys, and who accepts her exactly the way she is.

"It's all good news," he says. "I got him to double my salary *again*. They got no one else in mind, and I figured I had some bargaining room. We'll talk later."

I look at her after he's gone. "Wow. That means you can stay home, girl!"

"That's some fucked-up shit right there." She looks pissed as she searches for another cookie.

"What do you *mean*? Isn't that what you've been complaining about?"

"That's right. That means I have to reconsider all the decisions I've been coming to."

"Like Montreal?" I whisper. She shoots me a "shut up" look, and I do.

"I'm having all my cell calls forwarded to your phone," she whispers back.

"What? When?"

"Montreal."

"Why?"

"If he calls, you answer and tell him I'm in the bathroom. Then you call Marcus on his cell and ask for 'Muriel,' and that's our code to tell me to call Juan."

"This is insane," I tell her.

"Let's talk about you again," she says.

"I'm sick of me. How about someone else?"

"Okay. Let's talk about your lover Elizabeth."

"I'm sick of her, too."

"Can you believe that Selwyn bitch, *m'ija*? She just left Elizabeth with a baby. A lesbian all alone with a baby. It's crazy. Terrible. *Te lo juro*, that butch bitch has nothing but bad karma coming."

I listen to the news, horror-stricken. "What?" I ask. "Selwyn's gone?" I wonder if it's my fault.

"Yep," says Usnavys. "Left a *note*. That was it."

I hear the shower starting in Usnavys's master suite, and Juan's innocent and inexpert singing. He's happy to be home. I feel so guilty—for destroying the marriages of two friends. People should avoid me.

"What kind of woman would ditch her own baby?" asks Usnavys. "What kind of woman breaks someone in two like that?"

I don't suppose now is the right time to mention that Usnavys has just spent an hour telling me she plans to do the exact same thing to Juan that Selwyn did to Elizabeth? Not knowing what else to do, I grab a cookie and complete the binge. Next: purge.

"I'll be right back," I tell her. "I just need to use the bathroom."

elizabeth

IT HAS BEEN two days since she left me. I hurt for the failure of my marriage, but more than that I hurt because I held Lauren in my arms, after all these years of loving her, tried to breathe life into her, and now she's gone, sunken once more to the bottom of the pond. I can't sleep. These two women haunt me, the conversations I had with them but never should have, the ones I should have had but never did, all of it tied together in blood-red ribbon. I can't stop playing it all over again in my mind. I am empty, not solid anymore, a thing and not a woman. Depleted. I will not cry.

It is four in the morning, and I sit on the ergonomically correct kneeling chair at the white desk in my home office, working up the courage to call Sara to tell her I need a sick day. How can I possibly go to work when I don't know where my feet are or how to make them work? How can I work if I can't get up the courage to take a simple shower? I e-mail Sara instead. No need to wake her. She'll think I want to talk, and I don't. I want to be silent for the rest of time. I drink a Snapple peach tea and eat grapes and whole wheat crackers with organic peanut butter. I force it all down. I am so mangled with loss I don't feel like eating, but I have to take care of myself, for baby Gordon's sake if nothing else. He is counting on me, and I'm all he's got. He's all I've got, too. I can't let it all unravel now.

Gordon sleeps in the white bassinet next to me, oblivious to the fact that his other mommy is gone forever. She will not share in raising him. Her choice. Her *rotten* choice. When he is grown, the only evidence he'll have that there ever was another mommy named Selwyn will be the photos of two young women in love, bringing him home. He'll want to know who she was. I don't know what I'll tell him. A social worker? The truth? I do not know. Once upon a time I believed truth was the best policy. Now I know better. Look at what happened with Lauren. It would have been infinitely better to have her friendship for the rest of my life than to have this humiliating thing we have dangling between us now, this thing that makes me resent her and makes her want to be rid of me. Truth is not always best. I want to cry, but I will not. I. Will. Not.

"We'll be all right," I whisper, more for my own benefit than his. He stirs a little, and begins to suck on his lower lip.

I turn back to the e-mail. There's a message from Lauren, saying she talked to Usnavys about what happened last weekend, apologizing for leading me on. "I really wanted to be a lesbian," she writes foolishly. "If I could be one, you'd be the only woman for me."

It's a sweet, stupid note, but painful as a fist around my trachea. She has no idea how destructive she is.

There's also a note from Usnavys, with a link to a MeetUp.com group for single parents in the Beacon Hill area. "Don't waste time, *m'ija*," she writes. "Get out there and find you some support. Have fun. Wish I could come, too. No, seriously. You do not want to know. But I'll tell you anyway. Later."

I know why. She is cheating on Juan with Marcus from the resort. It was obvious to all of us. She thinks she's smooth and hiding it, but she is not. I don't know what to think, except that I want my friends to be happy.

I check the link. Everyone who's signed up seems interesting. I follow Usnavys's advice and sign up, too. It can't hurt. I don't have family here, and I can't raise a baby on my own. It's not natural to toil under the blessed burden in solitude. I am happily surprised to see that the group's next scheduled meetup is later today. I'm going, no matter how deflated I feel. It will be something to do and will get me out of the house, something like the promise of first light, to look forward to.

I surf the Internet for news from Colombia. My heart aches for my country. There is so much bad news, hardly any good, and yet I consume it all, greedy for my past, for my identity.

I go to the Viviun site, to fantasize about moving to Latin America. Somewhere that I would not be the woman with the funny accent, where my beautiful, fluid language would be everyone's language, where people would not rush past one another with cold, angry faces, but rather sit to chat on front porches or in town squares—warm, generous, lovely.

I check on Costa Rica. Mexico, too. Homes are cheap there. I could buy in cash there if I sold this house. The only thing keeping me in Boston is

Sara, and even she's been talking about moving to California. We're all out-growing Boston, it seems. That is the fate of this giant college town. No one stays forever, do they? At least not the transplants like us. Every year, hundreds of thousands of students swell this otherwise parochial city. I am getting too old for it.

I continue to waste time online until the sun comes up. The baby stirs a little with the glow of daylight. I lean over the bassinet and watch him sleeping there, his arms and legs bent at the elbows and knees in nearly right angles. He looks like a hieroglyph of a turtle. Mexico would welcome us, wouldn't it? He is so soft, with such smooth skin and such a tight moist seal of his eyelids, one against the other, such a sweet curve to his tiny lips. I am astonished that one day he is going to be taller than me, and laugh at the jokes of his friends. Knowing that he has already lost three parents—two to AIDS and Selwyn to apathy—makes me want to drape my body across his for now and forever. I don't want him to suffer anymore. I want to protect him from the world. He did nothing to deserve the life he got.

I am still surprised that he is mine. I continue to expect someone to burst into my home and take him because they figured out I don't know what I'm doing. There are so many people who think a woman like me should not mother, people within my own nondenominational Christian faith. They are the same people who don't care about babies from Africa, usually. So I suppose we are safe from them for now, as they couldn't care less what happens to black babies.

Gordon sighs in his sleep, and his jaw vibrates with intensity as he dreams of a meal. The cuteness of him is sugary, debilitating.

"I won't let you down," I promise him in a whisper. "I might not always know what I'm doing, but I'll work harder than any other mother ever has to figure it out."

I leave him sleeping and go to my bedroom to change into jeans and a long-sleeve T-shirt, red. Done with that, I settle in with a book until he rises. An hour later, he's up, wailing. I heat the bottle of formula for him under the hot running tap, and settle into a chair in the family room with him. I love feeding this child. There is something very Woman about holding a child as he suckles. Something essential, wonderful. I realize as he eats that I am nearly out of formula.

"You ready to go to the store?" I ask him, once he's slowed down.

"Mami!" he cries, his eyes joyous, followed by something I can't understand. Some adorable mumbling thing. Dear Lord, I think, thank you for the exquisite blessing of this boy who hopes and loves, this smiling human gift. Thank you, Jesus, thank you.

I change his diaper, dress him in a white jumpsuit with doggies on it, pack him into the stroller, and out we go, into the morning gloom, a family of two, on a simple trip to the market that, from circumstance, feels like the last terrible round of a boxing match. I am a single black Latina lesbian mother of an AIDS orphan from Africa, both of us abandoned and unloved, two warm brown exiles in the middle of this cold white city, with autumn, and then winter, coming.

But I am still standing.

And as long as Gordon looks to me for peace and comfort, I will not cry.

lauren

BECAUSE I HAD to make up a lie to tell my nitwit boss, Chuck Spring, just to get out of the office for this whole youth-mentoring thing, I arrive at the red brick school building two minutes late, just after three, running from the Back Bay subway station like a woman on fire. Why I wore high, strappy sandals is beyond me. No, that is untrue. I know why I did it. Amaury likes women in heels.

Plus, I think I wanted to look young and cool, but right now, as they wobble and the heel threatens to snap off, I feel nothing but silly. Chuck almost didn't let me go, because he's got all these tickets to some World Cup playoff kinds of things that are going on in Massachusetts this summer, and he wants me to go with him and his wife for some reason. There's a game this afternoon. He keeps talking about it, and if you know Chuck, the man who makes hamsters look smart, he can never quite tell when he's gone on too long. You could literally fall asleep listening to the man, and he would not take the hint. To get him to shut up, I agreed to go to another game with him another day.

I suppose I should be pleased that the man I once regarded as my archenemy on planet Earth has actually taken to inviting me to hang out with him and his family; used to be he only did that for the white men who worked in our department. I think it represents some kind of progress, but I'm not sure. Maybe it only marks my permanent servitude.

I go directly to the main office for the pass that will allow me to roam the halls. Then, with a pain in my chest that reminds me I ought to see a doctor and find out why I keep having heart attacks even though I'm in pretty good shape and relatively young, I walk quickly to the science classroom where the Latino students have been meeting after school all year long.

I find the teacher, but it takes a moment to realize that is what he is. My first impression is that he is a model or an actor. Even though he's not all that tall—maybe five nine?—he is a dead ringer for the salsa singer Michael Stuart, buff and bald, but bald in the way of gorgeous Caribbean guys who shave their heads because they're going for a look. He wears stylish black-framed glasses that make him look super smart, and trendy jeans with a form-fitting T-shirt and nicely cut blazer. On his feet are soft, buttery black leather loafers. I swear to you, he looks like he just stepped out of a Guess advertisement. The breath catches in my throat, which is a statement of monumental design, for the simple reason that no man has made me feel this inadequate since I met Amaury five years ago.

"Uh, hello?" I say, timidly approaching him. "Are you Mr. Segura?"

"Lauren Fernandez!" he says, recognizing me, I assume, from my column photo in the paper each week. He takes a couple of steps toward me with his large, clean hand outstretched. We shake. I feel foolish, and certain that I am the ugliest, most miserable woman to cross his path all day. Suddenly, I know it was a mistake to wear low-rise jeans and a Juicy T-shirt. I look like a total wannabe kid. He looks professional and clean, but not like he's trying to emulate the children he teaches. Me, though? It's just sad. I was trying to look young and hip, but at this moment it hits me that young and hip to a thirty-three-year-old woman might look desperate and pathetic to high school kids and those who see them every day.

"Call me Joe," he tells me, welcoming me to the large, airy room with the black-topped laboratory tables. Every inch of every wall appears to be papered with science posters and Latino pride posters. We know what he's about, anyway. Pigeons roost on the windowsills outside, and you can hear them cooing through the dirty glass.

When Joe Segura smiles I see he's got good teeth. He is dreamy, if I were ever to be hokey enough to use that word, which I'm not, so don't even act like I might be. "I'm so glad you came. It's great to meet you. I've wanted to meet you for a while. I mean, I'm a fan of your columns. You're really great."

"Thanks." I extract my hand with some effort. He wants to keep it. I don't know why. Can't he see how gross I am? I remind myself to relax, remind myself that I'm not in the market for a new man. Even if I were, I seriously doubt this one would have any interest in someone like me.

Joe—aka Mr. Segura to the students—introduces me to the dozen or so students in the room. The students seem impressed and happy, and one achingly beautiful girl shows me the clips of my articles that Mr. Segura photocopied and gave to them all. I bet Joe Segura lusts after her, but what do I know. Why do I care?

The girl is dark, taller than I am, with a model's body and a large, symmetrical face with wide-set green cat's eyes, framed by long, curly black hair. She picks at an open bag of Funyuns, and drinks a large red Gatorade, neither of which seem to have any impact on her perfect young body. She tells me, in slightly accented English, that her name is Marislesys Curazao, that she was born in the Dominican Republic and came to Boston as a little girl. I hold the laugh inside, because to me she is *still* a little girl, albeit a little girl with bigger boobs than mine and a perfect body. Mr. Segura tells me that Marislesys is only a freshman, but that her writing is good enough to have gotten her into the honors program.

"I write for the school paper, too," she says, all confidence and fresh as milk on a farm. Her innocence keeps the statement from sounding like bragging. I envy her in a way I recognize is sick and unproductive if we are to have a mentor-mentee relationship.

I know enough to know that women should not compete with one another, and that a woman in her thirties should not compete with a teenager for physical beauty points unless she enjoys losing. But it happens in spite of my best efforts.

The urge to compete with other women appears to have been burned with a cosmic branding iron into my DNA and there's not a shitload I can do about it. I hate her, even as I smile and admire and like her. Complicated. She has so much naïve enthusiasm for life, so much *hope*. God, I can't even remember the last time I felt like that. Lately, I feel like those strings on the old mop I saw the janitor pushing around the floor in the hall on my way here, graying, soft, powerless, and ineffectual.

"She wants to be a newspaper writer, like you," says Mr. Segura. He has a nice voice, sort of deep and calming, and he slips in and out of Spanish with ease. His Spanish, I should note, sounds much different than Amaury's. Put nicely? Joe Segura sounds *educated*. I am now getting fluent enough to tell that my boyfriend and I sound like country bumpkins when we speak Spanish, because I learned it from him and he's a hick and a hood, in Spanish. I am going to have to start reading in Spanish to fix my problem—yet one more to add to the list.

I interrupt him without meaning to. "Where are you from, originally?" He stops mid-sentence to look at me in surprise. Many people regard us rude and obnoxious journalists like that. We are used to asking invasive questions, used to interrupting in the name of a story or a deadline.

"I was born in Santurce, Puerto Rico," he says. "I was raised in Lawrence."

"Sorry," I say. "I shouldn't have interrupted you."

"Not a problem," he says, placing a hand on Marislesys's shoulder. I feel sick and jealous and disgusted. "As a teacher, I'm used to it." He pauses for me to realize he's kidding. "Anyway, I was just saying that I was hoping that in addition to mentoring the whole group once a month, that you might be open to being Marislesys's personal mentor once a week. If you want. If you have the time. I don't want to put you out. But you expressed interest in doing that when you filled out the paperwork, if you remember. You said you'd do it for an interesting journalism student."

"I remember." I just don't remember thinking the student would be hotter than me.

Marislesys bounces in her chair, excited, and bites her lower lip. Even with half her lip in her mouth, her lower lip is still bigger than mine. I am seriously considering lip implants. I never thought I'd be the cosmetic surgery type, until I turned thirty-three. All of your morals and your righteous indignation at the cosmetic surgery industry go flying out the window like a pent-up pigeon as soon as you pass thirty, girl. I promise.

"So you'll do it?" asks Marislesys. For a moment I think she's read my mind and is asking me about surgery. I stare blankly at her, and then I realize she's asking me to be her personal mentor. Do I have time for that? I didn't think I'd be getting in that deep with this, I really didn't. It's only my first day. I resent that Mr. Segura has asked me this in front of the student, because it really gives me no ground whatsoever to refuse.

"Sure. That'd be fine," I say.

"Yay!" Marislesys beams and squeals, then begins to dig through the stack of clips. "I especially liked this one," she says as she holds up a column I wrote four years ago.

"I'd really appreciate it, and so would her parents, if Mari had less time for certain unproductive after-school activities," says Mr. Segura. The girl rolls her eyes at him.

"They all hate that I have a *boyfriend*," she says. Of course she does. And of course Joe Segura hates it, because he probably secretly wants her. "But I get good grades and do all my work. He doesn't get in my way. See, I think I'm just like you." She hands me the article of mine that she loves.

I take a look at it, and wince. It was about how educational it had been for me to be in a relationship with a "boy from the hood." That boy would be Amaury. I don't mention his last name in the article, which was a big fight with the copy editors because in newspapers you refer to children by their first names only. I fought, and won, and now I see their point.

I cringe at the sight of this piece. I hate this piece. I am embarrassed to have ever written such crap. I would never put that sort of information about myself out there now. It was all about how I learned the barrio ways from Amaury, how we professional women are free to choose our men based upon all the shallow criteria men have used for centuries. It's all about how now that we professional women support ourselves just fine we don't need the men in our lives to be providers, that they can please us in all sorts of other ways, like in bed. Jesus, did I actually write that for the whole of New England to see? I might as well have written the headline myself, something like, "Lauren Fernandez Is a Delusional Slut." That would have worked.

Marislesys touches my arm and says, "We have so much in common. Even our boyfriends have the same name."

"Amaury?" I ask.

She nods and smiles at me with her perfect, young, white teeth. "It's a common name in the D.R. He is fine like your man, too. And *so* sweet. He's really amazing. I have pictures of him on my MySpace page, if you want to look at them?"

"Not right now," says Mr. Segura, with a roll of his eyes. "You see what I mean? She's boy crazy." I roll mine back in sympathy for his "those crazy kids" look. "I'm sure Ms. Fernandez has other things to do right now."

"Okay, but at least can I give you this?" she asks. She holds up a piece of paper, typed. I look at the title. "Learning to Cook Grandma's Rice," it says, "by Marislesys Curazao."

I take the paper. "Sure, no problem." I read the first sentence. It is overwritten, but lyrical and poetic. I hate her for that. That, and her boundless smile that threatens to take over the room, and maybe even the city of Boston itself.

Mr. Segura and I finish our rounds, and I meet all thirteen kids in this group. They are all good kids, you can tell, the kind who worked hard enough and were bright enough to gain admission to this school, a magnet school for the best and brightest in the Boston Public School System. They are humble, sweet kids and I like them all.

But none of them have the beauty or effusive energy of Marislesys. She is a far cry from my last mentee, Shanequa, who I met through the Big Sister organization. I lost touch with Shanequa four years ago, after she had her first baby at fourteen and decided to move in with her much-older drug-dealing boyfriend. I couldn't take the disappointment I felt around her, or the way she mistreated that baby, or the way she said that it wasn't fair that I could date a drug dealer but she couldn't. Of course, I never had anything to say to that one. Come to think of it, why am I a mentor? No one should strive to be like me.

No worry of that with this girl, though. I can see that Marislesys might in fact *surpass* me one day. I'm not sure I like that, sitting in the audience while the glorious Marislesys accepts her Nobel Prize and thanks me among the little people who helped make her who she is. But, you know, just as long as she's not like me.

Finally, I take my place at the front of the room, and take out the printout of the talk I've prepared for today. It's all about how I overcame a severely dysfunctional childhood—you know, the stoner white-trash mom and the self-absorbed Cuban dad, the sexist *abuelita* who thought I was inferior to all men and tried to get me to believe it, too—and how I dealt with it by deciding to study and excel in life, in spite of my parents. I don't know why I assumed these kids would also come from screwy backgrounds. As I read it, I take breaks to look at the kids. Most of them listen in respectful, uncomfortable understanding. Only one of them looks like she feels sorry for me. Marislesys. Of course. She doesn't come from a dysfunctional family. Great.

After I finish, the kids clap, and I gather my things to go. I get Marislesys's phone number, and give her my work number. I don't want her calling me at home or tracking me down on my mobile. She looks like the type. Joe Segura leaves one of the boys in charge of the room, excuses himself, and walks me down the hall. I thank him, and avoid shaking his hand again by walking quickly down the cement steps to the sidewalk leading to the subway station. I don't want him to think I want him, which I totally do, big-time. I call out my good-bye, and turn to walk away before he has another chance to realize I am a complete loser.

I hear him clear his throat. "Uhm, Lauren?" he calls. I don't want to, but I stop and look back. Right now, he reminds me a lot of Juan. They don't exactly look alike, because Joe Segura is a stud and Juan is just a good guy, but there is something in the way he carries himself, a submissive confidence that he has, a gentleness that I am not used to in gorgeous Latin men. He's the kind of guy who will make a great husband for a woman who won't appreciate him someday.

"Yeah?"

"Would it be all right if I called you sometime? I do a little writing myself, and I'd like to talk to you about it. If you want. No pressure." He cringes as he asks. Why? Does he have inappropriate motives? I'd like that. "I mean, I'm not a great writer like you," he says, clarifying his insecure behavior. He wants to write. He is insecure about that, and nothing else. I mean, a guy like this won't even be single, will he? Not in this town. Too many women on the prowl, many of them now younger and better-paid than I am.

"Okay," I say. "Sure. Whenever."

"Great," he says, chipper as hell. "Talk to you later, then."

I turn to walk away, wishing I could be happy to be helping a gorgeous scientist learn to write, but really just pissed that this is what my life has come to—hot men see me as a writing coach, and nothing more. And a whole new breed of Latina journalist is coming up through the ranks, born when I was nineteen, and hotter than me, nicer, and more talented.

sara

ABOUT TWENTY OF the people who work on my show *Casas Americanas* are here at my house to celebrate with a big Cuban-style cookout (minus the pig, for obvious reasons) the fact that we just got another spike in the ratings. The new Nielsens show that we are now the fourth-most-watched show on the House and Garden Network, up from eighth last season.

The only one from the show who isn't here is Elizabeth. She called at the last minute to tell me she couldn't make the cookout because she had agreed to go to some single parent support group in her neighborhood that Usnavys recommended.

"*Oye, pero* what am I, chopped liver?" I asked her. "I'm single. I'm a parent. I'm your best friend. How am I not a single parent support network for you?"

"I know," she said, sounding tired, *chica*. So tired I got worried about her. "But I feel like I need to vent with some complete strangers right now. There are some things so personal that you can only tell people you hardly know."

I'm at the big built-in grill on the brick patio of the spacious backyard of my new house. There's a counter with a sink out here, too, *chica*. Very convenient and fancy. People stand around with their homemade mojitos and Cuba libres, nibbling croquettes and olives. I love cooking for big groups, and I love that I have created all of this for myself—a real life, my own home, with a career and new friends. And all of it has nothing to do with Roberto—and I hope to keep it that way.

It's a split-level ranch-style house, like from the fifties, which, you have to admit, is not the most fashionable thing in the world. But it's what you get out here in this part of Newton, if you make what I was making when I bought it. I bought it mostly for the schools, which are incredible.

The house has three bedrooms, and a totally updated kitchen, but is about a third the size of our last house, a mansion Roberto thought was too small, if you can believe that, *chica*. It took some getting used to, but now I love it. Inside, it's beautiful because, you know, I made it that way. Back here isn't that bad, even, with the pool area fenced off so the boys don't accidentally fall in, and the grassy part in the middle for kicking a ball. It's all wired for music, and right now we've got my favorite old Celia Cruz album going. I have my little vegetable and herb garden along the south side of the house, and the big red tomatoes are popping out all over like crazy. Then there's the sandy part of the yard that the boys used to play in with little plastic shovels and buckets when they were smaller, which is now popular, unfortunately, with the neighborhood cats. We've got the trampoline set up there now, and the boys are both in there in their basketball shorts and T-shirts, bouncing around with Valentín, who, apparently, can do backflips, even in tight jeans.

"Mom!" shouts Sethy. "Look what Valentín can do!"

I look up from the burgers and kosher hot dogs just in time to see my young cameraman twirling through the air and nearly landing on his neck. He rolls over, then looks up at me like a kid, happy as can be.

"*Oye, pero cuídate*," I shout. "I don't want to have to call an ambulance!" The other people from the show are clapping for him, encouraging Valentín's craziness around my kids.

"He's amazing!" cries Jonah, my other son, standing facing me with his hands and face pressed up against the black mesh enclosure of the trampoline. "Mom! Look!"

Valentín jumps very high, and kicks both legs over his head, landing on his ass. The boys, *chica*? They're knocked over by his momentum, and they all roll around in there, laughing. I hate to admit this, but I really, *pero* really, feel happy for the boys. They so rarely get a chance to roughhouse with a man like this. I'm not exactly a jock, okay, and I'm not the kind of extreme mom who's going to get in the trampoline with them.

"Show me how to *do* that!" Sethy screams at Valentín.

"No, Valentín," I shout. "Don't. Don't you *dare* show them how to do that! I don't want them doing that."

"Oh, Mom, why not?" whines Jonah.

"C'mon, Mom!" seconds Sethy. "Please?"

"Yeah," echoes Valentín. "Why not?"

"Because they're little boys and I don't think they should get paralyzed at such a tender young age. If they want to paralyze themselves, let them do it when they're on their own and grown up. I don't want that on my conscience."

Valentín shrugs in defeat. "Sorry, guys," he says. "Mom's orders."

The boys begin to wail and moan. I cut them off, waving the huge barbecue grill spatula in the air like a stick. "Enough. You keep that up, you're not getting video games tonight. *¿Me oyen?*"

The twins look at each other and instantly stop complaining. Video games, *chica*, are their life. Video games, skateboards, and chess. These are the bargaining tools at my disposal.

"Video games?" asks Valentín, looking from one boy to the other in amazement. "No way. Which ones you got?"

The boys begin to rattle off the names of their favorites. I have no idea what they are, or what they mean. I only know that I can't figure out how a Wii works to save my life, *chica*. The last video game I understood was Ms. Pac-Man.

"Oh, dude!" Valentín raves in that cute Texan accent. "You have Red Steel? No way. I love Red Steel, man!"

"You do?" the boys ask in unison. They are stunned. They look at me to see if I've heard because, to my knowledge, no grown-up in my orbit has ever known about this stuff. I don't like that game at all. It's nothing but shooting and violence. I don't like them playing those games, not with the father they had, *¿sabes?* But it's like I don't have any control over it. I try to buy games for the boys that involve strategy and saving animals, that kind of thing, but they use their allowance to buy this other kind of game. All the boys they hang out with play these shooting games, and love them. If the twins didn't play them here, they'd play them at their buddies' houses anyway.

My boys continue to brag to Valentín about their prized games, and he listens, letting his eyes stray to me now and then, with a secret thrill in them.

He seems to really like them. I wonder how much of it is real and how much of it is show, for my sake. I think he wants me to see how much he likes kids.

"Mom! Can we play Wii with Valentín now?" asks Jonah.

"For fifteen minutes," I say, sterner than I feel. Since their dad left, I've had to become the tough disciplinarian. *Óyeme*, but do you know how hard that is? "Then we're eating."

"Yay!" cry the boys.

"Yay!" cries Valentín.

They all tumble out of the trampoline enclosure and scurry across the yard into the house. I wish Elizabeth were here to tell me whether she still thinks it's a good idea for me to consider dating this man. This much, *much* younger man who knows video games.

Twenty minutes later, as the rest of my staff and crew are helping themselves to burgers, frites, hot dogs, potato salad, *congri*, finger sandwiches, and homemade mojitos, I find my sons and Valentín sprawled out on the leather sofas in the cozy, cool finished basement, shooting and stabbing each other on the big-screen TV and yelling with excitement. They're laughing, too, and from where I stand on the stairwell, they can't see me. Valentín actually is having a great time, *chica*. It wasn't for show.

"Oh, man," groans Sethy, after Valentín kills his guy. "How'd you do that? No fair!"

Valentín reaches over, and shows him. "Dude, listen. It's all how fast you move this right here," he says. Sethy tries what Valentín shows him, and it works. My son beams with pride as Valentín pats him on the back. I think back to when their father lived with us. There were never fun moments like this. It was all about obeying orders and staying out of Dad's way.

Sethy watches, wide-eyed and amazed, as Valentín offers more expert pointers. Jonah watches, too, and I can see the admiration he has for Valentín in his beautiful green eyes. Valentín is teaching my sons something I have thought of as possibly dangerous because the game is violent, but he's doing it with affection, patience, and kindness. They are mesmerized. It's not the games boys learn from, I realize.

It is the men in their lives.

elizabeth

I **LOCK THE TOWN HOUSE,** and in the moody gray of a stormy summer evening in Boston, I walk up the hill toward the single parents support group meeting. Having Gordon in the carrier in front of me, my arms wrapped around him, one hand against his back, and one hand pushing the stroller with the stew, I imagine that this is what it would feel like to be pregnant. Before receiving Gordon, I sometimes wished we had gone the artificial insemination route, that I had actually had a child from my own flesh. But now that I have this child, I realize it would not be possible to love any other child more, regardless of shared genes. I was meant to have this child. He is mine, and I am his, and I will care for him for as long as I am alive, and, God willing, beyond.

As we walk, young couples with babies and dogs pass and smile knowingly at me. With the arrival of Gordon I have been ushered into the secret and understanding universe of parents, and they see me as one of them. The kinship I feel with other parents helps to ease the solitude I now feel as a single parent. I am not alone. Every night, all over the world, millions of other new parents rise to feed their babies. We do not see each other in those dark hours, but I feel their spirits all around me, supporting me in the honorable task of raising the next generation of human beings. There is nothing more sacred, nothing holier in all the world, than parenting.

I find the town house where tonight's potluck is being held. It is a lovely red brick house I have passed many times on walks around the neighborhood. I have often admired the geraniums in the pots on the steps in the warmer months, like now, and the tasteful holiday decorations in the windows in the winter. I have thought, upon passing this home, that the people who lived there must be very organized and responsible, and so I am surprised now to learn that the people who live here are actually a single parent named Margo and her children. I ring the bell, and wait.

Margo answers the door, and I realize I have seen this beautiful woman around the neighborhood. She smiles in recognition of me, too, and we have a brief and slightly awkward conversation during which we realize that we are neighbors with something important in common. I am surprised to hear she, too, has a Spanish accent in her English. She tells me she used to watch me on the news, and apologizes for never having stopped to introduce herself, explaining that she is from Paraguay, and that people there are friendlier than they are here.

"I guess I've become more of a Bostonian than I realized," she says, and then she invites me in. "Forgive me."

"I know what you mean about unfriendliness here," I say in Spanish, relieved to have a Latina who is not a colleague or a college friend to speak to.

Margo's home is tastefully decorated in a French Country style that does not dissolve, as so many do, into the kitschy, and I wonder what she does for a living. She certainly seems to have a lot of money.

She leads me to the kitchen, which is downstairs one level and opens onto a bright and cheerful family room done in pale blues and yellows. The sofas are stained with food and who knows what else, but otherwise the room is very tidy, which comforts me. People with children should not have spotless homes, but they should be clean.

Eight other single parents are here, six of them women and two of them men. The room smells of tomato sauce, steaming pasta, and baked goods, and everywhere you look there are children, of all ages. Two teens sit at the kitchen table taking turns with a handheld video game. Older toddlers play with wooden blocks on the floor of the family room area. Music plays from a stereo, classical guitar.

Margo takes my hand in hers and leads me around the room, introducing me to the other parents. One of the fathers gives me a testosterone-soaked look I recognize as romantic interest. Little does he know. I smile as politely— and coldly—as I can, anticipating at some point we will have the inevitable conversation.

Oh, how much easier life would be if I could will myself to be straight. Just as Lauren wishes she could will herself to be gay. I have tried it, in the past, tried to date men and even on several occasions attempted to sleep with them. But those bodies of theirs, with the hair and the hanging, protruding bits, did nothing for me. Nothing whatsoever.

After the last two other guests have arrived, the two hired babysitters take over care of the children in the family room and Margo leads the grown-ups to the formal dining room, which is surprisingly large. Gordon is still sleeping, and I reluctantly leave him in a playpen in the family room, with instructions for the babysitters to come find me the second he wakes up. They are patient with me and my nervousness to leave his side, and clearly competent.

The walls of the dining room are painted a dark shade of red, and the large, solid walnut table easily accommodates all twelve of us. We take our places with our plates of food and our plastic cups of wine. It feels so very good to be in the company of other adults, and to be rid of the weight of Selwyn's misery, I almost want to sing.

"Everyone, we have a new member with us this evening, Elizabeth Cruz," says Margo as she stands at the head of the shiny, solid table. She is a regal, Spanish-looking woman, with something of a younger Meryl Streep to her. She is about five eight, with a chin-length bob that is dark brown streaked with silver. She wears an outfit similar to mine, though somewhat more classically feminine: jeans with loafers, a white oxford shirt with a thick pale orange sweater made of soft wool. The pale, warm hue of the sweater reminds me of Creamsicles, those orange-flavored popsicles we used to eat during the summer in the Bay Area. My mouth waters.

Margo has a beautiful amber necklace with large, sparkling stones, and matching earrings, an assortment of jangling bracelets stacked at the wrists, and rings with large gems crawling up her delicate fingers. None of the jewels make her look overly showy, however. She is the sort of fit, middle-aged elegant woman I have always admired from afar, but never approached because I didn't feel refined enough. You might find her photo under the word "socialite" in the dictionary. She is very handsome, the sort of woman I could imagine holding court at a museum fund-raiser or knowing how to spot a fake at the many antique shops in the neighborhood.

I think Sara would like Margo because they each remind me of the other in some intangible, unobvious way, and I wonder if it would be possible to introduce new friends into our little circle. Probably not. Most of the *sucias* seem to have their two sets of friends—us, and then the friends they have collected in the years since we met.

One does not collect such a high caliber of friends, generally, as one ages, as we did in college. Friends in adulthood, at least in the United States and Boston in particular, seem to come and go as readily as do the people who change jobs every year or two and move on. Everyone in the professional world here always seems to be moving on with the idea of moving up, and friendships appear as disposable and replaceable as apartment leases.

Margo goes on to say, "I'd appreciate it if we could start tonight's meeting by just going around the table and reintroducing ourselves to Elizabeth, but this time tell her a little bit about yourself, how you got here."

"Oh, God," moans the man who made eyes at me earlier. He is very average, with a plain face and plain hair, an unspectacular shirt and nondescript pants. Like too many men, he is louder than he ought to be. "Shit, Margo! Do we have to expose our wounds again?"

"Gary," says Margo, with a scolding type of laugh. "You don't have to go into all the gory details, but as you might recall, it's helpful when you're just starting this process, or this journey of single parenthood, to hear tales of others who've been there, done that, who have survived." She claps her hands together and looks around the table. "So, who wants to start?"

Of course, Gary volunteers. Not to sound like Selwyn, but I sometimes wish men wouldn't invade these sorts of groups. They always seem to want to take over every group they participate in, and far too many women allow them to. Men seem to think everything they have to say is more important than what a woman might have to say, and I find the way in which most women simply let them take over to be incredibly frustrating. Usually, though I am not keen to generalize, the women who allow them to take over tend to be straight. I pity straight women.

Gary tells a story of a cheating wife "with the most incredible body," who ran off with the UPS man. I try not to laugh, hold the napkin over my mouth, and pretend to choke on a bit of potato salad. It's almost comical. I mean, I feel terrible for him, but there is something almost unbelievable about a wife leaving her husband—an attorney, no less, for, he assures me, a very prestigious firm—for the well-hung delivery man. I am not certain the UPS guy was well-hung, but I imagine he was because it makes the story all that much more predictable and maudlin. When it was discovered that his wife also had drinking and drug problems, the courts awarded Gary full custody of their two young children.

"But don't call me Mister Mom," he says, leaning back with his average hands planted behind his oval head. "I am one hundred percent Mister Dad, understand?" I fight the urge to roll my eyes and tell him to get over himself. Men can come across as *so* pompous, and I don't think most of them realize how full of themselves they are.

Once Gary finishes his tale of woe, the others begin. There are stories of infidelity, of growing quietly apart, of new loves found and the old one left behind after much soul-searching and misery. There is one woman whose husband was killed overseas in one of the many wars this country seems to be waging for no discernible reason; he was a military doctor killed in the line of duty when his field hospital was blown up.

Finally, the storytelling comes around to Margo. She stands and smooths her Creamsicle sweater out, takes a deep breath that appears to be calming and thoughtful and therefore moves me.

"Well," she says, looking us all in the eye, and smiling specifically at me in a shared-secret sort of way I don't understand.

"Where do I begin? I'm Margo de la Puente. I own an art gallery on Newbury Street. We specialize in Latin American paintings. I used to be a painter, and then I realized there was more money in selling other people's paintings. Now and then I manage to sell one of my own, too. Let's see, what else? I was born and raised in Asunción, Paraguay. I came here to go to the Massachusetts Institute of Art, and never left. I love this country, what can I say? I have a degree from there in painting, and a degree from Lesley College in accounting that I use mostly to make sure my business doesn't go in the toilet, and I'm pleased to report that in fifteen years of operation we have consistently been in the black.

"I'm forty-two years old, and I've got two children—Matt is from my first marriage. He's thirteen going on thirty and thinks he's God's gift to women now that he's shaving. You might have seen him out there with the video games." She stops to roll her eyes. "If I could get him to spend as much time on his homework as he spends on those damn games, we'd be in good shape." She smiles, and we chuckle with her. "He's a bright kid, but he doesn't direct the energy where he should. I guess you could say he takes after his dad that way." She rolls her eyes in memory of her ex-husband, and I feel the familiar pit open in my gut as I realize she is straight. I hadn't meant to find her attractive, but you can't control your heart or instincts. You like whom you like, whether you want to or not.

Margo seems to shake herself out of her reverie, and continues, "Enough of that. My other child is Daniela, who is two."

"That's a big age difference," I say. I hadn't meant to speak, but it just happened.

"Tell me about it," says Margo. She goes on to say that her second marriage ended when "Charlie, her other parent, found new love with one of her younger students."

Her? Did she just say *her*? I look at Margo and she is making very direct and meaningful eye contact with me, as if she wants me to be clear about the fact that her second marriage was to a woman.

"Charlie teaches physics at MIT," she explains. "And I guess she had a graduate student who was not nearly as much of a genius as Charlie was and could therefore worship her properly, as I'd failed to, I suppose. My mistake there was thinking that we were equals, in spite of my lack of a Ph.D. or understanding of string theory. I hear they're very happy together." She pauses for a moment, and laughs to herself. "The funny part is that this graduate student? It's a *man*."

Around the table the other parents look at their plates, or shift in their seats. They've heard the story before, and do their best to be at peace with it. I'm guessing that statistically it is possible that at least one of these people is a homophobe. Yes, even in liberal Boston, even in liberal Beacon Hill, you have people who think being homosexual is wrong, or a choice.

"So, basically, I left a man for her, and she left me for a man. It's been a year and a half, and me and the kids, we're getting by okay."

"How long were you together?" I ask, stunned at the similarities between our lives—both from South America, both formerly with women professors.

"That's the thing. We were together eleven years. So she basically raised Matt. She still visits him, but it's been really hard on him, as you can imagine. He's lost two parents. Which is why I don't make it a habit to date, or get involved with anyone. I want to wait until the kids are grown to try that again."

"Sixteen years, Margo?" asks Gary. "You sure you got that kind of time, sugar?" *Sugar?*

She blinks at him with a strained smile, and I get the sense that I'm not the only one here who finds him tedious. "I think I'll manage," she tells him, coldly enough to cut off his bombastic commentary.

I smile to myself, and then I smile at Margo. I know she doesn't have any intention to date, and to be honest, neither do I. Not this soon. Not after Lauren, and Selwyn. I need to take some time to heal. But I have to wonder what the odds are that there is a beautiful, elegant, artistic Latin American lesbian with children of her own living mere blocks from me, going through something so similar.

Margo smiles at me, and says, "Your turn, Elizabeth." She sits back down.

I push back from the table, stand up, and tell them my narrative. Each time I look at Margo, she seems to blush and look away, her eyes landing instead on her plate. But with each look away, and with each new chapter of my story, her secretive smile grows more and more pronounced.

"I have never raised a child," I tell them in conclusion. "But I love it so far, and I've committed myself to doing the best job I can. I know it won't be easy to do it alone, but I know it won't be impossible, either."

With that, I sit back down.

"You aren't doing this alone," Margo tells me as we all resume eating. "Remember, you have us now. And we're more than just a once-a-week group. When one of us gets sick, we know we can call on each other to help us, whether it's with childcare, last minute or whatever, or with help preparing meals."

"That's good to know," I say. "It's amazing, actually."

"Just know we're here for you, and we all live in the area. Anything you need, you call us."

I look directly into Margo's eyes, and at that moment I hear the recognizable wail of Gordon waking up in unfamiliar surroundings.

"Oh!" I say, setting my fork down and standing quickly. "That would be my baby boy. If you'll excuse me."

They all nod or tell me not to worry. They understand. I love this group already. I feel like I'm finally among family, as if I've found a warm community in the heart of this cold culture. Maybe I wouldn't have to move back to Latin

America to find what I'm looking for. Maybe I just have to get out more. This is one of the best decisions I've made in recent years, to attend this group. It's like Jesus says, you will only receive help once you admit that you need it.

I brush past Margo on my way toward my baby, and feel her reach out to touch my hand with hers. I pause and look down at her. She smiles up at me with an intense, knowing look in her large, beautiful brown eyes.

"Anything at all," she says softly. "You let me know. We're neighbors, after all. That means something where we're from."

Though I had not come here anticipating the closing of the pit in my belly, a start to the healing of the wound Selwyn and Lauren both left in the center of my being, it occurs. A knitting as the open sides find one another again, a fluttering up of a million butterflies as that old feeling returns, the one I thought I might never experience again. It has been so long since I felt it I am not sure at first what to call it. And then, as I squeeze her hand and release it to answer the call of my child, I recall.

This incredible feeling has a name: hope.

usnavys

My Favorite Outfit

Okay, so you *know* I don't get philosophical and psychological and whatnot all that much when the topic is sex, right? Me? I'm more like one of those women who just say "bring it on, baby," and the more the *better.*

But I got me some friends, right? One of them in particular comes to mind, with some curly red hair and a negative attitude, but I won't name her here because that wouldn't be nice. Anyway, *m'ija,* she thinks she looks fat and ugly all the time, and she's always looking in windows when we walk by a store on the street, and there's this big old frown on her face like she just looked in on an autopsy video or something.

No surprise, *m'ija,* that this friend has issues with men and sex, okay? Now, I don't know for sure that her sex life is bad, but I do know she has her some better sex with evil men who don't know her when the lights are *out.* This is the biggest problem I see for us women in the bedroom. If we don't love our bodies with the lights on, no one else will, either.

Take me, for example. I am ample and proud, and I don't let an extra curve here or there get in the way of me getting my groove on, okay? I don't hide in the dark, either. They say the average woman is bombarded from the minute she gets up to the second she goes to sleep with images of skinny women in this country, *nena,* and I happen to think most of us are plenty messed up in the head as a result. You gotta have some psychological armor up to get past all that starving Nicole Richie nonsense, okay? That's what I'm saying. What kind of world is it when good women like my redheaded friend are letting Lionel Richie's daughter dictate their sex life? No, no, no.

So here's what I want you to do for me. Listen good. Take off all your clothes, even your panties and your bra. Right now—unless you're reading this at work, in which case I recommend you wait until you get your ass home, and unless you're on your period, in which case I say wait you a week before you do this exercise. Now, walk around all buck naked like that. Don't do anything crazy, like jump up and down in front of an open window. Close them shades, okay, and then just live like you always do, get you a snack, watch you some TV, all nude and beautiful as the day you were born.

Next, get yourself to a mirror and just *look* at you standing there, looking back at yourself. Tell yourself you are beautiful and sexy. Say it loud and proud, girl. I don't care how big or small or whatnot and whatever you are—*look* at your body and say it over and over: I am beautiful the way I am and perfect the way God made me. If you ain't feeling it, do it again. Repeat until it feels real—fake it till you make it, girlfriend.

Next, once you believe the truth of what I've just told you to tell yourself—that you are beautiful just the way you are—I command you to *pounce* on your man when he gets home, like a cat on a little mouse. Do not say any of the following stupid things women ruin their sex lives with: *I feel fat. I look awful. Don't look at me. Don't go down there, I smell bad.* Just shut your damn mouth on complaining about yourself and act like a goddess, and your man will be crazy for you.

See, there's a secret the gay men who run the fashion industry don't want us women to know: Men desire us curvy and round and substantial and so on. They evolved to lust after us like that. They *like* how we look, they like how we smell, they like the whole thing. And all your man wants is for *you* to want *him, m'ija.* He doesn't care how flat your stomach is, or how toned your thighs are. I am *telling* you, it's only other women care about that nonsense.

All *he* cares about is that you think he's hot, and that you want him more than you ever wanted anything in your life, and you can't keep your hands off him. I promise you this is true. It's all a conspiracy, *m'ija.* The gay men who run the fashion industry think real women are threats, okay? They want to make us hate ourselves so that we all stop lovin' us our men, so the only ones *doing* men anymore will be the gay men who run the fashion industry. That's the big plan, and I am telling you, we need to fight for our right to be sexy in our own skin—no matter how much skin we have.

It's a Thursday, and I'm not at work. I'm not even in the country, *nena,* but I got it like that. I can leave whenever I want. I'd like to see them try to fire me, okay? They won't. I told them all I was working from home and they could call me on my cell if there was anything urgent.

I've worn my most French outfit for this trip to Montreal—a form-fitting Chanel summer suit jacket in black and white, with a long strand of pearls and fantastic clear-and-black Prada pumps. On the bottom, I've got long black linen shorts from Lane Bryant, but no one needs to know this. I wasn't about to wear the short-shorts Chanel is pushing on everyone this season. They weren't ladylike.

The flight attendant smiles her good-bye, and I give her a demure wave with one hand as I whip a pair of big black Chanel shades onto my face with the other. *"Au revoir,"* I tell her. *"Bonne chance!"*

I have checked bags. Of *course* I have, *nena*. You think I am going to Montreal, the most European city in North America, with a carry-on only? You must be mad. Luckily for me, my two medium-sized Vuitton bags are the first out of the chute.

I hire a man to pull them to the curb for me, and I hail a cab with a wave of my hand. I give the caddy a ten-dollar bill and fold myself into the taxi.

The driver asks me if I speak French, and I tell him I do not, but I tell him in *Spanish*, okay? I am certain that any French I could throw at him would not be adequate, and who cares, anyway? "Not a problem," he says, in perfect English. "Where are you headed this evening?" You see, *m'ija*? Why can't they do that in our country? Why can't they just make everyone speak English and Spanish? It's not hard. It's good for everyone.

"To the Hôtel Le St. James," I tell him.

"Fancy place," he says, impressed.

"I don't know," I say. "I've never been."

"Trust me, it's a fancy place."

"About how far is it?"

"We're twenty kilometers from Old Montreal," he tells me. "That's where it is."

"That's, what, about thirty miles?"

He laughs. "No, ma'am. That's about twelve miles."

He pulls away from the curb with a lurch. I *hate* these kinds of cab rides. I try to buckle in, but I realize pretty quickly that the seat belt isn't big enough for me. The airplane seat belt wasn't big enough for me, either. They had to give me an extension. I hold this one in place with my hand, as if that would do me any good in the event of an accident, right?

The twelve miles from the airport to the hotel slide by pretty effortlessly. It's a beautiful city, *m'ija*. I have never been here. Everyone always says it feels like Europe, and I never quite believed it. But now I see what they're talking about. There's an old-world kind of feel here, even more than in Boston, with old buildings and big green trees. It's also a very large city. We're over this canal, and that canal, and then we twist and wind our way through the city. Finally, we arrive at the hotel. I take one look up at it and whoop out loud. "Yes, sir, *that's* what I'm talking about!" It is regal, a narrow gray building eight stories high, with ornate details and stately red awnings. It absolutely screams "Paris," and I know Juan wouldn't even know what to do in a place like this.

"I told you," says the cabdriver.

"You just earned you a tip," I tell him. "For your obvious good taste."

I pay him, thank him, and take the doorman's hand to exit the cab. He nearly falls as he hauls me up, but I steady him. While he grabs my bags I sashay up the steps and whoosh my way through the front door, which another doorman holds for me, my head held high. Two servants. That's more like it. The lobby is incredibly elegant, with fresh flowers and dark, polished wood. I remove my sunglasses and try to look as though I belong here and have always been in such scrumptious surroundings. After all, I *deserve* this.

"Hello, can I help you, miss?" calls the gentleman behind the counter. I don't know how he knew I was American, or English-speaking anyway, but he did. I am a tiny bit offended, *m'ija.*

"I guess you don't see many gorgeous mahogany women up in here," I say in Spanish French. I switch to English then. "My name is Usnavys Rivera. I'm here for a reservation under the name Marcus Williams."

The gentleman looks scared of me, and that is just how I want it. "Yes, ma'am. Mr. Williams arrived a short while ago." He hands me a tiny folder with a key to the room and directs me to the elevator. "We are always happy to see him here."

"Thank you, sir," I say.

"You're most welcome, miss. Enjoy your stay, and let us know if there is anything we can do for you."

I find the room and knock on the door. Marcus opens it, with a big old smile on his face. He wears jeans and a simple black polo shirt, and looks like he belongs here. "Usnavys!" He pulls me to him and kisses me. I kiss him back, lifting my foot behind me just like a French girl swept off her feet. A man clears his throat behind us, and we turn to find a scrawny new bellman and my bags.

"Sorry," says the bellman.

"Don't be. This is a great day," says Marcus. "Please, come in."

I follow him into a room that is not just a room. It is a damn suite. I remember the trip Juan tried to take me on to Rome, when he got us the most horrible piece of crap hotel because it was the cheapest around. This is what

I'm talking about, *m'ija*. This kind of room. A suite, all in muted creamy tones and fabrics that look more expensive than caviar. It is breathtaking, but I don't want to get all country bumpkin on these people and start oohing and ahhing over everything. I sneak looks around and try to seem like a woman of style and grace who is accustomed to this level of luxury. And why shouldn't I act like that? I *am* like that. I could get used to this in a matter of seconds.

The bellman finishes placing my bags in the closet and stands to the side waiting for a tip. Marcus digs in his pocket and produces a smooth leather wallet, filled with crisp Canadian currency. He pays the man. Of course he does. Can I just tell you, *nena*? My heart goes pitter-patter when I see him tip the bellman, full of style and sophistication. I feel like I can't even catch my breath. I feel like falling onto my knees on this thick, soft, Persian-style carpet and just crying my eyes out, because this is how I imagined my life would be, what I am owed by life for what I've been through. This must be how Rebecca lives every minute of every day.

"You look great," says Marcus as his eyes drink me in.

"I missed you," I tell him. Why does it feel hollow, saying this? Why is it that I can't get Carolina's face out of my head, now that I'm here? I was able to forget about her all the way on the plane, but now? That little filthy tomboy just barged in on my brain.

"Are you hungry?" asks Marcus.

"I could eat a little something."

He wraps me in his arms and pushes me toward the bed, ever so gently, *m'ija*, but like he means business. "There's a wonderful restaurant downstairs," he whispers as he nibbles at my neck. "But we're walking distance from some of the finest restaurants in the city. It's up to you."

"How about we stay in for a few minutes?" I purr. I don't know what's wrong with me. I close my eyes to block it out, the whole wrongness of what I'm doing. I focus on the feel of him in my hands. I pretend. I tell myself this is my husband. And then I tell myself that he really could be, if I play my cards right. I wonder what Carolina would be like if she were raised by a man who could take her all over the world in high style.

We tumble onto the bed, and he begins to remove the Chanel. I let him. I am not feeling it, though. Not like the first time. I think it's all the e-mails and text messages. I feel like I know Marcus a little better now, and it's harder for me to be wild with a man I know.

"You know what?" I say, pulling my jacket back on. "I think I'd rather eat first. It was a long flight."

"From Boston?" he asks. "It's not that far."

"A long day, I should have said."

"No problem." He stands up and dusts himself off. "We've got the world here, anything you want."

"French," I say. "I feel very French."

"French it is," he says. He looks at me for a moment. "Are you okay?"

"I'm fine," I lie.

"You sure?"

"Why do you ask?"

"You seem sad," he tells me.

"Just hungry."

"Okay. I'm on it." He hurries to the phone and dials the concierge for advice. He handles it like a pro, like the pro he is, speaking fine French. There is nothing wrong with this man at all. Nothing. Except that he doesn't speak Spanish.

The feeling that this is all wrong persists, through the fancy French dinner we share, with the snails and the duck parts and whatnot, where Marcus doesn't understand any of my Spanglish, like when I say I'm feeling "*bien* satisfied" and he looks all confused, and he doesn't laugh at my jokes. The feeling of being alone gets worse on the walk along the street back to the hotel, when I try to bitch about my coworkers and the craziness of my *sucias* with all their problems, but he has no idea what I'm talking about, and really doesn't seem to care all that much. Juan would have been right there with me, hanging on every bit of gossip and news I had and asking me for more. He knows my life better than I do, and sometimes I think that man *likes* it more than I do, too. I never realized until this minute, right now, in Montreal with a former golf star, that I took the shared history and same sense of humor that I have with Juan so totally for granted.

By the time we get back to the hotel, a strange silence has crept up in between me and Marcus. I still think he's hot, and I'm still a red-blooded woman. So? So, we have sex, and it's pretty good. But afterward, when I want to watch a *novela* on the Spanish channel, my favorite one, girl, the one I have to follow every night—you know how we are with our stories, *m'ija*—he laughs at me as if this were absurd.

"You really *like* that stuff?"

I stare at him, ready to pop him smack across his French-lovely mouth, girl. "What? Yes. I do. *¿Y qué?*"

He doesn't understand what I've said.

"It means, *so what*."

"I mean, the women have so much makeup on, and that man. He has the biggest mullet I've ever seen."

"*¿Y qué?*"

"I don't know, I guess it's just not my thing." Except he says "thang."

"But it's *mine*." I hoard the remote.

He folds his arms over his chest and pouts. "But I can't understand anything they're saying. Does that even bother you? I mean, no offense, but it's kind of rude."

"Fine," I snap, throwing the remote at him. "Watch what you want."

And he does. He very happily and easily takes the remote, and turns the channel to golf. Golf, *m'ija*. He doesn't get enough the rest of the time? I mean, I know it's the sport of power. I know it's what you learn to play if you want to get ahead. But it's boring as shit. I didn't think anyone actually enjoyed watching this shit, okay? It's like watching dishes dry on a rack. *Dios mío.* Is it possible to love and hate your husband and your lover both, at the same time? What is wrong with me?

"Amazing," I say, getting up to go run a bath for myself.

"Are you sure there's nothing wrong?" he asks me, again. "You look upset. What did I do now?"

"If you must know, I just don't feel like you get me," I say, as I wrap myself in the luxurious hotel robe.

"I'm not sure I know what you mean." Marcus begins to pick his back teeth with his middle finger.

"Yeah," I tell him as I turn back toward the bathroom. "You *don't* know what I mean. *That's* exactly what I meant."

cuicatl

MY **LOS ANGELES** show is sold out. I was prepared to face an empty room, bravely. But I didn't have to. Rather, I stand on stage at the Staples Center, and look out at the endless crowd of bodies. After the other duds, I don't know what to make of it. Maybe it's just Los Angeles.

Maybe it's the column my friend Lauren wrote in the *Boston Gazette*, about the way the mainstream media tend to assume Latino artists represent all things Latino when they do anything at all, whereas other Americans never seem to have that problem. I keep playing a couple of lines from the column in my head: "When the Dixie Chicks raised hackles with their pointed commentary against George W. Bush, no newspaper ran headlines decrying the decline of white women in the country music industry. When Lauryn Hill released her esoteric experimental album, no one wrote about the end of black women in pop culture. So why is it when my pal Cuicatl tries something daring and new and meets tepid public response, idiot reporters coast to coast bleat about the de-Latinization of America? It's idiotic, wishful thinking by a handful of xenophobic losers."

"*Órale, Los Angeles, ¿qué va?*" I roar into the mike. They roar back, motherfucker. Like a million lions. I draw from their energy, and the memory of me and Frank at the top of the Sun Pyramid, and I play my ass off, dance my ass off, sweat my ass off—and rock *hard*.

After the show, *pues*, we're all hungry as shit, and after the guys decide to hit a taco place in La Brea, Frank and I talk about where we can go in the middle of the night. We decide on home cooking, seeing as we're going to be on the *pinche* road for the next two or three weeks. *Órale, pues*. At least we hope it lasts that long. But if it doesn't? *Ni modo*.

Frank takes me to his cute little Spanish-style house in Silver Lake. He's got it all tasteful, colorful, and Mexican inside, with art and big, soft sofas and chairs. We make miso soup—I'm craving something hot on my voice box—and a big old tofu scramble, with vegetables and homemade *pico de gallo* in it. We make whole wheat toast with butter. We settle at the living room coffee table, sit on big pillows on the hardwood floor, and we talk about how Lauren's column got picked up on the wires in dozens of other papers across the country. Cooking with Frank, hanging out with him, it's all so *bien* easy, you know what I'm saying? I could do this for the rest of my life and not get tired of it.

"She called to tell me they want to interview her on Anderson Cooper," he tells me as he sips his beer. "They're all over the story, 'discovering' us yet one more time, like we keep getting lost."

After the meal, we shower together and make love on his king-sized platform bed. He is tender without being wimpy, considerate without being passive. I think age is good for men, man. They lose that sense of urgency. They want to please the woman. Maybe it's just Frank. Whatever it is, I'm not complaining, right? I don't know what to tell you except that it's the best sex of my life, and the second time I've really felt like I'm making love instead of screwing.

I lie back on Frank's arm, and he bends at the elbow so his hand can play with my hair. "You okay with the whole sales thing?" he asks me.

"I think so."

"Because, I was thinking, what I did back in Mexico, it was inconsiderate."

I'm surprised by this. "No, it wasn't. ¿*Cómo que* you were inconsiderate? It was the most considerate shit anybody's ever done for me, man."

"No, I mean, I realized I didn't try hard enough to understand your feelings about it, to think about it as your manager first, and not just as the Mexica man who loves you."

"Shut up."

"Seriously. I was thinking, you know, if it's important to you, and I think it is, that we can find ways to get your name out there a little more and drum up some publicity for you."

"Are you serious?"

"Listen. I want you to be okay if it all ends, right? I know that you would be now. I've seen it in your eyes. But . . ." He pauses.

"But what, motherfucker?" I sit up, and look at him with wide eyes. "You backtracking on me? After Teotihuacan? Are you crazy?"

"No, no," he says with characteristic patience. "I'm not crazy. Just hear me out."

"I'm listening, *vato*."

"When you made it, whether you liked it or not, millions and millions of Mexica kids, and other kids, too, saw themselves in you. They saw their own power and possibilities in you. Just like they did with Selena."

"And?"

"And in a way, if we let this thing die, if we don't do everything we can to keep it going, it's like giving up on them, too. On the kids. It's not just about you."

I think about this. "But you said not to believe my own hype," I remind him.

"This has nothing to do with that. I'm talking about being aware of the impact you had. Of the power you have, and we should be thinking about ways to maximize that if we can. We got the door open a little crack, you know? And now, girl, instead of rolling over and dying like they want us to, we have to surprise the shit out of everyone and blow the fucking thing off its hinges."

"So they can't close it anymore."

"Exactly. So they can't keep pretending we just got here again."

"How do we do that?"

He studies my eyes with his own. "Well, I was thinking about it. You know what we need to do? Get your name out. It has little to do with the music, at the end of the day, a big part of it is how people see you. And even if this current album doesn't hit, you've been writing some amazing new shit, Cuicatl, so I think we should start working on raising public awareness of you now, so the next record makes all these fuckers eat shit."

"How do we do that?"

"The way everyone else does it," he tells me. He gulps like he's nervous. "With sex and babies. You get married, or you have a baby, or you adopt a baby, or something like that."

I consider it. "I don't want a baby right now. And I don't want to get married."

He looks hurt for a moment, and I realize he is fishing. Wow. Frank wants to marry me? He wants to have a baby with me? Why doesn't he just say so?

He says, "I was even thinking, you know how celebrities love adopting babies to rescue them? There's lots of babies in Latin America."

"What the hell are you talking about?" I ask him. "I told you, I don't want a baby."

He looks hurt. "I don't know. It's just an idea. I'll think of something else to get your name back out there."

"You're a crazy *viejito*," I tell him. I consider asking him what he's really trying to tell me, but I'm too burned out right now. Too *pinche* tired. Maybe tomorrow. "I'm going to get some sleep."

lauren

ON THE HARDWOOD living room floor of my condo, I shovel the contents of four large white cardboard containers of Chinese takeout into my mouth. Ordinarily, my man would be here with me and I wouldn't eat as much in front of him. Ordinarily, I am not the kind of woman to say something like "my man," but I'm in a white-trash mood at the moment. *My man.* My man Amaury, the recovered gangsta. God, am I a loser, or what? You should know, Amaury is still sick with something he says makes him puke and shit all day and night. He's a two-headed tube of toothpaste, squeezed to the max. I'm glad he's not over here, considering.

I wear the new Bebe outfit I got yesterday for the date Amaury and I were *supposed* to go on last night, until he called to tell me of his near-death state. I wore it to work today, just because it was there and smelled like new clothes, even though the disapproving looks I got in the hall reminded me that miniskirts with form-fitting blazers aren't really tolerated in the suspenders-and-bow-tie world of the *Boston Gazette*. They say they want Latinas in the newsroom, but they don't want us to dress like Latinas. They want us to dress like Condoleezza Rice.

Yesterday, Amaury and I were supposed to go to dinner and dancing at the Aguakate concert at the Wonderland Ballroom in Revere. Obviously, we refrained, considering the explosive rectal emissions of said boyfriend. Lest you think me cold-hearted, know this: I offered to make him chicken soup, but he reminded me that I can't cook. He never likes what I make him, which is why he eats at his sister's house all the time. I remember making him Southern-style fried chicken once, and he frowned after the first bite and told me, "I guess it's edible." Then there was the time I took his nephews to a public pool, when I made Louisiana trailer-trash-style hamburgers on the public grill at the neighboring park, and even the boys chimed in about how flavorless my cooking was. Amaury's sister, meanwhile, seems to dump an entire carton of Sazón Goya on everything she cooks, and it always tastes salty and good. What the fuck was I talking about? Oh, right. My *man*. Amaury wants to be alone tonight, he told me, because his illness is intestinal in nature and he doesn't want to harm me with his effluence. Pretty considerate, when you think about the fact that this is a man who cheerily separates his butt cheeks with his hand whenever he has to fart, whether there's anyone around or not, whether he's in public or private.

I dine alone, the bulimic's version of bliss, with only the rain battering the roof for company. Mu shu chicken, beef with broccoli, enormous greasy egg rolls, and shrimp fried rice. The takeout guy put four sets of plastic utensils in the bag for me. No one would believe one woman could eat this much, but I can. I shove it all in, chewing with my mouth open like a slob because no one's watching. I top the meal off with a bag of Funyuns and a red Gatorade. What can I say? They looked good when that glamorous fucking kid ate them. And then, for good measure, I add a bag of Oreos. Right before he handed me the bag of food, the Chinese guy at the takeout place down the street picked his nose and wiped it on his pants. I saw it all happen. A normal person would have refused to take the food after a thing like that. But I am not a normal person. I'm a binger-purger. A bulimic. There. I said it. Nothing is going to stand in the way of my binge. I had been looking forward to the food all the way home on the subway, and nothing was going to deter me from my rightful dinner. Not even stringy snot. At least I know the Oreos are clean.

No, I don't mean the small bag of Oreos. I mean the big bag. Thousands of Oreos, it seems, black like the night across my teeth, giving me all the unwashed oral appeal of a seventeenth-century English harlot. I wash them down with a large Diet Coke flavored with cherry and vanilla, sucked desperately through a straw, and feel instantly sick and overly full. Belching doesn't even help.

Ugh. I am so full now I feel like a pumpkin, the kind that wins fairs in quaint rural places for being so ungodly *huge*. The kind of pumpkin fat farmers pose with and look thin next to. I am surely the shape and shade of a pumpkin. I know I shouldn't make myself throw it all up, that it's stupid to keep doing this, but I also know that I will, in a few minutes. Feeling bad about being bulimic only makes me want to eat for comfort. How sad.

My cat Fatso circles the empty containers on her stiff legs, sniffing. "You're out of luck," I tell her. She's getting arthritic. I should put her on a diet. She's not as spry as she used to be. Note to self: Use "spry" whenever possible in upcoming columns. It's a hell of a good word.

To stall before the inevitable roiling purge, I get up, open the distressed wood computer armoire, which is painted green, pull up a dining table chair and sit in front of my Gateway PC. I got it on sale, in a box that looked like dairy cow skin. It's slow as hell and I don't know what's wrong with it. Every computer I ever get ends up like this. I have given up trying to fix them. I just tolerate their moods. I keep a stack of magazines next to the mouse—*Ella, Glamour, Redbook*—so I can read when the machine gets snoringly constipated.

I open Explorer and log into Gmail to send Cuicatl an e-mail letting her know how much I like the new song she sent everyone in a zip file. She's on this whole trip now where she wants to "straddle the balance between commercial and art." I don't know how you "straddle a balance," but I admire her efforts. If you think about it, and I'm just a big enough loser that this is the kind of thing I sit around pondering, anybody can make a crappy album and call it art. To really get a commercial hit, you have to hit something important inside lots and lots of people. That ain't easy to do. Critics like to pretend it's easy, but the truth is, it's not. She's done it before, though, and I am sure she'll do it again. She sent me some photos, too, of her and Frank in Mexico. She looked happy and fit, and so did he, and they seem to be in love, which is most excellent. She deserves a good guy, and Frank is definitely that, even if he's old. We're happy for her. I'm also envious. Frank is not a recovered gangsta. Frank is a lawyer. He's organized and loving. He'd be a good dad. I am not sure what sort of father Amaury would make, but I do know that I am in my thirties and need to start to think seriously about potential fathers if I want to have children.

I find an e-mail from Elizabeth, responding to the apologetic one I sent a couple days ago. "Dear Lauren," she writes. "Thank you for sending your e-mail. I agree, we should not let what happened in New Mexico stand in the way of our friendship. It will be hard for me to pretend it never happened, as you suggested, but I think I am mature enough to move past it without dwelling too much on it. I value your friendship over all else. I feel exposed, but I know this feeling shall pass. Sara and I are shopping at Copley Place to-morrow, if you'd like to join us. She has agreed to date Valentín, which is good, don't you think? Otherwise, I'd be happy to get together for coffee one of these mornings before work to talk. It would be good if another *sucia* could be there, too. I don't entirely trust myself to stay calm yet. I am terri-bly sorry things turned out the way they did. I'm glad everything is going well for you. Call me when you wish. Elizabeth."

I don't know what she has to apologize for, and I don't know why the note has to be so cold in tone, but it's a start. I tap out a quick note thanking Elizabeth for the invitation, but say I'm busy. Usually, this kind of thing from me would have been a lie. But this time? It's actually true. I have, have, *have* to work. Ever since the retreat, I've been lazy about getting my columns in on time. Chuck left me a voice mail earlier: "Fernandez? You there? Hello? No? Well, all right then. I haven't seen you around the office. I looked for you, but you weren't there. I'm wondering if you have chosen to leave us and did not let us know." He stopped to laugh that Waspy fake laugh, just to let me know he was kidding. "Surely you must know you've got a number of stories that need to be wrapped up. It's urgent you attend to this as soon as possible, provided you aren't off brokering a deal for Cas-tro or something." *Click.* He didn't even tell me who he was. Not that I wouldn't have recognized the voice. The one voice in the universe that strikes terror into my heart, you know. I would know it. But, still. There's this New England blue blood way he has of speaking that is at once arrogant and lighthearted. It drives me nuts.

When I called Chuck back? He did the unthinkable. He invited me to so-cialize with him again. That's how he said it. "How would you feel about an afternoon socializing with me and my wife?" What was I supposed to say? No? I said yes, of course. I was surprised. He invited me to another soccer game this coming weekend. I have to go. It's like an assignment. Isn't it bad enough that I have to see him on the weekdays? But now I'm spending the weekend with my boss, too? Oh, and here's the really disgusting part. He said, and I quote because that's what reporters do: "Jenny has a friend we'd like you to meet. He's a Hispanic fellow. We think you'd like him."

Excuse me? In Chuck's world, I will like someone not because they are nice, or smart, or well-read, or funny. No, sirree. He thinks I will like his wife's friend because he's *a Hispanic fellow*, like me, minus the fellow part. That's the common denominator. I am telling you, the entire United States mainstream media? All the people in charge of it? They all think like this, like we minorities are interchangeable and easily predictable. It's upsetting, but I am in no position to complain. Chuck signs my checks. Well, no, he actually doesn't. It's some machine with the name of the publisher on it. But he keeps the machine-signed checks coming. I need my job. I am not like Rebecca, with a rich husband and successful business of my own. I am not like Usnavys, who is getting ready to quit her job, I think. I am not like Sara, who is self-employed and famous, or Cuicatl, who has a recording contract. I'm not even like Elizabeth, who works for a woman—our friend Sara— who thinks it's cool to bring your baby to work, and has a nice new nanny anyway. I'm a mainstream media slave. One of these days, I'll grow some balls and leave to do something else. But not without a safety net. I could never just, say, write a resignation letter like a manifesto and quit to do something new. That would be stupid. That kind of thing never works out.

I scan the rest of the in-box. Somehow, spam is getting through. Gmail is supposed to be good about filtering that. No, I don't want to send money to a dignitary in Africa to claim my rightful inheritance. No, I don't want to watch a woman have sex with barn animals. No, I don't want to get a bigger penis—not on my own body, anyway. *In* my body, perhaps. But not a penis of my own, thank you very much. Tried that in New Mexico. Didn't work.

There is also a note in my in-box from Mr. Joe Segura, sexiest science teacher on the planet, thanking me for talking to the kids and giving such an "inspirational" talk, and also suggesting I might enjoy a reading by a famous lefty journalist who is coming to town to promote his book. He does not, I notice, invite me to attend the reading with him. Therefore, I don't reply. Surely he's not asking me out, if all he's done is provide the information on the talk and suggest I'd like it? I am not going to hurt my brain trying to figure this out right now.

Rather, I stroll to the commode, tickle my tonsils with my toothbrush, and barf my dinner up. *Kerplunk.* I do it two more times because it's getting harder and harder to empty the bag, as it were. I stop to cough for a while, rinse my mouth with water, and do it again. All better. Poof, like magic. Ah, yes. Such an easy fix to overeating. I'm surprised more people don't do it. I instantly feel better. I feel great, in fact. I wonder for a moment if I am addicted to this behavior, because it actually feels really good, like ecstasy good. I was fat when I entered the bathroom, and now I'm not. Amazing.

What now? Well, because I am compulsive and curious, I surf over to MySpace.com and search for Marislesys Curazao's page. I wonder what her boyfriend looks like, what kind of page she'd post. I wish I were her, with my whole life in front of me. I rationalize my behavior by telling myself I need to learn about my mentee. Her profile page pops up instantly. I guess hers is not exactly a *common* name.

On the profile page she has four slide shows of photos playing. One features her and her family, with cute, loving captions, like "My mom and dad, still in love!" Puke. There's a picture with a huge family, and the caption says, "Family reunion, in the D.R., baby!" They really are all very adoring and happy looking, and this makes me hate her more than I already do. She has the kind of family I deserved but never got.

The next slide show is of her and her friends at school. She has lots of female friends who seem to adore her immensely. "Me and my girls, look out!" And, "Jenna and Lisette—I'd do anything for you chicas!" More cute captions. She is. Nothing like me. I'm the kind of friend who literally screws her friends and leaves them wounded.

But nothing in the world could make me hate Marislesys Curazao more than the third slide show, which features her incredibly cute self and her boyfriend. The breath catches in my throat at the first shot. I continue to hold it through the six photos of the two of them together in various places around Boston. Her on his lap. Them kissing. Them on a Swan Boat in the spring. Them dancing dirty on a crowded dance floor, with a caption identifying the place as the Wonderland Ballroom, the date yesterday, the band Aguakate. His familiar eyes, hands, nose, lips.

No kidding that our boyfriends have the same name.

Her boyfriend is *my* fiancé. Same person.

MC. Marislesys Curazao.

"Fuck!" I shout. I slump to the side of the desk like I've been shot. Where is my heart? It has fallen straight through the floor of my belly, dropped out onto the creaky wooden boards, where it flops and spasms like a fish out of water. I have never felt pain like this in my life. *Never.* I grab my recharging cell phone to call him—my home phone was turned off for nonpayment of the bill—but my hands tremble and I drop it onto the floor. It lands with a clatter directly next to my heart, and breaks.

Like everything else I've ever touched.

sara

WE'RE GOING IN here," says Elizabeth. She yanks me by the arm of my Coldwater Creek light jean jacket, out of the mall and into the painful brightness of Arden B., a shop that I have walked past many times on my way to Chicos or Ann Taylor.

"I don't know about this," I tell her. In my chinos and basic brown short-sleeved sweater, I am not exactly the typical shopper here. I look at the clingy, slinky dresses on the mannequins, and at the other women shopping here. They seem to be about ten years younger than I am, with long hair, and remind me of ferrets, long, lean, and vicious. "Everything looks so . . ."

"Sexy?" asks Elizabeth, who herself wears simple jeans and an Eddie Bauer type of T-shirt.

"I was thinking tight. And short."

"That would be 'sexy.' "

"Yeah. I guess so."

"Then we're in the right place."

Fíjate, chica. I have never been comfortable with showy clothes. I was raised in Miami, where it's normal to show a lot of skin—it's hot there, *¿sabes?*—but even so, I always went more for the conservative look. That's just the way I am, I guess in part because my grandparents are pretty orthodox.

I touch a leopard print dress with a cowl neck. It feels sleazy and insubstantial against my fingertips, like a wearable condom wrapper. "I don't know, Liz," I say.

"Well, no, not that one. That's ugly. Here, look at this."

Elizabeth holds up a flowing black dress, silk or satin. It looks too short, but otherwise not all that slutty. It's got an empire waist and a low neckline.

"I'd like it longer," I say.

"Just try it on."

"I don't like my legs."

"Try the dress *on*, Sara. What size are you?"

"Ten."

She shoves the dress at me in my size. I walk across the store in time to the thumping house music, embarrassed and second-guessing myself. Should I really have agreed to have dinner with Valentín Saturday?

I strip in the little room, and look at myself in the mirror in my green lacy bra and matching panties. I look healthy. I remember the photos Usnavys showed me, and remind myself that I have every right in the world to have a date with someone who won't do that to me. *Imagínate, chica.* I'm in my thirties, and looking better than I did in my twenties.

I slip the dress on and look at myself. It doesn't look half bad, actually. Maybe it looks *good*. How is that possible? I step out of the room to let my friend see, and her face changes from bored to ecstatic.

"You have to get that," she says. "You look great."

"You think?"

"Absolutely. Turn around. Let me see. Okay, wow. Yep. You look great."

A woman checking out her *fundio* in the nearby three-way mirror looks at me in the mirror and agrees that I look hot. Then she asks me if her butt looks big, and I lie and tell her it does not. Never be honest with strangers. They might carry guns.

"You don't think I'm going to look like I'm trying too hard?" I ask Elizabeth.

Elizabeth shrugs. "If you do? God, Sara, I think it's sweet that you might look like you're trying. After months of blowing the man off, I think it might be good to let him know you are a little bit interested."

"He's a baby."

"He's a man."

I make a pained face, like I'm passing a kidney stone or something, and bend over as if I've been punched in the gut. "But twenty-one? Liz! He's twenty-*one*."

The stranger passes me with interest on her face and holds a hand up. "Younger man? High-five." This makes me think of Borat, but I high-five her anyway. Never leave a stranger hanging; you never know when they might have a gun. After the stranger leaves, Liz and I exchange the look. The one where we think someone's loopy but can't exactly say so at the moment because the loopy person might tackle us to the ground.

I retreat to the dressing room and put my old clothes on. I look ten years older, instantly. When I exit, I ask Elizabeth if she thinks I dress too old for my age. "I mean, I look a little like Margaret Thatcher."

"You look nothing like Margaret Thatcher," says Liz.

"Okay, but I dress like her."

"Yes." She does not hesitate to answer. "But I figure you have an excuse."

"I do?"

She puts her arm around me and we head back out into the store. "You married young, had kids young. Roberto never made you feel pretty, just dirty. You feel old because of all that. But the good news is, you're single and free and you're still young. You can have fun now, all the fun you never got to have before. Right?" She picks up a feathered boa and holds it out to me. I take it as if it were a live snake—unhappily, in other words.

"Right, but not *that* much fun." I put it back on the rack with the other assorted horrors that pass for accessories here.

I take the dress to the cashier, and buy it with my American Express card. Somehow, putting it on the card makes it feel like less of a commitment than if I'd used my check card, like I'm not *really* buying it.

"Now for shoes," I say, as we leave the store.

"Something sexy."

"Yes," I tell my friend. "Something sexy."

As we walk toward the Charles David boutique, Elizabeth casually mentions to me that she has met a great woman she finds interesting—in her single parents group, no less. "She's an art dealer. She's amazing."

"¡Dios mío, chica! You work fast!" I look at her, and she gives me a shy, silly sort of smile with a flinch, like she expects me to slap her. "Why didn't you tell me?"

"Do you think it's too soon to be thinking about someone new?"

"No," I tell her, clapping my hands together. "The sooner the better. You know the saying. Un clavo saca otro clavo."

"I never liked that saying. One nail replaces the other. It's awful."

"Usnavys reminded me of it the other day. I like it."

"I guess."

"But it's true. The sooner you find a new nail to hammer in, the sooner the old nail all stuck in the wood falls out the other side. That's why I'm going on this date with Valentín. He'll be the new nail to hammer me."

"I think straight women like that saying more than lesbians."

I laugh. "I see your point."

"Has he called you again?" she asks, her expression serious, and I know by "he" she means Roberto.

"No. It's weird, actually. I thought he would have by now."

"Why are the hairs standing up on the back of my neck now?" she asks.

"Don't worry about it."

"You have to tell the police, Sara."

"I know. I will."

"Couldn't you tell them now and they could trace your incoming calls or something?"

"I don't know. Let's talk about something else. Like these shoes. Look at them."

We stop in front of the window and look at the strappy, spiky things there. Some of them are hideous, with shiny chrome heels that look like weapons. But some are lovely. Almost at the same time, we both spot a pair of open-toed pumps with high heels, black and very sexy and elegant. They must have a four-inch heel. I never wear anything higher than two.

"Those," I say.

"You read my mind. They're super sexy, Sara. And young."

"Yes," I say as I lift my chin and sashay into the store. "I want them."

lauren

I WAKE UP HUNGOVER to the sound of rain. And banging. Someone is banging on my door. I look around my living room and try to remember where I am. White Chinese takeout containers and three empty wine bottles litter the floor, and it looks as though I ripped up a bunch of photographs of Amaury.

Oh, right.

I groan and push myself to sitting. I'm still in my Bebe date outfit, the one I thought I'd wear on a date that Amaury decided would be more fun without me. He has been cheating on me. For months, apparently. With a teenager. It all comes back to me now.

"Shit," I say. My face screws up and I feel the tears coming again. I don't want to cry.

Bang, bang, bang. Someone is knocking on my door. I think back, and try to remember whether I called any of my female friends last night. I don't think I did. But I do remember putting my phone back together and drunk-dialing Amaury's sister and yelling at her for not telling me. She admitted to knowing. She tried to give me some line about how we as women have to prepare ourselves for this kind of transgression in our men, that we need to work harder at keeping them at home. She sounded just like my Cuban grandmother in Union City, New Jersey. These women from the Old Country think it's the woman's job to stop the man from cheating on them, or, at the very least, it is the woman's job to tolerate the man's cheating as an inevitable part of female life.

Fuck that.

Groggy, a little dizzy, I push myself to my feet and stagger down the stairs to the front door. I look through the little fisheye peephole, and who do I find? The cheater. The asshole. The liar.

Amaury.

"Go away!" I scream. My voice is hoarse with having been drunk, and my throat feels like it is on fire. God, it hurts. And my chest! It's the heart attack feeling again.

"Open the door, *mi amor*," he calls. "I have something for you."

"Fuck you!" I scream. This prompts the woman upstairs to bang on her floor to shut me up. I look at the ceiling. "Fuck you, too!" I scream.

Suddenly, I wonder if it is a workday. Have I missed work again? Shit. Shit, shit, shit. I run to the computer armoire and look at the calendar. It's a Saturday. No work. But I'm supposed to go to the game with Chuck and his "Hispanic gentleman" friend. I pick up the phone and call Chuck's house to say I'll be too sick to go anywhere today. I try to sound sicker than I am, with sniffles and the whole deal. I'm relieved to get his wife instead of Mr. Chuck. I'll tell her, and hang up.

"Chuck's right here," his wife says. "Would you like to talk to him?"

My heart races in fear. "No, no," I say. "Don't bother him. I'm okay. Just tell him I'm going to rest and try to get better, but I probably won't make it today. I don't want to infect everyone with this, whatever it is." Bulimia and alcoholism are contagious now?

"But he's right here," she says. "I think he wants to talk to you."

Bang, bang, bang. Amaury continues his barrage against the front door.

"I'm sorry, there's someone at the door," I say, slippery and wimpy. "Tell him I'll call him later. Okay?"

I hear Chuck's voice next. "Hello? Lauren? You sick?"

I pretend I haven't heard, and hang up. Then I turn the phone off to gather my thoughts. They cannot be gathered. They are scrambled up. *Cheating asshole Amaury. I hate my fucking job. This condo is a mess. I smell like a goat. Cheating asshole Amaury. I hate my fucking job. Etc.*

I hear keys in the door. Shit. That's right. He has keys. Why didn't he just use them before? I sprint as well as I can with the room spinning around me, then rush down the stairs again. I try to hold the door closed.

"Leave me alone!" I wail. "I hate you! Go away!"

"*Mi amor*, I talked to my sister. She said you think I'm cheating on you. Don't be like this," he says, gently, so gently, and pushes the door open past me. Before I can run away, he has shut the door and captured me in an embrace. He's got flowers in one hand, and a bag of bagels from my favorite Jewish deli in the other.

"What is wrong with you?" I cry. I start to hit him in an attempt to get away.

"Calm down," he says, tightening his grip on me. "Calm down. Listen to me. You've been drinking. You're not well."

"No, I'm not well. That's because you've destroyed me." I begin to weep and I simply give up. I let go of my body and allow myself to slump out of his grasp. Dead weight, I am too heavy for him to hang on to. I drop to the floor of the entry, with the dust bunnies and the wispy cakes of cat hair. This place is a mess. Cheating asshole Amaury.

"I brought you bagels," he says. I look up and see him smiling at me as if some part of him is really enjoying this whole scene. I would have expected contrition. But there is none. It hits me that this is all some kind of game to him. He's getting off on it. It? Let me say that again. He's getting off on my pain.

"Get out of here, please," I say.

"But why?"

"Don't look at me like that! Don't look at me like you enjoy this."

"What are you talking about? I don't enjoy it." His eyes tell a different story. They dance with pleasure.

"Why, Amaury? Why did you do it?"

He sits next to me on the floor and smiles. He moves his hands in an hourglass shape. "She was a virgin until I met her," he says, as if this explains everything.

"She is fourteen!" I scream. I scoot away from him. He's licking his lips at the memory of her young body.

"Fourteen is a woman," he says. "Girls get their periods at nine or ten. If you can have a baby, you have a sex drive."

"You're disgusting."

"And you are too American. It's different where I'm from. You have to understand that. I'm not like you. You know, you really shouldn't call my sister. You got her very upset, saying you were going to kill yourself." I *said* that?

"Get out. Get out. *Now.*"

"Not until I'm sure you're not going to hurt yourself," he says. He scoots after me, and I get up and run to my bedroom. He chases me, fast, and shoves his hand through the gap before I have time to slam the door closed.

"You don't care if I'm hurt. If you did you would have never done this to me."

"I didn't do it to you, Lauren. What I have with Mari is completely separate from anything I have with you." *Mari.* He calls her Mari.

"You have nothing with me now, okay? Get out."

"You don't mean that," he coos as he opens the door and tries to wrap his arms around me.

"I do. I mean it."

"I love you," he tells me. "But you have to understand, we come from different places. I *do* love you."

"Don't touch me."

He touches me anyway. I scramble away and remember the nail scissors in my nightstand drawer. I have a whole manicure set in there, for those nights when I feel motivated and normal enough to actually do my own nails. This occurs about twice a year.

He lurches after me and forces a kiss on my mouth. I push away and run to the nightstand. He grabs me and kisses me again.

"I want you," he tells me. "I can't lose you. She was just for fun, you know?"

"Get off me."

He does no such thing. I see a new look in his eyes, a wild look, and I realize that there is a side to this man I have been voluntarily ignoring. He's a good writer, and he's a quick learner. But he is a former drug dealer. He is from the slums of the Dominican Republic, raised with a very different value system from my own, in extreme poverty, in complete machismo. There were signs. Usnavys was right. It was obvious, all the signs. But I ignored them.

Now, as he paws me and tugs at my clothes with that thrilled look in his eyes, I realize: This man is capable of rape. I would never have thought so before, because I romanticized him. I made Amaury out to be the perfect Latino for me to save, a ready-made Latino hoodlum from a prime-time made-for-cable movie. I was as guilty as any other member of the media in confusing race, ethicity, class, and socioeconomics.

"Get off me," I say again. But he pushes harder, and his hands are all over me.

"She doesn't care that I have more than one, and neither should you," he tells me.

"Please tell me you used condoms with her."

He shakes his head and smiles. "She was a virgin."

"That's what she told you."

He laughs as if I've made a joke. I take my moment and lunge for the nightstand again. This time, I am fast enough. I open the drawer and take out the scissors. I palm them in my hand, and turn back to him. This time, when he reaches for me, I slash him.

"Fuck!" he cries, looking at his hand.

I pick up the dead phone, the phone I haven't paid to have kept on, and pretend to dial 911. "Get out," I tell him. "I'm calling the police."

"You're crazy," he says, cradling his bleeding hand. To my surprise, he backs off, toward the door, shaking his head in disbelief. "My mom was right. American women are crazy."

"Yeah, we're crazy. You go around raping teenagers and I'm the crazy one?"

"It's not rape if she wants it."

"Get *out*."

"Hello?" I say into the dead phone line, for Amaury's benefit. "I need someone here. There's a drug dealer, he broke into my apartment and he's trying to rape me."

"Fucking bitch," spits Amaury, as he turns to run for the front door. "I'll be back. We're not finished."

I wait a couple of minutes after hearing the door slam closed, before venturing out to make sure he's gone. I feel like a heroine in a horror movie, moving slowly through my own hallways with a tiny pair of scissors in my hand. How could it have gone this wrong? Usnavys was right about him. I never trusted her, but I should have. She was right.

I check the closets, under the sofa, behind the chair. Nothing.

He's gone.

I find my cell phone and call information.

"Hello?" I say, my hands trembling. "I need the number for the locksmith on Center Street in Jamaica Plain, please."

"Of course," she says, her American accent and very calm demeanor incredibly comforting to me right now. "One moment, please."

usnavys

SOMETIMES, *M'IJA,* **YOU** wish the man would just stop talking already. But he don't. Doesn't. It's Sunday, I've been back a couple of hours from Montreal, and already this man's getting on my last nerve.

"Baby, and don't take this the wrong way, but maybe instead of spending every weekend helping your friends with their work assignments overseas, or every Sunday getting groomed like a poodle, you *could* do more to help around here," Juan tells me with that sour-ass look on his face. Then he smiles across the kitchen at me to let me know he didn't mean to hurt me.

"Canada is not overseas, baby," I say.

He gets all pissy now. "You know what I mean. I feel like I'm flying solo here. It's too much, Usnavys. I can't do it all alone. We need a to-do list or something. You just got here. I could use some help, and some time with you."

As *if, mamita.* Right? I done tried talking to him about how I feel about a to-do list when I'm the one staying home. *If* I'm the one staying home. Marcus wants to meet me again, next weekend, in the Adirondacks. I said yes before I could stop my damn mouth and don't know how I'm going to get out of it. I don't know if I *want* to. I need to make a decision here. Juan's not helping tilt things his way, either, by looking at me like all fragile and *cansa'o* that. Like he thinks I'm useless. He doesn't believe in my wifely skills. *Sinvergüenza.*

I look at him slouching there by the kitchen sink in his boxer shorts and yellowed T-shirt, with his hair all sticking out like one of them designer Asian roosters the men in my neighborhood growing up used to like to fight. Like he couldn't even bother to get dressed, right? The entire time in

Montreal, Marcus looked clean and dapper, with his shirts ironed and his pants just right, and the minty smell of gum in his mouth. I could get used to a man who made an *effort*. I could.

Me? I'm dressed to kill, in my red and white checkered sundress and espadrilles. Damn. It smells like old food in here. It's much too nice a kitchen to smell so bad, okay? Even though we live in a hundred-year-old house in Mission Hill, I had the kitchen redone all country style a couple of years ago, with one of them white farmer's sinks and the stainless steel everything else. There's granite on the counters, and recessed lighting. There is no excuse for it to smell like the damn projects, okay? I have come too far to go back to that, right? We got us a fancy dishwasher, but he's washing dishes by hand, while Carolina plays with pots and pans on the floor, pretending she's some baby again. She watches us fight with a sad, scared look on her face, but the overalls she put on, with those rain boots? I have had it up to here with *her*, too. We've been arguing more and more in front of her, and the last time she actually screamed at us to stop.

"What do you think a housekeeper is for, *nene*?" I ask him as I shrug into my white cardigan. For what it's worth, Marcus talked about his *staff*, okay? His staff of *housekeepers*. He has people to do his yard, and his laundry, and his cooking. He has everything. Me? I have Juan, and he thinks he shoulders too many of the responsibilities around here. "*Deja éso, ya*. All this cleaning. Pssh. Maybe if you weren't so cheap we could get someone to help out."

"She'd only come twice a week, probably. We eat *every day*. Some of us more than others. There'd be dishes no matter what."

"What's that supposed to mean? 'Some of us eat more than others'? What are you trying to say? You mean me? Is that it? I eat too much now?"

Marcus likes me large, okay?

He sighs. "I'm just *saying*, Usnavys. Someone has to do the dishes, and take care of Carolina, and make the meals. You act like I'm doing it to undermine you, but you're never here! Please! I'd *love* to stop. You know that? I'd like to sit down with a beer and watch a game, no matter what kind of girly man you think I am. You think I *like* this? I hate it, woman! But someone has to do the laundry and keep the bathrooms stocked with toilet paper. You act like these things just magically happen, Usnavys. You think fairies come and put your underwear away for you? No. I do it. That's me. Do you ever notice, or thank me?" He shakes his head and throws the sponge down like he's never going to pick it up again, but I know better. "You know, I'm tired of it."

"I think I do plenty around here," I counter. I try to think of things I do around the house. I take showers. I get dressed. I put the towels back after I dry off. I close the shades when the glare is too much on the TV and I can't see the *novelas*. I buy Carolina beautiful clothes she doesn't wear because he doesn't *make* her. None of this seems worth mentioning.

Juan shakes his head at me. "Well, when I start my job again next month, you're going to have to do a lot more around here than you've been doing."

"I'll use my extra cash to hire a maid."

"We're not going to have that much extra. There's the extra car and the gas."

"You want comfort, you have to pay for it."

"Well, that's lovely, Usnavys, but I think whether we hire a maid or not is a decision we both have to make, don't you? Seeing as we're married and it's our money, not *your* money?"

"Whatever." The wooden country clock on the wall over the kitchen table tells me I am bound to be late for my early evening manicure appointment. "Whatever, okay? I mean, what-*ever*. I still make more money than you will, to start with."

"What does that have to do with anything?" He is practically shouting now.

"It means she who makes a man's money gets to make decisions like a man. I am hiring a maid whether you like it or not."

"We can't *afford* that. I've done the budget, and we just don't have it right now."

Marcus can afford it. And more. Much more.

I glare at him. "If we can't, it *isn't* my fault. It's yours."

"Stop fighting!" screams Carolina, still in her Batman pajamas, the front of which is shiny with maple syrup spillage. Her hair looks crunchy with grime. Am I the only person in this family who believes in *baths*? She puts her hands over her ears. "I hate this. Stop it! Stop it!"

"*Mira*, see what you did?" I point at Carolina and stare at Juan. "You upset her!"

"Me? *You* did this!" cries Juan. He also points at her. She looks up at us, confused.

"No, I didn't." I put my hands on my hips.

Carolina begins to howl, in tears. The normal reaction would be to comfort her, but neither of us seems to feel the need to do that. It's sad, *m'ija*, because what we end up doing is both of us yell at her to stop. I say *"Cállate la boca,"* which is Spanish for "shut up," and Juan tells her to go to her room. She doesn't go, though. She's frozen with fear.

"Don't tell her that," he screams at me now. "Don't you tell my daughter to shut up! Don't yell at my daughter!"

"Your daughter?"

"I'm the one *raising* her. You think our money is your money, well then I say our daughter is *my* daughter."

"That's some bullshit right there," I say.

"Stop it, Mommy!" screams Carolina. "Stop it!"

"Go to your room!" I yell at Carolina.

"You're abusing my daughter," hisses Juan. He closes his eyes and puts his hands over his ears, like a child. "Stop, Usnavys. Just stop."

"Don't tell me how to talk to my daughter," I return.

"I hate you!" shrieks our daughter, as she stomps off to her bedroom, leaving me alone with Juan. He looks tired, and old, and I don't feel attracted to him at all. He's getting too *flaquito, nena,* all scrawny like Marc Anthony with his manorexia chiseling up his face. The more I eat, the less Juan eats. Walking side by side, we look like the number ten. Marcus is fit, but he's large, as in tall with broad shoulders. We balance each other out.

"What is wrong with you lately?" he asks me. "I don't even recognize you anymore. You're so angry all the time, and you can't even seem to be bothered to spend any time with us. It seems like you hate me. What did I do? Tell me."

"Maybe if you didn't complain all the time and try to make me feel terrible I'd make more of an effort."

He holds up a plate and that damn sponge he acted like he'd never touch again. *Told* you. The suds from the sink drip down his forearms. "Why do you think I do all this, huh? Who do you think I'm doing it for? Myself? Is that what you think?"

"I think you don't trust me to be a real woman."

"That's crap. God did not say 'only women shall wash dishes.' People made those rules, and they've been broken in every industrialized society in the world. I'm trying to help you. I'm trying to make life easier for you."

"I can handle it all, okay? Without your little list. I *said* I'm not giving up my manicures and pedicures and I want to hire a damn maid. This would be much easier if you'd *listen*."

"Then you should find another time to do your manicures, because I think Saturdays should be family days from now on. We could make it a fun family day, get the house in order, make dinner together, sort laundry with Carolina."

"Oh, like cleaning and laundry are such great family activities? Please. That's so ghetto."

"She needs to learn about responsibility. Responsibility is not 'ghetto.' "

"So we get her a credit card and make her sign the check to pay it."

"Don't be stupid."

"I'm not."

"A family day with laundry could actually be fun," he says. "If the parents made it fun. If you made half an effort to be an effective mother."

I stare him down. "Oh, no, you *didn't*. You did *not* just say that shit to me."

"Listen. Carolina needs to feel like a productive member of this family, she needs chores and responsibilities, too. And she can't see herself like that if she never sees her mom helping out."

"Please, I am *not* that tomboy's role model."

"Yes, you are, whether you like it or not. And I don't think she should grow up to think it's normal to depend on a man to do everything for her."

"I am not her role model, okay? Don't even say that shit. No, *nene*, she has Hulk Hogan for that. She has that lesbian from Clinton's cabinet, that Janet Reno."

"Janet Reno is married to a man."

"Whatever, *nene*. Don't lie."

"See? You see what I mean? It's like you hate us, you know that? Nothing we can do will ever be good enough. I see that now. I used to think you'd change, you know? That you'd come to your senses and realize that I love you, that your daughter loves you, but you're just too selfish to see that. And what if Caro does end up gay someday? Eh? What are you going to do then? Hate her? Are you insane? Are you that crazy?"

"I think *you're* selfish."

"Me?" he asks, all confused-looking. "How?"

"Because you won't relinquish control of this house to me, that's how."

He laughs out loud. "I'm trying to be a helpful husband, not like some macho asshole who doesn't understand his wife's needs! You complained because I didn't have a job, so I went out and got one. And then you complained I didn't make enough, so I got a raise. But have you said one kind word about any of it? Have you? No. You're never satisfied, you know that? I can do no right by you."

"Maybe if you quit trying so hard to be a woman."

He smiles as if this is both funny and terribly painful. "I don't believe this."

"Neither do I."

"You're crazy, woman!"

"Don't 'woman' me, Juan. I'm not in the mood."

"You're right. Maybe I should be calling you 'man,' because as far as I can tell you have embraced every rotten bit of the *machista* culture I've hated all my life, the one that ruined my mom's *life*, only you've flipped it, with me as your little wifey. I'm done, okay?" He throws the sponge down again. "Seriously. I can't do this anymore."

"What is that supposed to mean?"

"It means I can't stand this anymore, the way you treat me and Caro."

I glare at him. "I've had no choice, *nene*. You didn't step up to provide like a real man, so I had to. I'd say I'm the best *male* role model Carolina could ask for."

Juan drops a plate in the sink, his face twisting in annoyance. His voice rises in volume. "Is *that* how you feel?"

"I feel *late*," I tell him.

"What if, one of these weekends, I actually wanted to go out on a Saturday afternoon, what if I wanted to go out with the guys to play some soccer, what would you do then?"

"I thought you went to the Children's Museum with Caro yesterday. Now you say you were playing soccer?"

"No, we did go to the museum. I'm saying what *if*, Usnavys. Listen to me. You are missing the point. What if I wanted a day by myself, Usnavys? Do you realize you get both days to yourself practically every weekend? You take off with Lauren like you're still single, like you're not a mom. And why is that? Why are you able to do that? Because I'm here for you. Because I take it all on. I'm always the one watching Caro, or going to the store. Not that I mind. I love our child. But you know. Whatever needs to be done on a Saturday, I'm the one to do it. You don't even offer to help. You just carry on with your life as if we never had a child. It almost seems like you don't even think you're married, either. It's always about shopping, or your stupid plastic fingernails, or that disgusting *blog*."

He says "blog" as if it were some sort of a chicken virus. Juan is correct, of course he is. I don't feel married. I feel henpecked. I miss Marcus. I don't like being here, and I don't think I like Juan very much anymore. I take the guilt and push it out of my mind. When I do that, ignore my looming sense of guilt, I usually just end up getting angry over every little thing.

"I can't talk about any of this right now," I scream. "Stop trying to make me late. You're always trying to sabotage my beauty, Juan."

He laughs at me. "Me? *I'm* the one doing that, huh? Not you, with your donuts and your cookies and your *fritura* and *batidos de mamey*? With whipped cream on top, in the middle, *and* on the bottom! I'm the one shoveling every scrap of food in this house into your mouth, am I?"

My eyes narrow at him, and if I could shoot hot red lasers out of them to eviscerate him, I would. "*What* did you just say?"

He turns his back to me, and goes back to washing the dishes with that saggy ass just standing there. "Nothing. Just go. Go get your nails done." He says "nails" and "done" with all the maturity of a fifth-grade playground bully.

"I look good, okay?" I say. "You want to get ahead in life, you have to look good. That's something you'd know nothing about, obviously."

"Okay, Usnavys. Whatever you say."

"Lots of men like me like this, whipped cream and all."

"I'm sure they do."

I am so angry at him for insulting me that I actually feel my legs shaking. I hate him. I am sick of him. This is it. This is the moment. "They *do*. And now and then, I like them *back*. Like, when I was in New Mexico. I liked somebody *back*, okay?" There. I said it.

He freezes. I watch, and wait to see what he will do. He's a smart man. He knows what I mean. "What are you trying to say?" he asks, and his voice is quieter now, calmer than I'd expect. That scares me, *m'ija*.

"I'm saying that now and then I like a man, Juan."

"In bed? You like him naked?"

I make a face I know he'll hate, prissy and proud. "I don't kiss and tell. Now if you'll excuse me, I'm late."

"So you're kissing, then."

"Yes, I did. And it was good, baby, okay?"

"And I can only assume you're kissing someone else, because I can't remember the last time you kissed *me*."

"If you didn't insult me and call me fat, maybe that'd be different," I say as I move to the doorway.

"I didn't call you fat."

"Yes, you just did. You just did!"

"I said you eat too much. I didn't say you were fat. Jesus, Usnavys, your own doctor says you're developing diabetes! Don't you care?" He pauses, with a lost look on his face, then looks back at me again and yells, "You *slept* with someone *else*?"

"If you were nice to me, I wouldn't have had to do it, Juan. If you paid me half the attention you pay to this house or to Carolina, then maybe we'd still have a marriage."

His face twists in confusion again. "You don't think we have a *marriage*?"

"You said it, not me. You said I didn't act like I was married. You do the math, Juan. It's not my fault, okay? I did what I could. You knew my needs, and you never did anything to address them."

"Are you nuts? All I do, all day every goddamned day, is try to make a life for us. I am the glue that holds this whole fucking thing together."

I feel a tug on my shirt and look down to see Carolina, her eyes filled with tears, standing at my side. "Why is *papi* using bad words?" she asks me, bewilderment all across her pretty little face. "I thought you said we aren't supposed to use those words with people we love and respect."

I glare at Juan, and say to her, but mostly for his benefit, "You're right, *mamita*. People only use those words on people they don't love or respect. I think that's what your daddy is trying to tell me."

"Usnavys, don't drag her into this. It's not fair."

I hug my daughter, kiss the top of her head. "I'm going to the salon now. You have a good time at the museum with Daddy."

"I'm done, Usnavys. I am serious. I'm done. I'm not doing this anymore."

I turn to leave because I can't handle what's happening here. I don't do loss, *m'ija*. I don't. I never wanted it, and I don't want it now. You don't go into a marriage with someone, and have a kid with someone, thinking it's going to turn out like this. I don't want to think about it. I want to get away from here and be me the way I used to be. I wasn't cut out for this.

As I open the front door of the house, I hear Juan comforting our daughter by telling her it's going to be all right, that sometimes mommies and daddies argue but it has nothing to do with their children, that it isn't her fault.

He's wrong.

It's *all* her fault.

I'd never tell her that, of course, but it's the damn truth. Before we had this child, Juan and I had a real relationship, but not anymore. Now, it's all about the child, and Juan is so worried he's not going to do it right that he never spends time alone with me. I need attention, too. Anyone who knows me knows that. And I am *not* fat. I am ample, generous, welcoming.

I don't want to cry, *m'ija*, I don't, but as I take the steps down from the house to the sidewalk, toward the curb where my new BMW *del año* is parked, I feel the tears come anyway. My tears, like my husband and my daughter, don't care what I want. They do what they want, without checking with me first.

"Usnavys!"

I stand at the driver's side door to my car, and turn toward the woman's voice. It's coming from down the block. I see Lauren in her big, black raincoat with jeans and sneakers sticking out the bottom, running toward me, her own face distorted by grief. What is wrong with the world, *m'ija*, that everyone is crying? I wipe my tears away, sniff back the ones that are coming, and smile at her like nothing's wrong. But it's no use.

Lauren sprints toward me, all crazy looking, and when she sees the tears in my own eyes, she stops cold and stares. I have never cried in front of my friends, *m'ija*. Never. I am a strong woman. My own brother died in my arms, shot in a drive-by, and I think that was the last time I allowed myself to cry in front of people. I am not going to do it again, I always told myself, but here I am, crying, and I can't make it stop.

"Usnavys?" she asks. "Are you okay?"

"I'm late for my manicure," I tell her. "Get in the car. You'll go with me."

"You're crying because you're late for a manicure?"

"Just get in," I tell her.

"I was on my way to the office, but I couldn't do it," she says.

"On a Saturday?"

"I'm supposed to be meeting Chuck there at seven."

"Chuck? Your boss?"

"He wants me to go to one of those nighttime soccer games with him. Panama and Brazil. He's got some Hispanic friend he'd like me to fuck."

"What?"

"He's trying to set me up with someone, and so he picked his one Hispanic friend."

I'm getting annoyed by her talking. I'm late. "I'll take you by there after the manicure. Get in."

"Okay, but I can't be late. I tried telling him I was sick, but then he called and I sounded better and it's just too hard to lie anymore."

We both get in the car, and after I take the box of Cheez-Its out of the backseat and prop it open on my lap, I drive away from my personal hell. I feel her staring at me as the tears roll down my cheeks. I will not wipe them away, because that's like admitting I'm crying.

"Please tell me you're not crying because you missed your manicure," Lauren says.

"I'm not crying. I have allergies."

She looks at me doubtfully. "What's going on, Usnavys? You can tell me. You tell me, then I'll tell you about how I stabbed Amaury this morning."

I glance at her in shock, and see that she knows I don't have any stupid allergies, *m'ija*. I am not even going to comment on her stabbing someone, because if she did it, I don't want to know, and if she didn't do it, I don't think it's a funny joke. I hope she *did* stab that lowlife.

I turn my eyes toward the road again, and then I do it. I tell her that I broke up with Juan today, that I finally told him I cheated on him in New Mexico, but I didn't tell him about Montreal and so I expect her to keep lying about it for me.

"Oh, my God. What did he say?" She reaches over for some crackers.

"Nothing." I begin to cry again, but not as hard as before. It helps to talk to a friend, *m'ija*. And when you consider all them times I've come to Lauren's rescue and listened to her stories of woe and misery, you will agree with me that this bitch owes me, okay? And I don't call her that as an insult, I call her that because I love her, now more than ever. "He was totally quiet and wouldn't even look at me. That's the part that scares me."

"Wow," she says again through a mouthful of crackers. "So why are you sad? I thought this was what you wanted."

"I don't know. I thought I did until he told me he was done with me, and now I feel like I'm going to die."

I lay it all out, and by the time we get to the Roxbury salon—where the girls really know how to do them some nail tips, okay?—Lauren is speechless. Speechless, *m'ija*. Just staring at me with her mouth a little open. This is *Lauren* we're talking about, okay? The girl who can't seem to shut her damn mouth most of the time, the girl who thinks all of New England wants to hear what she has to say every week, even if it's to complain about Cinco de Mayo being not really for Mexicans or whatever.

"I had no idea you could cry," she says, at last, as we enter the salon.

"Yeah, well, now you know. Okay? Now you know."

I dry my eyes, throw my head back, walk up to the receptionist, and demand two new appointments—one for me, and one for my friend who now knows entirely too much about me.

lauren

WITH A MILD, weird pain in my chest and this persistent sore throat, I sit in the pedicure chair next to Usnavys, who, in her gingham checkered dress, wears her chair like a throne. She looks like someone could serve a meal on her back at an Italian restaurant. She demands service from the technician. Me? I guiltily allow the haggard little skinny Vietnamese woman with the sad eyes and slouched shoulders to tend to my corns and calluses the way you might allow a doctor to do a colonoscopy. Poor woman. She's so pale she looks bloodless. The pedicure corpse.

She sighs, and I feel like apologizing.

It's cruel to do this to her. She needs a blood transfusion, and a bowl of spinach. She does *not* need these feet of mine, my freakin' feet that look like they might belong to David Beckham after a marathon, rather than a professional woman. But it's her job, the pedicurist's job, and I have to remind myself that she is actually making money from it. Still, I have guiltily mixed feelings about her indentured servitude. I mean, she's performing a service, but I know she's underpaid and there is no way in hell any human being with any shred of dignity wouldn't hate the job of shaving dead skin off someone else's stinky-ass feet. I worry she'll shave too far. What if she did that with the last customer, and that person had AIDS? Can I get AIDS from a pedicure shaver?

You can see why I don't get pedicures much.

The only thing worse than the state of my feet is I can't seem to stop belching. Gross, I know, but lately this has been my disgusting new habit. I am queen of the burps. They come all day long lately, which makes me wonder what the hell is wrong with me. Stress. It's gotta be stress.

"Now, what's your story today, *m'ija*? I've been talking so much I didn't even stop to find out why you were all sad as shit when you came over. It had to be something major to get you over on a Sunday evening instead of calling me." Usnavys closes her eyes like a TV psychic. "Let's have it."

I tell her that I tried her cell, but it was turned off and went directly to voice mail, and then I tell her that I called her home phone but it was busy, as if someone had taken it off the hook.

The women kneeling at our feet act as if we haven't spoken. They are the picture of discretion, but there's a part of me that wonders what they really think of us and all our problems. They're like silent bartenders.

I lean back in the black fake-leather of the chair and feel the massage machinery beneath the skin of it, attempting to knead the stress out of my back. I have a serious pain, yes I do, in my chest today, just beneath the sternum, and I don't know what it is. It's stress. Damn Amaury.

I begin the tale at the meeting of the Latino students at Boston Latin. I progress to finding Amaury all over that little girl Marislesys on her My-Space page.

"No, you *didn't!*" Usnavys sits up in fury and astonishment.

"I did."

"Fourteen years old?" She's wild-eyed.

"Fourteen years old. Seven times two."

She thumps the armrest with her fists. "They need to throw his ass in *jail*."

"Yeah." I nod. "It is true. How could I believe he was so perfect? What did I miss?"

"They need to throw his ass in *jail* so he can find himself a big-assed hairy man to make *him* the girlfriend."

"Yeah."

"Fuck *him* up the ass for fourteen years, see how he like it."

"Yep."

She looks at me like I'm a puppy in a pet store window on a rainy night. "I'm so sorry, *mamita*. That's horrible."

"Yeah. Pretty horrible."

Usnavys stares at me, in shock. "Are you sure it was him, *m'ija*? I mean, I know he's done some bad shit, but this is *really* bad shit."

"Oh, I'm sure. I finally talked to him about it this morning. He forced his way into my house and tried to rape me, and I stabbed him in the hand with manicure scissors."

The pedicure corpse raises one eyebrow toward the other nail tech, almost imperceptibly.

"Did you hurt him badly?"

"I don't think so."

"That's too bad."

"He left saying he'd be back. I had the locks changed this morning."

"Good."

"You think he'll come back? I'm kind of freaked out about it."

She shakes her head. "No way. He's out of his league now. You could send him to prison. You know too much about him. My guess is, he'll disappear now. He'll move to New York or Lawrence or something. You don't have to worry about it."

"I can't believe he did this."

She shrugs. "I don't know why you're surprised. Sounds familiar, *m'ija*. Don't you think?"

"I know," I tell her as I painfully recall that every man I've ever loved has cheated on me and lied to me.

I look at her for a moment and realize that my friend is a manizer. The way that my last two boyfriends have been womanizers, she is a manizer. She is a cheater. Is it weird that I've picked her for my best friend? I mean, why do I pick people who don't value what they've got? It's my disease, to always try to please people who don't quite approve of me.

Whoa.

"Why do you do it?" I ask her.

"Do what, *m'ija*?"

"Cheat. When you've got a perfectly good man at home who loves you like crazy."

I can tell from her facial expression that Usnavys knows I am asking her for an answer mostly so that I can understand what is happening to me—happening to me *again*.

"*M'ija*, it's different than what Amaury did. Okay?"

"I don't think so. No, it's not. It's not."

"No, it is. First of all, he's a Dominican."

I make a disgusted face at her. "What does that have to do with anything? Plus, your dad is Dominican. Why are you always talking shit about Dominicans, when you yourself are Dominican? Jesus, Usnavys, come on. You know better than to slam a whole group of people. That's what we fight against every day, girl."

"Who better to know the workings of the mind of a Dominican male than the daughter of one, *m'ija*? That's all I'm saying."

"Just because your dad was a jerk doesn't mean all Dominican men are jerks."

She shrugs. "Amaury wasn't raised in the United States, *m'ija*. He has these ideas about love and romance that are very different than the ones you and I were raised with here. What you saw today? Very normal interaction where he's from. You being a white-trash hillbilly from the bayou and whatnot would not understand that shit."

"Like what?"

She gets a philosophical look. "Okay, like this. He thinks about women as possessions, and that's part of the reason I never wanted you to get involved with him in the first place. I can see it in the way he walks. He thinks he can own you and that once he does, he can do what he wants to you. He's not the only one, okay? Our men are groomed for that shit."

I dislike Usnavys's tendency to lump all people into groups depending on where they're from or their skin tones, but she does it all the time and right now I am feeling far too weak to protest. If I'm honest about it, I realize that she's got a point, to an extent. I tell her she's right. That in fact, Amaury even defended himself by saying that in his country, fourteen is not considered too young for sex. That he even bragged to me that Marislesys was a virgin when he first started seeing her, and he showed me the reason he liked her by using his hands to outline an hourglass in the air between us.

Usnavys whistles and shakes her head. "I told you he was no good. From the *start* I told you that. I told you that, *m'ija*."

"Yeah." I am starting to sound like a parrot, but it's all I can find to say right now. Yeah. "I know."

"Damn, Amaury. I thought for a while that maybe he was different, because he was making you so happy, girl," she tells me. "I thought it for five seconds, but I *thought* it, you know? For *your* benefit I tried to give the man the benefit of my doubt. I will not do that shit again. My instincts are good like that."

"I know. He was so good in bed, Usnavys. I'll never find anyone like that again."

"Bullshit. Yes, you will."

"I don't think so. You don't understand. We clicked that way."

"Why? Because he was rough with you?"

I swallow and say nothing. It sounds sad to hear her say it like that, even if it's true.

"You need a dose of self-respect, *m'ija*. That's what you need. To 'click' with better men, okay?"

I look away, miserable. She's right, of course.

"Don't you be getting all sad about this, *m'ija*. Losing him is the best thing ever happened to you. But you better get you tested for some STDs up in there." Her finger twirls in the air.

"I know. I already made an appointment." My chest is *killing* me now. I wonder if I'm too young to have a heart attack. It's getting harder to breathe. I hear my breath coming in wheezes, like an asthmatic.

"*Ay*, Lauren. I'm so sorry. *Mira*, the thing is, most people don't change. You can *want* to change, but it takes a lot to make a person change. I think we all come as we are, pretty much, and so if you don't like someone the way they are when you meet them, better keep on moving and find someone else."

I think about it, and realize she might be right. I hate that. I hate when other people are right and I'm wrong. My heart keeps thundering in my chest, and I feel like I can't breathe. This is bad. I know this is bad, but I hope it passes. I don't need to have a heart attack right now. It's the last thing I need. I pretend it's not there, hoping it goes away.

"Look, you have to be morally bankrupt to be a drug dealer," she goes on to say. "You have to be—at the very least—a damn moral *opportunist*. That's what Amaury was when you met him, so you shouldn't be totally surprised that this happened the way it did."

I stare at her, amazed once more by how easily Usnavys can sound erudite if she wants to.

"What? I can't use me some big words now and then? You the only one gets to use them big words, *m'ija*?"

"I didn't say a word about your words."

Her eyes search mine and slowly turn away. "It's not like he was volunteering at church, *nena*. That boy was poison."

"Or helping people get off drugs," I say, referencing the job Juan had for years as the director of a rehab center for Latino men and their families. He was amazing at his work, and at everything he does. "Or taking care of young children."

"Low blow," says Usnavys. She looks terribly sad now, and stares out the window at passing cars.

My sternum feels like it's being dipped in lye. Beneath it, my heart feels tight, like it might be straining. Maybe I *am* having a heart attack. I slam my hand to my chest with a choking sound. Usnavys looks at me again, as if she hadn't noticed something before. Her face is worried. "You okay?"

"Yeah, I'm fine. Don't worry. Just a little heartburn or something." I smile and shake my head no. I wouldn't know how to even tell her something so pathetic as the fact that I can't control my life. Hell, I can't even control my *body*.

"You don't look good, *m'ija*. You look all pale."

At that moment, the pain escalates, and I feel it spread from my sternum down my arm and up into my neck, on the right side, and into the ear. "Whoa," I say. I feel dizzy. Lightheaded. The room starts to spin. "Oh, shit."

"Hey, Lauren, you all right?" she asks.

"I don't know," I say. "I think talking about all this got me worked up. It's weird, I have this weird feeling right here," I shake out, pressing my chest with my hand.

Usnavys asks me to describe the weird feeling, and when I do, she cuts the pedicures short, before the polish. "Sorry, ladies," she says, gathering her purse and stuffing her feet back into her espadrilles. "We have to go."

"What?" I ask. The pain is getting worse. "Go where?"

Usnavys looks at me as though I've lost my mind. "To the hospital, *m'ija*. Where else? When your best friend has a heart attack, you take her to the damn hospital. For all I know, that lowlife done poisoned you or some shit. Now get your shoes on, girl. Let's go."

I tell her I'm not sure I need to go to a hospital. But the words ring hollow, because at the moment I speak them, my heart squeezes in a way that sucks the breath out of me. "Ow. Okay, okay," I say as the weary pedicurist shoves my shoes onto my feet. "Let's go."

Usnavys pays, and holds me by the arm on the way to the car.

"Call Chuck for me, okay?" I mumble. I am nearly delirious, but I am not crazy enough to get fired for missing the game.

"Sure, of course. Don't worry about that goofy motherfucker right now. You're gonna be fine, girl, okay? Just keep breathing. Yeah, like that! Good girl. You're okay. You're gonna be okay. I promise."

The pain escalates as we drive to Brigham and Women's Hospital. She pulls into the drop-off area in front of the emergency room, and asks, "You okay to walk in there by yourself, *m'ija*?"

I nod.

"I just have to park the car. I'll be right back," she says. "You sure you can make it?"

"Yeah, I can do it."

She jogs around to open my door, and, out of breath, pulls me from my seat. "Just that way, *m'ija*. I'll be right back. Don't you die on me, *¿oíste?* Don't you *dare*."

As I walk slowly and unsteadily down the bright, tiled hall toward the reception area, I wonder how Chuck is going to react when she tells him I can't go to the soccer game after all. I guess it won't look like I was lying about being sick, now that I'm in the emergency room. He won't think about that, I bet. He'll think about how he won't get to introduce me to the only other Latino he knows.

Pity.

I wonder how it is that I can continue to be a smart-ass in my own head, even as I stagger toward certain doom. Once an ass, always an ass I suppose. Not even death could fix me.

sara

I SIT IN my new sexy black dress at a table for two in Tajadas, a trendy, crowded Panamanian and Spanish tapas bar in Harvard Square, with the oh-so-young Valentín, watching him pour dark red sangria from the pitcher into my glass. He wears khaki slacks and a burgundy guayabera. I'm trying to focus on the evening at hand, and not on the fact that Lauren and Cuicatl won't return my calls. I wish they'd be more understanding.

"What's wrong?" asks Valentín.

"Nothing."

"So? What do you think?" He gestures to the room.

"I like this place," I say. "It's got a nice feel. It's not like there are millions of Panamanian restaurants around."

He leans toward me, grinning. "I know, *right*? Panamanian. Who would have thought?"

"The people who own this place?"

"Panamanians."

"Ah."

"I thought you'd dig the décor," he says.

I had half expected the *jovencito* to pick a college sports bar and spend the evening watching a game with his mouth open. I swear, *chica*, I tend to underestimate people.

Valentín could be Mark Ruffalo's younger twin right now. He's got the adorable slouching thing to him, the downturned, intelligent eyes, the posture of a hot guy who has no idea how hot he is.

He pours some of the dark red, smoky, fruity sangria for himself now, with a very masculine hand. Earlier, we ordered several plates of tapas to share; some, like the garlic shrimp, of a decidedly Spanish origin, and others, like the cinnamon-baked plantains and the boiled yucca roll stuffed with meat and boiled eggs, more Panamanian.

He looks tall, and warm, and rumpled, and smart, and I really—I mean really, *chica*—love the way he's looking at me right now. With half a grin on his face, and a whole lot of intent, sexual intent, unspoken and kept at bay behind his eyes.

"You look amazing," he tells me. At the last minute I bought a lacy shawl at Neiman Marcus, to wear over my shoulders, so I didn't freeze or look too desperate. I also got a little black clutch, extremely subdued. I got some new jewelry at Tiffany, nothing too expensive, but nice nonetheless.

"You look like Mark Ruffalo," I tell him.

"Who?"

"He's an actor."

"A good actor?"

"I think he's very handsome."

"Can he act?"

"Yes. He's a good actor."

"What's he been in?"

"This movie with Reese Witherspoon." I can't think of the name, and hit myself on the forehead with my palm as if this might help. When that fails to help I look at the ceiling and bite my lower lip. That seems to do it. "*Just Like Heaven*. The movie is called *Just Like Heaven*."

"Huh," says Valentín. "Never saw it. What else has he done?"

"He did *Rumor Has It*, with what's-her-name from *Friends*, *la flaquita esa*."

He laughs. "Which one?"

"Jennifer Aniston."

"Ugh." He looks like he's detected a foul odor and tries to wave it off. "Can't stand her."

"Why?"

He chews with reckless abandon, a real epicurean, shrugs, so confident in his youth. I don't remember feeling that confident at twenty-one. "I don't know." Valentín speaks with his mouth full, but it is not gross when he does it. He keeps his lips close together. It's sexy, and sensual. "Something about her. She's too skinny, for one, and I don't like her nose. She reminds me of a puppet from *Sesame Street*, one of those twin blue monsters with the big, red nose."

"Oh, c'mon! That's awful. She's adorable," I counter. "Everyone knows *that*."

Valentín shakes his head violently, "No, no, *no!* See? That's the thing. I *hate* when everyone thinks someone is adorable, and so you feel guilty if you don't agree, you know? I don't think Jennifer Aniston is adorable. I think she's frighteningly birdlike, and manly."

"Manly?"

"*Sí*, Sarita. She looks like a man."

"If she looks like a man, I hate to think what I look like. A wookie?"

"You"—he points at me—"look a hundred times better than Jennifer Aniston."

"Such hostility toward Jennifer," I joke. "Hasn't she suffered enough, losing Brad Pitt?"

"Pussy."

"Who? Brad Pitt?"

"A total pussy."

"Yeah, right!" I pick another shrimp to eat. "You're so jealous. Just like I'm jealous of Jennifer Aniston."

"You have no justification for being jealous of her. You over Jennifer Aniston, any day." Valentín spears a marinated mushroom from one of the six plates of tapas in front of us, puts it in his mouth whole. "Mmm," he says, savoring it. I swallow the shrimp, down my sangria for courage, and pour another glass.

"Done already?" he asks, smiling in a playful, mocking way.

"I'm a little nervous. This helps."

"Nervous? Why?" He eats another mushroom and looks at me with a sparkle in his eye, because, I think, he already knows the answer.

"Because you won," I tell him. "Because I think you're adorable."

The slight grin turns into a full-on smile, *chica*. He sucks the end of his fork, to get the last bit of juice off, and watching his mouth makes me light-headed. I want to be that fork.

"What are you thinking?" he asks.

"Nothing."

He sits back, cocky, and smiles at me. "I won, huh?"

I give him a smile to say yes, he has very much won, and tackle some more garlic shrimp. We both fork bits of the food onto our respective plates, and spend a few moments quietly eating and observing our surroundings.

"So, what's the craziest place you've ever had sex?" he asks, finally.

"What?" I almost choke on the shrimp, and freeze, not knowing whether to laugh or not.

"Just a simple question."

"It's a loaded question." And just the kind of question you might expect from a man his age, *¿no?*

He shrugs, but looks hurt. "So don't answer it. Sorry I asked."

"No, hold on. That's okay. I'll answer it. Give me a minute to remember."

"Been that long, huh?"

"You have no idea."

I down more sangria and after I start to feel its effects—a lifting out of my own self-consciousness, mostly—I decide to stop being nervous and shy about this whole thing. Now, I'm the one leaning back and smiling at him. It catches him off guard, and he seems uncomfortable with the shift for a moment.

"What?" he asks. I'm staring at his mouth. He notices, and touches it with his fingers. "Do I have something on my lip?"

"No."

He looks at me quizzically, waiting for an explanation.

"On a hotel balcony in Chicago."

"What?"

"That's the weirdest place I had sex."

"It doesn't sound that weird."

"It was right next to the freeway. It was rush hour."

"Okay, maybe a little weird. Who was it with?"

"My estranged husband. He was on a business trip. He got a promotion, and wanted to celebrate."

"That's how he celebrated?"

"He was a little strange," I say. He looks at me with sympathy because he, like everyone in my orbit, knows all about the legendary murderous husband who dropped off the face of the Earth. We've never spoken of it directly, but Elizabeth told me that he talked about it with her. He knows.

"No! I think it's great," he says, uncomfortably. "If I had a promotion to celebrate, I'd want to do it like that."

"On a balcony?" I ask, grateful he's not asked more about Roberto.

"*Donde sea*. With you."

I am speechless. So I drink a little more and look around the bar. "Nice place," I say.

"You're funny," he tells me. "I'm glad we're doing this."

I drink more, and when I feel a little less nervous, say, "I can't believe I'm here." I feel sexier the more I talk. "With you. I've wanted to do this for a long time."

"Really?" He looks quite surprised, *chica*.

"*Oh*, yeah."

"Coulda fooled me, girl." He hides behind his goblet of sangria, a smile in his eyes.

"I know. I'm sorry about all that," I say.

Valentín shrugs. "All that what? The coldness? The unresponsiveness? Or the constant rejection of my advances?"

"All that."

"Huh." He eyes me with interest, as if he's rewriting our entire history now, with the new information factored in.

"It wasn't that I wasn't interested, okay? You're beautiful. You know that, right?" I say.

Valentín shrugs, but I can tell he knows he's attractive. It's not false modesty; it's more like he's tactful.

"Women have told you that before, right?" I insist.

"Once or twice." He grins.

My blood speeds up, heats up. "I just didn't think, I mean as your *boss*, it just felt weird."

"You look sexy when you're talking about being my boss."

I feel a blush coming on. "That's gross."

"No, it's erotic."

"Next topic." Only a *jovencito* would think an affair with his boss was erotic.

"Okay."

"You didn't tell me the weirdest place you've done it. I mean, *if* you've done it."

He looks mock-offended. "What do you mean 'if'?"

I smile, teasingly. "Well, being so young, I don't know."

"You're hilarious." He's more offended than I expected, probably because he's so young.

"So you're not a virgin?" I tease, relentless now that I've gotten to him.

"I'm not even going to dignify that with an answer," he says. He seems to think for a moment, drinks his sangria, and says, "In the ocean."

"In the ocean what?"

"I did it in the ocean. I was in San Diego with my girlfriend at the time, and we did it out in the water, with our heads up, and pretended all we were doing was hugging."

"How the hell did you do that, *chico*?"

"Just moved her thong out of the way, me behind her."

"You have a girlfriend who wore a thong?"

"Had. That's right. Had."

"And you just stuck it in right there in the ocean?"

"With surfers and kids and everything all around us."

"That's crazy!"

"It wasn't very productive. Salt water stung like a motherfucker, and she itched for days."

"I bet."

He looks at me with longing in his eyes. "Next topic."

This time I say, "Okay. Your choice."

"How long I've wanted you."

"No, no. How about this? How long I've wanted *you*."

"You want *me*?"

"Since the first day I interviewed you." Yep. Must be getting drunk to tell him *that*.

"Oh, really." He seems pleased with himself now.

"Really."

"But? There's gotta be a 'but' in there."

"*But* you're so young. My God, you were only *twenty* then! I'm an old lady already, with kids. I'm your boss. You understand my dilemma here?"

"No."

I glare at him.

He lights up. "Okay, yes. I do. But when there's chemistry, there's chemistry, right? Age smage."

"You think we have chemistry?"

He scoots his chair closer to mine. "I know so," he says, leaning toward me. "But there's only one way to know for sure."

Ay, Dios mío, chica. His hand is on mine, and the simple touch sends waves of excitement along my spine. Now he's touching my cheek, gently stroking it, and the smile on his face has been replaced by something more intense and focused. I feel this look of his in my core. He looks at me with an expression more animalistic than he has ever given me before, and I like it. My body shivers as a thrill passes along the nape of my neck, raising the little hairs there. His eyes zero in on my mouth, and he leans in, no longer a boy at all, not at all. In this moment, Valentín is all man—without any wrinkles.

Oh, my God.

He's about to kiss me. I want to come up with some super-clever reply, no, to what he just said, but my mind is a little hazy, comfortably numb so to speak, and all I can do is focus on those lips coming toward me. *Oye, pero* this is unwise, right? So why does it feel so good?

His head is turning a little to the side, and then, like that, like the softest moon landing of all time, his lips touch mine. It is a gentle kiss, just a peck, really, and then another. Three little pecks in a row, and then he's moved away from me and his eyes are open, looking at me.

"Yeah," he says. "I'd say there's chemistry."

"You think?"

He closes his eyes. "God, I love your smell."

"It's Carolina Herrera, 212."

"No, not the perfume—which is nice. I mean your smell. Your mouth, your breath, your skin. Your natural smell. I like it."

"You like my *smell?*"

"Don't say it like that, Sara! Smell is essential. If you're not smell compatible, there's no hope, no matter how much you like someone. And what about you? You like my smell?"

"I think so." This time it is me reaching out for him. I grab him behind the neck and pull him closer. "I think we need to do that again to be sure."

I kiss him. A couple more pecks, then they turn into nibbles, and yes, I like his smell. Very much. There is something very musky and manly about it that excites me. He puts his arms around my shoulders, and we sit facing one another, kissing, and then his lips part, and the kiss becomes deeper and more passionate. I move closer, and open my legs toward him, under the table, and he moves one leg right in between them, takes one hand from my shoulders and places it on my thigh. I think I squeak a little bit, but the music in the bar makes it impossible for anyone but us to hear.

It has been years, *chica*—and I mean years—since I made out with a young man in public. I feel sort of humiliated, but not enough to stop. Mostly I just feel turned on.

I move my hands along his legs, onto his belly, to his chest, neck, along the sides of his face, touching lightly and feeling the electricity flowing from his body to mine. He feels solid, powerful, and all I want right now is to touch him *there*. I move my hand back to his thigh, and up, toward the center. I stop just short.

"Scared?" he asks, with that laugh in his eyes. He looks amused, cocksure.

"Too many people around."

"They're all drunk."

"Not all of them. The waitress isn't drunk."

"She's seen worse."

"I'm sure."

He starts to stand up, and pulls me with him. "Where are you going?" I ask.

"Come with me."

"Where?"

"Just come with me. Take your purse."

"We leaving?" I look around, confused.

"Not yet."

I trip along behind him as he weaves through the crowd with my hand clutched in his. He stops when we get to the door to the women's restroom.

"Uh, Valentín? What are you doing?"

He knocks on the door. No answer. He looks behind us, then down the hall. "Okay," he tells me. "C'mon."

He opens the door to the women's room, and pulls me in with him. I am so nervous, *chica*, I feel like I could cry and laugh at the same time. "What are you doing?" I hiss-whisper as he shuts and locks the door.

"I thought we both needed a new public sex story."

I look at the bathroom. It's a single room, fairly large and clean. The walls are painted red, with art hanging on them, and the light is dim. I look good in the mirror. Dim light will do that. A real, healthy ficus tree stands in one corner, and an automatic air freshener spews chemicals that smell vaguely of bubblegum into the air. Valentín looks around, too.

"I swear, women are so much cleaner than men," he says. "Look at this place. It's like a palace. You could eat off the floor."

"I wouldn't."

"Men are pigs. Men's restrooms are disgusting."

He grabs me, kisses me again, and pushes me up against the wall, next to the shelf with extra paper towels and toilet paper on it.

"Men *are* pigs," I joke, referring to him. But *chica*, I am telling you right now that this feels amazing. I have always wanted to have a man like this push me up against a wall like this, and just do what he's doing, which is hold me in place and kiss the hell out of me. Valentín takes my wrists in his hands and lifts them over my head, pins them against the wall, and he kisses me expertly, hungrily.

"You're so fucking sexy," he tells me. "I don't usually do this kind of thing."

The bad word makes all my latent bad-girl neurons fire, *chica*, and I kiss back, hard. He responds instantly, and escalates the kissing back. He kisses my chin, my neck, my earlobes, my collarbone. I realize that there is a big difference between truly masterful lovers, like this young man, and bullies like Roberto who only *think* they're masterful. To be truly masterful with a woman, a man cannot be selfish. I can't believe it took me this long to realize.

Valentín slides my shawl off and tosses it onto the shelf. I now understand why the straps of this dress tie on top of the shoulders. Easy access. He uses his teeth and fingers to untie them, and they just drop off. The dress falls to my hips and stays there, tentatively. I worry about the stretch marks on my belly, evidence of having had children. Those scars, those horrible wormy little scars, are never going to disappear.

Valentín does not seem to notice them. Or if he does, he does not seem to care, he does not let on. What he does do? Admire my breasts, compliment them, touch them, squeeze them, trace them with his fingers. Then he pulls the tops of the cups of my bra down to reveal bare skin, which he kisses.

"I guess you're not a virgin," I comment. "I wasn't sure you were telling the truth."

He smiles up at me and takes a nipple into his mouth. Roberto never took so much time on me; not in all our years together can I remember him taking this much time to please me.

"*Ay, Dios mío,*" I say. I had no idea what I was missing.

Someone knocks on the door.

"Just a minute," I call. "I'm, uhm, I'm a little sick, so I might be here a while."

Outside the door, a woman says, "Fuck."

"If she insists," whispers Valentín.

He kisses my belly, the stretch marks and all, and keeps one set of fingers clamped to my breast, kneading more or less just the right way. With his free hand, he hikes up the skirt and presses his face to my panties, breathing in.

"Oh, my God," he says. "You smell so good."

Through the lace, he bites me, gently. The skirt falls over him, and he stops to tuck it up into the waistband of my panties, then returns to work. And what work he does, *chica.* Slides the crotch of the panties out of the way, and licks and tickles just right, enters me with his fingers, finds the g-spot almost instantly, which is so shocking I cry out.

"Sorry," he says. "Did I hurt you?"

"No, no, no," I say. "No pain. Felt amazing. Don't stop." Roberto didn't like to do this. He told me it made his jaw hurt. So I stopped asking after a while.

I still wear the heels, which help with the tensing of my calves and thighs as I quickly—surprisingly, almost embarrassingly quickly, *chica*—tilt toward climax.

"Yeah, girl," he says, "do it. Come for me."

"Now?"

"Right now."

He continues, and I obey the orders. He knows exactly what he's doing, and does it beyond well. I come easily, and efficiently; probably after all those years of neglect my body was surprised to be paid any attention at all. As soon as I stop, he knows, and withdraws his hand and tongue. He removes my panties, takes a condom from his wallet, rips the package open with his teeth, puts it on quickly but carefully, turns me around, and bends me over toward the wall. I know exactly what he's doing, and it's what I'd hoped he'd do. Sex feels amazing after I've come. I know some women want to stop, but not me. I want to keep going, and going, and going, like the Energizer Bunny.

We keep going.

As he slides into me—a perfect fit, *chica, Dios mío*—I let out a little scream. It's like a roller coaster, *chica*. I can't help it. I wish I could, because someone else—or the same person, *quién sabe*—is knocking at the door. Loud. I should yell something like "just a minute" again, but it turns out I can't think very well right now. I can only feel. And I feel amazing. I don't want it to end.

"I hate to do this," he says, as he starts to pump faster, blindingly fast, which I love, "but I'm gonna have to speed this up. We can go for slow and sweet later, Sarita."

"*Vente, ya*," I tell him. "*Vente ahora, mi amor*. Come."

And he does. Afterward, he holds me, hugs me, kisses me. "Now you have a better public sex story," he says. "Right?"

"Much better," I say as I readjust my clothes. All he has to do is pull his pants up and zip up. Oh, my God, *chica*, I can hardly walk. It was *that* good.

I look in the mirror and see mascara has run all over my face. "I look like a drowned raccoon," I wail.

"You look beautiful," he tells me with a playful slap to my behind. "You have never looked more beautiful to me than you do right this instant." He kisses my cheek, then gives me a peck on the lips. He is smiling. I hadn't realized men could do that after sex. Roberto was always so angry. I got used to seeing his anger after sex, his disapproval of me.

"Okay," I say as I fix the damage to my makeup with a moist paper towel. "But how are we gonna get out of here without getting arrested for public indecency?"

"Walk with our heads held high?"

We laugh, and then, with great bravery, I open the door, smooth my skirt over my hips, and smile at the young, nubile and, frankly, shocked girls waiting to pee.

As I walk back to the table hand in hand with Valentín, I hear one of the girls say to the other, "Damn, he's hot," to which the other answers, "Wish that had been me."

As we cross the floor, me practically prancing with *orgullo*, back toward our table, a suited figure at the bar catches my eye. It's Roberto.

I get the angry stare after all.

rebecca

BOB MUEHLER SCOOPS his thick white clam chowder *toward* him in the cup, thoroughly uncouth. Across the table from him in the woody darkness of Legal Sea Foods, I scoop mine *away* from me in the cup, as protocol dictates. He doesn't notice my effort to teach through example. But this is not a surprise. Since meeting him here half an hour ago for dinner to discuss the possible sale of my magazine to his company—for nearly $150 million if I give him half the shares, or close to $300 million for the whole thing—he seems to have noticed little but the rear ends on the waitresses, most of whom are pretty and, I assume, putting themselves through college by working here, making them at least forty years younger than him.

It is important to me to sell my magazine, if indeed I am to sell it, to a man or woman capable of learning through example, a person able to understand the pleasures of good company and polite behavior. It is also important, considering that this is a women's magazine, that the owner respect women, especially young women—the future of our readership.

"Tell me how you see the magazine evolving in the event that your company were to take it over," I say. "As you know, there have been some issues in the sale of *Essence* magazine to Time Warner, editorial changes and a loss of focus now that the magazine is no longer black-owned. I don't think I need to tell you this is a pitfall I would rather avoid."

I cringe as he gulps down the last of his second beer and wipes his mouth on the sleeve of his blue button-down shirt. He is a bald man of about sixty, with the look of one who has had too much red meat and too many cigars, however buttoned-down he may be in his trousers and high-end dress shirt. He joins his hands over his belly, leans back, and sizes me up with his shrewd brown eyes. He looks at me as if he knows I'm bluffing him, which I am not.

"Oh, c'mon, Rebecca," he says in a patronizing tone of voice. I half expect him to pick his teeth as if he were at a rural barbecue, but he does not. "You know as well as I do that I won't be the one overseeing day-to-day operations of the magazine. You know I'm not exactly qualified to be the visionary Latina in charge of *Ella*."

"I am surprised that you believe you know what I know," I tell him with a friendly smile that reveals none of the irritation I feel at his smugness. "But comforted somewhat that you don't think you're a visionary Latina."

He changes his approach now, perhaps sensing that he's getting nowhere with me by using his usual bullying. "You know me well enough by now to know that I'd hire someone qualified to do any restructuring for me. Hell, I don't even speak Spanish. Not that it should matter. I own properties in France, in China. My wife and I are looking to relocate to China at some point, for good. We got multinational properties out the wazoo. I'm not the guy you need to be an expert at running *Ella*; I'm the guy you need to trust to find the experts in your little community. You know our track record, the success we've had with all our other properties."

Little community?

I consider what he has told me. It is true. He has been successful at getting good people to do the jobs that must be done within his media empire. But there is something about thinking of *Ella* magazine as one of Muehler's multinational "properties" that unsettles me. I have worked my entire career to build the magazine, and unlike Bob, I have been the person at the head of the company and the visionary behind the success of the product. I have watched it grow from nothing at all to a magazine with consistent growth in both advertising sales and circulation. It feels like a friend to me, not a "property."

"You don't have to worry," he says now, his eyes softening a little. I don't know much about him, but I do know he has a wife and three children that he adores, some grandchildren somewhere. With regards to his treatment of me at the moment, however, I cannot tell whether he is sincerely sensitive, or whether this is yet another negotiation strategy for a man who has made a fortune through little else. I decide it is most likely the latter. "We'll take good care of the magazine. There's nothing we'd like to change about it, as far as I can tell, because you're making a lot of money. Hand over fist. How do you say that in Spanish?"

"I'm not sure I know." I wonder if he has forgotten that *Ella* is an English-language magazine.

"What the hell, doesn't matter. You're making money. That's why we want to buy you out, obviously. If it ain't broke, I always say—"

"Don't fix it," I finish for him.

The waitress returns with yet another basket of bread, the third. I have not had a single bite of bread. Muehler pops some into his mouth and continues his attempts to sell me.

"We've been waiting months on this, going back and forth, me and you, dancing like Fred and Ginger. I think it's getting to be close to decision time, Rebecca."

My spine grows rigid at the hint of a threat. "You think so?"

"I don't want to sound ungrateful, but I have to tell you that the board is getting antsy about the whole thing." He breaks off a chunk of sourdough bread from the lump in the basket and uses it to sop up the last of his chowder. Ugh. "I don't want to pressure you, but I do think it would be best for me to go back to New York with a decision this week. There are some other properties that have come up, some speculation going on, and there are new directions some on the board would like us to follow. You know the amount we're ready to give you?"

"Yes, it is more than fair."

He leans across the table like he's sharing a secret, his eyes darting around. "We've never offered this much to a minority publication before. But the writing's on the wall, with all the illegals in the news and the way the country's changing whether you like it or not, and we know what side of our tortilla is buttered. I was amazed myself when the board approved the amount, and it'd be a shame to keep them hanging too long and upset them, you know what I mean? They might not be willing to stay so high unless they get some sign that you're willing to play."

Tortilla? What is he thinking? I look at his eyes and don't like what I see. "All right. Well, then, let me make this easy for you."

Muehler's face lights up in anticipation of my selling. I could slap him right now. Illegals? Is that what he thinks? He thinks *people* can be illegal? He thinks this is my target audience? That all Hispanics are the same? Does this man have no idea that most of the Hispanic women in this country were *born* here? That the majority of us are just as American as he is, if not more so, that we live our lives in English most of the time? Is he really this ignorant? I realize with a shock that I have been so focused on having a baby that I haven't allowed myself to really pay attention to what Muehler has been saying all these months. I was so flattered by the offer that I refused to see the moneylust behind it. He knows nothing about us—and even though we scare him, he is more than happy to make money off of us. It is exactly the kind of thinking that would, in fact, destroy *Ella* magazine, if Bob Muehler ever got his grubby hands on it.

I hold his gaze and do not flinch. "I'm not interested in playing."

He stops himself from taking another hunk of bread into his open mouth, and his eyes narrow. "What did you say?"

"I don't want to sell, Bob. I'm sorry I led you to believe otherwise. There have been some changes in my thinking."

"You made me come up here during the weekend for nothing?"

"I was interested in seeing your eyes. I wanted to talk face-to-face before making any decision. Now we've done that. Besides, I hear there's a home game for the Red Sox," I offer with a smile. I put two tickets to the game on the table, a gift.

"Rebecca, listen. Don't be foolish." He eyes the tickets, but does not thank me.

"That's exactly what I was thinking," I tell him. "I don't *want* to be foolish, and at this point in my career, and in the development of *Ella* magazine, I don't think it would be wise to hand the property over to an organization with an unproven track record in addressing the needs of the women in the community I serve."

"What do you mean unproven? We have several black magazines that do well."

"It's not the same, Bob. Surely you must know that."

"Of course I know that." He pauses. "Let me ask you—did you receive a better offer?"

"No," I say. "I am keeping *Ella*."

"You sure?" he asks.

I smile at him. "I admire what you've done, and have nothing but immense respect for you and gratitude for your interest in my magazine. But I am not comfortable with this deal at this time."

Muehler's jovial attitude is gone, replaced by bitter arrogance. "You're going to regret it," he says with a shrug as if he didn't care, pocketing the tickets. He continues to eat, smiling as if none of this bothers him at all. "And when you come back to us, when you realize you made a mistake, don't count on the deal still being there."

"I would never expect anything of the sort," I say. "I am not naïve."

Mercifully, my cell phone rings. I would normally have remembered to turn it off before starting a meeting like this, but tonight I forgot. I have been a little distracted lately, with the discussions with Andre about possibly using a surrogate. I look at the caller ID and see "Rivera." Normally, I wouldn't take Usnavys's call at a time like this, but right now I would like any excuse not to have to share an entire meal with this man.

"Bob, if you'll excuse me, I think this is an urgent call."

"No problem, babe," he says, probably using the word because he— wrongly—assumes it will bother me.

The "urgent call" words are not true when I speak them, but as soon as I step outside the restaurant to take the call, as soon as I hear the panic in Us-navys's voice, I realize they were less a fib than a premonition.

"Lauren's in the emergency room," she tells me. "She thinks she's having a heart attack. I know you have a meeting, but if you can get here, it'd be good."

"Emergency room?" I ask. *Heart attack?* "What's wrong?"

"They're not sure yet. Can you come?"

I promise her I'll be there just as soon as I can, hang up, and take less than two minutes to praise Bob Muehler, shake his meaty, sweaty hand, thank him, and beg his pardon as I have an emergency to attend to, in my "little community."

sara

MY HEART IS POUNDING as if I were being chased, which in a way I suppose I am. I can't believe Roberto is here in this cheerful restaurant, star-ing me down. I try not to look directly at him, pretend not to have seen him yet. Think, Sarita, *coño*. Think. I have to get this situation under control. But I don't want a scene between Valentín and Roberto, so I lie to my new lover in order to get him to leave me behind at the restaurant where we've only just made love in the bathroom. Mostly, I don't want Roberto to hurt Valentín.

"I know this is going to seem strange," I say to Valentín. "But I'm feeling a little weird now, about this whole thing."

God, it's a horrible lie. In truth, I think I am falling in love with this man. But in fairness to him, I have to make him think I don't like him now. For his own good.

"What do you mean?" he asks. He looks scared, and hurt.

"I mean, I'd really just like to be alone right now."

"Are you serious?"

"Dead."

"You want to be alone?" He looks flabbergasted.

"I'm sorry, Valentín." I hold my hand out to shake his, businesslike, already concocting the lie I am going to tell Roberto later. "But I think you should leave."

He looks at me, stunned. "You're serious?" He shakes my hand, as I hoped he would, but his eyes betray his confusion.

"I'm sorry. I'm like this. I need time to process what just happened."

"Time."

"I'd appreciate it if you'd leave now."

"You want me to *leave*?"

"I want you to quit repeating everything I say, and just go."

"Go."

"Now. Get out of here. Hurry." I turn away from him as if he held no interest for me at all.

He shrugs, awkward, and starts to walk away. "You're sure?" he asks.

I ignore him now, just watch him from the corner of my eye. I hope to God he doesn't try to kiss me or something. That would be a death sentence for him. For me. He comes back. Fuck. I didn't want him to do that, *chica*.

"Can I call you?" he asks, keeping a safe distance.

I try to look bored. "I'll see you at work. Please leave. I can't stand the sight of you right now."

"Oh." His face flushes red, and he looks more angry than hurt now. *Ay, Dios mío*, it hurts to do this to him. "I'll see you at work."

He leaves, and I try to stop my heart from hurting. I'll explain it all to him later. I know he'll understand.

Once Valentín has left the restaurant, I look up and see Roberto still staring me down like a bird of prey. He is not pleased, I can tell by the firm line of his mouth and the way his dark eyebrows push together over the bridge of his nose. It looks like he's guzzling a gin and tonic. That's bad news, too, *chica*. This is the drink he turns to when he's *requete* angry. I walk over to him, without smiling. I don't want to lead him on anymore. I don't want him to think he has a chance in hell. The seats at the bar on either side of him are taken, so I stand before him, shaking like the fronds of a Florida palm tree in a breeze. *Coño, pero* I didn't think I'd be this wimpy.

"What are you doing here?" I ask in a forced whisper, trying to sound stronger than I feel. "I thought you were in Buenos Aires."

He looks right at me and says, straightforwardly and in a low voice, "There is a gun in my jacket pocket, Sara. And if you do anything stupid, I am pre-pared to use it."

"You wouldn't do that to me." As I say it, I know it is untrue.

"But I might do it to myself," he says, and I can see him fishing for pity now. He looks at me with wounded eyes, a man who feels supremely sorry for himself.

"Why are you even here? Are you crazy? Someone will see you."

"Making sure you meant what you said. You know, I had a feeling, Sarita. I saw that you bought a black dress on our American Express card, at a store I never saw you shop at before, and I just got a little sinking feeling."

"You don't still use that card! Your name was taken off the account."

"True, but I can still access the statements online."

"How?"

"I have some friends in Miami, Internet people, police people."

"My God, Roberto. How could you spy on me like that?"

"Me? How could *I*? Is that what you just said?"

"You heard me."

"No, it should be how could *you*, eh?" He fingers the shoulder strap of the dress as if it were a rotten banana peel. He speaks softly, near my ear. "You look like a whore. And you *are* one. I saw that tonight. I knew it, too. As soon as I saw that, I got the feeling. The kind you get when you're not sure someone has been straight with you? I got that feeling looking at the statement in Argentina, and so I decided to come here, hang out here for a while and keep an eye on you."

"That's horrible."

"I don't want to talk about it here," he says. "Too many people. *Vamos.*"

"No, we're not going anywhere. I'm not going anywhere with you."

He grabs my hand and places it on his jacket, over his heart. I feel the hard metal of a pistol inside. He runs my hand along it so I understand.

"We're going."

I turn to walk away. He captures me by the arm and drags me across the restaurant. I see the girls from earlier, and they stare at me in amazement, whispering to each other. I can only imagine what they're thinking. I was in the bathroom with a fine young man earlier, and now here I am, being forced out of the place by a gorgeous man in a business suit.

"Ow," I say as his grip tightens on my arm. "You're hurting me."

"Not as much as you've hurt me."

He hurls me out the door and onto the sidewalk. I look around nervously, afraid that Valentín might still be nearby and will somehow want to get caught up in the middle of all of this. He knows the story of my "ex" husband, the same way everyone in Boston knows about it. It was on the news. And now, here is Roberto, out in the open with me. I consider running, but know he'll only chase me. He is faster and stronger than I am. I am not sure he'd refrain from shooting me.

"Someone might recognize you," I say, trying to reason. "You should go back to Argentina."

"That's why we're getting into my car," he says. He grabs my arms again and starts to push me along the sidewalk toward the parking lot. "Just smile and play nice, Sarita. Just make it look good, or you know what will happen."

As he speaks near my ear, I can smell the alcohol on his breath. He's steeped in it. He has been drinking a *lot*. *Mira*, I know him well enough to know that he smells like this only when he's had at least four drinks.

"You shouldn't drive like this."

"Did I ask your opinion? No, I didn't." We stop in front of a red SUV, an American car of some kind. A Jeep. A rental. I hear the locks disengage as he presses the key fob. "Get in."

I do as he tells me, even though part of me is sure this is the worst decision I've ever made. I don't want to die. He'd kill me if I ran. He would. He gets into the car, too, and immediately starts the engine.

"Why don't we just park here for a while and talk?" I suggest. "I think you're a little drunk, Roberto." I am terrified now. This is not where I wanted to end up. How does this man scare me into doing his will? How is it that he has done this to me since we were kids? I can't stand it anymore.

"Drunk with anger, Sarita. You fucked him, didn't you? That kid in there?" He charges the car out of the space and peels out in a squeal of tires. This is one of the things I hated the most about him. The way he drove like a maniac when he was angry at me. A couple of times he even did it with the boys in the car. It's like he enjoys scaring us.

"Please be careful," I cry as he narrowly misses swiping the side of a parked car. "You're in no shape to drive. And no, of course I didn't have sex with him. Don't be ridiculous."

He looks at me for a second, calculating whether he believes me or not.

"I swear to you, I did not sleep with him. He's a colleague from work. He's engaged to a woman in the office and we were talking about the wedding."

He looks at me suspiciously again.

"That's why he was all over you?"

"He was not. You're drunk. You're paranoid. You don't know what you were seeing. He doesn't have a mom, and he looks up to me to help with that kind of role."

God, I sound like a fool, for the second time tonight. I am going to have to stop lying to men, and my friends, trying to keep everyone happy and calm and doing the right thing. It just isn't worth it.

Roberto speeds ahead, like a maniac.

"Slow down! You'll kill us driving like this!" I shriek, in Spanish, my language of panic.

"And what do I care, eh? You think I have a lot to live for? You call this a life, what I'm doing?"

"You have plenty to live for."

"And your little boyfriend there? Is he good at driving, eh? Is he good? Does he drive you like I do?" Roberto speeds ahead, and through a red light. I shriek, and he smiles like a madman. "I find out he fucked you, I'll kill him. I'll do it in front of you. I'll stuff his balls in his mouth."

"*Please* slow down," I say. "Please!"

He speeds south along Massachusetts Avenue, toward Boston, weaving through the other cars, continuing to scream insults at me, using his right hand to punch me and slap me now and then. He grabs my hand and bites it at one point, drawing blood. I am seeing it happen as if it were a movie of someone else's life. I ask him where he's taking us, and he tells me he's taking me home, to tell the boys what a whore their mother is before he sends me to heaven. This is when I realize that this will be the end of me. I have to do something. Something. I have to get out of this car, or I am going to die. I begin to cry and hope he slows down enough for me to jump out of the car and run.

"You're not thinking right," I wail. "We need to talk about this. Things have changed, Roberto."

He continues to curse at me. Frantic, I take my cell phone from my bag and start to dial 911.

"What the fuck you think you're doing?" he roars, in Spanish.

"What I should have done a long time ago," I say. He grabs for the phone and I try to crawl into the backseat. He is swerving all over the road now. I feel him clawing my legs, breaking my flesh with his fingernails. I scream as his hands batter me, as the lights of the night and other cars smear past us, as others honk at us. Please, I think, let a cop see us now.

He manages to wrestle the phone away from me and throws it out the driver's side window. It is gone. I begin to sob, so, so scared. "Don't fucking get cute on me, Sarita," he says, his hand finding my throat and closing in on it. "I loved you, and you destroyed my life. You understand me?"

"Yes," I whimper. I don't know what else to do. I need to calm him down. He will crush my windpipe if I don't. I caress his arm, his hand, and tell him I love him. I promise him nothing has changed. This is the way it had gone with us in the past. He releases my throat, but doesn't slow the car down at all. He runs another red light, causing a crash between two other cars when a car with the right of way slams on its brakes and the car behind it hits them. "Stop, Roberto! You might have killed someone."

"That's all you think of me, eh? After all we've been through? You think I'm a killer, is that it? You know what? If it were the reverse I would *never* have done this to you. You're *evil*, Sara. That's what you are. You are trying to destroy me. I've finally figured you out. Well, you're not going to do it to me anymore. Understand? You will not do this to me again."

When we get near the intersection of Massachusetts Avenue and Memorial Drive, there is a line of traffic waiting to get on the bridge and Roberto has no choice but to slow down. As he's cursing the traffic, and the car is crawling along at about fifteen miles per hour, I seize my opportunity and open my door. He lunges for me, but it's too late. I've fallen out of the moving car, landing on one knee, in the middle lane, on the blacktop. Cars honk at me, and I can only imagine how crazy I look. It hurts, oh God, I have never felt such pain.

"He's going to kill me!" I scream, but my voice is hoarse from being strangled. "Help me!" My leg gives out under me. It feels strange, maybe broken. I can't put much weight on it.

Fighting back the overwhelming pain, I run the best I can in the opposite direction from traffic, sure that Roberto won't be crazy enough to turn around in the jam to come after me.

I am wrong.

I hear the engine gunning as he furiously turns the car around in the small space he has, the scraping of metal as he crashes the rental into other cars to turn himself around. And then, there he is, stabbing his red Jeep through the middle of the traffic, through the tiniest of spaces, racing toward me, pushing other cars out of the way as he goes. I hurry as well as I can along the lawns of MIT, straight ahead toward the intersection. The light has just turned red in the direction Roberto is traveling. If I can get across it, he'll be behind cars and have to stop. Then I can go into one of the buildings, and find a phone and call the police. I have to find someone to help me.

I limp through the intersection, cursing my lame leg. The light is red. I hobble up onto the sidewalk in front of a building at MIT. I turn my head to see if Roberto stops. He does, but only for a moment, only long enough to nose the car in front of him out of the way. Then, as he has done twice before this night, he runs a red light.

But this time, he is not as lucky as before.

A flower delivery truck, driving much faster than it ought to, barrels through the intersection, right into the driver's side of Roberto's rental car. I watch the whole thing happen as if in slow motion. The screeching of the brakes, the honking of the horns, it all seems a million miles away. The nauseating crunch of metal as the truck plows into the side of the rented car. It happens so fast, yet feels completely slow and unreal.

I stand on the crowded sidewalk, my leg on fire, and watch as the truck pushes Roberto's rental in front of it, losing control. With a sickening smash of glass and metal, the Jeep is accordioned between the truck and a light post, smashed completely, forced around the pole. I stare in disbelief. Somewhere near me, people scream. It happens so fast it almost feels like I am remembering it as it occurs.

Airbag or no airbag, there is no way a human being could survive something like that. This is what I mutter as people stop their cars, get out, and come to help. They scream and make calls on their phones. I wander now. I am dazed as I stumble from the sidewalk into the street and toward the wreckage. The delivery truck has burst open on one side, scattering flowers across the broken glass and spilled oil in the road. They are not just any flowers. I recognize what they are. Wedding flowers. White calla lilies and pink hydrangeas are still held together with elegant hand-tied silk ribbons, for handheld bouquets. Bridesmaids? There is a larger hand-tied bouquet in the middle of all the mess, more white calla lilies, with white and off-white roses. How can there be beauty in this horror? How is it that these delicate flowers survived, bounced through the glass, while the metal caved in? There are huge, clear glass vases shattered across the road. Green apples roll away from them, and more calla lilies, tall on their stalks. Other vases empty themselves of white orchids and floating candles. These must have been the centerpieces. It is funny the images that imprint themselves on your brain during a crisis. Somewhere, a bride's dream has been shattered on this night. Maybe she is the lucky one.

"There's no way," I say, over and over. A black woman in jogging clothes with headphones around her neck comes to me and asks if I am all right. She's sweaty and has a kind face. She says she's a doctor and tells me I am bleeding from the arms and legs, that my lip is split. I put my fingers to my face, then draw them away to look at them. They are shiny and wet with dark blood. I *am* bleeding. I had no idea. I look at my feet. I've lost my shoes somewhere, and the toenails are torn on the right foot. It bleeds too. My leg looks like raw ground beef.

The doctor helps me to the curb and tries to find out how I ended up bleeding, walking in a daze down the street as a car crash happened. I can't find the words to say, so all I tell her is "He wanted to kill me in front of my children. The man in that red car." She puts her arm around me, and soon she tells me the ambulance has arrived. She talks to the paramedics who've come to see me. I watch in horror as they use giant pliers to rip open the side of Roberto's car. His body is slumped inside, smashed, bloodied, limp.

"Is he dead?" I gasp.

"It appears so," says one of the paramedics. "I'm sorry."

They rush me to the waiting ambulance and shut me inside. Outside, there is no rush to remove Roberto. Is this because it would do no good? Is he in that bad a shape? He is dead. Just like that. This is a bad dream, all of this, happening again. How? I did not believe it could be this bad.

I close my eyes for the ride across town, and feel nothing. Something has been poked into my arm, and it is all so, so fuzzy, so far away. I do not open my eyes until they've hauled me out of the ambulance and rushed me through the doors of the emergency room. I look around, and see Usnavys and Rebecca in the waiting area. I blink, and think I must be dreaming, until they see me and rush over.

"¡M'ija!" cries Usnavys. "What the hell are you doing here?"

"Me?" I ask. "How did you know I'd be here? Were you following me again?"

"No, no, girl. We're here for Lauren."

cuicatl

As I **BOARD** the plane out of Seattle for Boston on a Sunday morning after a decent show, it hits me that I need to pay more attention to my friends. For a while, when I believed my own hype, I thought we were all so different. But really, we're not. Now, two of them are in the hospital and I realize they could leave me at any time and I won't have had the chance to tell them how much I love them. Even Sara.

I take my seat in first class with my sunglasses on. I don't want anybody to recognize me, so the sunglasses are pretty fuckin' big. I have a baseball cap on, too, with my hair back in a ponytail, and I'm not wearing any makeup. I'm wearing your basic jeans, with a sweatshirt sent to me by the good people at Rock & Republic. They send me free shit all the time. That's one cool thing about being a celebrity, I suppose. You never have to pay for your clothes. It's cool, but it's also fucked up, because if anyone has the money to pay for this overpriced designer crap it's celebrities, right? But it's the celebrities who get it for free. Great country.

Not.

I ignore the flight attendants because I've heard their whole spiel a million times. All I want is to get up past ten thousand feet so I can turn on my iPod. I don't like the noises airplanes make. I am finely tuned to every vibration and buzz, and even though I'm not exactly afraid of flying I could do without the changes in frequency and volume that go along with the pilots steering this thing through the sky.

Once we're up and I've got the Latin Playboys churning out of my headphones, I crack open a *People* magazine. So sue me, *vato*. I like to read it. This is one of my guilty pleasures, checking in on what everyone else is doing. I would say that of all the magazines that write about stars, this one and *Entertainment Weekly* are the only ones that come halfway close to telling the truth.

I flip though the magazine. The cover story is about babies. I mean, it's about celebrities having babies, adopting babies. There are all these shots of women with their babies, or their pregnant bellies.

I read the whole magazine, cover to cover, and then I just kind of zone out on the music for a while. It's a long flight. When they offer me the free wine we get in first class, I turn it down. I think this whole thing with Lauren and the bulimia and drinking—Rebecca called me from the hospital right as I was boarding, with an update that said Lauren's excessive use of alcohol contributed to her problem with her throat and digestive system—is like a *pinche* wake-up call for me. I'm not getting younger. I'm not sure I need to be high or drunk all the time, just because I'm a musician. I want to see if I can stop smoking dope, man. I'm not a kid anymore. It's about fucking time.

AS THE PLANE lands in Boston, I get that old familiar feeling, as the song lyrics go. I love this city for no other reason than it was the city where I really found myself. It's the city that gave me my start in the world. I love the clubs and the college scene here, and I even love the red bricks and green trees and cherry blossoms in the spring. I've been all over the world, and Boston is still one of the prettiest cities I've ever seen. And, last but not least, it's where I found my best friends.

I get in the cab, and we zip underground through the city's massive system of tunnels, coming out near Kenmore Square. The driver recognizes me, even with the hat and glasses. How do people do that? *I* hardly recognize me. I try to be nice to him, because the one time I was rude to a cabdriver (I'd been three days without sleep, on tour, and I was high and sick with a cold and just wanted to get home) it ended up all over the *National Enquirer* or one of those stupid tabloids. I say stupid, but the truth is they basically got the whole exchange right. It made me look like a total bitch, but I *was* a total bitch that day. When you're famous, you can't have bad days without everyone knowing about it.

I get out at the hospital, and give the driver a nice tip and a signed copy of my latest CD. I carry a few around for moments like this. People never forget a thing like that, and they tell everyone they know how nice you are.

In the hallway outside Lauren's room, I find Usnavys on her phone.

"I never told you I was married because I was a lying sack of crap, okay?" I hear her say. She notices me, but does not curb her conversation in any way that I can tell. It looks like she's been crying. She says into the phone, "I should have told you, but I wanted it both ways, cake and eat, you know how it is. So, no, we can't see each other in the Adirondacks, or anywhere else. I'm sorry. That's just how it has to be. I'm sure you'll find someone worthy of you."

She hangs up and stashes the phone in her large handbag.

"What was that all about?" I ask her.

"You look good, Aztec," she tells me. "Love done you good."

"You okay?"

"I'm fine. My best friend is dying in the hospital, and I almost ruined my marriage, but I'm fine."

I don't know what to do, so I hug her. To my surprise, she hugs back, hard. Usually her hugs have that *pinche* air-kiss quality to them, you know? But not this time. Something in this woman has changed.

"I don't know what's wrong with me," she says softly. In all the years I've known this woman, she has never had that tone of voice with me. She has never admitted to doing something wrong.

"You're too steeped in consumer culture," I tell her.

She laughs. "I didn't say that so you could diagnose me, okay?"

"But it's true. If you gave up thinking money would make you happy, you'd discover that you already have everything it takes to make you happy."

"Easy for the rich girl to say."

"I was happy before I got money."

"But it helps," she says.

"Not really."

"Come on," she says, and pulls me into the hospital room. "Lauren's in here."

I find Lauren in a hospital bed, in one of those horrible thin cotton hospital gowns, open to the front and slipping off her shoulder, with an IV drip in her arm. Rebecca is in the room, looking tired from having been here all night. I expected to find Elizabeth here, too, but they tell me she's in Sara's room at the moment. I knew Roberto had kidnapped her, but now Rebecca tells me they just found out Roberto was killed in a car crash last night.

"So the motherfucker's dead?" I ask, just to be sure. Rebecca flinches. I know I piss her off, but I don't care.

"Roberto perished in the crash, yes," she says.

"Isn't that awesome, Amber?" asks Lauren. I let the name thing slide. I don't get too stressed about what people call me anymore, because it's my own fault in a way that they're all confused.

I go to Lauren and give her a hug, careful of the IV drip. "You okay?"

Lauren laughs. "I'm okay. I think."

As she says that, a doctor enters the room. Elizabeth follows her, saying Valentín has come to be with Sara for a while. She waves at me and I smile back. The doctor is very efficient, an older woman with silver hair pulled back in a low ponytail. She looks fit, like she runs every day, and her blue eyes have a warmth and humor to them that make me like her instantly. She introduces herself to me, because apparently I am the only one of our group who has not met her yet. Dr. Campbell. There was a time in my life when I would have distrusted her instantly, simply because of her extreme whiteness. But I'm over that now. Traveling around the world cures you of prejudice, if you're smart. People are just people, everywhere you go.

"We've got the results back," the doctor tells Lauren. "I can share them now, or we can ask your friends to step out."

Lauren looks at each of us quickly. "No, it's okay. They can stay. Anything you have to say I'm going to tell them anyway."

Dr. Campbell gives us a glance, and smiles. "You're lucky to have such good friends," she tells Lauren.

"Yeah. I know."

"You'd be surprised how many people come in here and they don't have a friend in the world."

"That's sad," I say.

"I love you guys," Lauren gushes at us. Tears brim at the edges of her eyes, and I can tell she's expecting the worst. I grab her hand and stand at her side. Usnavys takes my cue, and takes Lauren's other hand; and Rebecca, to my great surprise, takes mine. For years, she and I have been frenemies. No more.

I hold Rebecca's hand tighter, and smile at her. She smiles back with a sadness and softness in her eyes I've never seen before. Órale. I don't know what's going on with her, but I plan to find out. It might just be that she's worried about Lauren, but it seems to be bigger than that.

The doctor looks at us all, and smiles. She seems truly moved by our support of Lauren. "People heal much faster when they have love and support like this, Lauren," says Dr. Campbell.

"So I've got something to heal from, then."

The doctor nods, but her smile is comforting. "We did the upper GI, and even though we knew from the early visual that your esophagus looks inflamed, and there's an issue with the sphincter from your esophagus to your stomach completely closing—it doesn't—the good news is there doesn't appear to be a major rupture. The bad news is you've suffered some serious erosion of the esophagus already. But nothing deadly."

"Oh, thank God!" cries Rebecca.

Dr. Campbell holds up her hand in caution. "*Yet*," she says. "You have a small hiatal hernia, as well. That means your stomach has come into your chest cavity through your diaphragm, at the esophageal opening. You have literally vomited your stomach into your chest, Lauren. Your stomach acid is like battery acid in your esophagus. At the rate you're going, unless you drastically change your behaviors, it can eventually lead to changes in the esophageal cells, which can, in some cases, lead to throat cancer. Which is nearly incurable and a miserable way to die. Something to consider."

None of us says anything. Lauren's face turns red and her eyes take on a worried look I have only seen in her regarding men. I realize that one of the best things about having friends for a long time is that over time they become different people, like, metamorphosis. You have the same friend, but over the course of fifteen years she becomes many different people.

"Bulimia and drinking are a terrible combination," the doctor continues. "Either one would be terrible on its own, but together they are a deadly combination. You need to really, really understand this. A lot of bulimics function on the assumption that what they're doing isn't really bad because they're not overweight, but the truth is most bulimics are of average or above-average weight. They don't die of starvation the way anorexics do. Bulimics die two ways. From heart failure, after they get dehydrated and screw up the balance of salts in their body. The heart basically just misfires and they drop dead. Or like this, with GERD and esophagus ruptures. When and if your esophagus does rupture, Lauren, what will happen is that all the food you eat will drain into your body cavity instead of into your stomach, and you will die. You will die quickly, and painfully. The chest pain you've been feeling is because of the GERD, or gastroesophageal reflux disease. It can feel like a heart attack. Basically, what you've done is paralyze your own esophageal sphincter, the little thing that keeps your stomach closed. It's a one-way valve, and what you've done over the years is force it to be a two-way valve, until it simply gave out."

"All that from throwing up?" I ask.

The doctor turns to face me. "Remember, vomiting is meant to be an emergency tactic. We are really only designed to do it a few times in our lives. Repeatedly forcing oneself to vomit is unnatural and can be deadly. It's very serious."

Lauren gulps, and puts a hand over her chest. "So, will I ever stop feeling this pain?"

"Medications will help the pain go away, but the only real way to treat this is to stop throwing up, and to start following a low-fat, healthy diet. Small, frequent meals. No bingeing."

"Sounds easy enough," says Rebecca, cheerful.

The doctor looks at her now. "For you, and for me, it would be easy. But for the bulimic, these issues are harder to grasp. There's a genetic component to this disease, we're discovering. It's not just a lack of willpower."

"I never really thought I was fully bulimic," says Lauren. "Because half the time, or more than half the time, I keep what I eat down. And I go for months without doing it at all."

"You are the typical bulimic—very driven and accomplished professional woman, a perfectionist, harder on yourself than you are on the others in your life. Am I right?"

Lauren nods sheepishly.

"There are some very good treatment programs for eating disorders in the Boston area," says the doctor. "I'd recommend an inpatient program for a couple of weeks, to help you get your digestive system back on track. So after I give you the prescriptions for the GERD stuff and the sore throat—which is only a temporary solution to the discomfort, and they don't work on many of the people we give them to, okay?—I need you to follow up with your primary care physician, and we need to get you into a program right away."

She looks at us now, and says, "I need you guys to promise me you're not going to let Lauren slack off on this. If you love her, you have to make sure she gets help."

"I'll get help," says Lauren, tears streaming down her face now.

"You mean it this time?" I ask. I look at the doctor. "We've known about this for a while, and she always said she was stopping."

"Well, sometimes landing in the ER with chest pain and vertigo is just what a person needs to understand how important it is to really get help. And to really stop." Dr. Campbell touches Lauren on the top of her head and looks lovingly at her, like a mother. "You're a smart woman, Lauren. We all know that. I need you to tell me that you understand the gravity of this situation."

Lauren lifts the hand with mine in it to her cheek and wipes the tears away. I feel the wetness of them on my own hand. "I understand, Dr. Campbell," she says.

"Good," says the doctor. "I want you to be in touch with me, Lauren. Let me know how it's going."

"I will," she says.

Dr. Campbell hands Lauren a stack of prescriptions, explains them to her, and says her good-byes to us. She tells Lauren she is free to go home now, once the nurse comes to take the IV out. She starts to leave, but stops at the door, turns, and says, "Lauren?"

"Yes, Doctor?"

"I don't usually divulge personal information to patients, but in this case I feel I have to."

I brace for what might come next. It's always weird when doctors become human beings. You want them to be better than human beings.

"My sister died from this," she says bluntly.

No one speaks. We just sort of look at each other.

"Ten years ago."

"I'm sorry," says Lauren.

"She didn't think it was a big deal."

We remain silent, awkward and silent.

"I loved her. She left three kids, and I'm raising them myself now. So, you can see this is an important issue for me."

With that, the doctor walks out of the room with a slightly embarrassed look on her face, probably from having broken the whole doctor-patient wall that they teach doctors to keep up all the time.

Lauren looks at us, wipes the last of her tears, and gets a determined look on her face. "You hear about people hitting rock bottom, right?" she asks. "Well, I think this is finally it."

Órale.

rebecca

WITH AMBER BY my side, willowy and wild in her designer Goth wear, I walk from the hospital all the way past Kenmore Square, to the Espresso Royale coffee shop, on Commonwealth Avenue near Boston University. It was my suggestion, for old time's sake, to go hang out near our alma mater. Even on a Sunday, late morning, the place is overflowing with college students. The rain of the past few days has begun to clear, replaced by clear, strong sunshine. Kids are out in shorts, basking.

"They look so young, don't they?" I ask her.

"I can't believe we looked that young when we were that young," she tells me. "I feel like I looked the same then as I do now."

I look closely at her, and see that of all of us, she has remained the most youthful, at least in attitude. "Actually, you kind of do. You haven't changed that much."

We order our drinks—I get a decaf nonfat latte and she gets Red Zinger tea—and find a table near the back, where it's a little quieter. We discuss Lauren's situation, and agree that she seems like she finally wants to get help. We also agree that we're going to do everything we can to help her. We talk about Sara, and Cuicatl tells me she thinks this will finally turn her around. "But she might end up attracted to the same kind of guy for the rest of her life. Who knows?"

I watch the students, the way they laugh and socialize with the arrogance of youth. I miss those days. I'd like to chat with them a bit before leaving, just to see what issues are on their minds these days, for the magazine's sake. I am so pleased I did not sell it. I believe it was the right thing to do.

"Rebecca," Cuicatl says. "Tell me what's going on with you. You seem different. I noticed it back at the hospital. I noticed it in New Mexico, actually, truth be told."

I freeze for a moment, trapped. I raise my eyes from the top of the table to meet hers. "You think I seem different?"

Cuicatl nods and fidgets. "I have to tell you something. It's not that I'm a psychic or something. I overheard you talking to Andre on your mobile phone, back in New Mexico, at the resort, that first night. You were waiting for the elevator, after you left us, and I went to the bathroom."

"So?"

"So, you were talking about morning sickness. I *know*, Rebecca."

"You know what?"

"I know that you're pregnant."

She looks at me steadily as a wave of emotions washes through me. Surprise, shock, anger, confusion, and, finally, amusement. "You don't know," I tell her simply.

"No. I do. I heard you. Loud and clear. You don't have to hide it from me. Actually, I've been thinking a little about having a baby myself lately, in a way."

I laugh bitterly and stir a bit of artificial sweetener into my latte. "You don't know as much as you think you know," I tell her. "I was pregnant, if you must know, but I lost the baby. I can't ever have children, that's what they tell me."

"Wow," she says, with more sympathy than I expected. "I had no idea. Why didn't you tell us?"

"I'm not like you guys. I'm private, Amber. It was just between me and my husband, and I didn't feel like sharing."

"I'm sorry I made you," she says.

"You didn't *make* me." I hesitate, and smile at her. "It feels good to tell someone, honestly."

"Damn, man. I'm so sorry, Rebecca. Shit. That sucks."

"It's something I've wanted for so long." I fight the tears.

"What about a surrogate?" she asks.

I shudder as she says this, and try to appear normal. It feels good and awkward to share so much with this woman. "As a matter of fact, we've discussed it. But we aren't decided. The Church is opposed to it."

Cuicatl rolls her eyes now, but mercifully says nothing.

"We haven't ruled it out. It's just the whole idea of a stranger incubating our baby for us. It gives me the creeps."

Cuicatl traces a ring around the top of her cup. "Unless it wasn't a stranger," she says suggestively.

"I don't know anyone who does that sort of thing," I say, hoping she won't offer.

Cuicatl looks at me and lifts her eyebrows. I'm not even going to touch it. Certainly she wouldn't be brazen enough to volunteer, considering her history of drug use and her unstable lifestyle?

"I'll do it," she tells me. "I'm perfectly healthy. I've been pregnant before. Back with Gato. I had an abortion."

I feel sick. Abortion is absolutely repugnant to me. I wish she had not shared this information with me. That is one Church rule I would never, ever consider thwarting, and I've never understood it more than I do now. A human life is a human life. And now, here is Cuicatl, suggesting that I hand over my child to be raised in her uterine graveyard?

"That's very generous of you, Amber, but I don't think I could place that burden on a friend."

"I'm not kidding. I'll do it. No burden."

I shake my head gently, but firmly. "No, Amber. I don't think so."

"Why not? Who better to have a Mexica baby than another Mexica?"

"As I said, I am moved by your generosity." I want to run out of here. She reaches for my hand, but I move it away.

"Seriously, Rebecca. I'm happy to do it." Cuicatl looks wounded.

"I appreciate your offer. I really do. It's so generous. It's incredible, really. But I can't."

"Why not?"

"Because, Amber. I don't know how to put this without offending you, but if we do it at all, Andre and I are really looking for a surrogate who is healthy."

"I'm healthy."

"You are a marijuana user," I say calmly. "I am not judging you for it. I admire how you've been able to function so well, considering. But you must surely understand why we feel this way. We want the best possible start, if we do it at all, which we haven't decided."

"I'm clean now," she tells me. I stifle a laugh.

"I saw you just last week at the resort, and you were stoned out of your mind, Amber. Please."

"True dat," she says. "I've stopped since then. And I'm in love, too. We're talking marriage. That's what got me thinking babies."

I blink back my horror. "Then why on earth would you want to be a surrogate now?"

"Oh, we've got plenty of time," she says.

"Very kind of you to offer, but let's drop it now." She's talented, possibly even brilliant, but completely mentally unhinged.

"I'll get a physical, the whole thing. I want to do this for you, Rebecca. I'm not on drugs. I promise you that."

"I don't mean to sound condescending, Amber, but it is very hard for people to kick the drug habit. We have run many articles about addiction at *Ella*."

"Weed is not addictive."

"Of course it is."

"Okay, *órale*. Even if it is? I could kick it. No problem, homes. Of course

I could. That's something a lot of people don't realize about musicians, is that to be halfway good at it, you have to have incredible discipline."

She is exhausting me with her persistence. "Why are you so adamant about this?" I ask her point-blank. "What's in it for you? Not too many rock stars tour around the world pregnant."

"Look, it's what you need, and it's what I need," she explains, without sugarcoating her own motives. "My career isn't exactly great right now, Rebecca. I need to jump-start the publicity thing, and this would be the perfect way to do it."

So that's it. I feel disgusted by her. "I don't know what to say," I tell her. "I am speechless."

"I know, it sounds cheesy and shit. But it'd be good for both of us. Think about it. I know what you're like. I've known you for almost twenty years. You're a control freak, right? I'd be willing to live in your house with you during the pregnancy, and you could keep me under lock and key and monitor everything that went in my mouth. That boy in the bubble? I'd be the girl in the bubble, only the bubble would be your house. You could have me there like a prisoner, and I'd use the time to write music and relax. A sabbatical. If I had to go somewhere? You come with me."

I hold my hands out in front of me, the way you might to stop traffic. She is coming on way too strong. I think she is sickening and foolish, but I value her friendship and our history enough to not tell her this directly. I think of how to extricate myself from this conversation. "We're very private people, Andre and I. We don't need that kind of attention. And our baby wouldn't need to come into the world that way, either."

We sit in silence for a little while. "Okay," she says, finally. "I understand. But know that the offer stands, if you change your mind."

"I'll think about it," I say, more to be polite, I think, than because I actually plan to think about it. As soon as I leave here, I will not think about it at all.

"Talk it over with Andre," she suggests. "See what he thinks."

"I will."

I am certain he will laugh as hard as I do at the very *thought*.

usnavys

Gone.

I came home from the hospital all excited to tell Juan I was sorry, okay? I wanted to explain it all to him, now that it made some sense to me. That's right, I said I was gonna say *sorry*. You heard it right. *Mira*, I can count the times I've said I'm sorry on one hand, right? And maybe that's part of the problem. But here I was, all ready to apologize and atone for my sins, but Juan, my best friend in the world, was gone—with no immediate plans to return. Ever, okay? *Ever*. And I already broke up with Marcus. Can you believe my luck? I'm like the little girl who cried wolf.

I was going to tell Juan all about how listening to Lauren's problems with Amaury, and seeing my two friends face their damn mortality at the same time, made me realize I was being a *sinvergüenza* like that cradle-robbing idiot, Amaury. You don't live forever. I wanted to tell him I loved him and promise him I was going to grow up this time. I wanted to tell Juan about how hearing all my friends describe my husband as this *santo bendito* who saved people's lives made me remember all the reasons I fell in love with him in the first place. I let the stress of parenthood and work and everything else push him away. I'm embarrassed to say I regressed.

I blamed him for things that weren't his fault, like how we seem to have a lesbian daughter. You don't pick how they come into the world, *m'ija*. They just come as they are and it is your job as a parent to put up with it as much as you can before you drive yourself crazy.

I have loved Juan for years and years, and sometimes that love has gone into hiding, but it always comes back. I wanted to tell him that, and hug my butch little girl because life is precious and people get sick and you never know when you're going to see them for the last time.

And they were gone.

I was too late.

While I was tending to my crazy friends, Juan took Carolina to San Juan on the last plane out of Logan, to stay with his mother, who hates me and has always hated me. He wrote me up a nasty note, saying it was for "a while," and said he'd be back in a couple of weeks to tie up loose ends with his new job, but that in the meantime I could just count on him living with his mom from now on, where he and Carolina wouldn't bother me or my "boyfriends" anymore. He was really pissed off, *m'ija*, I could tell because he wrote the letter in pencil, and it was all dark like he'd been stabbing at the paper with all his might.

Gone.

I sit on Carolina's bed in my now-filthy sundress, and stare at the little pink dresser. I feel very starlet, and very dramatic and sorry for myself. The dresser is a mess. My girl went and wrote all over it, drew cars and airplanes on it with angry black marker, like graffiti. She draws like her daddy wrote that letter tonight. I don't know what's going to become of that girl, I really don't. The drawers hang open, and I can't believe how empty they are, like starving mouths, every last one of them. He can't do this, can he? Just pack up all her clothes and most of her toys, and leave the city for Puerto Rico? With the money in our shared account? He can't do that, can he? It's kidnapping, isn't it? She's enrolled in the best day school in the area. Is my husband an idiot? Yes, he is. He should not have taken her. Did he even call the school to say she'd be absent? Did he even cancel her play dates? I will have to call the French teacher on Monday to find out. He probably did call everyone, I bet. He's that organized. He meant it. I am in shock.

Shock.

I find a phone and call Lauren at home, where she's staying for a couple of days until she goes into that rehab for bulimics.

"You can't be alone right now," she says. "And I don't want to be here."

"I can't see people. I don't want to see people."

"I'm coming over," she tells me.

"Don't."

"You can't stop me. You saved my life, so, basically, it's your fault that I'm on my way right now."

She hangs up on me. I go back to Caro's room to play drama queen on the bed again. I take the letter with me to read it again. Juan left it on the coffee table in the living room, trapped underneath the black shiny statue of the panther that I got from my mom and haven't been able to get rid of even though Juan insists it is the single tackiest piece of non-art in the entire city of Boston. He weighted his letter down with the panther as a final fuck-you to me, I can tell you that, *m'ija*. I know him well enough to know that.

I walk out of Carolina's room feeling enormously sorry for myself, go back to the living room and point the sound system remote at the unit in the black entertainment center, press Play for the CD player again. I've played this same CD seven hundred times already probably, but I can't get enough of it. It's Héctor Lavoe's *La Voz*, and even though some of the songs are upbeat and salsa, the fact that Hector had one of the saddest lives of all time helps me to stay miserable. I love Jen and Marc for making that movie. They could have done anything, but they did that. Mad props for that.

I cry as I sing along. I can't believe this is happening to me, *m'ija*. I never thought he'd go. Ever. I thought that Juan was the kind of man who might stick around with me forever, no matter what I did to him, and to tell you the truth that was part of why I hated him lately. He was such a *flojón*, *m'ija*. But now that he's standing up for himself and telling me to fuck off, it's like he's a man again, *mamita*. You know what I'm sayin'?

I listen to *"Emborrácheme de Amor"* and sing along until the song is over, then I press the song on from the beginning again. When I'm finished, I turn the volume down and dial Juan's mother. She answers, *la suegra del infierno*, the mother-in-law from hell.

"Let me talk to Juan," I say, in Spanish.

"Who is this?" she asks, as if.

"Put him on the phone, *suegra*."

"I don't think so."

I can hear Carolina in the background, crying. "Why is she crying? What did you do to her?"

"I don't know what you're talking about." Okay, so that's how she's gonna play this. The *suegra* won't tell me.

"Do not disrespect me with regards to my daughter," I tell her.

The *suegra* hangs up on me. I throw a pillow across the room. I feel like I'm going completely insane. I call back.

"Hello?" she calls out in Spanish, sweet as can be, as if she didn't just dis me.

"Tell me why my child is crying."

"She was laughing," she tells me. "There's nothing to worry about."

"Oh, yes, there is. If you don't put that man on the phone, I'm going to give you plenty to worry about."

She hangs up again. I call back.

"Do not hang up on me, unless you want me to come and stop you in person," I warn her.

"You'll be hearing from my Juanito's lawyer in the morning," she assures me. "I have nothing more to discuss with you."

Click.

Her Juanito. I am telling you, *nena*, do *not* marry Latino men, because their primary loyalty will always be to their mothers. They will have been spoiled by them all their childhoods, and then when they grow up they'll still run to them when there's the smallest problem. Not that this problem—my cheating and telling him about it—is small. It's not. But it's not that bad, now that I've realized why I was doing it and have ideas about how to fix it. Juan just needs to talk to me.

I call her once more.

"Put your Juanito on the phone," I hiss.

"I'm sorry, but my son is unavailable at the moment."

"Your son is unavailable? Drag his ass out of the bathroom, then."

"He's out on the porch talking to some of the girls from the neighborhood, *mujeres decentes*," she adds, decent women, implying that I am anything *but*.

"Listen, *mala suegra*," I tell her. "You go out and get him, now, or I'm going to fly out there and kick your ass myself."

There is a pause, then a click as she hangs up on me again.

"Fine," I say to the empty phone line. Then, quicker than you can say "cat fight," I dial my corporate travel agent and tell him to get me on a flight to San Juan in the morning.

elizabeth

SARA HAS GIVEN me a whole week off, because she herself is taking a week off to focus on healing, and explaining as much as she can to her children, who are catching all sorts of grief from the other kids at school who have heard the story about their father's death on the news. I welcome a paid vacation. We all need a vacation after the maelstrom set off by our vacation in New Mexico. They call it the land of enchantment, and from the way things have gone lately, I would say we've all been under some kind of spell. Seeing Lauren in the hospital, I found peace with it all—with her, with us, with how we must focus on rebuilding our trust and friendship. I am strong enough to do that, because now, more than ever, that woman needs friends.

I'm on the thick navy blue Pottery Barn rug on the floor of the family room, playing with Gordon. Doggedly, he stacks blocks in small, unstable towers of two. They fall over. He stacks them again. He is a person who doesn't give up easily. This character trait will serve him well in his lifetime.

Outside, the green leaves on the trees sway, like hands waving good-bye. I feel good that I am able to provide Gordon with a safe place, a happy place, a place where he can focus on growing and learning. God only knows what he would be like now if he were still in Sierra Leone.

I am pulled from my imaginings when the doorbell rings. I freeze, and try to remember if I've forgotten something, or someone. No. I'm not expecting anyone, so, being a single mom on her lazy day off, I'm still in my pajamas (leggings and a huge Bruins jersey) even though it is nearly noon.

When the baby napped from seven to ten, I napped with him. I am barely diving into my morning coffee. My hair is nappy and a mess, tied up in a do-rag, and I quickly try to find a rubber band for it so I can put it back. There are none to be found.

So, looking—or at the very least *feeling*—like a slob, I pick Gordon up, and together we open the door to find Margo delivered to me on a wind that smells of warming grass and flowers, showered and dressed in a beige linen skirt and tank top. It's the hottest summer but this woman makes it feel like spring. She looks very natural and wholesome, without makeup but rosy in the cheeks and quite lovely. She has her youngest child in a costly stroller, the girl's cheeks pink with good health. Margo is one of those people who looks pulled together, even on days off.

"Good morning," she chirps in her lovely Paraguay Spanish. I can tell by the way she bows a little and blushes that she senses my discomfort. I try to correct the surprised horror I think I wear on my face. I have the baby balanced on one hip, and use my free hand to touch the rag on my head. "Am I catching you at a bad time?" she wants to know, wincing as she watches me behave self-consciously.

"No. Well, sort of." I try to laugh it off, but she looks horrified that she might have offended me.

"I'm sorry. I should have called first. I thought I was being neighborly. You mentioned how nice it would be if people acted more like neighbors in Boston. I have the day free, too, and thought I'd drop by. It's not Bostonian of me, I know. Sorry. You can take the girl out of Paraguay—"

"No, it's okay. I'm just—we're being lazy this morning, right, baby?" I say to my son. Somehow it's easier to confess if I'm not alone in it. Gordon gurgles at me as if to say, "Speak for yourself." For his part, Gordon has been hard at work.

"I can come back another time. I know we've only just met. I should have called first." Margo takes a step away from the front door, and I feel like reaching out to pull her back in.

"No, it's good to see you. You want to come in?"

Margo considers my offer for a moment. "You sure?"

"Of course! Please. I was just drinking some fresh coffee if you'd like some."

Margo takes her child out of the stroller, and they come inside. I lead them to the family room.

"What a beautiful home," says Margo. I am embarrassed by my lack of real art. I have framed prints that I imagine look tacky to an art dealer, but she does not let on that this might be the case. Her daughter instantly heads toward the big plastic toy chest in the corner of the family room. "Play with whatever you want, sweetheart," I call out to her. To her mother, I ask, "So, coffee?" and silently add "tea, or me?"

"That sounds perfect," she says as she unwinds the lightweight scarf from her neck. "So, let me explain. We were out walking, and I saw a sign for a great play this afternoon at the Children's Museum, one where they teach children all about plays, of all things. It's meant to prepare them for going to live shows later on. I thought it'd be fun to go, but I thought it might be even more fun to go with you and Gordon, if you're not busy."

I consider the invitation, and ask her when it starts. She tells me we have two hours, and suggests getting lunch and then heading over. She offers to drive. I want to go, but I don't want to go like this, and tell her I'd need some time to get dressed.

"Of course. I mean, I think you look great. Don't get dressed up for *me*."

Why not, I think to myself. Doesn't she find me attractive?

"Well, I should clean up anyway. I don't usually go out like this," I say.

"Sure, go ahead. I can watch Gordon if you like."

"Oh, wow," I say in Spanish. "Do you know how long it's been since I had a shower in this house without him in the playpen in the bathroom with me?"

"I know what you mean," she tells me with a smile. "Go on. Enjoy it."

"Thanks, Margo. That's very sweet."

"What are neighbors for?"

"I guess you're right."

"Of course I am. I'll expect you to pay back the favor one of these days."

"Any time."

As I walk down the hall away from the family room, I hear Margo talking to Gordon in comforting, experienced tones. I stop, and just listen. Goose bumps rise across my arms and along the back of my neck, because this is precisely the way I imagined Selwyn would one day come to talk to our child, with love and patience, with an understanding of the weight of the job of raising a child, an understanding that nonetheless you must never lose sight of the fact that even with the huge responsibility of it, you must never forget to have fun, so that your child grows up happy.

I take care choosing the outfit, a variation as most of them are on my basic theme of jeans and a shirt with comfortable shoes. I choose jeans that I know make my body look trim, and a short-sleeved T-shirt in a shade of green I know complements my eyes. I don't usually wear makeup on weekends, or ever, really—but today I apply a dash of color to my cheeks, and mascara to my lashes, and Sephora lip gloss with gold sparkles in it that I got for Christmas from Usnavys two years ago. I spritz myself with perfume. I put on earrings and a necklace, too, turquoise from New Mexico that I got last weekend, in a Southwestern style I think Margo would like.

I return to the family room and find all three of them on the floor, playing together. Margo's little girl seems smitten by Gordon, and my baby, for his part, cannot seem to take his eyes off this fascinating little person, so close to him in size and yet so much more capable of walking, talking, and roaming about the world on her own terms.

I should not think this, but I do anyway: They look every bit like a family.

usnavys

JUAN'S MOTHER LIVES in a pink square house like a big old buttermint in the jungle, with gnomes and stone lions in the front yard. Now, that's some tacky shit, okay? Juan tries to make it all like I'm the tacky one, but *look* at this bullshit, *m'ija*. She's got a cottage by the ocean, about two blocks from the beach, one of those typical Puerto Rico homes with shutters, made out of cement with a little carport attached to the side. It's a little tiny-ass house with these idiot lions on either side of the front door, like that's gonna trick the neighbor into thinking she got her some kind of palace.

I park the rental Taurus—did I not *tell* you all Tauruses are rentals?—in front of the house, and check my lipstick in the rearview mirror. I have to look good when I slap my *suegra*, *m'ija*, because this is Puerto Rico and that means the whole neighborhood is going to come out to see what all the yelling is about. I have to make an impression.

I check the straps on my high-heeled *chanclas*, and open the door of the car and step out, like a lady, into the humidity and heat, in my sundress and shades. I can hear Carolina laughing in the backyard, and then I hear Juan yelling at her not to touch the big yellow bug because it might be poisonous. *Ay, Dios mío, m'ija.* I should have known my daughter would be out here in the jungle getting all Steve Irwin on everyone. I imagine her trying to pet snakes and all sorts of dangerous things, and it actually makes me smile. Missing her like I have has made me realize that I wouldn't want her any other way. She is Carolina, plain and simple, and that's good enough for me.

I prance across the brick walkway to the front porch, adjust my hair, ball my fist, and knock exactly three times on the door. Then I stand there between the lions and wait for the inevitable. Through the door I hear old bolero music and I can smell steak and yucca cooking. I'm starving, too, girl, so maybe I'll hold off on fighting with my mother-in-law until she's fed me.

The door opens, and I see her. She is petite, and in good shape, with a yoga suit on. It takes her a moment to recognize me, but when she does, okay, she's all, like, "Oh, no. Not you. You're not welcome here."

So I'm all, "Listen, woman, I am not here to ask your permission for anything. I am here to get my daughter, and if you don't let me in I will force my ass in, and you won't like that."

She stares at me like she's scared now, and I can see her trying to think of something to say. I don't give her time.

"Open the door, *suegra*, or I'm'a open it on you."

"Juan!" she shrieks. "Juan, get over here."

"Oh, okay," I say. "*Now* you're gonna let me talk to him, huh? Now that you think I might *hurt* you. You're not so tough *now*, are you?"

"Juan! Get over here!"

I hear the sliding glass door in the living room open, and Juan's voice chimes out. "Mami? What's wrong?"

"Daddy!" I hear Carolina calling after him. "The yellow buggy likes me!"

"Put that thing down, Carolina, now!"

Then, there he is, behind his mother, towering over her even though he's not a tall man. She's just short, *m'ija.* Short and butt ugly. I don't know how such an ugly woman produced such a handsome son, I really don't.

Carolina comes running up behind them, in shorts and a tank top, all covered with dirt and her hair a nappy mess all over her damn head, with a big-ass yellow insect crawling all over her hand. I scream. The evil *suegra* screams. Juan screams, and then he does what a good parent should do, and grabs that nasty-looking thing off of her and throws it into the yard. This makes Carolina cry. She stops as soon as she realizes I am here and I am me.

"Mommy!" she cries, and runs over to me. I hug her and kiss her, even with all that dirt and buggy grime on her, and I don't even tell her to go get cleaned up, which is what the old me would have done. I don't care. I don't care if she's a dirty little girl, a *sucia*, a real *sucia*, *ensuciada por la jungla*, with bugs and *animalitos* crawling all over her. She's going to do great things, *m'ija*. You'll see. She just won't look like a girl when she does them, but who cares? *I* look like a girl, and look where it got me. Nearly divorced from this amazing man.

"I love you so much, baby," I tell her. "Mommy missed you and had to come see you."

I look at Juan, and he gives me a pained smile. "How was your flight?" he asks.

"Fine."

"Good."

The *suegra* retreats back into the house with a snarl, and leaves me and my family, or what's left of it, on the porch, in plain view of all the nosy *viejitos*.

"Juan, we have to talk."

He sounds like a robot, *m'ija*. "I don't think we have anything to discuss, other than custody arrangements. I'm happy to do that, as I told you in the note."

"You're not going to fight again, are you?" asks Carolina. "I don't want you to do that."

"No, baby," I tell her as I cover her stinky-ass head with kisses. "We're not going to fight. Daddy and I are going to take a walk to the beach and we're going to talk and you're going to go back inside with *abuelita* and help her make dinner."

"We are?" he asks.

"I *hate* cooking," pouts Carolina.

I don't do what I would have done before, okay, which is tell her that every girl needs to learn how to cook. I smile at her and say, "That's okay, *m'ija*, just go in and keep *abuelita* company, then. Tell her a story."

"I like telling stories."

"Good. Now go on, go inside."

Juan looks at me doubtfully, like I'm a prisoner swearing I'm innocent even after that DNA test said I did it. "You might not want to talk, but I do," I say. "Now let's go."

"Usnavys." He sounds weary and hurt. "I don't know. I told you. I'm done. I'm not doing this anymore. Twenty years is too much. I can't take it anymore."

I take me a big old breath and brace for the unthinkable. "I will start this conversation by saying I'm sorry. Okay? I am. I'm sorry. I'm stupid, and I made a mistake, and I should have talked to you about how I was feeling instead of being passive-aggressive and shit, and I'm just plain sorry."

I have never seen a man's eyes bug out so far that they actually fall out, *m'ija*, but this thing that Juan is doing now? It's close. I'm worried about his eyeballs. I know people who saw that shit happen on a TV show once, and they told me about it, and ever since then I can't get that mental image out.

"Get your eyes back in your head," I tell him. "Just push 'em back up in there."

"I'm sorry. Could you—can you say that again? That part about how you're sorry."

I wince at his amazement, and tell myself not to get huffy. "I'm sorry. I am truly sorry."

His eyes go back in his head and retreat behind slit lids now. "I don't know who you are, or what you did with my wife, but when the police find out where you put her, you're going to be in big trouble," he says.

"If I'm not afraid of your mother, I can handle the damn police, okay?"

Juan cracks a reluctant grin. "Yeah. Okay."

"Does this mean we can talk?" I ask him.

"We can *talk*," he says, and I can see the love he still has for me in his eyes. There is nothing I could do to make this man stop loving me, and this is a blessing that few women will ever know. "But I'm not making any promises."

"Roberto's dead," I tell him.

"What?"

"And Lauren almost killed herself by barfing her insides out."

"What?"

"Roberto tried to kill Sara, and she got out of the car and ran away, and then he got hit by a flower truck and died." Girl, it feels good to talk to this man who knows my world as good as I do. As *well* as I do. It feels damn good.

"You're kidding," he says, all surprised.

"No, I'm not. I didn't come home the night you left because I was in the hospital with those girls, and I left you a message, but I don't think you got it."

"Roberto's dead? Really?" His eyes look like they want to pop out again.

"Dead."

"It's about time," he says.

"That's awful," I say, crossing myself.

"*He* was awful."

"So was I," I say. "I'm really sorry, Juan." A tear plunges out of my eye onto my cheek. I am actually overcome with remorse right now, okay? That's amazing right there.

"Mami!" Juan yells through the screen door, the way people always do here. "We're going for a walk."

"If you're not back in an hour I'll call the police," she calls back.

"Stop it, Mami," he yells.

"Why is *abuelita* calling the police?" cries Carolina, in loud-ass public Spanish, getting the hang of communication, Puerto Rico style.

"She's joking," I yell.

"No, I'm not," yells the *suegra* from hell.

"Yes, you are," Juan and I yell back at her, in unison. We laugh.

"Let's go," he tells me. I try to put my arm in his, but he pushes me away. "Not yet," he says. "I'm not ready for that yet."

"But you think you will be? Eventually?"

"I don't know."

We walk, side by side, in the street. Long grass grows everywhere, and palm trees wave in the breeze overhead. The humidity is getting to me. I'm starting to sweat. "But I can tell you love me," I say as I mop my brow with my sleeve. "I see it."

"That's fine." He hands me a tissue from his pocket, ever the prepared daddy. "I do love you. But I don't hate myself enough to keep getting crapped on by you."

"So you think we might not make it?"

"Maybe not."

I don't want to cry, *m'ija*. I didn't think I'd come all this way and apologize and he'd tell me some shit like that. I mean, I knew it was a possibility, but I didn't think he'd actually do it.

"Please," I beg. My voice is all choked up and shit, and I sound like the saddest overactor in the world.

"I don't know."

"Don't you love me?"

"Yes. But there are limits. You took it too far this time. We were supposed to be a family, Usnavys."

"I know. I fucked up, okay? I know that. Sometimes they say cheating is a symptom of something wrong with a relationship, but it's not the actual thing that's wrong."

"You're saying cheating isn't *wrong*? How much airplane wine did you *have*?"

"No, it's *wrong*. *Obviously* it's wrong. But sometimes that's not the bigger picture. And I didn't have any wine."

"There's a bigger picture?"

"I was stupid. And I'm sorry. But I think I know why I did it now. It was the stress of being a parent, and all that whatnot and what-have-you, and me being scared and us having a bad sex life."

He looks taken aback. "You think it was bad?"

"It didn't exist."

He nods, admitting what we both knew but didn't talk about before. "That's pretty bad."

"I should have tried to talk to you about all that so we could fix it, but instead I went back to all my old ways and started looking for attention from other men."

"That's one way of putting it." A polite way.

"I'm *sorry*. Okay? I can't promise you I'll never do it again, because I know how bad that would sound and how insincere, but I can promise you I want to try to change, and that I'll go to counseling and do whatever I need to do to make this work, if you can get past it and try to understand that it wasn't about you, it was all about me and me being insecure and an idiot and I'm just really sorry, okay?"

We walk the remaining block to the beach in silence, but as the roaring of the sea gets louder, Juan does something I don't expect.

He reaches out, and after a tiny hesitation, holds my hand.

"So it's not over?" I ask.

He sighs, and stares out to sea. "Usnavys, Usnavys, Usnavys. Even if I wanted it to be over with you, it never would be. It's like a curse, loving you."

I look out to sea, too. "I realize that. And I guess that makes me pretty lucky. To have you."

"You have no idea," he says. He looks at me, and I can see he's fighting tears. "But this has to be the last time. I'm serious."

"It is," I say, realizing as I do that he doesn't believe me. "I swear."

lauren

IT IS MY second-to-last day living for two weeks in the inpatient treatment hospital for eating disorders, and I lie on the bed in the comfy sea-green yoga pants and matching long-sleeved shirt Cuicatl brought me a couple of days ago. I told her something like, "Oh, you shouldn't have," because the fabric was heavenly and it was such a thoughtful thing, considering that I've taken up meditation here, but she told me something like, "It was free. They all send me crap all the time."

The shirt has the words OM ANANDA on it, which means something in some more spiritual language than English. Cuicatl thought it might help me focus. She thinks I should take up yoga. I'll give anything a shot at this point. I'm waiting for my counselor with the frizzy black hair to come and give me discharge instructions. I'm a little afraid to leave. The real world is a scary place, full of fried food and cheese and cookies.

I don't want to go back out there. I truly am alone. All alone. I mean, I have my *sucias*, but I don't have any men in my life to speak of, and it would be cool to have male friends. This is one of the things I've been meditating on.

The counselors here have taught us about the twelve-step method of overcoming addiction—and I have an *addiction* to food—but I have been un-comfortable with the whole "God" thing. I am not religious. I prefer science and reason to God. So I've been focused on the things I want, and I've put these messages out to "God," while really thinking just "the universe" and science. I've asked for freedom from my illness, freedom from my addictions to food and men. I've asked to have men in my life whom I can see as friends, as people, who might provide the masculine presence without the pain, so that I can learn to relate to them in a different and less desperate way. I've asked for the strength to learn to live as a truly single person, without focus-ing on a man—and my counselor has agreed that this is what I need, to form an identity that is entirely my own and has nothing to do with the man I am attached to. A lot of bulimics seem to have dependent personalities—even though we're strong we look for confirmation of who and what we are in the eyes of the men we are involved with. I have "prayed" for the strength to trust my own opinions of myself as being just as valid as those of the men around me.

So, yeah. I will work on having men around me, in a new way. Not as boyfriends, but just some men in my life that I could hang out with and talk to. If only I could have that, and continue to live here at the hospital, every-thing would be hunky-dory.

First off, it's not really a hospital. I mean, there are doctors and nurses and counselors, but this place is more like a really upscale girls' prep school from the movies. It is a collection of lovely Victorian houses arranged at pleasing angles in a twelve-acre compound with a gym, horses, and large trees whose leaves drift to the ground with Oscar-worthy grace in the after-noon sun. It is just the sort of place I always wished I could have gone to school when I was growing up in Louisiana, the daughter of a Cuban exile and a trailer-trash mom. Don't balk. I can call her that because, after all, they're my people.

My room is more like a luxury hotel room than a hospital room, with a pillow-top queen-sized mattress atop a solid dark-wood bed with four spiral-ing posts pointing toward the ceiling. The head of the bed is eight inches above the foot, specially built for bulimics who've ruined their esophageal sphincters. An elevated head like this prevents GERD from eroding the esophagus in the night, supposedly. I have slept well in it. I've also been on this medication that stops stomach acid from forming, and I feel a lot better, without the chest pains and less coughing. *And* I have not purged. Not once. I am proud of that.

The bathroom is outfitted with elegant brass fixtures, and restocked each day with soaps and shampoo and conditioner from the Bliss salon in New York City. Part of the treatment program has been to help get me to think of alternate ways to reward myself than food. Taking bubble baths is one of the things that is supposed to substitute for a bag of Chips Ahoy! I've taken a lot of baths these past two weeks. And, I'm pleased to announce, I have eaten exactly zero cookies.

The first week was miserable—all I could do was think about all the food I wasn't allowed to have anymore. There's a dining room in the house I'm staying in, and a kitchen stocked with fruit, vegetables, and lean meats. Counselors sit in those spaces round the clock, to monitor what we eat or, in the case of the anorexics among us, what we do not. We have to carry these little food journals around with us and mark down every last crumb that goes into our mouths. The idea is to get me used to eating small meals every two or three hours, no real meals anymore because of the acid reflux, just snacks all day long, but small ones. It's good for me to never get hungry enough to want to binge. I can't eat foods that cause acid, like mint or chocolate, or spicy foods, or greasy foods, and the good people here have done their best through classes and readings to help us understand that while moderation and stable blood sugar are among the keys to avoiding bingeing, bulimia ultimately has less to do with food than it has to do with how we feel about ourselves and our lives.

This last part was hard for me to accept. Of course, I knew it was right on target. But admitting that you hate yourself and that you can't deal with your own emotions, to a group of other people, without a hint of humor or sarcasm, is very difficult. The stories I heard from other bulimics here were so similar to mine it spun my head. Many of us were neglected as kids. Many of us were very accomplished professionals with higher degrees. Many of us felt inadequate, even though there was no real reason to believe we were. We were just convinced that no one would like us. Watching other women, beautiful women with incredible careers, talk about how disgusting they felt they were, made me start to understand that I was probably a lot like them. I wasn't nearly as bad as I thought I was when you looked at me objectively.

A knock comes on the door, and I look up expecting Cheryl, the counselor. Instead, I see my *boss*, Chuck Spring, a man I have come to loathe in myriad ways over the ten or so years I've worked for him. He is a man once deemed by *Boston* magazine to be among the most eligible bachelors in town, a blue-blooded New England trust-fund baby who made it through Harvard mostly because all the other males in his family since time immemorial had also gone there and later contributed lots of money to the school.

"Chuck! What are you doing here?"

"I wanted to see how my favorite columnist was holding up," he says. Seeing him now, with an almost submissive posture and a look of concern on his face, makes me realize just how much our relationship has grown over the years. Where his limited worldview of women and minorities was once a source of tension, the mere act of having had to work with *me* for so long has informed him in ways he never expected. I have to say that having him edit my work has also made me much more aware of the dominant worldview than I ever was or could have hoped to be, and that if I am honest with myself about it, his influence has helped to make me a better writer. He is not as dumb as people at the paper think. He's got some interesting ideas about writing, and storytelling, that I've used to my own benefit.

"Can I come in?" he asks.

I nod, and he settles himself on the rocking chair near the fireplace. Did I mention my room has a fireplace? "Nice little place you got here," he says. He seems jumpy.

I sit up on the bed and try to seem professional. In truth, it feels weak and strange to see him in this context. Here, now, he looks like a man, not an editor, just a simple person like me. And it seems like he has something to say.

"Listen, Lauren. I've been in touch with your friend Usnavys since she called me from the hospital. She calls me to fill me in on you, now and then. I like her. She swears like a damn sailor, but I like her. She's . . . colorful."

He likes Usnavys?

"She's the one who thought it'd be good if I came to see you here. She called me from Puerto Rico, apparently, to ask me to visit you, actually, be-cause she couldn't be here."

"Really." I am going to have to have a talk with my so-called best friend when she gets back.

"She wanted me to know you really were sick the day we were supposed to go to the soccer game."

"That's nice of her."

"She also wanted me to know you've been sick a lot of other days before that, days when you came to work and got pissy at everyone."

Pissy?

He looks uncomfortable. "Listen, Lauren. I know we haven't always seen eye-to-eye on everything," he begins. "And I know I've been hard on you, and sometimes it seems to you like I'm not listening to what you have to say."

I pick at the fringe on one of the decorative pillows on the bed so that I have something to distract me from looking at him.

"But I want you to know that even with all of that, I think you're a pretty good writer. You've got a lot of loyal readers out there, and there's got to be a good reason for that. I know you don't always feel like you fit in at the pa-per, and you're not always happy there, but I want you to know that everyone at the *Gazette* is really concerned about you, and we're hoping you get over this, and we're willing to do whatever we can to help you. A big part of your not fitting in has been that you didn't let yourself. You put these walls up. I want you to know that we care about you. That's all I wanted to say."

I'm speechless. I don't know how to respond at all. If there were a list somewhere of the things I expect in life, this situation with Chuck would not have ever appeared on it at all. Anywhere. Regarding Chuck, the expecta-tions I might have had would have included things like "tittie bar" or "stupid racist comment." I would never have expected him to come humbly to my hospital room to tell me how much he appreciated me.

"Wow," I say. "Thanks, Chuck. I don't know what to say."

"Here," he says. He opens his backpack and takes out a red gift bag. "This is from the folks in the department."

I don't mean to, but I start to cry. I have never considered my coworkers to be the kind of people who would get me a present. I've thought of them as the kinds of people who would make fun of me behind my back.

He holds the bag out, but I am too overcome with emotion to get up and walk across the room to take it from him. Chuck gets up and brings it to me. He sets it gently on the bed next to me, and places a hand on my shoulder. I see a box from the Sharper Image inside, and wonder for a moment if the department got together to buy me a vibrator. That would be hilarious and pathetic at the same time.

I almost, upon having this thought, tell myself something about how I think I *myself* am hilarious and pathetic at the same time, but I consciously stop the negative thought from taking full shape. One of the things I've learned from Cheryl this week is that negative thoughts about ourselves, even if said jokingly, affect the subconscious as though they were affirmations of our character. The subconscious mind, apparently, does not understand sarcasm and has no sense of humor. I replace the thought with one of my new mantras: *I am smart, and beautiful, and kind to myself, and I am good enough to be loved and to love.*

This makes me cry again.

"Hey," he says softly. For the first time since I've known this man, I can see that he is kindhearted. "Hey, it's okay."

"Thank you," I answer. "I'm sorry. I don't know. This has been an emotional week for me."

"I can imagine."

"It's not you."

"Oh, you know what they say. I make all the girls cry," he jokes.

I laugh, and realize that Chuck's New England Waspy humor has also been influential on me, even when it has made me cringe. I have loathed him, but I think it has turned into the sort of loathing you have for your misguided parents when you are a teenager. Right now, as he comforts me, I wonder if I'm not, in my mid-thirties, pulling out of the snarky attitude I've had toward him and warming to him in a more forgiving way. I have spent all this week learning to forgive myself for not being perfect, and now, as I deal with Chuck, it seems easier to forgive him his imperfections, too.

"It's been a hard month," I tell him.

"You're a strong woman. Shoot, you've put up with me for a boss. That's worth something. So, I promise you. You'll get through this just like you've gotten through so much other stuff."

Stuff. Ordinarily I would have cringed to hear him use such an unimaginative word, but right now I focus on the meaning of what he has said, rather than the details of word choice.

"Thank you, Chuck. Coming from you that means a lot."

"You know, if you wanted to do a column or two about this whole experience, it would probably go a long way toward helping a lot of women." He takes his hand from my shoulder and returns to the rocking chair.

"I don't know. I don't know if I want the whole world to know I am bulimic. It's sort of disgusting."

Chuck keeps a neutral face. "It's up to you. I can understand that you wouldn't want the whole world to know. But you know, Fernandez, after half the stuff you've already told everyone, this wouldn't even make them blink."

I laugh again. It's true. I have been overly confessional in my columns. I've embarrassed myself without realizing it, like with the column that Marislesys brought out to show me. "So, how was the soccer game?" I ask, hoping to change the subject.

"You missed a good one," he says, all excited like a small dog that's been cooped up. He goes on to describe the game to me, and I understand nothing he says. Then, to my surprise, he says, "Jenny and I were disappointed you didn't get to hang out with Joe."

"Joe?"

"Joe Segura."

"The science teacher? Is that who you wanted me to meet?"

"Well, I said that before I realized you two knew each other already."

"How do you know him?"

"He and Jenny run with the same jogging club in Newton, and she told him she knew someone he'd like, and when she said your name he got all excited. He seems to really like you."

"No, he doesn't."

"He said he found you interesting."

I will the negative thoughts away. *I am smart and beautiful.*

"That's crazy," I say.

"Yeah," he jokes. "What could possibly interest him about you? You're only, what? Smart, pretty, nice."

"You did *not* just call me nice."

"I did."

"I think you came to the wrong room by mistake."

He smiles. "Could be. But I don't think so."

I warm to him. For the first time in my life. "Chuck, how is it you've put up with me?"

"I put up with you because you're *good*," he says. "Even when you're shocking everyone. Even when you sound a little crazy. Okay, a *lot* crazy."

"Thanks, Chuck."

"I'm not as much of an asshole as you think. I mean, I *am* an asshole. I'm just not as much of one as you think." He surprises me with the curse word. I don't think I've ever heard him do that. He's always cheerful.

There is another knock at the door, and we both look up to see Cheryl and her big hair. "Hey, Lauren," she says. "Can I come in?"

"Sure." I wave her in. "Join the party."

Cheryl focuses on Chuck, and holds her hand out to shake. "I'm Cheryl," she says. "Lauren's counselor. She's made a lot of progress these past two weeks."

"We were just talking about Lauren's progress," he says. "I'm Chuck."

"Nice to meet you," says Cheryl. "How do you know Lauren?"

Chuck looks at me, and I take it as my cue to answer for him.

"Chuck's my friend," I say.

He smiles at me and nods in agreement.

Cheryl, a big proponent of God and the twelve steps and well aware of my request to the universe to deliver me male friends, gives me a knowing, possibly triumphant look. The power of positive thinking and all that . . . *stuff*.

Yeah, yeah. I know.

Sometimes, the universe has already given you what you need. It's just up to you to recognize it. And when you don't the first time out, sometimes the universe gives you a second chance. And maybe that's what this year is all about for me and my friends, I think.

Recognizing our second chances when they arrive.

SAME TIME
NEXT YEAR

usnavys

The Best Things in Life Are Hard

I know that over the course of this blog I have given out a lot of advice, *nena,* and today I am going to admit to you that not all of it has been good, okay? Most of my advice and counsel on matters of sex and passion has been *incredible,* okay, so don't get all hyped up thinking I'm recanting nothing or whatnot, because that's not the case.

Rather, I am talking about love and marriage, *m'ija.* I felt like, for the longest time, marriage was a kind of a sexual prison for me. I felt like I couldn't get excited about the same little man over and over again because, and I have to be completely honest with you here, for all them years before I got married I had a bunch of things cooking on the back burners—you know what I mean—and variety was the spice of life.

Well, and I am going to be honest again here, and it ain't gonna be easy. I almost lost my husband because of how immature I was about sex and lust, and even though I thought I wanted to lose him for a while because I couldn't stand him and the way I thought he was acting, I almost destroyed my life with that nonsense. If you have a husband, there is a reason you married that man, and unless it's something huge, like he got himself another family all hidden up in Puerto Rico somewhere or something like that, you owe it to him and yourself and your kids and God to try to work that shit *out.* I'm embarrassed to say I wasn't doing that that lately. I wasn't. I was ready to leave my husband for a man I didn't even know, a man who wasn't right for me, because I was too afraid to feel the uncomfortable feelings that come with working on a difficult spot in your relationship. I was the kind to cut and run, and that, girl, is a mistake.

So, here I was, giving you what I said was a Latina's counsel, and the truth is it was 100 percent gringo. I was ready to divorce my man because we had us some hard times after we had us a kid, and that is complete nonsense. You can't give up on a lifetime commitment or something like that. You marry someone, they are your family now, okay? You can't just give up on your family, girl, I don't care how many times Liz Taylor or whoever got her ass divorced, okay? These gringo values, *m'ija,* they tell you to just pick up and move on to the next best thing, but I am living proof today that there is nothing better than what you got, if what you got is your best friend.

Nobody stays the same. Not even the man you marry. You marry a man, he's going to be ten different men before you retire. So I guess that's what I wanted to say today. Your man is going to grow and change, and any problems you got with him, in the bedroom or out, you just have to work on it. A good marriage is hard work, just like good sex. That's what too many people don't understand, and I count my former self among those people. People expect good sex to take effort and work, but they think marriage is going to be easy. It ain't nothing but foolishness to live like that.

Ain't *none* of it easy, *m'ija. None* of it. And that's the point. It's hard to like our bodies the way we are. It's hard to keep the flame of desire alive. And it's hard to make a marriage work when you're both tired and there ain't enough money to go around or whatever the problems are. But it's *worth* it to try. Nothing worth doing is easy, okay? And I think I might have just landed us up on my final point.

I've been too easy, because I mistook sex for love. Just like I used to think money was the same as commitment. But we learn as we go, and I wanted to share what I learned with you all, even though I am aware that you can't teach somebody anything like this and that we all have to go through our own nonsense to figure it all out.

Nothing good is easy. Not marriage, not friendship, not sex, not work, and, most of all, not women. Maybe our *abuelitas* had that part right, *nena*. And I'm not saying keep your panties up or anything *idiota* like that. I'm saying: Take them panties down only for the right man, and once you got him, hold on to him and put the same effort into listening to him and understanding him that you put into keeping yourself sexy and gorgeous. Ain't *nothing* good that's easy, and I am proud to say to you today, in bad grammar—yes, because that's how I feel it right now and I, of course, know the difference, because I am refined like that: *Usnavys Rivera ain't easy no more.*

So, here I am, in a full-service seaside resort outside of Montego Bay, Jamaica, one year since the last *sucias* retreat in New Mexico, and I'm *not* cheating on my husband Juan. I will never cheat on him again, *m'ija*. Don't look at me like that. I'm serious.

Lauren picked the spot this year. She gets a ten, okay? Ten out of ten points. This place is beyond beautiful, *m'ija*, right on the north coast of the island, 150 acres of luscious gardens, sparkling swimming pools, gourmet restaurants, a world-class spa, tennis, golf, you name it, we got it goin' *on* up in here.

You ask me, I think Lauren went a little overboard booking this place, like she was trying to show us how it ought to be done, right? She didn't like New Mexico last year, girl. This I *know*. So she got us a mega-resort, with mega everything, including cabaña boys that are cute enough to bite and so on. But I ain't biting, no matter how delicious the bait. I am a one-man woman now. It ain't easy. I am not saying it is. But it's the right thing to do. I love Juan, even with his problems, and I am getting too old to keep thinking something better is going to find me. It don't get better than Carolina's daddy, okay? Not that I approve of the way she's asking me to get her signed up for Little League like Sara's *sons*, okay? She's all, "Mami, I want to be a baseball star." *Dios mío, chica*, but some things never change. It gives me a headache to even think about it. But Juan's all, "Have you seen this girl's arm,

Usnavys? Have you seen her throw? It's amazing." So, whatever, whatever. My daughter, a future Red Sox pitcher.

No, I'm not cheating on Juan anymore. You heard me. And it's not just because we're expecting another baby. What? That bug you out? I'm a fertility goddess. You know that. And it's not that there haven't been opportunities to cheat, okay? I mean, look at me, girl. What's not to want? You better believe that there are a lot of fine Jamaican brothers out here, all following me around under the four-story palm trees and whatnot with their trays of Champagne glasses and fluffy green beach towels, asking me if there's anything they can do for me, anything at all. They want me, know what I mean?

Like this morning, right? There was the snorkeling guide, this Jamaican who looked like a buffer Wesley Snipes, and I could tell by the way he helped me down the steps of the boat into the water by that coral reef and called me "m'lady" that he wanted me. I should tell you, I do *not* ever want to snorkel again, and I don't know how that girl Lauren talked me into it, okay? It was a nightmare, being out in that salt water that makes your hair extra nappy, swimming over all them spiky black sea urchins the guide told us would paralyze us if we stepped on them. Why the hell would they even take a lady out there to swim around over something nasty-ass like that, huh? Tell me. Tell me why that's a good idea. I could have *died* out there, with water up my nose and all them blue and yellow fish looking up at me all terrified like they didn't want to be my dinner. I will never do that again, okay, *m'ija?* I am not meant to live in the sea. I like it right here, in the chlorinated pool, at the swim-up bar, with the nachos and the cold *non*alcoholic piña colada.

Uh-uh. I don't have the time and energy for cheating anymore. I have to save my energy for family housecleaning day. No, I am not kidding. We wrote us this big old chart, all up on a big white poster board, and at first I hated it, but now it's kind of nice to have the salsa music going in the house and all of us busy scrubbing our own things. The change in Carolina has been amazing, girl, I have to tell you. I don't mean she thinks she's a girl yet, but she doesn't seem to have the same drive to beat up her classmates anymore. She needed to feel like part of a real family, which I think I did, too. That is why I have decided to be a one-man woman.

No, really. Just ask my friends. You could start with Sara, who's sitting next to me at the swim-up bar in her white bikini. I have a one-piece, with a skirt on the bottom, and I still feel like I'm showing a little too much, okay? Sara doesn't seem worried that her shit is hanging out for the whole world to see. She looks good, though. Ever since she moved to Encinitas, California, to shoot her live show with the studio audience, and ever since she sold her line of home design items to one of those big linen retail stores, she's gotten very into the whole liposuction culture out in Southern California. She's all into Pilates and yoga, too, and it shows. She's always getting something fixed now, and it truly does not bother me the way it bothers some people. When and if I start to look bad, I might do it, too. I said *if*, okay? It's not likely.

We are drinking virgin piña coladas, because Cuicatl wanted to see if we could do a retreat without alcohol and we took the challenge seriously, and I know that ain't very imaginative, but we've tried lots of the nonalcoholic drinks around here this weekend, and this one here is da bomb, okay? It is candy in a glass, and even without the buzz, I am telling you, you are feeling no pain. I need it, too, to keep my patience right now, because Sara keeps asking me the same damn question, like I haven't already answered it forty-seven times. She's like a Cuban-American parakeet.

"You don't think he's too young? Really?"

"No," I sigh, watching a group of muscular men and women playing volleyball in the pool around us. It should be criminal to be at a place like this, to relax this much, to have this much fun.

"But twenty-*two*? *Chica, ¡por el amor de Dios!* That's too young to get married." She stares at the engagement ring on her left hand. I've seen bigger rocks, okay, but this one isn't that bad. Considering a little boy got it for her.

"You're not marrying him until he's twenty-three," I remind her. Next year, at this time, at a golf resort in the boy's home state of Texas. Oh, and get this. He's converting to Judaism for her. His parents are evangelists of some kind, and they're all mad at him for damning himself to eternal hell. I am telling you, *m'ija*, the stupidity of intolerant people, it makes me crazy. Why believe in a God if it's not a God who loves all mankind? What use is a vindictive God? I don't know. Rebecca's family is the same way. Bigots. I was lucky enough to marry a man from the same background as me, so we don't have to deal with that kind of thing, but we got our own issues with my mother-in-law, mainly that she thinks I'm the devil and so she has these glasses of water behind every door in her house to capture the bad spirits she thinks I'm sending her and whatnot and so on. Whatever. I have limited Juan to one phone call a week from her, no more. If she had her way, she'd talk to him twice a day, the way she used to before our recommitment ceremony. That's one of the concessions he's had to make, okay? Letting go of Mama. So he can hang on to *me*.

I have been trying to convince Juan to take him some golf lessons, and if you'd believe it he finally agreed. That's part of the new Juan-and-Usnavys show. Less bickering and shit, more compromising. What? Don't look at me like that, okay? It's not just him compromising, even though I did finally get the marriage counselor to convince him that he ought to dress for *me* now and then, and stop dressing like a college student on welfare cheese. I got him some nice shirts at that store PINK, you know? And he looks good in them, *m'ija*.

He's still working at that job with his old boss, making five times what I make part time, and you know what? He got me to do some compromising, too—giving up other men being the big one—and many of them compromises seem to be freeing up a little bit of cash. For instance, I traded him the new Juan wardrobe for me cutting up two of my credit cards and paying down the balances. Best thing about it? Now that he doesn't resent me as much for spending too much, and now that I don't think he's a complete girly man because he gets up and goes to work in a nice shirt every day, we have our sex life back. It's not perfect. He's still got some work to do. But it's getting there.

"I *can't* marry a man this young, Usnavys. It's not smart. He'll leave me for someone younger when I start to get wrinkles." Her face shows no expression from all the Botox. She won't get her no wrinkles, okay? Not at this rate.

I slam my plastic drink cup down on the bar. (They don't use glass in the pool bar, *m'ija*, okay?) It doesn't sound as tough as I hoped. It was more of a pop than a bang. She is getting on my last nerve.

"Was I right about Amaury?" I ask her.

"Yes."

"And you all told me I was negative about him, that I should support Lauren more, remember that?"

"How could I forget? You bring it up every single day."

"Okay. Answer me this one. Did I marry me a good man?"

"Too good, if you ask me."

"What is that supposed to mean?"

"I can't believe he stayed."

"Why not?"

"I mean, I'm glad for you. You guys seem to have it all figured out. But I'm amazed a man could have that much patience."

"That's because you don't think women deserve it," I snap.

"Don't start with that."

"Okay, fine. Moving right along. Answer me this one. Was I right about that little man-woman Selwyn that Elizabeth married before she found the lovely Margo?"

Sara sucks down the last of her icy drink, and talks into the cavern of her cup. "I don't remember what you said about Selwyn."

"I said she was a cold butch bitch," I remind her.

"Oh, yeah. Right."

"And she was."

"Yes, she was."

"And did I not predict that Amber would end up with that sexy *viejo* way back in the day, when she was still living in poverty with that Aztec rat man, Gato?"

"You did."

"And all of you were like, 'No, Amber is a lone wolf,' and some bullshit like that."

"I never called her a lone wolf."

"Whatever, *m'ija*. Okay? I am not even going to ask you to repeat what I told you about Roberto."

"Thank you."

"Then you must admit, Miss Sarita, by default, that your friend Usnavys has a pretty damn good sixth sense about men and marriage and all of that other shit?"

"Selwyn wasn't a man."

"Might as well have been, okay? Might as *well*."

"Granted."

"You must admit that everyone would be better off listening to me most of the time, if not all of the time."

"I guess."

"Then why, I ask you, do you doubt me when I tell you Valentín Garza is one of the best men on the planet?"

"I don't doubt you. I just don't want to drag the boys into another failed marriage."

Now, *m'ija*, I have *seen* Sara's twin eleven-year-old boys with Valentín, at barbecues in her backyard, and there will be no dragging involved. They love him. They love his energy, the way he jumps on the trampoline with them and swings them up in the air. They love the way he eats as much pizza as they do and knows how to play the same video games they like. Valentín is the fun-loving, easygoing father they never had. And I mean never. And best of all? That man loves their mother the way a man ought to love a woman. Gently. This is why I don't even say a word to Sara now. I just give her the stare.

"I know," she says.

I continue to stare.

"Stop looking at me like that." She puts her hand up like a shield, smiling.

"Not until you relax."

Sara finishes her drink, and thanks me for reminding her about relaxing. "I have a massage appointment at the spa in ten minutes," she says. "I better get going."

I watch her swim across the pool to the steps, get out, and take her towel from the beach chair among the six beach chairs we've got side by side near the outdoor stage area, where they have sexy dance shows every night. Me? I had my massage yesterday. Two hours, girl. It felt *good*.

Lauren is still in her chair, in the shade of a giant palm tree, reading an activist *chica*-lit novel by Sofia Quintero, with her big hat and sunglasses on, and that gauzy cover-up thing with the long sleeves. She is pale as shit, right? It's the white girl in her. She never used to protect her skin from the sun, girl. That's another thing about her that's changed. She used to get sunburned and joke that it was the fastest way to a tan, because once the dead skin peeled off, she was what she thinks is brown. She's still got issues with her esophagus, and I feel bad, too, because we'll be getting down at the breakfast buffet here, the rest of us, piling up the eggs and the oranges, and she's there with her Prilosec pills and bottled water, with a little slice of watermelon for later. She says it doesn't bother her anymore. She's just happy to be alive. That's what she says.

I'm not so sure Joe *Segura* is happy she's alive, though. She went nuts on him and slashed his tires a while back. I think she ripped up his clothes, too, or set them on fire. After six months of dating the hot science teacher, she moved in with him in his house in Newton. She also joined his jogging club, and if you can believe this, they started to go on double dates with her boss and his wife. She was feeling all normal and happy, she said. I don't know, *m'ija*. There are some people I never thought she'd be friends with, but coming this close to death can shake you out of your own prejudices sometimes, that's all I can think of. Or coming this close to losing your husband, as was the case with me. You never know how people will react.

Anyway, don't get all carried away thinking her life turned around and got all normal and shit all of a sudden. It didn't. She found out the wonderful Joe Segura was cheating on her, just like the other men she'd picked. Every damn man this woman has been with has done this to her, in almost the exact same way. It's a sad thing to watch.

I didn't see the one with Joe Segura coming, though. I really didn't. I don't know what the hell was wrong with my sixth sense radar, but I have to tell you I actually thought that he was going to be different for her. I was so disgusted with him that I swear to you I almost went over to his house and kicked his ass my own damn self, but I realized that would have looked bad. Besides, I had Lauren to take care of. Girlfriend had her nowhere else to go, she ended up staying in my guest bedroom for a while, until she got herself another apartment, in Jamaica Plain again. I was all, like, get something in another neighborhood. Shake it up a little, step out of the rut, right?

I asked her why she didn't buy something, make a sound investment, right? And that was when I realized the old Lauren was gone for good. She said something about giving several months' notice at her job, so that she could move to Mexico and write a novel. At first? *M'ija*, at first I thought the bitch was joking because I told her to move to a different neighborhood. In my world, doesn't anybody in her right mind, thirty-four years old, leave her lucrative career as a rising star in the United States press corps, to start all over again in a third-world country, okay? *Mira*, I tried to talk sense into her, but she told me it was what she was going to do, and that if I didn't like it I could keep my thoughts to myself. So, I am keeping my opinions to myself, but only because the bitch asked me to. The overwhelming opinion I have on the situation is that I don't know what I'm going to do without my best friend around to brag to, especially with all my *sucias* moving away, but I predict she'll be back. Not even the Mexicans want to stay in Mexico, okay?

From where I sit, I have a view of the bay. Somewhere out there right now, Rebecca and Cuicatl are deep-sea scuba diving. Don't ask me why any sensible Latina would want to do that crazy-ass shit. I would never hook my lungs up to some tank and drop my life down to the bottom of the sea, just for the thrill of it, you know what I'm saying? But those two? Peas in a pod these days. I know they don't think they have all that much in common, the way they fight about things Chicano or Spanish and whatnot, but they're the two most ambitious women I have ever known.

I'm happy they're out there, too, in those rubber suits with the face masks, swimming around with the sharks. Know why? Because, for several months last year, after Rebecca refused to allow Cuicatl to be her surrogate and went out and found some washed-out-looking borderline Amish woman from Ohio to do it, they didn't even talk to each other. Cuicatl was all defensive, thinking Rebecca picked a white woman because she wishes she *were* white, which I thought was unfair as shit and mean on top of that. Rebecca explained that she and Andre had chosen the woman from an agency that did background and health checks. Rebecca said she found it easier to handle if the woman lived in another state, if she didn't have to watch the pregnancy unfold up close. When the baby is born in a couple of months, Rebecca and Andre will fly to Cleveland for the birth. Then, *m'ija?* Then they're moving to Santa Fe for good. She decided it wasn't all that unhip after all, and he scooped him up a bunch of hot talent from where Intel laid a bunch of people off out there.

Cuicatl isn't bitter about it anymore, because she got what she wanted anyway. After Rebecca found her unfit for surrogacy, Cuicatl went nuts and went and found herself a couple of Chicano activists out in Houston who couldn't have a baby, friends of a friend of hers, and she went ahead and cooked that baby for *them*. Just to prove something to *Rebecca*. I swear to you, it is not good to live your life in reaction to things. It is *not good*. They have a sibling Mexica rivalry thing going on. Cuicatl had the baby a month ago. So, if you can imagine, all the time Rebecca and Andre were searching for the perfect surrogate, there was Cuicatl, all pregnant already, being a surrogate! Tell me this ain't a crazy world, girl. Go on. *Tell* me. Uh-*huh*.

Her manager, Frank, who is also her man now, had the gossip press in on it from the start, and all the stories talk about what a great humanitarian Cuicatl is, and about how when all these other famous women are busy adopting babies and taking them into their homes, Cuicatl was selflessly willing to offer her body to a friend in need. Nowhere in any of them stories did anybody mention that the whole thing began with Rebecca, and not a one of us *sucias* talked about it to nobody either. *Any*body. Sorry. Rebecca wants privacy, and we respect that. Cuicatl wants publicity, and I respect that, too. What's friendship without mutual respect, no?

I'm not so sure the others here share my respect, but if they have a major problem with the way the whole thing went down, didn't none of them want to talk about it with *me*. All that publicity went pretty much the way Cuicatl hoped it would, too. Her new album *CHANTICO*, all these soft, beautiful pop ballads and lullabies, landed pretty high on the charts this time around. I should tell you, Chantico is some Aztec goddess of domestic life. Cuicatl explained it all to us the other night. She's the embodiment of the mix of pleasure and pain or some crazy nonsense like that. I still have my doubts about the damn Aztecs, okay? They were a little *too* into punishing people, if you ask me. But don't tell her I said that. Chantico's all right with me, because she's brought good luck to Cuicatl, right? This album looks like it might be her biggest seller yet.

Cuicatl's been a guest judge on *American Idol* a few times, and she just told us last night that MTV asked her if she and Frank would like to star in a reality show based upon their real-life May-December romance. He's one of them touchy-feely hippie men certain women like, all rubbing her pregnant belly with oils so she wouldn't get stretch marks, and chanting to some Aztec goddess to get in touch with his feminine side and whatnot and what-have-you. Hell, he even sat with her in the hot tub when she pushed that baby out into the world, while the Aztec drummers played in the backyard of his house in Silver Lake. Having that baby made her want one of her own, she said. So now they're going to start trying. I'm happy for her, *m'ija*. I really am. I can't wait to see how many Mexican *x*s she can put into her child's name.

Which just leaves Elizabeth. That's her over there in the Jacuzzi, the one overlooking the bay on that little bump in the hill. Why she wants to get her body into something hot right now, when the rest of us are hoping to cool off, is one of life's great mysteries. But that's how it is with Liz, right? We yin, she yangs. It's all good. She and Margo moved in together about six minutes after they started dating, got themselves a big old house in Cohasset, of all places, near the ocean. They have all them kids roaming all over the place, and Margo has enough money—the woman is rolling in it, okay?—that Elizabeth decided to leave her job producing Sara's show and stay home with Gordon full time.

She dropped a big old bomb on us the first night we were here, *m'ija*, and said they've been talking about buying a house in Baja, Mexico, on the ocean. Those South American lesbians are sick of the cold weather up in New England. Margo wants to move her gallery from Boston to San Diego. Liz wants to write poems. But that's not a surprise. That's all she's ever really wanted to do, and even though I'm going to miss her if she leaves, I know she'd be happy there. Besides, Sara's out there now, and Cuicatl is only a few hours' drive away from there. It's not like the Colombian *sucia* is going to be alone, living on the other side of the world like some crazy-ass half-Cuban disaster areas we know. Or alone in Boston like one Puerto Rican diva we know and love. I been talking to Juan about getting him a job offer up in Los Angeles somewhere, just talking it up a little something-something. You never know, *m'ija*. I think Carolina might like her some surfing and rock-climbing. And what's the point of your sisters having all these babies if they don't grow up together, anyway?

I finish the last of the piña colada, and the handsome bartender is over just like that, fast as a seagull diving for clams. He asks me if I'd like another. In the background, the reggae beat changes to merengue, *m'ija*. I didn't think I'd hear me some merengue all the way out in Jamaica, but I guess the world is getting smaller. I guess that's what happens when you got people from one place moving to another place, and the Internet, and cell phones, and airplanes and so on and so forth and what-have-you. The world shrinks up on you, like plastic wrap. Yes, it does.

"Excuse me, m'lady," he asks me. "Would you like another virgin piña colada?"

"Of course," I tell him. "Bring it on."

She just wants the perfect guy—but she keeps falling for married men!

Vanessa Chavez has a successful career, is rich with friends, and is loved by her family, but she has one giant Achilles' heel: she keeps falling for married men. What's a girl to do but take a vow of celibacy and figure out why she makes the ultimate bad choice of boyfriend over and over again?

the husband habit

alisa valdes-rodriguez

The *New York Times* bestselling author of *The Dirty Girls Social Club*

"Valdes-Rodriguez ... has once again written an extraordinary and impressive book."

—*Library Journal* on *Dirty Girls on Top*

St. Martin's Press   www.stmartins.com